Reason

by Victoria Elaine Jones

A Novel

N'TYSE ENTERPRISES LLC
Division / *A Million Thoughts Publishing*
3501 Gus Thomasson Rd. #87-2002
Mesquite, TX 75187
asst.amillionthoughts@yahoo.com

Reason is a work of fiction. It is not meant to depict, portray, or represent any particular gender, real persons, or group of people. All the characters, places, incidents, and dialogues, are products of the author's imagination, or are used fictitiously and are not to be construed as real. Any resemblance to actual events, locales, or persons living or dead, is entirely coincidental.

Editors: N'TYSE & Ann Karnes
Admin. Liaison: Tiffani Brown
Acquisitions/Creative Consulting: N'TYSE
Cover Design: Deshawn Taylor
Cover Layout: Designs By SheShe

Library of Congress Cataloging-In Publication Data: 2014943944
ISBN-13: 978-0985166434
ISBN-10: 0985166436

This book is dedicated to the teachers of the world, whose encouragement and support can change the course of history. And in particular, to Judy Logan and to Ms. Lenigan, both of whom I hope understand have written chapters in my life.

Acknowledgements

Many thanks to my publisher, N'Tyse, for her support and vision and unwavering confidence in the success of this novel. Thank you to Larry Thornton and Janet Fitch, who taught me the tricks of the trade, and namely, that there were no tricks to substitute for practicing your craft. To Sonia Sanchez, you'll never know how much that car ride meant to me. To Sapphire, who was the first to challenge me to write seriously, though I'm sure you don't remember the question you asked that night.

Thank you to Dina, my friend and right hand, who made it easy for me to live in two worlds at once.

And finally, to my family: my boys, Yomi and Kay, who knew enough to see when mama was spacing out and to leave me alone to write. And to my husband, who was perfectly happy holding up the walls of our home on his shoulders while I went dancing through our life. You are amazing, everything for which I prayed and many, many things for which I did not. Who knew that a second chance could be better than the first?

Oh, and lest I reap his wrath for forgetting, my cat Rockstar, who plopped down determinedly on my keyboard when it was past time for me to take a break.

Justice

People live and die in Reason. Babies, delivered in the old elementary-school-turned-hospital out on 68th and Main, grow up, grow old, and pass, but their memories remain. A small few leave, taste life outside of town, return wit a bit more money and a little less dignity, but they always come back. Most never leave to begin wit. There's nothing about the lay of Reason, about the wide and tree-lined streets or falsely-brightened buildings, compelling people to stay, but they do all the same. 'Round here they say, you been here a day, you like gon' stay a year. An if you been here a year, you might as well settle in and let be. 'Cause this where you gon' be, least as long as God leave you on this earth.

On occasion, a young boy, just beginning to feel himself, or a girl, just thinkin' she know something, will go. Usually, they get no further than Courtney, just twenty minutes northwest of Reason, before they give up and come on back. To a boy or girl born and raised in Reason, Courtney is enough. The lights of the city, bright enough to obscure the moon overhead, and the people, quietly and quickly shifting through corridors and alleyways, are enough. In Reason, streetlights politely submit to moonlight and people smile before passing by. In Reason, confusion is somehow less chaotic and life progresses along a preexisting path, continuing without pause inexorably toward death. There are few decisions to be made, and those, too, are predictable.

"Mid-Town" is a set of four two-story buildings, each occupying a separate corner at the intersection of 66th and Main and sporting cheery pastel coats of paint and shiny marble stairs to hide the wear and tear of decades of use and service. Those stairs, even now, are the most costly thing in the entire town. They stand as the first invitation into Reason, welcoming visitors into City Hall, the library, and even the two churches that sit caddy-corner from one another in both physical location and philosophy.

Wilson's Grocery & Trade, just a few blocks away, is one of Reason's more modern attributes, a chain grocery store with brightly-lit aisles and wilted fruit. The manager, imported along with the franchise name, makes brisk surveillance of the aisles, looking for anything that might expose the store to liability or attract the notice of a health inspector. Years ago, Wilson's was local-owned and proud of it, but even in Reason, change can't simply be stopped. Slowed, yes; fought and chastised and resisted, but still it can't be stopped altogether. And so in Reason, as in the rest of the world developing beyond the borders of the town, change comes in soon and catches folks unawares, if for no other reason than to fulfill its nature and mix things up.

Justice is a fluid concept in Reason. It depends on a number of factors like the circumstances, the means, and, most importantly, the people involved. Like when that young girl at Kelly High got knocked up a few years back. She had been kept tighter than a preacher's daughter and then one day her belly just 'on swole up. By two months, you could see a mile away that she was carryin', all that baby just a swayin' in her hips.

Her aunts, Reason born and raised, every one of 'em, hunted that boy down with such calm precision you woulda thought it was they occupation. Folks was more surprised when he returned than they had been when he come up missin'. And didn't nobody ask where he got that long, uneven scar across his left eye or why he now walked about with a limp, hiding his eyes and his face from view. That was just Justice gettin' her own. And then, later, when it came out how that girl had sniffed behind him for months before like a bitch in heat, how she had invited him into her home and conceived that baby right on her grandmother's sainted bed, well, that didn't change a damn thing. What was some poor trash from across the way doin' bein' somewhere about to attract her notice? That girl was one of Reason's best-kept, most well-guarded secrets, and didn't a body question Justice when it came in the form of those three women. They were, after all, Reason born and raised.

Justice is God's way of balancin' things out, makin' sure everyone wins and loses all the same wit everyone else. Problem wit Justice is, it ain't always selective. And it don't ever quit. Sometimes it stirs the pot on up years after you thought the fire'd gone out, blown out, been stamped out, and danced on top of. As the Bible says, the sins of the father get visited on the children. In Reason, folks say that's just Justice gettin' her own.

Like what happened in the house on the corner of Starlite and Lane somewhere goin' on nineteen years ago. But back then it was the mother, rather than the father, who sinned. Sandal and his wife, Reba, lived in the peach house with their daughter. She was about eight at the time, a lil' bit of a thing, beautiful. Dark, smooth skin and thick brown hair always done in two plaits, one pinned above each ear. The kind of child old men like to rock on their knees, innocently, when they think no one is looking. Her daddy called her Baby Girl; her mama never called her at all.

To be fair, though, she mighta had good reason. Reba

had been a beautiful child, too, before life got aholt of her. She'd graduated from high school valedictorian of her class and then up and married one of the most handsome and eligible bachelors Reason had to offer the very next day. Didn't nobody think that was right. The whole town had had plans for the both of 'em. Parents of other young teens kept their kids inside, afraid such foolhardy independence might be contagious. Some of the preachers and elders put pressure on Reba's momma and daddy to stop such foolishness, but neither one was young enough to have it declared illegal. And so the two of 'em, both stupid and headstrong, settled down to married life.

Not a year'd gone by when Reba gave birth to a child, a baby girl. And then, less than ten months later a sickly boy, who died a few days after birth. Two miscarriages and too many late nights and early mornings later, she began spending time in bars, listening to women sing out their sorrows over some triflin', ungrateful man who done 'em wrong. Enough of all that, Reba decided her man had done her wrong.

By then, she was not that strong young woman she had been, but she was still stupid and less than honest. She didn't leave. She didn't even tell Sandal somethin' was wrong. Instead, she took up with Ray Jenkins, a hardworking and lovely brother who had stepped out on his wife more than a few times before. Cassandra, his wife, was too busy raising five children to notice that her husband had taken up with a woman almost twenty years her junior. It seemed natural that Ray should go walking his little girl over to play with her best friend, and right, too, that he should stay and visit behind closed doors and curtained windows until the girl was ready to return home. More than that, his relationship with Reba re-

4

leased Cassandra from the burden of caring for her fifth child and from the constant fear that her husband might get it in his head one day to try an' conceive a sixth. Ray's sudden interest in his youngest daughter and her friends left only four children for Cassandra to correct and discipline and teach and look after.

Sandal, when he knew, wasn't nearly so nice about it. In Reason, hot news is old news, so word spread fast. Sandal came home one day to find his Baby Girl playing alone in the yard, making mud pies and setting them on the front porch. She musta thought he looked hungry 'cause she offered him one. He kept goin', though, to where his hunger could be satisfied.

They say two things this side of heaven a woman die for: love and hate. Two more things a man'll kill for: hate and love. When you think about it, we ain't so different, men and women. We both go through life lookin' to find the same emotions, same passions, both willin' to kill to protect it. Somebody like Sandal is no less human than you or I, maybe more so for the experience. It's that moment, caught between passion and love too thick to let thought dilute action, that we all been waitin' for, searchin' and looking and yearnin' for. Most of us just ain't found it yet. But if we blessed and we seek hard, we might just turn around one day, look up, and there it is. Love, the kind so deep it take oceans to drown it out. If we lucky, we ain't never got to kill for it. But if it's good, if it's real good and strong, not a one of us wouldn't. That's that edge of passion, what lovin' really is, what separates us from the animals and keeps us from becomin' gods. And Sandal, well, he really whatn't no different from the rest of us.

By the time the police arrived, the house was already tainted. Reba's body lay, quietly misshapen, on the kitchen floor. Blood covered her hips and thighs and turned the faded pink flowers of her dress an unnaturally bright red. Between the police, the paramedics, and the coroner who pronounced her dead upon arrival, not a one of them wanted to lift her dress and find out exactly where Sandal had put the barrel of that gun before he squeezed the trigger. He was in the bedroom, half-sitting, half-laying on the bright yellow comforter covering the bed. From the entrance, when you walked in, it looked as if he might have just taken a moment to rest his eyes. There was a brown substance around his mouth and a small hole above his ear. From the other side, the view wasn't nearly so pleasant. Half of Sandal's face had been blown off, presumably by the shotgun lying on the floor.

Ray was found a day later outside the bar where he and Reba had met, separated in two by the jagged violence of a knife. You could tell right off it whatn't no easy death. Of course, he whatn't alive to say who did it, but nobody in Reason doubted just who had graced him with Justice. The police did not try hard. Cassandra quickly and quietly collected the insurance money and final pay from Ray's job, and settled down to raise her five children on hard labor, social security checks, and food stamps. Sandal and Reba's beautiful Baby Girl, having been found next to her daddy's body, mud staining her hands, was packed up by her mama's parents and taken away to live somewhere out near Courtney or beyond. Everybody knew they was still pissed off about it all, 'bout how their daughter's foolishness had cost them their dreams and disgraced their names. But none of Sandal's family was willing to take her in, afraid she might be infected with the stupidity or foolishness or dishonesty or selfishness or love that had made their ambitious young boy turn crazy and kill his wife. Everybody in Reason agreed that Justice had been done. It had been predetermined from that moment the Sandal and Reba, the two of 'em both full of arrogance and selfish pride, thought they knew better than those who'd come before them. The violence of that act, the deaths of those two, even the disappearance of their Baby Girl, all of that had been necessary to set things back to right and to balance out the world. Justice had been served, and whether folks liked the outcome or not, all agreed it had been comin' on for years.

Mistake everybody made was in thinkin' it had come. No, Justice wouldn't be satisfied wit handlin' business so quickly in just a few short years. Justice took her time, let memories hush and wither, waited out through cold winters and brutal nights. Justice lay stretched out on coarse mats and concrete streets and curled up to sleep on the wooden benches in train depots, watchin', waitin', plannin' her homecomin', knowin' exactly when and how and why she had to do what had to be done. Justice didn't return to Reason to get her own until much, much later. Nineteen years, to be exact.

Chapter 1

It was the slow, sleepy time in January when the little peach house on the corner of Lane and Starlite gradually began showing signs of life. First, there were the hollow, silver chimes that appeared suddenly above the front porch, singing a soft melody with the passing of each breeze. They were welcoming, but the landscaping was not. Tall weeds that had long since choked out every struggling blade of grass remained, now dead and brown and frozen into stiffness by the cold, guarding closely the privacy and identity of any occupants within. No car was parked in the driveway, no lights burned brightly in the windows, and there was no movement from within. Mama Kinney began watching the house, only to report to the ladies that gathered on her front porch a week later that there had been no other signs. Tricee suggested maybe the chimes had been there all along, and perhaps nobody had ever noticed. The women nodded slowly, tasting the possibility, but still uncertain. The paint on the house looked fresh, newer, but Mama Kinney would have noticed if someone had been painting. The gate connecting the fence around the house swung back and forth, no longer secured by a thick padlock. But surely any residents would show themselves, come out to meet and greet the folks that lived on the block. There was no call for rudeness, no way in which someone might have offended them. No, everyone decided, the house might be renewing itself, but it was as empty as it had been for the previous nineteen years.

Just to be certain, on a chilly Saturday afternoon in

early February, Jody and Sincere took their Bibles and the last month's issue of Watchtower someone devout had left on Mama Kinney's doorstep and walked on across the street. The women on Mama Kinney's porch stood silently for a change, patiently waiting, but expecting nothing. Almost a month of silence had convinced them to doubt their first impression.

To their collective surprise, a petite, slender, dark-skinned woman answered Jody's knock. The woman stepped out onto the porch and held the door closed behind her, despite the way Jody shifted onto her left foot, easing closer to the house. The women on Mama Kinney's porch shifted and drew forward, still silent, trying for a better view. The woman at the door smiled slightly, and cocked her head sidewise a moment, listening. A light wind briefly toyed with the hem of her baby blue housedress, then settled it again to brush teasingly against the skin just below her knees. She hugged an off-white cardigan closer, standing into the wind.

The conversation between the three women continued too quietly for the spectators across the street. Jody and Sincere pressed forward, offering a copy of the magazine. The woman shook her head, held her palm out flat against Jody and, turning, went back into the house. The door of the peach house closed quietly, softly behind her with finality. There was no movement within, no twitch of the curtains. Just that quickly, she was gone, with only memory to prove that she'd ever been there at all.

The women on the porch leaned back, waited, and resentment warmed the street between them before settling in their midst. Returning, Jody only shrugged. "Well, who here really wants to hear it, anyway? I mean, half the time y'all don't even answer the door, and y'all know who's knockin!"

"That's exactly why I don't answer the door, Jody!" Lady showed a broad and full-toothed grin, despite the moment. "Shit, it ain't got nothin' to do with religion, I just don't wanna talk to yo ass all the time." Lady eased away from her post and settled heavily into a brown folding chair, despite its protesting groan. Of all the women, she alone managed to look disinterested in the goings on across the street.

Jody shot her a speaking look. "Some of us need it more'n most, Lady, otherwise you couldn't *pay* me to visit that heathen home of yours. All those men..." and she shuddered delicately, either from the cold or the thought.

Mama Kinney stood leaning against the doorframe with arms crossed, sucking her teeth and rocking backward on the balls of her feet. "Still..." she said, and looked back out over at the house.

Jody turned suddenly, eagerly toward the other women, her earlier neutrality seemingly gone. Now she spoke persuasively, lobbying them. "Well, I will say this: before now she coulda come on over an said hi. I mean, I know she seen us out here before. Acted a bit siddity, too, the way she just refused, if you ask me."

Lady laughed loudly and said, "See, and that's why ain't nobody ask you. Sincere, girl whatchu think?" Everyone turned to Sincere, who stood quietly on the edge of the porch.

Sincere considered briefly before she shrugged. "I don't know no more'n Jody," she said, passing, and held her Bible more closely to her chest. Mama Kinney saw the movement and tucked it away for further analysis.

One of the women made a disgusted sound and, as a

group, they all turned back to Jody. She rose quickly to the occasion, used to being the center of attention. "I'm just surprised anyone is over there, I have to say I thought all of y'all was crazy." Reese reached behind to scratch her neck and her French-rolled hair shook briefly on her hand before settling. "I mean, *how* long that house been empty?"

Everyone looked at Mama Kinney and waited for her response. As the eldest woman in the group, she was by default the timekeeper, and she had the added benefit of having lived across the street from the house in question. She rolled her eyes back and thought a moment. "Seem like is been at least twenty years. Yeah, round 'bout that many. Since that thang between Sandal and his wife," she finished, wagging one finger in the air in recall. She looked past the women to the house across the street.

"Hm? What "thang?" Tricee, the youngest of the women on the porch and the only one who hadn't lived in Reason since forever, leaned forward. The other women ignored her, as they usually did, waving her to silence.

"Well, what she look like? How she act? Look from over here like she had a way about her, acted real pretty." Joyce, with her short, round frame, burnished orange complexion, and flat hands and feet had never come close to being beautiful. Still, she couldn't help but admire beauty, whether male or female. She was that unselfishly honest type and everyone liked her for that, even if her honesty was occasionally disconcerting.

Jody neatly avoided the first portion of her question, unwilling to be truthful, but knowing Sincere would contradict her openly if she wasn't. "Girl, how somebody "act" pretty? I'd like to know that!" Jody laughed lightly, then shivered as a brief gust of wind

11

rushed heavily past. Jody had decided today to sacrifice practicality for fashion, and so she was dressed somewhat lighter than everyone else in a gray A-line dress with a lightweight but pretty red half-jacket, tied at her waist. The combination served to highlight her slender but shapely figure and complimented the sweet caramel tones of her skin. "Like I said, I don't like her attitude. I mean, how she gone move into the house without sayin' so much as a hello-goodbye to her neighbors? Don't seem quite right to me. If she'da been nicer, I mighta even told her it ain't quite kosher, livin' in that house. What with that thang that happened..."

"What *thang*?" Tricee said again, and again the group ignored her. But this time Reese leaned over and whispered in her ear, and Tricee nodded, satisfied.

Now Sincere spoke up again, this time sharply toward Jody. "Don't nothin' seem right to you, Jody, especially when another woman is involved." She turned to the other women. "She was polite, courteous even, but not real welcomin'. Anyhow, since we don't know nothin' about her, it seems to me like we oughtta hold off speculatin' and not be carryin' tales 'til we find out more." Satisfied now, having said her piece, Sincere disappeared into the house. Mama Kinney was her godmother and she had as much access to the house as any natural born child.

Her reprimand suddenly reminded each woman of what she'd been about before stopping to converse. Reese was the first. "Luke'll be home soon. Don't notice if his dinner is cold, nasty, burnt, but he'll be pissed as hell if it ain't on time." Reese stood, gathering her handbag before she turned to Tricee. "C'mon girl, I'll tell you 'bout that *thang*. And you can watch me and learn a lil' somethin' 'bout cookin'."

12

"I *can* cook," Tricee replied, but gathered her things and turned to go just as well. With no family of her own in Reason, she rarely turned down an opportunity to spend time with someone else's.

Lady slapped a pack of cigarettes against her palm and pulled one out. She stood and slipped it between her lips. "Gotta go have me a smoke or two before the Boys get home, get ready for tonight," Lady said, smiling as she stuck one cigarette between her teeth. "Got me an itch startin' an' I ain't decided yet who I'ma let scratch it."

Jody looked at her disgustedly. "Thas nasty, Lady, just downright nasty. We good, God-fearin' folk, we don't need to hear 'bout all the carryin' on in yo house."

"Girl, speak for yourself!" Reese threw over her shoulder, stepping down from the porch. "Some'a us wouldn't have no life at all if it whatn't for Lady's stories. Lady, save me some for tomorrow!"

"Now you know I don't believe in savin' nothin' if I can spend it today," Lady replied, laughing. "But if you lucky, ladies, I might bring y'all some leftovers. Mama," she bent and kissed Mama Kinney on the cheek and quickly sidestepped her playful swat. "I'ma see you tomorrow." Lady waved before she, too, walked down the steps. For a woman as large as she was, Lady was quick and agile on her feet.

Mama Kinney called loudly toward her swiftly-moving form. "If y'all gon' be talkin' that raunchy nonsense, y'all can do it elsewhere tomorrow! My home ain't gon' be sullied by all that street gossip." Mama Kinney made that same threat at least once a week but her house still remained the spot for gathering. Now she looked meaningfully at Jody, who dutifully rose and gathered her things to go. Mama Kinney watched all four

13

women scatter in different directions before she stood, balancing carefully on her cane, and slipped into the house.

Sincere was in the kitchen, sitting at the table and sipping a cup of hot tea, staring at the peeling wallpaper. A small line of steam before her reached upward toward the ceiling, clutched briefly at the air, and then dissipated into nothingness. Her Bible lay, discarded, in front of an unused setting, along with the rejected issue of Watchtower. "Well?" Mama Kinney demanded immediately upon entering, barely pausing at the door.

Sincere sighed before responding. "Yeah, it's her. She a little bit different now, calmer. She used to have all this nervous energy..." Sincere stared at the wallpaper, remembering, then visibly shook herself. "People change, I guess. She grew up."

"That mighta just been youth." Mama Kinney said, but her voice was questioning. She pulled out the chair across from Sincere and sat.

"I suppose. You'd remember better'n me. I was just a girl back then. Imagine I've changed a bit, too." Sincere closed her hands around her cup and stared inside.

"Jean didn't seem to recognize you then." It wasn't a question. Mama Kinney had almost thirty years of reading into what Sincere wouldn't say. "Guess we'll do just what we said, right, and wait and see. See what the Lord done brought to bear. Can't be no worse than what happened last time in that house."

But Sincere wasn't so sure. "Miranda. Thas what she say her name is now." Sincere avoided her godmother's gaze. "Mama, I was thinkin'-" she began, but Mama Kinney interrupted before she could finish the thought, already knowing what she was going to say.

"You were thinkin' what, girl? I done already tole you,

14

I don't need no babysitter. And you a grown woman, you don't need me hangin' around, invading yo privacy. I don't want you bringin' it up again, Sincere, ya hear? You got yo place, I got mine."

"Still, I would feel more comfortable if I was here a little more…"

"To do what? Protect me?" Mama Kinney stared at her skeptically. "Girl, I got a good hunned, hunned-fifty pounds on you. I might be old, might can't move too quick, but I can use this here cane and put every one of them pounds behind it. 'Till I meet King Jesus, that'll have to be enough 'cause it's all the protection I'ma allow."

Sincere let it go, knowing it was a loosing argument. The two women sat in silence, each contemplating her own thoughts. Nervousness had settled inside Sincere, and she couldn't seem to shake the feeling that the woman now calling herself Miranda had known exactly who she was, and why she had come. What's more, there was still the lingering question of what Jean was doing here, and why.

Chapter 2

Moresha arrived on a Thursday not long after that. A broad-boned, thick-skinned Jewish woman with wide hips and more presence than seemed justified, she pulled into Reason and unhesitatingly announced her arrival to the entire town and the world beyond. "Miranda!" she yelled, pulling into the driveway of the peach house and honking. She popped open the trunk of her old brown Buick and stretched one moccasin-clad, blue-veined foot out of the driver side door. Her voice was startlingly loud, as if she thought someone in Reason on this quiet, slow day might not have heard the loud screech of her brakes or the loudness of her engine.

Miranda appeared in the doorway of the house, again dressed inappropriately for the cold again in a simple, faded black house dress, fuzzy blue slippers dwarfing her slender feet. Mama Kinney watched from her kitchen window as the two women stood in silent contemplation of one another, then quietly spoke. Something about the way they stood closely together, foreheads almost touching, conveyed an intimacy that made Mama Kinney's eyes narrow. Miranda helped herself to a suitcase from the trunk and stood waiting. Moresha closed the trunk and looked up at the house, holding another. Mama Kinney felt her acceptance from across the street before she nodded and went in.

The next time Moresha made an appearance was two days later. It was one of those rare days in February when the sun is out shining in full force, putting on its most glorious display but still fallin' short of heatin' up the earth. Just a few minutes before noon, she came quickly around the side of the house, balancing a wheelbarrow laden with bags of soil, plants, and other gardening paraphernalia. Mama Kinney squinted her eyes and moved closer to the window, repositioning a mug of hot chocolate to better warm her arthritis-ridden fingers. "Well, what she gon' do wit that?" she asked out loud to the room. No one answered. Moresha, in a faded yellow sweatshirt and loose-fitting blue jeans, halted the cart, knelt beside it in the dirt, and determinedly, systematically began yanking at the weeds that decorated the front yard.

Sincere arrived a few minutes later, stopping by although it was her day off from work. She paused briefly on Mama Kinney's porch to stare at the strange white woman across the street. Mama Kinney could not hear her question, but she understood it just the same. "Don't she know it's still February?"

She found her godmother in a chair pulled close to the living room window with an old and worn quilt wrapped firmly around her body from the waist down. The chair was an old folding one that got brought out to the front porch when the women gathered. Sincere leaned close to Mama Kinney and looked out the window. Down another block, a slight figure struggled against the bite of the wind. Sincere pulled back. "Look like I better make some hot chocolate, Mama."

"Make enough 'n then some," Mama Kinney called to her retreating figure without bothering to turn around. "They'll all be here soon. I ain't never known the cold to keep 'em away, specially when somethin' talk-worthy's goin' down."

Sincere was still heating hot chocolate in a large silver pot on the stove when the other women arrived, all curious about the presence of a white woman in their small black community, and even more curious about what she was doing with gardening equipment so late in winter. Whether cold, rain, or snow, they all knew better than to ask Mama Kinney if they could sit inside so instead they'd all dressed appropriately and stood shivering on the front porch. From the kitchen, Sincere could barely make out the their shivery voices. "Might be neighborly of you to invite us all in," Lady prodded Mama Kinney, speaking for the group. Her wide smile belied any offense her words might engender, even as her teeth began a slight chatter.

"Might be," Mama Kinney agreed and nodded. "But then, when you take in stray dogs, sometimes you get fleas." Mama Kinney gave a pointed look at the women.

"Who you callin' a flea?" Joyce said in mock offense.

"Not you, girl, not you." Mama Kinney patted her softly on the knee, but her voice gave lie to her words. As the oldest in the group, Mama Kinney could say just about anything. It was, after all, her house and her front porch, and with things happening across the street, none of them wanted to get kicked off, even if it was winter and colder than hate.

Sincere carefully balanced a tray of hot chocolate and moved out to set it on a table on the porch. All five women leaned forward, but before any could help themselves, Sincere grabbed two cups and moved fluidly away.

"So the question of the hour: what in God's name she *doin'* over there?" She gave the largest cup to Mama Kinney and took away the one she had already finished before taking her usual spot balanced on the pane of one large living room window. The cup she'd given to Mama Kinney was the older woman's favorite: colorful, ugly, and made with the distinct imprint of a child's enthusiastic hand. Sincere, herself, had made it for Mama Kinney when she was just a small girl.

"I don't know, but it'll be a wonder if she can get anything in, much less get it out in a month or two! I mean, what kinda crazy nonsense got her diggin' in the ground wit bare hands and that itty-bitty shovel at the edge of winter? What she think she gon' do, ground hard as it is, and this bein' February!" Jody sat close to Mama Kinney, sheltered against the wind by the jutting structure of the house and Mama Kinney's large body.

"Ain't we bein' just a trifle rude, sittin' over here staring at her while she work? I'm just sayin'…" Tricee trailed off when everyone turned to look at her like she'd just grown another head.

"God bless you, darlin', you jus' as sweet as this hot chocolate." Lady tapped her cup with one manicured nail and laughed loudly, teeth gleaming brightly in the sunlight. "Jody, girl, tell 'er what she done won."

Jody looked at Moresha, struggling in her yard, and then at Tricee, and smiled with intimation. "Girl, after all this time, you still don't know when to keep yo mouth closed. Why'n't you go'on on over there and take her some hot chocolate? Warm her hands a little, maybe then she can actually use 'em out in that frozen yard."

"Me?" Tricee asked, startled by the suggestion. Her dark brown eyes grew large in her face.

"What you scared of, girl? Don't look like she bite." Lady stretched her legs out and crossed them at the ankle, then winked at Tricee and threw her a sly smile. "Although, you might like it if she do."

"Lady!" Joyce seemed genuinely shocked at the suggestion.

"Y'all cut all that out, now, you hear? Y'all know the girl scared'a her own shadow. And she way too young to

19

be hearin' 'bout yo past and present endeavors, Lady. Y'all know she pure an' innocent." Mama Kinney's thick lips hid just a hint of a smile as she looked back at Tricee. "Now, an idle mind is the devil's workshop, so get on up, girl, and go'on handle yo business," she said encouragingly.

Left without choice and a direct edict from Mama Kinney, Tricee bravely crossed the street, still trying to prove to the women gathered on the porch that she was not as young or as timid as they all continued to assume. It'd been the same since she arrived in Reason, going on three years past. Because of her age and unmarried status, all the women assumed things about her: that she was naïve, innocent, less-than-capable. No matter how often she showed herself to be otherwise, their prejudices did not diminish. After three years of their assumptions, resignation was beginning to replace the frustration she had initially felt.

With both hands, she tightly gripped an oversized, dark blue mug of lukewarm chocolate that grew colder with each step she took toward her goal. Staring straight-forward in determination, she didn't see Lady shake her head or Jody's broad smile.

Moresha didn't look up, but her posture changed noticeably when Tricee stepped into the driveway and leaned over the fence. She cleared her throat and her voice, when she spoke, was cheerfully bright. "I'm Tricee. Mama Kinney over there, your neighbor, she sent this over for you." Tricee reached out, offering the cup and ignoring the lack of interest apparent in Moresha's posture.

Moresha finally looked up, balancing her weight carefully in the dirt. Her face was streaked with varying shades of brown and sweat made her short, dark hair

20

cling to her forehead. Tricee had never known a white woman to look so unconcernedly unkempt in public. The white women Tricee had encountered in her various jobs and in government positions had always smiled with calm superiority, their higher-priced and more fashionable threads making Tricee feel awkward in their presence. Moresha, on the other hand, seemed comfortable in her skin.

Despite the filth on her hands, she reached up and pushed red-rimmed glasses, large enough to hide the finer features of her face, further onto the bridge of her nose before peering at Tricee over them. "Tricee, you say?" She quickly glanced across the street, then back at the girl standing, shivering, just beyond her fence. "That Mama Kinney sitting down?" Tricee nodded.

"You tell Mama Kinney I said thanks, but I'm not at all very thirsty." She smiled to take the edge off her words.

"It's more to warm you up," Tricee said, and offered again, but Moresha shook her head and looked up at the sun significantly. Despite the awkwardness of her position kneeling in the dirt, Moresha placed her left hand on her hip and stretched backward. "You know, I'm plenty warm right now, thanks to this gorgeous weather. Maybe some other time, though. Right now, I got to get these flowers in the ground."

Tricee, frustrated by the exchange, briefly toyed with politely insisting, but she had the feeling that would get her nowhere fairly quickly with this stronger-willed woman. In the end, there was nothing to be done but to gracefully accept defeat and return with her offering back to Mama Kinney's porch. To show that the failure of the meeting was not her fault, and that she had not been intimidated by the older woman, she deliberately walked with unhurried patience, back straight and head held high, as if the meeting had been successful, despite the cold cup of chocolate chilling her fingers.

The women, of course, had watched the exchange wordlessly, waiting for her report. Noticing the cup she still held, Jody clucked her tongue disgustedly and sat back in her chair. "Thas why you don't send a young girl to do a woman's work."

"Seem to me like she did what all she needed to," Reese replied, and then to Tricee as she drew closer. "Well?"

"Well... she don't want no chocolate." Despite herself, Tricee found herself uncomfortable once again as she faced the women.

"Well, we *knew* that! But did you find out what she doin' over *there*?"

"She say she plantin' flowers." Tricee sat and perched one knee awkwardly on the railing. She took a small sip of the chocolate to hide her discomfort, but then choked as she remembered it had cooled. She held the cup out to Reese and waited until she took it before continuing. "She plantin' something, don't really seem like she care to engage right now, but she say she might come over some other time."

"Some other time!"

"Sound rude to me!"

"She coulda came an' said hello, at least!"

"Well, what she look like up close?" Joyce leaned forward, listening avidly.

Tricee warmed to the spotlight, more confident now. "Same as from afar, 'cept a lil' bit closer. What y'all expect? She white, not alien!" Tricee stared them down in silent rebuke, wondering what the fuss was all about. The most interesting thing about the woman was her

22

spirit, her manner of being, but otherwise she seemed a bit lacking. Her hair was ugly, her shape unremarkable, and she was, after all, white. Why anyone would be interested in her was beyond Tricee, but the other woman, the Black one, she could clearly see why everyone was so amazed. Even from across the street she could see that the woman had a pure and natural beauty that few women were born with, and fewer kept past puberty. If you asked her, she was by far the more interesting of the two women living in that house.

"Tricee!" Joyce shouted, recalling her to herself. "Whatever you thinkin', you obligated to share. Now out wit it. Tell us what you thought!"

Tricee could see that she would need to say more to satisfy their curiosity. She struggled to think of something else, then brightened as she remembered. "Got pretty eyes. Very blue. Talk real correct, too. She seem..." Tricee paused, unable to find the right words. "She seem impressive, I guess you say. Like if she come in a room, you can't help but know she in there." She leaned back, satisfied with this final description, and unable to think of anything more.

Everyone else, it seemed, was also satisfied. As a group they seemed to settle again as Tricee took her seat at the table. There was quiet a moment, and then, "I jus' wonder what they doin' over there *together*. I mean, I ain't never yet known a grown woman could share her home wit another."

Lady nodded. "Thas why it's just me an my boys. When Reggie got old enough, started thinkin' she was grown, she had to go. If I'da had a son, he coulda stayed forever. But daughters, soon as they start smellin' they own panties, they got to get the hell on. It's they mouth. You can always hear it in they mouth."

23

"You ain't lyin', that's why I been making sure ain't a one of my girls openin' they legs. I'm not anxious to see how they gon' turn out, and the Lord won't blame me for prolongin' the day." Reese had thirteen-year-old twin daughters.

"Ain't nobody anxious to see how those two gon' turn out, but we already got a good hint. And you 'bout the only one in Reason think either of them girls is virgins, they both been gettin' it regular *least* two years now. The both of 'em 'bout as subtle as rattlesnakes in the grass!" Mama Kinney alone could say what everyone else already knew.

"Rattlesnakes! I beg yo pardon. If either of my girls was doin' the do, I'd be the first to know." Reese stood in agitated indignation, but Mama Kinney waved a hand in her direction.

"Girl, sit back on down. You can recognize truth as well as I, maybe better cause they live in your own house an you ain't got no cataracts to blind you. But," Mama Kinney swiftly changed the subject, "that still don't say nothin' 'bout these ones across the street, since they ain't related." She looked over at the peach house and the large woman struggling alone in the yard.

Sincere spoke into the gap. "Time will tell the truth, better'n we ever could. But stranger things've happened than two women abidin' under a single roof. Ruth and Naomi did it back in Bible days, and the Word say ain't nothin' new under the sun."

"The Word ain't never lied," Joyce echoed, and nodded. Still upset by Mama Kinney's insinuations, Reese sat back in her chair with her arms folded across her chest. It was clear, though, that she would get no support from the other women, who all looked up to Mama Kinney as if she, too, had never lied. She wisely held her tongue rather than cause a confrontation, but wondered if she ought to stop coming by. Mama Kinney was worse than a gossipmonger. She spread rumors that simply weren't true!

Sincere noted Reese's continued anger and made a mental promise to talk and smooth things over with her. Mama Kinney was no fool, but age had made her too outspoken. Diplomacy, she often said, was another word for wastin' time. And seein' as how the Lord might call her home any day now, she didn't have a whole lotta time to waste. She had abandoned tact for efficiency, but Sincere knew that this particular time, Mama Kinney might have gone just a bit too far. Any woman who refused to see what was goin' on right under her own roof wasn't ready, yet, to have the truth spoken out loud. And the girls, though promiscuous, hadn't yet done any harm. Mama Kinney might not have the patience for tact, but Sincere surely did.

Sincere took her leave of Mama Kinney much, much later, when Mama Kinney finally insisted she go home. It was a recurring argument between the two women. Mama Kinney was about as close as Sincere got to family; the woman who had raised her when her mother was too burdened to see to her needs. After her father's death, Sincere had moved in with her godmother. Mama Kinney had taken her shopping for her first training bra, and when her menses started, Mama Kinney was the first to know. As she got older, she hardly ever saw her older brothers and sisters, and she suspected that was as much a relief to them as it had been to her. Mama Kinney had been her world, day and night, and Sincere suspected that the grief she had felt when her mother passed a few years back would be nothing compared to the grief she would feel when Mama Kinney finally went home to glory. Sincere fretted and worried that Mama Kinney would have an accident, or some other unforeseen tragedy would take her away, and she knew the only way she could calm that worry was to move back home, but Mama Kinney would have none of it.

So Sincere had done the next best thing: she'd moved into an apartment a few short blocks away. Now she visited almost daily, whenever life took her past Mama Kinney's house. Despite the comfortable arrangement, Sincere always made clear to Mama Kinney that she would move back in a second if only she would permit. But her answer was always the same. And Sincere, was almost satisfied that she was within close reach.

Chapter 3

Mama Kinney had been a widow goin' on forty years now. Her husband, Wilson, had married her when she was only nineteen, and he, already, sixty-two. She had been grateful for his intervention, pregnant as she was, with a child by the newly-come preacher over at Bethune Baptist Church. He had courted and seduced her, then decided a woman who gave her chastity over so easily could not possibly be a pastor's wife. In had stepped Wilson, a dignified, sober, older deacon in the church, a widower, and one of very few privy to the situation. He had taken pity on the young woman and offered to marry her and acknowledge her child, although his own children were long-since grown and out the house.

The child, unfortunately, had never come. She had carried the baby through the first trimester, loved it through the second, and miscarried in the third. Years later, when she was old enough to appreciate the hastiness of her marriage and what it had cost and gained, she resented the almost-baby for forcing her hand. There had been many a beautiful man who'd cut eyes at her, both in and out the church, who might've made good, vigorous young husbands. Instead, she had been tied down to Wilson, who had treated her with polite respect, but was incapable of deeper passion. Intimacy had been difficult in their marriage, given their difference in age, and the two had not attempted it often.

They had waited until after the miscarriage before attempting to consummate the marriage. She still remembered the humiliation of that first night, how she

27

had tried hard not to be repulsed by the wrinkles in his skin and the way white hair covering his chest brushed abrasively against her skin. He, for his part, had been quickly efficient, pushing into her dryness without pause, moving once, twice, a third time, and then stopping. It had been nothing like her experiences with the preacher, how his soft whispers and gentle caresses had made her unfold, like a flower, to the joy of his entry. Still, after being hurt by his defection, Wilson's non-attempt at seduction had been exactly what she needed to push home the brutal fact that she was married, finally, without recourse. This would be all life had to offer. It had been a painful realization, but she had drawn strength from it nonetheless. She had stood dutifully in church, dressed in unremarkable modesty, resentfully eyeing both the preacher and Wilson as they conferred together. They acted for all the world as if they didn't share the truth of that awful secret or the knowledge of her body, and resolution was all that had kept her standing upright. She had waited, even without knowing why.

Then one day the hospital had called the grocery store to report that her generally-healthy husband had slipped into a diabetes-induced coma. She hadn't even known that he had diabetes, that's how little they spoke. She sat by his bed for three days, praying piously for his life, and guiltily hoping for his death and the release it would provide. His children had come and gone, unsurprised by this development, unsympathetic to either their father or their young stepmother. Three days later, on a Sunday, Wilson awoke from the coma, to her surprised disappointment and relief. He sat straight up in the bed, looked at the clock, then narrowed his eyes at both her and the waiting nurse as if they were somehow responsible for his condition. To their collective surprise, this dignified and spiritual man who she'd never heard use profanity or even a harsh word, had yelled out "Shit!" before he passed into glory. And with that, she, after ten years of a loveless marriage, was a young and wealthy widow, with no inclination at all to tie herself to another man.

If only things had remained that way, she might have been satisfied. Wilson had left nothing to his children, telling them instead through post-mortem letters that they should build character through their own financial struggles, and had given everything to his young widow. She had sold Wilson's Market, the grocery store her husband had owned and she had managed until his death, and settled down to live quietly in the home her husband had so thoughtfully provided. But the money had attracted more than a few men and even one or two pursued her out of simple liking. Untouched for so many years, she had been excited by the attention and barely tried to resist. There had been warm nights, painful memories, including two embarrassingly brief, but discrete relapses into an affair with the penitent preacher who was now convinced of her virtue and more than willing to marry her, but despite giving into the enjoyment of physical love, she had safeguarded her independence and her wealth with unshakable determination. And so here she was at sixty-eight, childless but for her goddaughter, alone, still quite wealthy, and with few regrets.

Of course, when all was said and done, Sincere would end up with it all. The money, the house, even her love. She was as close a daughter as any woman could have, certainly more appreciated and loved than those vipers Reese had spawned, or the clueless and ungrateful daughter Lady no longer tried to teach. She was more attentive than Mama Kinney's step-children had ever tried to be. She'd been raised without a father, but the benefit of two mothers, both of whom loved her. Secretly, though Mama Kinney thought she'd probably loved Sincere more. Because Cassandra had also been busy raising her other four, she had always been more mother to her than Cassandra, and that was just how she had wanted it. Sincere had spent so many nights snuggled closely to her beneath the comforter, and sometimes Mama Kinney had turned the heat down low so she could hold her as she slept. Sincere had been her small piece of heaven, this side of eternity, and life had taught her not to be subtle about claiming her own.

There was this passage in the Bible, somewhere in Isaiah, where God had commanded the children of Israel to sing. Long ago, back when Mama Kinney had spent time in church, playing her part of the deacon's wife, she had been convicted by those words reaching out to her, compelling her to sing. God's promise, that though she was barren, she would have more children than the housewife. But she had never wanted many children, she had only wanted Sincere. And that's exactly what God had given her, a little bit of heaven, wrapped up in the form of a tiny baby girl. To boot, what with four brothers and sisters, all old enough and smart enough to fight harder than she could for Cassandra's love and attention, Sincere had needed her, too. How could she have not fallen in love?

Despite her love for Sincere, she couldn't help at times

30

being exasperated by the girl's stubbornness. Sometimes she had to remind herself that *she* had taken care of Sincere all these years, and not the other way around. Otherwise, Sincere would try to completely order her life, taking charge as she did for the patients in her care. Mama Kinney almost felt sorry for them, left as they were to the tender care of Sincere's managing personality, and with no one to gainsay her.

Mama Kinney didn't bother cooking tonight, preferring instead to await Sincere in the front parlor. She would come, as she always did, on her way home from work, stopping in to make sure her godmother was all right, as if Mama Kinney was somehow in danger of starving or otherwise whenever Sincere wasn't around. She would cook, making something nutritious and healthy, tsking at any request Mama Kinney made for something that might agitate her diabetes.

Older now, and wiser, Mama Kinney could appreciate the difficulties Wilson must have faced exposing his aged body to such a silly young girl. Her skin had long since lost the even smoothness of youth, and small blueberries peppered the back of her neck. Wrinkles formed one-lane highways across her face, one for each year of her life, it seemed. Her hips had widened with time, and she avoided looking downward even in the shower, for fear of what she might see. Her hair had begun the process of graying when she was twenty-three, and she'd been forced to dye it monthly since age thirty. Four years ago, when Cassandra's death had reminded her that life was too short to spend hours with her head bent over a kitchen sink washing youthfulness into her locks, she had finally stopped. There was no point in fighting the gradual process of aging, and it took far too much energy to try.

31

Still, she was not completely saddened by what had happened to her over time. Though diabetes was slowly stripping away her health and vitality, her mind remained agile. Some of her friends and contemporaries could not boast as much. And, with only the slightest support from her cane, she was still able to get about, although she had not left her house now for almost two years. She was still capable, but a little bit reluctant. Besides, there really was no one to go see. All of the women in town at some point or another sought to congregate on her porch; Sincere brought her groceries and medication, and her doctor still made good, old-fashioned house calls. She supposed there might yet be good reasons to leave her house, but she hadn't come across one anytime to soon. And until she did, this was exactly where she would remain, shut up behind these walls, living mostly in memories. It was not a bad life at all.

Sincere arrived early in the evening, bringing swirling cold and wetness in with her. From her seat in the living room, Mama Kinney yelled out, "Girl, don't you track nothin' into my house!" although she knew Sincere would not. Sincere rolled her eyes in the hallway and stomped extra hard against the mat to show that she had, indeed, wiped her feet. The house was almost as cold within as it had been without. Sincere removed her shoes and left them in the hallway, padding on bare feet into the living room.

"Mama! Good Lord, what you tryin' to do, freeze to death?" She located the control for the heater on the wall and listened as it roared to life.

"Hmph! Girl, you too young for your bones to be so sensitive to the cold. That ain't at all natural, you ought to get Dr. Martin to check that out." Sincere smiled at the thought; Dr. Martin would have retired years ago but for the access his job gave him to visits with Mama Kinney. Not that Mama Kinney ever noticed.

Sincere flopped into a soft, cushioned chair, grateful for the heat beginning to wind its way through the house, and the relief of another day's work completed. She looked down and clucked her tongue disgustedly, realizing that her uniform would have to be cleaned before she could wear it again to work. The crisp whiteness of it was now splattered with gray and black streaks from passing cars on her walk from the bus stop. The light mist that had begun after noon had become rain by sundown, and she had been unable to avoid completely the waterfalls each time a careless driver got too close.

"Long day?" Mama Kinney asked, already knowing her response. It was there in the rigidity of her spine and the way her hands dug into the arms of the chair, as if she needed something, anything, to anchor her in this world.

"No longer'n most," Sincere replied, taking a moment's break before she went about her chores. Mama Kinney sighed. Lately it had been this way between them. The routine was comforting, but less than exciting, and it seemed as if Sincere was no longer sharing her life. It was not the way it had been when Sincere was a girl and she and Mama Kinney had stayed up on long Friday nights, speaking their dreams into being. She had been young enough then to still have a few, and Sincere had been uncertain of her direction and so in need of guidance. Or the closeness that had been between them, even while Sincere was in college, when she saved every happening of her day to discuss with Mama Kinney in the evenings, dissecting and explaining them and seeking her godmother's wisdom. Now, routine had deprived them of their camaraderie, making their visits too frequent to merit more than summaries and casual words. Mama Kinney wasn't completely sure how to stop this process, but she was certain that allowing Sincere to move back in, as she continued to ask, would only hasten it. The two of them, both grown women now, would be bored every day staring at one another and each would try to manage and control the other. The short distance between them, though, was all that had preserved even this much of their relationship.

Then, too, separate homes had allowed Mama Kinney to keep alive the hopeful expectation that Sincere might one day do something scandalous and wake up with some strong, beautiful and infinitely sexy man beside her, hoping to marry her and immediately produce babies. True, Sincere leaned more toward virtue than scandal, but anything was possible. All it needed was a little bit of hope and the unwavering nagging that only a mother could provide. Since Cassandra had died four years ago, Mama Kinney would have to do. She hobbled behind Sincere into the kitchen, watching her gather all of the things she needed to cook.

"So that new supervisor of yours, he make a move yet?"

It was Sincere's turn to sigh. "Mama," she said, spooning cornmeal batter into a pan small enough for just the two of them. "For all I know the man could be married."

"And yet, you ain't so anxious to find out. Take him for lunch or somethin', get to know him. Ask him why ain't there no ring on his finger, an whas his idea of a good woman."

Sincere laughed in helpless admission. "Yeah, you and me both know I am *not* that bold. What do I do then if he says no, he ain't married? Sit in his lap? Put his hand on my breast?" Mama Kinney laughed, too, caught by the incongruous image of Sincere boldly seducing a man.

"I keep tellin' you, baby, you don't use it, you sho' will lose it. And that's the truth! Only reason I'm still in such good health is cause I made sure I didn't waste what the Good Lord gave me, and I had more'n a good time doin' it." She took a seat at the table, propping her cane against the back of another chair. "You might be well-served to do the same, get a coupla free slices, so to speak, 'fore you go'on an buy the loaf of bread."

But the suggestion only reminded Sincere of all the reasons why she had chosen abstinence. She instantly regretted having told Mama Kinney about the tall, handsome young man who had newly been appointed supervisor of County Hospital. Since coming, he had caused more than his fair share of lovesickness among the nurses. Sincere would not demean herself by joining them. She spoke quietly in rebuke, the moment of laughter having passed. "You and my mama didn't raise me to be no whore, Mama Kinney, and I ain't about to play the part now. I'm not like that. You know that."

And therein was the heart of the matter. Mama Kinney could remember brief lessons on chastity, but she knew they did not explain Sincere's prudishness. No, that could likely be laid squarely on the shoulders of Ray Jenkins, and maybe even the errant preacher of Bethune Baptist who couldn't keep his hands beneath his own damn robes. Sincere had seen first-hand the pain that could be caused when a good woman let her guard down enough to love a man, and she wanted to be good and damn sure her man loved her, too, before she let herself go. Having told her otherwise throughout childhood, Mama Kinney couldn't seem to convince her goddaughter that love was worth the risk, or that even being touched by a man, physically, could be done without love. She wasn't entirely certain she should try, knowing she was just as likely to shoot a man for causing Sincere pain. The thought of waiting out her golden years in a prison cell was singularly unappealing, but the thought of Sincere's trusting heart being broken was worse.

Funny, Wilson would have commended her for taking a girl who'd come from such a loose upbringing and instilling in her the "correct" morals. But she had never been as religious as Wilson, and she'd always thought morals were only as good as the behavior they inspired. There were more than a few women she could point to who exemplified this in one way or another: Jody, with her sometimes religion; Lady, with honor that ran deeper than her scandalous living arrangement; and even Sincere. For Sincere, religious mores were useful only as long as they excused her actions to the world. But even without religion, she'd still do what she thought was right, others be damned. It was one of the things that Mama Kinney loved and admired most about her goddaughter.

Still, even morality could be taken to the extreme. At twenty-seven, virginity was no longer becoming, and certainly not expected, but even Mama Kinney knew when to give in. "Well, the least you could do is pretty yourself up, look nice. You ain't got to fall out at his feet, but you could make him want to catch you if you did. You a beautiful girl, Sincere, don't know why you hide it behind those frumpy clothes."

"Frumpy clothes! Mama, this is my uniform. I can't exactly show up to work tomorrow wearing hot pink." Sincere laughed again at the thought, shaking her head.

"Even a uniform could look sexy, givin' some

touchin' up. Take up that hem, bring in the waist a bit, show yo figure off." She reached up and tugged at the uniform, but Sincere swatted her hand away. She peered more narrowly at her goddaughter, imagining and evaluating the shape of her uniform with a few alterations. "Then again, maybe not. Girl, ain't I told you to eat a bit more, you about as skinny as a stick."

"Well, what, you want me to look like them fat heifers always sittin' on your porch? Lady damn near broke your chair last week an Joyce gon' fall right through the floorboards one day, I swear!" Sincere tasted a spoonful of spaghetti sauce and decided against adding any more sugar. Knowing Mama Kinney, she'd likely had more than a few illicit foods today.

"You ain't got to get that big, Lord, no. But you could stand to gain a few pounds in the right places, let everybody know yous a woman." She stood and moved subtly toward the counter and the box of sugar on it. Sincere was deep in the refrigerator, her attention focused on locating some illusive item. "I said it before and I'll say it again, girl, only a dog wants a bone. You'd best be watchin', too, cause even you ain't immune to gettin' bit."

Sincere moved quickly to grab and put away the box of sugar before Mama Kinney could add any more to the sauce. "Mama, you 'bout the only one still sayin' that today."

"Hmph," Mama Kinney said, snorting. "Just cause they ain't sayin' it don't mean they ain't thinkin' it. Trust me on this one, Sincere, you ain't never knowed me to lie!" Having said her peace, Mama Kinney escaped while she could, unwilling to see how many other "healthy" alterations Sincere would make to what had used to be a deliciously simple recipe.

With dinner ended, Sincere took her leave, feeling as if some misunderstanding lay between her and Mama Kinney, but unable to define it. For her part, Mama Kinney was stubbornly silent, unwilling to ask Sincere to stay but a little bit lonely when she left. She sat in her parlor listening to the hush of her goddaughter's absence, wondering how silence could reverberate so loudly within the walls of the house. It was as if the house missed Sincere, too, having fallen in love with her during the awkward stages of her development. "I will *not* ask her to come back," she said aloud to the house in reprimand, stubbornly crossing her arms over her breasts.

"I must confess, I'm so glad to hear it. Would be much more difficult to have this conversation with her hangin' around." The woman spoke from the doorway, stepping into the room with assumed invitation. Mama Kinney startled, then recognized the face.

"Reba..." Mama Kinney said, then shook her head to clear away the memory. "You look jus' like yo mama."

"I'll take that as a compliment," Miranda said, and moved to seat herself. "I remember she was a beautiful woman."

Having recovered from her surprise, Mama Kinney snorted. "As beautiful as she was stupid! A more foolish girl, I ain't never knowed. Hope to God all you got was her looks, cause it'd be a shame if the earth produced two such silly women in my lifetime. This town ain't yet recovered from the first."

Miranda's lips tightened but she did not respond. It struck Mama Kinney that she might well be starting something dangerous, but she pushed the thought aside, refusing to be intimidated by this girl in her own house. "So I hear you callin' yoself somethin' different now. Miranda or some such nonsense. Yo daddy woulda had a fit!"

"What he got to do with my name? All he ever called me was Baby Girl, and hardly that." Mama Kinney caught the hint of bitterness lacing her voice and wondered at its source. She remembered Sandal as a thoroughly doting father.

"He ain't got nothin' to do wit it, I suppose, 'cept for the fact that he named you himself. Jean Marie, jus' like his mama." Mama Kinney could see her surprise at the revelation.

"Marie," Miranda sounded out the word, tasting each syllable with new interest.

Mama Kinney nodded. "Thas what we used to called her, too, Marie, back when we was all young." Mama Kinney laughed. "Girl had a wicked sense of humor, too, yo grandmama. Used to do some scandalous things, just to get a good laugh outta folks."

Miranda shook her head, as if to clear away the words and the images they invoked. The two of them were silent, both contemplating one another. The ticking of a clock sounded loudly within the house, punctuating their thoughts.

Mama Kinney finally sighed. "What you come back here for, girl? Ain't nobody left in this town who mighta loved you, they all been gone for years now."

"You sure 'bout that, Evelyn? You ain't got just the smallest place in your heart for me?" Mama Kinney snorted again in response and Miranda shrugged. "Oh, well, I guess that's that, then, maybe I should pack it all up and go'on back home."

"And where's that? Underneath a rock somewhere?"

"Home?" Miranda lifted one eyebrow and stared at Mama Kinney. "Ain't never had one, not really, not since I left Reason."

"An' yo grandparents? The Lord take 'em home yet?"

"He didn't get there soon enough. The devil came an collected them first." Her face closed as she said this, and Mama Kinney struggled to hide her response. "Guess the Lord *ain't* always on time. I been out on my own these past few years, makin' my way back to Reason."

"You don't look too bad for the journey. You know what they say 'bout cats and cockroaches, the two of 'em always land on they feet."

"That they do. Too bad for me, I was just a girl. It took more'n a few tumbles for me to catch my footing." Miranda said quietly, and Mama Kinney had the impression she was still thinking about her grandparents. She wouldn't ask. She'd never liked either of them, and wasn't the least bit regretful that she'd not seen them again after they left town. They were the kinda people that stirred up shit at night, under cover of darkness, an hid their hands in the morning. Miranda stood now, signaling an end to the brief conversation. "I'll be more than happy to leave this town behind, Mama Kinney, soon's I get what belongs to me. Nothing but pain and old memories here for me now, anyway."

Mama Kinney felt awkwardly disadvantaged looking up at Miranda, and she instinctively wanted to rise. But she was afraid Miranda might guess her reasons so she kept in her seat. "Well, I wish you speed in getting' it, and goodwill toward whoever got it. Maybe you'll be gone as quickly as you come?"

"Mmmm…" she said, not answering the question. Instead, she smiled down at Mama Kinney with sinister promise, making her want to hug herself. Miranda was looking at her as if *she* owed Miranda somethin'. She finally spoke. "I'ma be packin' my bags to go real soon. In the meantime, Evelyn, you might take some time to think, think real hard, and wonder if you might not be in possession of a thing or two that was never yours to keep."

"Now hol' on a minute, girl," Mama Kinney said, struggling to rise, but Miranda disappeared into the darkened hallway. Mama Kinney hobbled after her, but she knew the endeavor was futile. Even if she could catch up to Miranda, she had no way to make her explain that comment. Mama Kinney stood in the hallway, waiting for the sound of a door closing, but she heard none. She frowned, uncertain.

If Miranda wanted to frighten Mama Kinney, she had certainly succeeded. As she undressed for bed, she couldn't shake the feeling that everything said tonight had been carefully planned and orchestrated, even her own responses. But she still didn't understand. She combed her memory, wondering if there was anything belonging to the woman that she might inadvertently have in her possession. She relived each of the girl's visits with Sincere, but she could find nothing that would cause her to return after all these years. If anything, she had been a bit dismissive to the young girl. It had been obvious, even then, that she whatn't all good. If Sincere hadn't been so in love with her, Mama Kinney never would have allowed the girl around. Certainly she'd never kept anything that belonged to her.

The questions stayed, plaguing her, but she could find no answers. Instead she prayed, asking the Holy Spirit for revelation. Miranda's presence had made her uneasily expectant, and despite herself, she couldn't help praying more fervently for God's protection. Soothed by that promise, she drifted off into a dreamless sleep, vowing to put aside the comment and all its implications in the morning. Whatever Miranda was about in Reason, it certainly had nothing to do with her.

Chapter 4

In Reason, the rain came down without pause in torrential sheets of gray and black, reminding everyone that even God Himself was subject to the occasional tantrum and fit of anger Few animals ventured out, and fewer humans. Those who did found their senses obscured by the heavy and sudden downpour. The loud sounds of water hitting pavement made hearing impossible; the thick clouds and heavy rain made visibility irrelevant. So, like the most basic creatures, those individuals who could not get excused from work or who insisted on defying nature moved along sluggishly on the sidewalks, or encapsulated in their cars, wholly dependent on a sixth sense, a feeling of progress. Those who had not, through repetition and perseverance, finely honed such a sense, felt the full weight of the rain as they wavered uncertainly between the lines dividing each street, desperately trying and failing to resist the tug of the tide that coursed noisily past.

In that moment, with the residents of the small town locked warmly behind closed doors and tight windows, the rain gave each person traveling through the street a sense of solitude. In the midst of it all, unseen and unremarked, Miranda stood singing, humming air through the rain as if, by some strange evolution of nature, she could actually hear herself where she stood. Drenched with rain, alone, she sang in complete harmony with God, understanding in that moment that God was a woman and that she and God both knew, *knew* without questioning, exactly what note to sound.

Undeterred by the intensity of the downpour, Sincere made her way over to Mama Kinney's house, as she had every day after work for the past five years. In Reason, there was no such thing as spring. Winter eased right into summer, bypassing the joyful serenity of spring, and so she took the rains as simply God's way of reminding everyone that summer was still a long way off in coming.

She knew an umbrella would be useless in the deluge, and heavy, protective clothing would only have weighed her down, so Sincere didn't bother with either. Consequently, her white shirt and pants lay against her body in transparent honesty, seeking her curves and clinging to them with insistent familiarity, but the rain helpfully provided shelter from observation by curious eyes and improper thoughts. She kept dry changes of clothing at Mama Kinney's house for this reason, and for the rare nights when Mama Kinney actually allowed her to stay. It had been a long time since the last, but Sincere was ever hopeful.

Now she stood under the awning of the porch, leaning her sodden weight precariously against the doorjamb, pulling saturated sneakers and peeling thin socks from her wet and frozen feet. The wind whispered sharply between her toes, insistently reminding her that it could be as brutal and unfeeling as the rain, and she hurried inside, unwilling to submit herself to the abuse.

The house inside was silent, unmoving. Sincere stood a moment by the door, listening, trying to gage her location and proximity to her godmother. Mama Kinney had not left her house in over two years now, and old age hadn't yet made her senile enough to try such a thing today. No, she was here, waiting for Sincere, expecting her to come. Sincere stood in the hallway removing layers of wet clothing, still listening, unsure and uneasy, but unable to articulate the reasons even in her own mind. Surely Mama Kinney had heard her come in, and if so, why had she not called out?

She made her way through the house on quiet feet, alert now to changes and inconsistencies, wondering at her precautions. Doors stood closed off, as much to keep out the cold as to protect Mama Kinney's privacy, and Sincere briefly looked into each room before she finally approached the single downstairs bedroom that was her godmother's own private space. She stood a moment, leaning against the door and tried to discern any hint of movement within. Her heart skipped and slammed into her chest, making the moment more dramatic than merited; until Sincere finally threw open the door, afraid of what she would find.

The sight of Mama Kinney, cozily tucked beneath several layers of comforters and quilts, dispelled some of her anxiety, but not all. Her heart began to beat again, this time slower and with less force. Still she went forward with unjustifiable caution, approaching the bed on silent feet. She could not hear Mama Kinney snoring, and her hands were unstable and justifiably rough when she reached them out to her godmother.

"Mama?" Sincere said softly, shaking her.

Mama Kinney struck out in sudden awareness, screaming. "Aieeeeeee!" Her fist connected with Sincere's stomach, causing the younger woman to double over and lurch back. Mama Kinney, still confused from the awakening, tangled in the blankets and fell, her body connecting solidly with the wooden floor and making a sickening thud. Her voice was muffled by layers of material, and Sincere could barely make out her words. "You... don't owe... mine...," she said, and Sincere frowned in confusion. The words, and the sequence, made no sense.

Despite the pain that had settled hard within her belly, she moved forward again, untangling blankets and seeking her godmother's face, even more concerned now than she'd been when she arrived. "Mama?" she said again, finally finding and looking down into the dark brown of Mama Kinney's eyes.

"Oh, baby..." Mama Kinney said, her face collapsing in relief, and her lungs began filling with short, shallow breaths of air. Worried now, Sincere quickly sat beside her on the hardwood floor and pulled her godmother's head to her chest, waiting for the attack to subside. "Sincere... baby," she said between gasps, and Sincere hushed her, her index fingers automatically drumming a light and calming rhythm onto Mama Kinney's temples. As a nurse, she could readily recognize the symptoms of an anxiety attack, but she was helpless to explain its cause. She had never known Mama Kinney to suffer from anxiety before.

"Oh, baby," Mama Kinney said again when she finally calmed enough to talk, but her voice shook and broke and for a moment Sincere was afraid she would cry. "I thought you were..." but then she frowned and looked closely at Sincere, her words breaking in midsentence and hanging in the silence.

"Thought what, Mama?" Sincere asked jokingly, her confusion deepening. As far as she knew, she was the only person who'd entered this house for some time now.

The silence stretched out so long Sincere almost didn't expect her to respond. And then she sighed and said, "It don't really matter. I'm jus' glad it's you, baby."

Sincere laughed, completely at ease now. "Who else would I be? I'm the only one with a key, Mama, 'less you been entertainin' nighttime visitors of late."

Mama Kinney rushed to respond. "No, no, nothin' like that. No, nobody at all."

But Sincere caught the tension in her voice and frowned now in disapproval. "Mama, I thought you was over men in general. After all you been through, I thought you'd had your fill. I know you ain't back into that foolishness again."

Suddenly Mama Kinney realized that Sincere had not been referring to Miranda at all, but had assumed any nighttime visitors would necessarily be male. The thought made her laugh, too, considering. Not that she was too old to attract a man, but wisdom had long since replaced that fascination young women seemed to have with all things male and the concept of togetherness. She pushed away from Sincere and sat up, looking her goddaughter in the eye. "Girl, if I was entertainin' men at night, it sho wouldn't be none of yo business to say somethin'." Sincere opened her mouth to disagree, but Mama Kinney intercepted with a wink. "But jus' so you *do* know, I keeps my front door locked past six, jus' to stall off temptation." It wasn't exactly a lie; she had no idea how Miranda had gained entry. But she knew Sincere's innate prudishness was rearing its self-righteous head. Innocently, she continued, "'Less the good doctor come on by, makin' his evenin' rounds. He's a good lookin' man, an I ain't so blind yet I can't appreciate beauty, even in a man."

Sincere frowned again as if she would say more, but apparently changed her mind. Uncertain again, she asked, "You all right, then? Feelin' okay? Your heart slowed down?"

"Would I be talkin' to you if it hadn't? Girl, if my heart kept goin' like it was when you got here, we'd be having this conversation through a layer of clouds. Sweet Jesus, sometimes I think you deliberately tryin' to bring me closer to the Lord!"

Sincere looked hurt at the comment and Mama Kinney sighed, suddenly regretting the remark. For some indefinable reason, Sincere had grown sensitive of late. "Come on, girl, an help me back on into bed. Don't know where I put my cane."

So Sincere reached out to her, supporting Mama Kinney's heavier weight despite the disparity in their sizes. She was suddenly reminded of Mama Kinney's age, and the weaknesses that had so recently crept in these past few years. Sincere had to help her more often lately, it seemed, as her godmother became less capable of doing things herself.

Mama Kinney finally looked fully at Sincere and her mouth dropped open in shock. "Girl, what in the world you doin' standin' here in yo skivvies? It's colder than the devil's heart outside, girl, and it ain't much more warm in here."

Sincere looked down, ruefully eyeing the way her lacy bra and panties clung to her figure. Angles jutted out from awkward places, defining the shape she'd had since puberty. Mama Kinney had assured her then that the angles would fill in and become curves when she grew into a woman, but she was a woman now and time had proven the prediction untrue. "No, Mama, I didn't walk over in my undies, though nobody've noticed if I did. The rain is comin' down so hard, all the good folks stayed inside. Everybody all holed up behind closed doors, actin' like we ain't seen heavier rain than this just a few short months ago!"

"They might jus' have a bit more wisdom than you got, girl. I really wish you'd use that truck I got you and not go walkin' roun' town in soakin' wet clothes. Speakin' of which," Mama Kinney turned and angled her neck to peer out into the hallway, "I *know* you didn't leave them layin' in my hallway, stainin' my hardwood floors."

"Course not," Sincere replied with solemn indignation, and headed quickly to the door.

Mama Kinney tsked behind her, seeing through her response. "Twenty-seven years," she said quietly to herself. She called out loudly to Sincere, her voice echoing into the hallway, "You too old to need a mama, Sincere, you ain't no little girl no more."

Sincere's response was muffled by distance, but after raising the girl for twenty-some-odd years, Mama Kinney didn't have to hear it to know what she'd said.

Her clothing safely in the dryer machine, Sincere quickly and efficiently heated a pot of water and poured it into two cups, then used a tray to carry them both into the bedroom. Mama Kinney sat, propped up in bed, Bible open on her lap, reading glasses bringing the clarity of her eyes into sharp relief.

When they had finished their tea, Sincere borrowed an oversized cotton nightgown from Mama Kinney and washed her undergarments by hand before she hung them in the bathroom to dry. She crawled in bed beside her godmother, for a time feeling like the littlest girl, snuggling closer to Mama Kinney's warmth and pulling the blankets up high beneath her chin. They lay that way, foreheads touching, talking about life and nothing in particular, remembering moments like this when they'd both been much, much younger. Soon enough, Mama Kinney drifted into a light sleep, and Sincere decided this was as good a way as any to laze away a rainy evening.

Though she closed her eyes, Sincere found herself unable to reach that comfortable relaxation that preceded sleep. Her skin felt sensitized by the contrast of cold wetness, followed so quickly by warmth and cottony softness. Her mind, having rested well the night before, kept speaking, thinking. Her thoughts made no sense at all, words strung together in incoherent nothingness, fractions of images and thoughts. By and by, she drifted into a meditation, allowing her mind to freely associate words and images and actions.

Jean had returned to Reason. Sincere's first reaction had been a sweet remembrance of the time they'd shared together as children. She had been conflicted then, aware of Mama Kinney's strong dislike for the girl, the way she sided with the other adults in town about Jean's regrettable parentage. Sincere's loyalties to her godmother had made her wary of forming a friendship. Nonetheless, she'd been drawn by the girl's dark beauty, the way she smiled so sadly, always alone on the school grounds, always seeming so lonely. Though most of the children in town had not been permitted to play with her, Cassandra had always been too busy to carefully mind the actions of her youngest child. Sincere found herself sneaking through the shadows across streets on late evenings, just to talk and laugh with her friend. In daylight they had diligently ignored each other, not fooling anybody, until, Mama Kinney finally invited the girl over to play one day.

From then on, the two had been inseparable, openly preferring one another's company. Sincere had always had an innate shyness and insecurity, the inability to relate to her peers that was the product of spending too much time with old folks. Jean had been the type of girl that was destined for popularity, but handicapped instead, by her parent's unfortunate marriage. They'd spent Saturday afternoons making friendship bracelets and promises for growing up, and talking about how great friends they would be then, and choosing which of the local boys would be their boyfriends and their 'old man'; they called out "Mama!" and threw rocks into the air whenever an airplane flew loudly overhead and captured ladybugs with bare hands. It had been one of the most wonderful times of her life, a welcome relief from the loneliness of being a final, unwanted child and the only time when she'd ever connected with someone other than Mama Kinney.

Then one day, her mother had left home early for work, leaving her in her father's care. He had wanted to go out, and his restlessness was almost tangible in its palpability. She'd suggested, with innocent artlessness, that he take her to visit her friend, knowing he would not care about the rumors or even the facts, expecting he'd be grateful to leave her there. Standing at Jean's fence, overjoyed to see her friend, she had barely noticed the look that passed between Jean's mother and her father, but she had felt him relax and his restlessness suddenly depart. He had pushed her toward her friend, smiling lightly at Reba and telling his daughter that he would just go find out what kind of family the girl came from. Sincere had been uneasy for multiple reasons, not least of which was her desire *not* to have her father know the truth about Jean, but there her friend had been, laughing, smiling, inviting her to play, and she had put the anxiety away, dismissing the thought.

For a moment, then, it had been even better than before. Neither she nor Jean had been subjected to the awkwardness of Mama Kinney's watchful eyes; her father had insisted on taking her to visit Jean several times each week. They had even stopped for ice cream a time or two on the way back, and her father had been relaxed in a way she'd never seen before, as if the world had suddenly fulfilled every pleasure promised from his birth. He'd been affectionate and loving toward her mother, even, happily offering to take the kids off her hands so she could rest a bit, or have some "girl time." Exhausted and overworked, she never questioned his sudden attentiveness. He'd send her teenage brothers and sister off with money for their various activities and turn and look at his daughter with a smile. "Honeycake, you wanna go see your friend?" he'd asked with a ready smile, and Sincere had laughed with him, excited by the prospect. She, of course, knew the truth. But there was Jean, and guilt at betraying her mother was nothing compared to the fantasy of the world they had created together.

None of it had lasted long, of course. Suddenly, things grew tense at home; her mother looking with narrowed eyes at her father and telling him she'd had enough "girl time" for now. She delivered Sincere personally to Mama Kinney, sitting with her in the living room, the two of them watching the house across the street. Mama Kinney forbade her to visit Jean, and she instead stood leaning against the fence, talking with her friend as if no street lay between them. They stopped each time they were interrupted by a passing car, until finally Jean's mother came out, yelling at her for whatever reason or no reason at all, calling her back into the house. Or Jean's father would return, and laughingly catch his daughter up into a bear hug, his evident love for his daughter only reminding Sincere of her father's absence and making her feel lonely all over again.

Jean stopped attending school. Sincere would ask her about her absence when she got home, but the girl only shrugged and said nobody had taken her. Dirty, dressed in yesterday's clothing, Jean had seemed more than happy not to return to the place where children ignored her and teachers spoke in sharp words. Sincere had been worried. Then one day, the principal had come to her classroom, conferring quietly with her teacher, and the two of them had cast pitying glances her way. Mrs. Beckson called to her, pulling her out of class and taking her to the office where her oldest brother, Carl, stood waiting. He said their father was dead, breaking the news with abrupt impatience and telling Sincere that it was all her fault. "That little girl you liked to play wit, now she got yo daddy kilt," he said, walking quickly through the hallways of the school as if he expected her to follow. Stunned by the news and confused about why Jean would hurt her daddy, Sincere had run away instead through the streets of Reason without pausing, until, sobbing, she'd finally reached the comfort and safety of Mama Kinney's arms. She collapsed there in them, crying out her grief over the loss of her father and the conviction that her selfishness was the cause of it all. Even believing Jean had killed her father, she still wanted to be with her, wanted to share with her the awful knowledge she undoubtedly already possessed.

But the peach house across the street was empty, the windows quickly boarded up against intrusion. Mama Kinney explained that Jean's parents were dead now and she had been taken away by her mother's parents. Sincere didn't understand what that meant, except that her friend was gone. "What about the Nielsens?" she had asked in innocence, referring to Jean's father's parents, but Mama Kinney had simply pursed her lips tightly in response and told her not to question grown folks. Sincere wished she could go, too, but Mama Kinney reprimanded her sharply for suggesting as much. She reminded Sincere to be grateful that she still had a loving family, with one living parent. Silenced, she had stood alone in her grief, feeling even lonelier than before she'd had a friend, now that she knew what she was missing. She snuck over to the house one more time that night, falling asleep beneath the kitchen window, barely noticing when Mama Kinney's arms carried her home in the morning.

Now here they were together as women, again with only a street between them, but it felt as if that street had grown by lanes and miles. A lifetime of experiences had formed a deep gulf between them, a chasm that separated them far more effectively than mere time and space. Their lives had developed in such divergent ways. Sincere had grown up sheltered from the unpleasantness of her father's death by Mama Kinney's stalwart determination, as well as Cassandra's leftover, sometimes love. Her memories of childhood had faded along with her grief, but she still missed her friend. She was certain things had not been quite so easy for Jean, or Miranda now, and for that she was infinitely sorry. She'd heard enough whispered about Reba's mother and father to understand that they had been spiteful, mean, and self-righteous. Something in Miranda's eyes had told her they'd taken the full weight of their disappointment over their daughter's fateful marriage, out on her child.

Somehow, though, Sincere sensed that the truth of things had been much worse. There was this look in her eyes when she spoke with Sincere and Jody out on the porch, the absence of feeling. Coldness, like she'd had enough of life's pain and wanted to give some back. Or like she hadn't had enough of love. Either way, Sincere had seen a keen and calculating ruthlessness there, and she had been disappointed by Jean's unwillingness to acknowledge their remembered relationship. Maybe things would have been different if Sincere had gone over alone, but somehow she didn't think so. For whatever reason, Jean had not wanted Jody to know who she was, and while Sincere would not out her without knowing why, she was troubled by the thought. Why would Jean return to her hometown, only to act as if she'd never been there before? It didn't make sense.

Looking down at her godmother sleeping, Sincere instinctively knew that Mama Kinney had not told her everything she knew about Jean's sudden departure so long ago. But she had been a child then, and perhaps Mama Kinney had felt she was too young to understand. Had that been the reason behind her anxiety attack upon awakening? Were old memories rising, refusing to stay dead now that someone was around to give them new life?

She couldn't be certain, but she didn't immediately discount her feelings. It was possible that the anxiety attack had been due to something more mundane, but she didn't think so. Somewhere in her consciousness, having lain dormant for years, was the insistent belief that Mama Kinney knew more than what she'd ever told and had done more than she'd ever own up to. Sincere absentmindedly twisted the small friendship bracelet she wore around her slender wrist, her only tangible reminder of her childhood best friend. Well, it *had* been until Jean had come back. She looked down, watching her godmother sleeping, and prayed. This new woman, Miranda, bore little resemblance to the light-hearted, imaginative girl who had once been her best friend. She had hardened into a shell of a woman and there was something burning within, looking out at her with intensity that made Sincere uncomfortable. Sincere couldn't help the coldness that made her shiver briefly.

Chapter 5

Every fad has a beginning, some unknown person who first used his voice a certain way, or said a certain thing, or wore his clothing in a certain fashion. Rich Saunders was the kind of man who had unwittingly started a few. He was the type of man, confident in his carriage, upright, and completely, honestly, and unconsciously sexy. With a smile that flashed white against even, smooth honeyed skin, he had this unaffected way about him that always made women want to peel back the layers and expose his deeper side. Tall, lean, and with a body that hinted of long, rigorous nights in bed, he made women young and old go searching for a cool drink of water to calm parched throats and suddenly-thirsty tongues. All that and a bank account that testified of good sense; the women who managed to get his attention felt the glow of it right down to the ends of their polished and manicured toenails.

And yet, none of those women had yet joined Rich for a trip on down to the altar. After a time, every woman discovered the uninteresting, unmistakable truth about Rich; that he was too honest, had no layers to speak of, revealed everything and held nothing back. What he felt, or thought, or believed, was there on his face and in his demeanor, if only they could bring themselves to trust the truth of it. Instead, every one of them thought there was more, suspected it, but came to know otherwise. And when he proved to be just Rich, everything lovely about him simply faded away. They got bitter about it, too, thinking first that he had tricked them and later coming to realize that even that much deception was beyond his capabilities. Rich was just Rich, and that truth was too honest, too revealing, to be anything other than boring.

But Rich whatn't the type to hold a grudge, so he kept goin' through life, attracting women he never saw, loving women he never understood, losing women he never knew. A mere thirty-two years young, he still wasn't overly concerned yet about his inability to find a partner. Ever optimistic, he expected she might well find him when the time came round. For now, though, he was content to spend his time with the temporary women who granted him their company, if only for a short second. One day, whenever his good woman did come, she would undoubtedly end the parade.

On this particular day, Rich folded his lean body into a booth at Rainey's Diner, letting his long legs span the length of the table underneath. Rainey's was the type of place where people gather more for the company than for the food, and a waitress never arrived before a friend. So it was unremarkable that Jody came to be seated at Rich's table long before Jenna brought over their menus. Rich held up a hand. "Naw, Jenna, you know me better than that. Just bring me some a that chicken-fried steak, a coupla biscuits, an tell Rainey don't be skimpin' on the gravy. I come here way too often for y'all to get over on me." He looked up at Jenna openly, smiling. "An don't let him put none of that healthy stuff on the side, Jenna, you know I gotta keep my weight up."

Jenna nodded briskly, all professional for the moment, and folded the menu back at her side. She turned and lifted a brow toward Jody without speaking. Jody smiled, knowing she had the upper hand. She mighta been Rich's sweet thing months ago, but Jenna never had and never would be on his plate. "Just some water, please. A salad would be good, no dressing. Gotta keep my weight *down*," she said, winking at Rich.

"That's all right, Jody, some women got to work harder at it than others," Jenna said, and quickly walked away before Jody could respond. Jody managed to keep her mouth closed at the woman's cattiness and instead sat there seething, imagining a proper response.

Oblivious to the undercurrent of hostility that flowed between the women, Rich shrugged. "Rabbit food," he muttered, and glanced down at his watch.

"Sumptin' do, Rich?"

"Naw, not really. It's a slow season." He toyed with his cufflink, awkward in the presence of this woman, still uncertain as to why she had just up and left one day without explanation.

Jody nodded and smiled slowly. "Gooooood. I wanted to ask you somethin'."

Jenna arrived then with Jody's water. Shooting Jody a brief, challenging look, she turned to Rich and smiled, placing a large glass of Coke in front of him. The smile transformed the plainness of her features until she was almost pretty. "You forgot about yo drink, but I know what you like." Since Jenna made it a point not to speak beyond what was necessary, her voice was husky from being largely unused. The words were slowly-spoken, sensual, and even Jody got a chill as she heard and understood the other meanings Jenna no doubt intended to convey.

Rich, on the other hand, was peacefully oblivious. "My everlasting gratitude, Jenna. Ain't many women know what a man likes," he said, raising his glass.

Jody watched the byplay between the two and felt herself loosing ground. "Rich!" she interrupted loudly,

59

breaking the communication before he could reach understanding. She ignored Jenna and continued. "Rich, you hear 'bout what's been going on? That house, I mean?"

Rich looked at Jody over the rim of his glass in that same way that had first turned her eye. He carefully considered his words before speaking, knowing immediately of which house she spoke. "Yeah, yeah, I mighta heard a thing or two. Why, you know somethin' else?"

Jody waited until Jenna faded quietly from the table, still unnoticed, to answer. "I mighta been over to visit."

"I heard somethin' 'bout that." He looked down at his Coke, waiting, but Jody realized she had nothing. If he had heard that much, then he must know it all. Jody frowned. Well, there really was no all to know, not really. It had been a short visit, and even Jody knew nothing more when it ended than when she'd first gone over. But the visit had left her curious and unfulfilled, and with a strong suspicion that she didn't like this new woman, but without a reason why. And then that white woman had appeared, bringing her own questions and curiosities. Jody had given it all some thought, and then finally realized that a man could often get in where a woman could not. She quickly changed tact.

"She's a lovely woman, this girl. Skin color of—" she looked around for inspiration but only saw food. "Chocolate! Hot chocolate! She got the most beautiful, even skin I done seen in a long time." Jody wondered briefly if the enthusiasm in her voice sounded more like desperation, but pushed the thought aside.

Rich cocked his brow at her, wondering at her game. It was unlike Jody to give any other woman a compliment. Oh, she might say something about the woman's clothing or shoes or even her jewelry if she felt generous, but never the woman herself. He looked narrowly at Jody but she didn't meet his eyes.

"You know, Rich, you might like her, this woman." Now he really knew she was up to something. Rich might have been a simple man, but he was far from stupid. Jody and he were a thing of the past, but she had not been gracious about the breakup and would never be selfless enough to find him somebody else. He looked down into his drink, wishing Jenna would come soon with his food.

"Rich! You listenin'?" Jody was insistent this time. Her voice turned sweet, slippery. "Rich." That one word was a song. "I thought maybe you might want to go on over, you know, share the Good News with her."

Caught off guard by the request, Rich blinked at her a moment and then laughed loudly. A few of Rainey's other customers, sitting nearby, glanced at him, noted Jody's presence, and nodded before turning back to their own food and conversation. No doubt some of them would assume that the two were back together, but Rich was too amused to be concerned. Jody glared at him while he winded down to a few chuckles, and Jenna threw him an appreciative glance from her post behind the register. "Good News! Good News, indeed," he said in that deep, rich way he had, and laughed a bit more. His laugh continued, unabated, until he realized with some surprise that he was laughing alone. He stared at Jody. "Girl, I *know* you ain't serious!"

"And why not?!?!" she questioned, visibly bristling.

"Well, for one, assumin' you *had* some Good News, you wouldn't ever share it wit another woman. Jody, how long I knowed you? All yo life, and intimately, too. An I can tell this much from experience: if you personally held the keys to the pearly gates of heaven, you'd stand there and watch while the flames got to lickin' at the rest of our toes. Girl, you ain't ever share a damn thing wit me or anybody else this side a heaven, much less the Good News! You just ain't the sharin' type, an that's a fact."

"That ain't true! I go door-knockin' all the time!"

"The only reason you ever started door-knockin' was so you could see what everybody else is doin' behind closed doors. You ain't ever been religious, ain't never gon' be. Girl, give it up, it's me you talkin' to. You forget, I know you better'n most." He smiled at her and sat back, unfazed by the beginnings of her anger. "I still ain't forgot how you came a'knockin' on my front door to "share" the Good News. As I recall, there was more good news to see than there was to tell." He gave her a pointed look.

Jody pursed her mouth, looking at him disapprovingly. "I have often tried to tell you about the Lord, Rich, you jus' ain't never had time to listen." She leaned forward over the table, passionately defending her position. "An don't act like I was the only one doin' more than talkin', Rich, I seem to remember you started it!"

Rich leaned forward now, too, and met her halfway. "But see, Jody, I'm just a man. You the one holy, s'posed to be about yo father's business. Or was that it, then, anything to win me to the Lord? With such passionate witnesses, it's a wonder that church ain't pourin' out the doors wit new converts. I know I felt real religious afterward, myself." He sat back again, savoring the play of emotions on her face, and pressed his advantage. "So tell me true, Jody, if I hadna answered was you gone move on to Mr. Willy downstairs? Old as he is, you coulda taken him right on through to meet the Lord."

Jody was hot. Anger wound its way about her neck, choking her throat, burning her tongue. She opened her mouth to speak, but then she suddenly felt the attention of a half-dozen curious eyes watching. Anger gave way to the realization that she and Rich had been fiercely arguing in this very public place, and although they had kept their voices down, no doubt her business would be all over Reason within the hour. She sat back in her seat, reconsidering and praying for calm. She took a deep breath and tried again. "Okay, okay, Rich, you right to be suspicious, I'll admit that much. I'll even tell you why I want you to go."

Rich waited, satisfied that he had provoked her into some bit of honesty. He had no doubt that she would keep her full motives to herself, but he wanted to have some amount of insight before he would do her bidding. And he would he knew, if not now, then eventually. He always did. Despite himself, he still had a thing for Jody, even six months after she'd gone.

"I *might* be just a tiny bit curious. It's been a while since somebody new came into town, an I got this feelin' that somethin' ain't right in that household, somethin' funny's goin' on. So I wanna know, just sos I can be prepared. Is that such a sin?"

Rich again raised a brow and Jody backed down. "You'd know that better'n I, Jody, you the one claimin' salvation."

"Well, it ain't. I done read enough to know that much." But she smiled, again coaxing. "It's two women, you know, livin' in that house. Alone. *Together.*" She let that word ride on the air a moment while she tried to gauge his interest and figure out what more she needed to say to convince him to go. For a brief moment she crazily considered flirting, but dismissed the thought immediately. Given their history, he might well think she was for real.

Just then, Jenna arrived with the food. She set a large plate heaped with double portions of everything in front of Rich and a much smaller plate of wilted lettuce and a few dangling carrot strips in front of Jody. Jody eyed it with disgust. "Excuse me, Jenna," she said, as the waitress turned to leave.

Jenna turned again to face Jody and the younger woman reconsidered. The look Jenna gave spoke as clearly as words. Jody knew, *she just knew*, that Jenna would spit in her food if she sent it back and gave her a reason. If she hadn't already. Jody stared down at her lettuce, searching for anything white and bubbly. She wisely decided against speaking up. "Thank you, Jenna, um...could I get a little more water?"

Jenna smiled as if Jody's thoughts and her reaction had been completely transparent. "Comin' right up, gimme two seconds," she said, and quickly disappeared. She returned a minute later with a large tinted glass of water, decorated with a lemon slice on the rim.

Jody cautiously eyed the liquid and swirled it in the cup to make certain nothing was there. The brownish tint of the cup made it impossible to know for sure, so Jody pushed it and the salad toward the center of the table. Her appetite having waned, she turned her attention back to convincing Rich.

"That don't sound just a little strange to you, Rich, the two of them livin' *together?*" She stressed that last word, hoping even he would catch her meaning.

Rich calmly shook a bit of salt onto his plate and took a bite, ignoring Jody's urgency. He closed his eyes and savored that first bite of steak. Jody drummed her fingers against the tabletop, but managed to wait for his response.

Having finished that first bite, he finally gave her the courtesy of a response. "And how you know they ain't family?"

It was Jody's turn to look skeptical. "Cause one of 'em is white!" Frustrated, Jody snapped. "Rich, be serious, you know you about as curious as I am!"

Rich considered a moment, then decided to end the game. He nodded, admitting, "I confess to being slightly curious myself about the woman. An I might could help her out a bit, too, and get myself some business. Tell you what, Jody," he said, carefully selecting another bite. "I'll go on over, see what I can see."

Jody smiled and, in her triumph, reached out for her water and took a sip without thinking. "Plus," Rich continued, looking down in concentration while he cut his food. He held another bite up to his mouth. "You ain't the first person to tell me that girl is gorgeous."

The water went down the wrong pipe and Jody choked. As she tried desperately to clear her throat and find a napkin to cover her lapse, out of the corner of her eye she saw Jenna watching with a satisfied smirk. Jody's eyes again searched the contents of her cup, while she silently prayed the woman was simply savoring her momentary lack of composure. She could only hope the water had been clean but, if it wasn't, she knew she was better off not knowing. With that in mind, she firmly ignored Jenna and pushed the glass away, finished now with Rich and this tedious, but necessary conversation.

The Hallelujah Club

Rich mighta been a simple man, but he whatn't stupid enough to make his visit while Jody was around to see. He knew she'd be out, watchin' an waitin' to see what she could see, but he was determined that she would have to wait for his report. He would tell her as much as he himself knew, but he'd do it in his own time, just to make sure she didn't take his compliance for granted. He was, after all, no longer beholden to her or any other woman, for that matter, and this time he would make sure she knew it. He mighta loved Jody for a second, but the feelin' had gone right along with her when she up an walked out his door. He would do what she asked of him now, but for his own reasons.

Feeling defiant, Rich waited an additional two days before he cleared his calendar and told his secretary, Lorna, he was going out. She looked at him funny, and he knew she wanted to ask "Out where?" But he would not answer to her, either, and so he casually ignored the unspoken question and let himself out the door. Behind him, he heard the jingle of bells she'd hung above the door to welcome clients looking to buy a home in the small town. He made a note to have Lorna remove those bells later; they had a homey feel to them that he knew was off-putting to some of their classier clients. Not that he hadn't told her before, but this time she would listen. It was, after all, his office.

Rich took his time driving the few miles to the house on Starlite and Lane, eyeing with personal satisfaction the changes time had brought about in Reason. He had grown up here, in a tiny house on the West side, but the house had been like the community then, dilapidated and sad. His mother and father had been proud to own it, though, and had scrimped and saved and sacrificed to keep it. Rich remembered the resentment he'd felt wearing faded clothing and holey shoes to school, going to sleep on an empty stomach, but in thirty years the mortgage on that house had never once not been paid. And on the first of the month, too, not the fifteenth, lest anyone should accuse his parents of being ignorant spendthrifts like all the other poor families nearby.

Rich's lips tightened with the memory. That house had been the first one he'd sold, as soon as Bernie, his oldest sister, called him with the news. She'd barely stopped crying long enough to tell him that their mother was finally dead, as if the news was somehow unexpected. His mother had been battling cancer for the past four years, and he had been waiting to hear this for years. He'd started making plans to sell the house and use the money to set up his own business before he even boarded the train to return home. His sisters had been angry, emotional after losing their mother, but he had patted and soothed them and sold the house anyway. As the only son, he'd had every right.

And he'd been smart to do it when he did, too, and to get what he could. He'd suspected even as a child that they lived on the wrong side of town; now, his own intimate knowledge of the local housing market confirmed as much. His parents might have loved that house more than they did their children, but the neighbors hadn't been so careful. The neighborhood was an eyesore, a criminal part of what was an otherwise clean and peaceful town, and Rich always did his best to steer his clients away from homes in that area. If they were too stupid or too cheap to appreciate the favor, though, he might yet bring them around; he knew firsthand how someone could find a home in even the most rundown and unfortunate of places. It was just that sort of romantic ignorance that kept him in business.

Surprise took him as he pulled up to the house on Starlite and Lane that had been an eyesore in the community for as long as he'd been workin' it. The paint looked fresh, and boards had been removed from the windows. From the street, he could see that someone had painted the attic windows to look like stained glass, and the windows had been hung with bright, lacey white curtains. The house looked almost welcoming, and Rich was glad of the improvement. It would only enhance the values of surrounding homes and that would mean more money in his pocket.

In seven years of selling real estate, Rich had always avoided this particular house. Not that it wasn't worth money, he'd even submitted serious offers from one or two out-of-town clients. But the offers had waited, unanswered, and Rich had been unable to locate the owners of the house. The house sat on a corner lot and had been built in the prosperity of the turn-of-the-century so it was bigger and more stately than most. The neighborhood was more established, one of the better ones in Reason, and had been the last hold-out of white landowners back when they still hoped to resist the influx of well-to-do Blacks. It was not surprising that the house attracted attention. It dominated nearby homes with both its structure and its history.

But that history was shameful enough to ensure that nobody in the know would touch it. Rich was not a superstitious person; he was, after all, a businessman, but even he found himself a little intimidated by the house. He was glad the boards had been removed from the

68

windows; covered the way they were, the two in front had stared out at him each time he passed through, laughing at his discomfort.

Even cleaned and brightened, though, the house was still stained by its history. But that much couldn't be helped. Obviously, the new owners or renters were fine living there, and the fact that they'd done so for this long belied any possibility that there might be lingering ghosts.

Rich knocked briskly on the front door, unwilling to loiter in the driveway any longer, afraid he'd give the neighborhood enough to talk about already by being there. Everyone would, of course, recognize his car. Not for the first time, he regretted not having chosen something a bit less noticeable, something that would blend in with the other cars in town. But the car said what he would not, that despite the local prediction, he had, in fact, made something of himself. As he waited, he stomped his feet against an off-white WELCOME mat to dislodge any lingering dirt. It wouldn't do to track filth into this woman's house, especially when he hadn't yet given her a reason to like him.

The door went unanswered and Rich found himself leaning over the banister to peer into the living room. Frothy, off-white curtains obscured much of it from view, but he could still make out the general shapes of couches, chairs, and tables. Nothing moved inside. It was midday and so there was every possibility that the occupants were at work or otherwise occupied. The thought of returning this evening under the curious eyes of too many neighbors made Rich shudder.

Rich turned to knock again and nearly tripped, instead, when he found himself being observed by a woman standing at the door. He had not heard it open.

She had dark, even brown skin and thick hair that was pulled back and lay draped over one shoulder in a heavy plait. Wisps of hair fell lightly around an oval face and tucked behind perfect, small ears, and her lips were upturned in a slightly-quirky smile that was echoed in her eyes. "You like the view?" she asked, and he had the impression she was referring to more than simply his looking through the window.

Rich might have turned a shade darker, but he couldn't be sure. He had not been shamed this way in his adult life. "I- I apologize, I didn't mean to be rude, I..." He hoped he didn't sound like as much of an idiot as he felt.

"No offense given, none taken. That is, after all, the purpose of these curtains. By all means, look your fill." Her arms, which had been folded across her chest as she admonished him, finally fell away, and her smile somehow deepened and became more genuine. "Then again, you might get a much better view from inside," she said, and walked into the house, leaving the door swaying openly behind her.

As a real estate broker, Rich was used to being invited into people's homes. Still, he was struck by the fact that this woman had not yet inquired about what he did or who he was, and she didn't seem the least bit hesitant in her offer. Never one to look a gift horse in the mouth, Rich quickly entered the house and looked around as he shut the door behind him.

The house was no different inside than it had seemed from without, and Rich was at once both disappointed and relieved. He almost spoke his feelings aloud, but instead held back, realizing that this woman may be unaware of the house's history. He would not want to be the one to cause her sleepless nights and restless days.

70

Well, at least not in that way.

"Come," the woman said, moving forward through the hallway. The word seemed more a command than a request. Still, Rich followed behind her, through the darkened corridor, past closed doors and a stairwell, intrigued by the evident sway of this woman's hips. Rich wondered if she were deliberately avoiding the sheer transparency of the living room, where he had expected to be seated. But, trying as he was to avoid gossip, he would not object. She was as beautiful as had been rumored, but there was something more complex, something he wanted to, but could not yet define.

Once again, they entered into brightness. The kitchen was warmly decorated, and the sunflowers on the curtains were a small part of a recurring motif. Rich laughed aloud, pausing in doorway. "It almost feels like it's growin' up in here!"

The woman looked at him, amused. She filled a teakettle while he took a seat at the table and set it on a burner. "Moresha's touch, not mine." She sat across from him, crossing her legs at the ankles. Even her legs were beautiful, smooth and unmarred. A lavender-colored housedress covered her knees, but he suspected they, too, would be beautiful. Everything about this woman seemed perfectly made, and Rich had a vague memory of a passage in Proverbs, some warning to men about the dangers of a "strange" woman.

"Moresha?" Rich echoed, realizing that he was staring. The woman rose again and rummaged through a cabinet over the sink. Almost as if she'd intended it, her position served to strain the fabric of her dress over full breast and pulled it higher to reveal the tendons of her knee. As promised, they were perfect, and Rich shifted in his seat, willing his body to resist response.

71

She finally withdrew a bag of cookies and arranged them on a plate before setting the plate before him in the middle of the table. Behind her, the teakettle began to emit a slow and broken whine, and she moved briskly through the kitchen, filling two cups with tea and placing one in front of him before she resumed her seat again.

"Moresha, my partner. She had to handle some business today," she said, watching him as she took a small sip of the tea.

The speed with which she had moved, as well as the inherent sensuality of her movements, had both served to throw Rich off a bit. The smell of peppermint rose from his cup. Her answer confused him further, and he tried to remember the question. Moresha? Partner?

Rich frowned, understanding all at once. Of course. Every good woman was unattainable. He took a quick sip of his tea, then choked as his tongue was scalded by the heat. "Damn," he muttered, and reached for a cookie to soothe his injured taste buds.

The woman simply watched him as she calmly drank tea, which he knew had to be as scalding hot as his own. He was absolutely, irrationally angry at her, and he wasn't quite sure why. She had done no more than invite him into her home and treat him with politeness.

"Miranda," she said when he was once again composed, and reached toward him with her right hand.

"Richard," he said, feeling the need to regain some measure of formality with this woman.

"Rich-ard," she said, sounding out each syllable and letting each linger on her tongue. For a moment, Rich's wayward body rose in response, but then he remembered the implications of her earlier words. "Lemme guess, they call you Rich?"

Deflated, he nodded. She would not allow him even

that distance. He suddenly felt crowded in by her, as if his manhood was being dissected and deconstructed in their conversation. So this was what they meant by man-eaters. This having been his first time meeting a lesbian, the term seemed completely appropriate. That scripture from Proverbs came to him again, this time with clarity.

"So, Rich, what brings you here today?"

"I-" Rich was again confused, thrown off by the simplest of questions. What exactly was he doing there, besides ogling a woman who apparently had no interest in him? "Oh, I just stopped by to welcome you into the community! And to offer my services, should you have a need." In his professional persona, Rich was again at ease. He even managed a smile as he fished in an inside pocket, trying to locate a business card.

"I assume you mean a certain *kind* of need, Rich," she corrected, and laughed at him as if she knew that his suddenly fervent search was simply an excuse to avoid her gaze. "I mean, women always have all kinds of different needs, and I wouldn't think you're available for every one of them, varied as they might be."

A hot feeling shivered down Rich's back and his hands immediately fell to his sides. Everything this woman said seemed to have multiple meanings, as if she anticipated being on this earth too short a time and didn't want to waste a word. Rich wasn't sure exactly how to take her comment, especially given what else he knew of her and her lifestyle. Surely, she couldn't mean *that*.

"Drink your tea, it oughtta be cooler by now." Rich did, despite feeling emasculated by the inference. She reached over and took two cookies off the plate and set them in front of him. "Go on and have more. I only brought them out for you."

"Uh, thank you, but I, I probably should be goin' now. I have all kinds of things goin' on this afternoon, a coupla clients to meet with, lot goin' on." He looked down at his watch and painfully noted that he had another three hours before his next appointment. For a moment, he felt a sense of regret. If the meeting had gone differently.... Still, he felt an urgent need to remove himself from this woman's house, despite her welcoming attitude, before he lost any more of his dignity. Belatedly, he remembered to answer her question. "I'm an agent, a real estate agent, I sell houses."

Feeling stupid, he nonetheless continued, trying to sound more coherent. "I also help my client out with a variety of *needs*," he stressed the word, "that new homeowners sometimes experience. I set them up with gardeners, handymen, even recommend a good church or the best restaurant. Anything I can do to make their purchase more satisfying."

"Sounds like you're a good businessman," she said, propping herself on one fist and looking at him.

"I do try," Rich said, and quickly finished his tea. The desire to leave became even more pressing, and the history of the house suddenly weighed on him. The kitchen. Wasn't this where they had found the wife's body? Rich peered down at the floor closely, imagining that he could see some remaining streaks of reddish-pink.

"I might actually take you up on that offer," Miranda said, recalling his attention back to her. She stood and held out her hand to him. At first, Rich almost thought she was offering to assist him in rising, as if he were the woman and she the man. But then, "Did you find your card?"

"Oh!" Rich stood, patting his breast pocket. "I'm

afraid I didn't, I'll have to drop it back by some other time."

"That'd be lovely," she said and turned, leading the way back through the maze of darkness and into the brightness of the foyer once again. As she opened the door to let him out, she continued. "Bring it back by on Thursday, 'round 'bout six o'clock. We'll be expectin' you," she said, and closed the door in his face while he was still too surprised to demur.

On his way back to the office, Rich thought of a number of different excuses for why exactly he couldn't attend. But he already knew he would attend. He had always had difficulty refusing women, the legacy of growing up the lone boy among so many sisters. That's what had made the sale of the house so satisfying, the lone time he had told them all no. Rich had an inkling that by "we," she'd meant herself and Moresha, and the thought filled him with trepidation. He would be lucky if he left that meeting with all his parts intact.

As it was, he found himself, having delayed as long as possible, knocking on Miranda's door at ten minutes after six pm. The door was opened promptly by an older, stout white woman with straggly brown hair and a tight expression, as if she had swallowed something that disagreed with her intestines. Rich had the distinct impression that he might have been that disagreeable something.

She barely greeted him with a short "Humph!" before crossing her arms over her breasts. Given his earlier trepidation, Rich had to stop himself from turning tail and running back to his car. So this was the "partner". She was nothing less than formidable, and her attitude forecast that the dinner would be uncomfortable, at the least.

Rich cleared his throat and reached into his pocket to retrieve a business card. This time, thankfully, it was there. He offered it to the woman, who looked at it disdainfully but did not accept it. "Um, Miranda is expectin' me?" he said questioningly, almost hoping the woman would deny it.

From the area of the kitchen, he could hear Miranda's light voice call out. "That him, Moresha? Let him in!"

The woman at the door grunted again, but stepped back to allow him into the door. For a moment, as he passed her in the hall, he was afraid the woman might physically assault him. Instead, she closed the door with a quiet, but definite click behind him, and led him through the hallway, now lit by a dim overhead light, to one of the rooms that had been previously closed from his viewing.

Rich noted with some surprise that the house smelled of cinnamon and warmth. Despite himself, Rick could not prevent his stomach's answer. If the smell was an accurate indication, Miranda was apparently as good a cook as she was beautiful a woman, and he had just been invited to dinner. He might have guessed.

If it were not for the silent, intimidating presence of Moresha, the scene was almost normal. The dining room was also dimly lit by two tapers and a small chandelier that hung low over the table. The lighting only served to emphasize the beauty of the settings, which were white and trimmed with gold, and which matched perfectly the cloth covering the table and the upholstery on the chairs. Several covered dishes graced the table and the smells they emitted reminded him that he had been too busy all day to eat.

Miranda bustled in, wearing a frilly white apron over her clothing, with small dishes in each hand. One dish held pats of butter, arranged symmetrically in a pyramid, and the other contained some sort of brown gravy. "Y'all go on an' sit down, I'll be in in just a second, right after I remove this apron." She set the dishes on the table then turned and looked at the two of them, still standing awkwardly near the entrance. "Sit," she commanded quietly, and both Moresha and Rich immediately moved to take their seats. Miranda softened the order with a smile before, again, leaving the room.

She could not have been gone more than a few seconds, but it felt much longer with Moresha watching him closely from between narrowed eyes. Her arms were still firmly covering her breasts, as if she thought he might otherwise be tempted. Rich almost snorted aloud. He wouldn't touch her if she, herself, was being served as tonight's main course.

Moresha had opened her mouth to speak when Miranda returned, effectively ending the opportunity. Miranda took a place at the head of the table and held her hands out, palms up, to Rich and Moresha seated on either side of her. Rich was confused by the religious moment, having assumed the two wouldn't observe any religious tradition, given their preferences. Still, he obediently placed his hand in Miranda's and reached out for Moresha's to complete the circle. He did not so much see as feel her skeptical glance and his hand fell awkwardly to the table. He was keenly aware of the three empty seats at the other end of the table and wished that anyone else had been invited to relieve the tension. Even Mama Kinney or Jody would have been a welcome addition, gossips though they were, if for no other reason than to make him feel more at home and less like a stranger in a foreign land.

Miranda spoke and her voice whispered through the quiet, recalling him to the moment's task. "Grace, mercy, peace," she prayed. "Amen." Her warm hand dropped away from his as she and Moresha began to pass dishes.

Rich silently stressed the word *mercy* in his personal discourse with the Lord. That much he knew he would need if he were going to make it through this night. He eyed the thinly-sliced layers of beef Miranda was passing him with trepidation. His rational mind conceded that he was imagining menace where there was none, but he still couldn't shake the idea that the food could be poisoned, or worse. Who knows what two crazy women, living alone together in a house with ghosts, could think to do to a normal, sane man like himself.

"I didn't think to ask your preferences!" Miranda exclaimed, and withdrew the dish. "You don't eat red meat?"

"Hmph!" Moresha said again, unimpressed. "What man don't eat red meat?"

Before Miranda could respond with any further assumptions, Rich grabbed the plate and helped himself to a large serving, anxious to reassure her and her lover that there was nothing wrong with his manhood, or with him. "I eat anything, jus' about," he said, heaping on a serving of mashed potatoes and another of green beans. "My only rule is that it don't look like what it is by the time I get 'round to eatin' it."

"Very refined of you," Moresha said sarcastically, but Miranda only laughed. "Then it's a good thing I didn't let Moresha cook tonight. She's an excellent cook, but her meals aren't always pretty."

"So both of you do the cooking, then?" he asked, and then realized the implication might be rude. He was more than a little curious as to the division of labor, and who was the "man" of their house.

But Miranda, if she understood his assumption, gave no indication. "Moresha and I both have a variety of talents. We each do what we feel like at any particular time, there's no need to divvy up each chore."

"Miranda tells me you came a'knockin' just a few days back," Moresha said, with a tone as confrontational as her manner. "You find out what you needed to know?"

"We certainly appreciated the offer of help," Miranda cut in, preventing his answer. It was a good thing, too, because he had no idea how to respond. "Spring'll be here any day now, and we may well need a gardener. Those weeds have got to go!"

Rich laughed, for the first time that evening feeling some amount of ease. Both women stared at him expectantly, wondering what had set him off. "I'm sorry," he said, sobering. "It's just, y'all must not be from around this way. We don't really have springtime in Reason. Our weather goes from one extreme to the other, without pausing in between. One day there's snow on the ground, next day you got to turn on the air conditioning. No warning either, summer just come when it good and well feel like it."

Miranda frowned at him as if the absence of spring was his fault. "I hadn't anticipated that," she murmured, and the statement implied she had anticipated much more. But even Moresha seemed confused about the statement, and Rich decided not to ask. The ice broken, his initial hesitation disappeared and he ate heartily, without pause. The food was delicious and, but for the reminder of Moresha's presence, the company was lovely. He could almost imagine that Miranda was attracted to him, for the lowered glances she gave him and the way her fingers brushed against his own each time they passed a dish. Rich remembered the outline of her body as she had reached for the cookies just two days past, and found that his mind had recorded each detail of her figure. Even now, slightly more covered in a gold, sleeveless blouse that bunched at each shoulder and gracefully draped her neck, and concealing black slacks, Rich could make out the peaks of each breast and the narrowed curve of her hips.

"You lived in Reason long, Rich?" Miranda began the conversation, and Rich found himself speaking unreservedly about the beauty of his hometown and the people there. He described with affection the changes that time had wrought, how even the small town was becoming more populous and, consequently, more worldly. Chain stores had come recently to Reason, but already they were all over the place.

"And the nightlife?" she inquired, watching him as she finished her food. He had long since finished his own, and even Moresha had stopped eating to listen.

"Nightlife?"

"I mean, what do folks around here do for fun, exactly? When they want to be scandalous, that is?"

Rich stopped himself from reading more into that one word, scandalous. "Well, there's a few bars over out on 10th, a place or two up in the mountains where folks go to hang out, but that's beyond Reason proper. Mostly, though, people go an kick it at the Hallelujah Club. That's where all the action is on a night like tonight."

"The Hallelujah Club?" Moresha asked, frowning at the strange name.

80

"Over near the train tracks, just beyond Town. They call it that because the experience of it is certainly sinful, but almost religious." He forgot himself enough to wink at her before continuing. "Plus, it has the added benefit of being situated right between two churches. On church nights, the patrons at the Club try to make enough noise to give the holy rollers a run for they money."

"That sounds like so much fun!" Miranda said, smiling brightly in that way that seemed to portent problems. She didn't disappoint. "Let's go there. Tonight."

Rich choked on his surprise. "Tonight?"

"Yes. Me and you. Together," and Miranda's eyes bore into his own, denying him a refusal and promising much more.

Moresha's dishes clanked noisily to the table as she stood and pushed her chair back. Without speaking, she gathered them up and left the room.

Surprisingly, Rich found he was not happy to see her go. He had the feeling that she was taking with her any ability he might have had to resist. Moresha seemed outwardly formidable, but Rich was finding Miranda with her suggestion-demands and flirtatious glances to be a far more deadly threat.

Still, knowing she would find a way to override any objection he made did not make it easier to give in. If anything, his mind searched even more frantically for an excuse that might hold up to her strength of will.

"We'll have fun," she said, and leaned closer. Rich's eyes were drawn to the sweet curve of her lips and the way they seemed to taste each word before speaking. He felt her hand move to cover his on the table, and he was paralyzed with expectancy. Her fingers moved warmly to his wrist, resting there a moment and then softly massaging his pulse. He looked down, mesmerized by the movements of her darker skin against his veins, the way her nails parted and toyed with the light hair dusting his hand.

"We'll have fun," she said again, still moving in that rhythmic and seductive way. "I promise."

Rich found himself speaking without thought. "Yessssss," he said, and his voice was a whisper-thin hiss in the room. Any desire he'd had to refuse was gone in that moment, along with any reservations. What was left was only promise, her promise, that the night would be memorable. Suddenly, Rich wanted nothing beyond that.

Loud music blaring from the Club and muted only by the wind was Miranda's first confirmation that the Hallelujah Club would live up to its name. Rich was relieved. Having brought her here, he did not want to disappoint her expectations with a less-than-lively evening.

Despite himself, he could only savor the surprised envy on the faces of many of the bar's patrons, especially the men. New women in Reason were not rare, but few were as beautiful or as undeniably sexy as the woman who came in tonight on his arm. She had left on her gold top, but exchanged her slacks for a black skirt which stopped just above the knees he'd found so enticing only days before. Rich had waited for her in the living room, imagining what must be occurring right above him in the bedroom. He could almost see, in his mind's eye, Miranda pulling her blouse up and over her head, her back arching with the movement and her breasts pressing forward. He had imagined her thighs, freed from the confining fabric of her slacks, topped by what had to be a lovely, full and round derrière. Rich's hands had felt heavy with the desire to hold it, to cradle it in gentle hands while he plunged inside her, and his tongue thickened so that he could almost taste her nipples. The image had been only enough to tease, and Rich had taken the moment alone to discreetly relieve the aching fullness in his pants. It was not enough, though, and he still had high expectations for this night.

His mind scattered around Moresha and the implicit contradiction of her presence until he'd heard her voice, raised and agitated, muffled by the walls. His ardor immediately chilled and grew a bit less urgent. He couldn't make out her words, nor Miranda's quieter response, but he could almost feel the anger vibrating through the house. Doors slammed and furniture moved against wooden floors. For a moment, Rich thought Miranda might back out of her promise, and he couldn't tell whether his body had flooded in response with fear or relief. But then she appeared, eyes and smile beckoning, all excited and ready to go. And God forgive him, he was hard all over again.

Her top caught what bit of light there was in the interior of the club, reflecting it, drawing eyes and appreciative glances. Smoke and laughter surrounded them both as they made their way to a booth against one wall and sat side-by-side. The red vinyl of the booth seat slid cold against his skin, served as a reminder that they were in a public place.

The Club was set up such that several small booths lined the walls and all were visible from the dance floor. People had been known to handle private business in the booths, but every activity was on display, offered up for the residents of Reason to gossip about and speculate on. Never having been an exhibitionist, Rich was almost disappointed by the lack of privacy, knowing that it would impede the expectations he now harbored for the night.

A waitress arrived to take their order, and Miranda asked Rich to order her drink, since he was more familiar with the specialties. After thinking a moment, Rich ordered her a drink known as The 23rd Psalm for its smooth flavor and calming effects, thinking it would help to ease his way. For himself, he ordered a simple beer, not wanting to drink himself beyond the ability to enjoy this night.

When the waitress took her leave, Rich sat there eyeing Miranda in anticipation, but unsure of how to proceed. He was not usually awkward around women, but this woman seemed to intimidate him more than most. Still, she'd already intimated that she would be a more-than-willing bed partner, and so perhaps his persuasive powers would not be so necessary this night.

"So tell me more about this place. I know you must come here a lot, you knew what drink to order right off, without even looking at a menu." Miranda smiled at him, propping her head against one fist and looking at him expectantly. The pose was decidedly feminine, and a bit youngish, but there was a sharpness in her eyes that was more honest.

Rich thought back, trying to remember any bit of folklore that might assist in his pursuit. "Well, let's see. Club's been here many years, since long before I was born. It's a staple of this town. Over there," he pointed to a darkened corner where you could just make out the shape of drums and various other instruments. "Over there was where some of the biggest blues bands used to play, way back in the day. This used to be a hot spot back then, still is. In those days, the bands used to come on out to play for the white crowds in Courtney, and when that was over, they made a little extra money playin' to their own a night or two in Reason."

Rich saw Miranda's eyes shift and sweep across the room. Afraid he was losing her attention, he rushed on. "Didn't used to be the Hallelujah Club then, though. Changed ownership a few years back, when I was just a teenager, and the new owner dubbed it that."

"Really?" Miranda asked, and Rich could see that he had recaptured her interest. Rich continued. "Used to be owned by a man folks called Simple, great big giant of a man. People said it never seemed like much was goin' on up there." Rich chuckled and tapped his forehead in remembrance. "Sold out maybe goin' on 'bout seventeen, eighteen years ago. There was some...unpleasantness...police started sniffin' around." He shook his head. "Simple was a businessman, but I don't think he always ran things above the law, if you know what I mean."

Miranda nodded encouragingly and Rich continued. "Anyways, he closed up shop real quick and left town, never saw him again. Coupla years later, bar got reopened under new management wit a new name. Been The Hallelujah Club ever since."

Rich didn't elaborate further. Truth was, the club's history wasn't quite so nice and sanitary. That "unpleasantness" had been a dead body, and Simple had left town to avoid some questioning in the death. The case had never been officially solved, though everybody in town already had it figured out, what with the murder-suicide that had occurred the day before. But Rich didn't want to say anything that might lead back to Miranda and the house she now occupied.

After Simple left, two churches had moved in next to the closed-down bar: a Pentecostal church on the left and the only local Church of God In Christ on the right. The Baptist church was stately, the people reserved. They casually ignored the bar next door, except when they were patronizing it. The COGIC, on the other hand, was newer and less established, with a woman pastor to boot. Named it after her, too, despite the whisperings.

For a long while, it seemed the church would be quiet like the Baptist church next door. But they shoulda known better. COGIC philosophy was only one part Bible and two parts common sense and they were not known to back down from a fight. They wouldn't ignore the sinners next door. On Wednesday nights, when musicians in the Club made music, the church made it louder. When the Club advertised a featured singer, the COGIC brought out Sister Geraldine, a round woman whose overabundant flesh had squeezed the contents of her voice box into a high-pitched wail. When the Club's patrons stumbled out into twilight each morning at closing, drunk on wine and women and the pleasures of life, the church's congregants stumbled out as well from prayer meetings and late-night revivals, drunk on the Spirit of the Lord. Both groups had been glassy-eyed and speaking in tongues, the women outdoing one another in brightly-colored dresses and large, chandelier-shaped hats, and in the darkness you'd be hard-pressed to know who was who.

The church had declared war on both the bar *and* the Baptist church next door. To their way of thinking, if you wasn't COGIC, you was on your way to hell. On

New Year's Eve of that first year, the church's congregants finally revealed the coup they'd quietly been planning over prayer and praise. After surrounding the Club in a hand-holding round of prayer, they began passing out tracts to the Club's patrons as they entered in, urging them to spend the night in prayer instead of drunken revelry and upbraiding those who were known around town. More than a few of the women members of the church found their husbands going in, some on the arms of other women. The woman pastor had stood in their midst, preaching damnation and hellfire to those who ignored the tracts and went inside, shaming some into turning away. It had been a tumultuous climax to a story everyone knew was just getting started.

Finally, the Club's manager had come out to investigate the noise and he and the pastor had stood toe-to-toe, she with the Bible on her side and he with a stubbornness born of greed. The more heated their words, the more bets began to fly. The two of them were too busy yelling at each other, though, to notice the church folks and bar patrons co-mingling together, money and odds flying between them with quiet speed. The pious ones bet on whose business would close first; the practical folks, some of them in the church, bet how long it would be, exactly, before the bar owner would have the headstrong preacher-woman sinning with him between the sheets.

Rich was lost in his memory, thinking how many people had lost money on that particular bet. On the following Sunday, the barkeep and a few of his most dedicated drunken patrons had been out in front of the church, passing out flyers and advertising an upcoming event. They looked a sore lot, most of 'em wearing rumpled clothes from the day before with beer and old food staining their shirts, stumbling from the prior nights libations. Most of the congregants had feigned offense, but more than a few skipped church and came out on Wednesday night to hear the soulful crooning of an out-of-town big name band that'd been booked at the last minute, just for effect.

They called an uneasy truce in the end, the barkeep and the pastor, and went back to trying to outdo one another on the noise. Most nights, the church won hands down. But the sounds of tambourines and the vibration of church-folk stompin' that could be heard through the walls only comforted the patrons of the bar, who were reassured to discover they could enjoy the momentary pleasures of sin along with the eternal promise of salvation, all in the same place. The question of whether the barkeep and the pastor would end up in bed, however, was still outstanding.

The waitress arrived with their drinks, and Rich's mind was again captured by the sight of Miranda's lips as they curved around the straw. Those lips were made for kissing, and for more. "You wanna dance?" Rich asked when he could think of nothing else to say.

"Not really," Miranda said, and let the silence lengthen between them. She sipped contentedly, watching the bar patrons watching her. They were obvious in their curiosity, and Miranda seemed completely comfortable under their scrutiny. More than that, she seemed to be the one woman in the world, or at least the first in Rich's acquaintance, that didn't feel the need to fill each second with inconsequential chatter just to avoid the awkwardness of silence. Rich recognized and stifled the desire in himself to do the same, and instead allowed himself to enjoy this moment, and this woman, who so far had turned out to be unlike any he had known before.

Using an old trick, Rich slid closer and casually draped one arm around her shoulders. With his hand, he began to stroke her bare arm. Her skin was warm and seemed to hold lingering traces of the cinnamon she'd used to cook. Her lashes fell, and Rich softly kneaded before gradually increasing both the pressure and the rhythm. Tonight the jazz at the Club seemed to complement his seduction.

Miranda's head fell back, resting on his shoulder, and he could see down her blouse to the sharp way that her chest rose and fell with every breath she took. She moved unconsciously, surely, for no woman could ever have contrived the effect her movements were having on his senses, and on his body. He had never experienced such simple enjoyment, the way their breathing seemed to mimic the process of making love. His movements grew faster, more agitated, and her breathing changed accordingly until he knew that in a moment more he would embarrass himself, right here in this public bar, without having touched any more than her arm. Her hand fell to his thigh and her palm pressed against him under the table. The movement almost made him cry out for sensitivity. As it was, he backed away from her suddenly, recalling himself to the reality of where they were and in front of whom.

Miranda looked up at him with heavy-lidded eyes and smiled, but that smile said enough. Rich quickly rifled through his wallet to locate a pair of bills, then threw them unceremoniously onto the table and stood. Without asking, he pulled her with him through the bar and out the front door, unmindful of the eyes that followed his movements in knowing speculation. His business would be around town before noon tomorrow, and yet Rich couldn't bring himself to care. He could think of nothing beyond the sweet pleasure of this woman, here, beside him, and the anticipation of what it would be like to have her holding him tightly within her body.

He barely noticed how she stood, shivering in the cold while he unlocked the car, but he did think enough to turn on the heat as he pulled out onto the street. She seemed content to let things progress and he did not want to jeopardize that by verbalizing what was on his mind. Instead, he drove with single-minded determination, quickly and boldly through the streets of Reason, determined to get her home before she changed her mind.

He paused at the stop sign on the corner of Sparrow and Lane, suddenly unsure of his direction. He knew nothing about this girl other than her name, and he was reluctant to bring her into his home, his own private sanctuary, without more. On the other hand, returning to her house meant facing Moresha and the uncomfortable questions her presence would arouse. Worse, she might put an end to the culmination of this night. The thought of the large, mannish woman decided him, and he made a sudden left, pulling up to park alongside a deli. He sat a minute in the car, letting the engine idle, reminding himself over and again that patience was a virtue. If he kept on at this rate, he would be no good for her, little better than a youth.

He felt her hand move insistently across his thigh, searching, and he moved away. He wouldn't last another minute with her touching him. Getting out, he felt the rush of wind in his face, cooling him, but that, alone, was not enough. He rushed her up the stairs, his hand pushing gently at her spine, compelling her to hurry. He followed closely behind, moving forward when they reached the door at the top of the steps and brushing against her body. His finger fumbled with the key and he took a deep breath, willing himself to slow down. They moved hurriedly into the apartment, kicking the door shut behind them, both pairs of hands busily exploring one another. Rich tried to kiss her but she pushed his mouth away, instead pushing up her skirt and grinding hard against his hip. He could feel her wetness and heat, even through his pants. She tugged at the waistband a moment, then pushed them down, urgently seeking his hardness. His cock had a mind of its own, springing forward from its confinement to meet the openness of her hand.

He cried out when she touched him, but she only circled him, sliding tight hands along the length of him. His hips bucked beneath her, pushing upward, toward her warmth. He was afraid he would come, right there, and spill himself onto her hand and his clothing. But before he reached that point of utter disgrace, she finally released her hand, and instead raised herself into position, balancing on the arm of his couch and opening herself fully to his entry.

All at once, Rich had the impression of being plunged, fully, into water. Water that gave and moved with him, but surrounded him, holding him tightly, pushing and pulling and driving him insane. It swept over him in tides, revealing itself in the femininity of her embrace. She rode him, her hands gripping his hips, demandingly, meeting each thrust even in the awkwardness of her position. His hand reached up to cup her breast but she pushed him away, instead holding his arms in one hand above her and using them to support her balance. Her thighs wrapped tightly around

91

him, refusing his retreat. He surged against her and moaned, feeling her close around him, and the experience of it was pure ecstasy.

He could feel himself reaching that crest and tried to hold back as long as possible, wanting to prolong their dance. But then he felt her tighten and contract around him, and he could see her face just long enough to realize she did it deliberately. She smiled as she watched him come, spilling his seed within her, unable to hold back. His head fell backward on his shoulder, denying him the image, and he cried out with surrender. Somewhere in his mind, he understood that he was alone in this passion, but the thought was too insignificant to ruin the moment.

It was not until afterward, staring down at her face as he raised his head above her on the couch, that the thought returned, taunting him. He unfolded himself from where he'd fallen atop her, and awkwardly apologized for the cramping of her body that he knew she must be feeling. She only smiled at him forgivingly, and her eyes fluttered closed. Her legs still lay bent awkwardly over the armrest; his shoulders had been resting in the apex of her thighs. Now he pulled her gently forward onto the couch, settling her into its cushions, and knelt beside her. He could smell the scent of her sex rising, warming the air, bringing remembrance.

The last he could remember in their hurried coupling was the sensation of release and the vision of her smiling up at him, and gripping him from within. He frowned, looking at her closed eyelids. His passion-fogged mind had registered but not comprehended that smile. Looking back at it now, though, Rich knew with certainty that while he had been losing his mind, falling into ecstasy, Miranda had been in complete, absolute control of herself and her body's response. While he had been drowning in the pleasure of making love to her, she had merely been going through the motions.

Rich frowned in confusion. This was certainly not the first time he had failed to bring a woman to fulfillment, but for the life of him, he couldn't see how things had gone so wrong. Unless he completely misread her actions in the Club, she had wanted him as badly as he had wanted her. And later, when they entered the house, she had been as hot and eager as he. The stain of her wetness on his pants confirmed as much. She had been in command of the situation, and by her movements had controlled the pace, so he knew he had not gone too fast. He had been anxious, true, and perhaps a bit hurried, but he was almost certain he'd been gentle, and he had touched her in the same places all women like to be touched.

Maybe that was it; Miranda was not like the other women he had been with, and so maybe he shouldn't expect her to respond in the same way to the same stimuli. He would have to learn her, figure out what turned her on, and control himself in the meantime. That would be the most difficult part. Even now, having just spent himself inside her, he could already feel himself rising, returning to life. Something about this woman turned him on beyond belief.

They made love again, this time more slowly and with gentle progression. Rich touched and tasted her, and the knowledge of her filled his senses, edging him toward that peak. With his hands and body, he tried to possess her, reaching deeper into her and trying to touch that part of her he could sense but could not see. But he lost himself within her, somehow allowing her to possess him, while in his impassioned fog he again noted that she remained unsatisfied.

He drove her home in twilight, watching the sky shed the skin of its midnight blue and clothe itself instead with royal purples and the faint orange tinge of coming dawn. Miranda stared out the window, noting the scenery of the town, and Rich stared at her, wondering at the play of emotions across her face. He wondered, too, about the small puckered scar across her bottom lip, but she had refused to let him kiss her mouth. There would be time enough for questions, he supposed, but right now, he would not interrupt the comfort of their silence. He could hear her breathing, inhaling the scents of nighttime, and even that slight flaring of her nostrils was intensely erotic.

He parked behind the powder blue Buick, noting its presence and wondering when they would speak about Moresha. Perhaps Jody's intimations and his own impressions had been mistaken. If she was interested in him, how could she possibly want Moresha? But he knew such things were done elsewhere, in the world beyond Reason. He would not share her, even with another woman, but he was loath to cause disagreement so soon in their budding relationship. Questions and demands could wait, at least until he made her love him the way he was sure he'd come to love her, unhampered by the constraints of time.

When he would have left her there, Miranda pulled him with her through the house and up the stairs, to a spare bedroom. Rich was relieved. For a moment, Rich had been afraid that she had some perverse desire to share him with Moresha.

He spent the rest of the night trying to push her over that peak, and never quite feeling as if he had. He tried every trick he could imagine, and held out beyond endurance, but by the time the room began brightening with the dawning sunlight, Rich still felt as if he had failed to reach some unattainable part of her pleasure. He had never known a woman so controlled in her passions, and the knowledge only made him want to possess her even more. Eventually, though, even her beauty and inventiveness could not provoke him to arousal. It had been too much and he was exhausted. Rich's mind had barely a moment to register disappointment that she had outlasted him before he fell into a deep, uncomfortable sleep, surrounded by the taste and smell and feel of this woman he could not seem to master.

Chapter 6

Moresha awoke to the sounds of whispered touches and the pungent scent of sex. Despite herself, she could feel the slick wetness between her thighs, the evidence that her unconscious mind had already processed and absorbed the events with more than detached fascination. There was a hush, followed by a feminine giggle which long familiarity identified as belonging to Miranda. Her voice had always instantly distracted and soothed and, without really understanding why, even today it made Moresha smile. But then her voice was followed by the tenors of a masculine laugh, and Moresha's smile faded quickly from her face. He was here, then, in their home, making love to Miranda beneath the same roof in the middle of this night. Moresha shifted on the bed and turned her face to the wall, angry. Let him come, then. Better men had tried.

It had ceased to be a spoken tension in their relationship, this need Miranda had to be with men. In the beginning, Moresha had been hurt, confused even, and had tried to persuade Miranda that she was enough. She had given good love, caught up in caresses and sweet sensations, and the kind of emotional connection that men were incapable of truly knowing. She had touched Miranda with close attention, fine-tuning her responses, following each performance with the reminder that she, alone, could make that happen. That sweet rainfall when Miranda came, pressing together red baby walls and brown thighs, squeezing love-juice thickly within. She had been right, too. No man, no woman, either, had ever touched that part of Miranda, not like that, she was certain of it.

But still, it was not enough. And every so often, Miranda let her know.

She was never intentionally cruel, not since that first time, when she had kissed Moresha and brought him into their bed. Moresha had fallen asleep, naked, waiting for Miranda to return. The week before had been tumultuous, and she could physically feel the restlessness that kept Miranda up each night, tossing and turning in their bed, prowling the confines of their apartment. Strange things were happening, and Moresha was alert to the change, but then she hadn't yet known enough about Miranda to understand it. She was caught off guard by the fingers walking up her thighs and the rough insinuation of insensitive hands parting the creases of her vulva. When she had opened her eyes, it was Miranda's face that she saw, eyes darkened with desire, lips curved in anticipation of a kiss. But she had known instinctively, immediately that the hand was not Miranda's. Her thighs had clamped together quickly, causing the hand to withdraw, and the light had flickered on to reveal honey-golden skin tainted by the faint shadows of a beard and amused, deeply brown eyes. The man had looked at her, but spoken to Miranda.

For the first time in her adult life, Moresha had lost control. Feeling violated and at a disadvantage in her nakedness, she had beat black tattoos across the man's ribs and thighs, aiming for his groin (of course) before sanity returned and she heard the distant sounds of Miranda's cries. By then, the man's eyes were no longer amused. They were fearful and shrinking in the same way Moresha's had been just minutes before, and the moment's regret was tinged by an unholy satisfaction. The balance of power had been restored, but Moresha's thighs still remembered the moment of his touch.

Miranda had been incapable of genuine apology, not understanding, willfully so (or so Moresha suspected), the cause of her distress. Unable to fully articulate her anger and distress, Moresha had left. The separation had been brief, but speaking. When she returned, they had agreed. Moresha had resolved to ignore the occasional men, while Miranda had never again tried to bring Moresha into the experience. There had been subsequent fights, though none were physical, tears, and anger. Moresha had tried in every way she could to change the situation. But Miranda remained unchanged and, unfortunately, so did Moresha's feelings. Moresha would not leave again, bound to this woman as she was in love too deep to be deprived of its object. She knew without understanding the need within Miranda that prevented her from speaking her love and drove her into physical experiences with other men. And yet she loved Miranda still. So the two women continued in this uneasy existence, loving and fighting in seasons.

Still, in the morning, Moresha made a point to leave the house early, before the two lovers awoke. She had not yet reached the level of maturity where she could sit and speak civilly with a man Miranda was fucking. It made no difference who he was, simply that he was a man, and that he was someone other than she. Moresha was no longer insecure about the arrangement. She knew that the men were temporary and that Miranda would quickly be done with them. She was, however, still slightly bitter and (perhaps) a little bit jealous. Her jealousy was not directed toward any one individual, not even the man whose muscled but hairy leg she'd glimpsed hanging over the sheets on her way out of the door. He was merely a temporary fixture; he would be gone soon enough. No, if she was completely honest with herself, she would admit that her anger and emotion was directed at a more stable source of enmity: Miranda.

It was, after all, she who kept that part of herself back, reserved, waiting. She refused the open love Moresha offered, taking far more than what she needed but giving nothing in return. Whatever the man of the month, it was Miranda, herself, who intentionally kept Moresha on a constant diet of deprivation and longing. And it was Miranda, ultimately, who refused to stop her physical encounters with men, even knowing how much it hurt Moresha. One day Miranda would freely come to admit her love and she would leave behind this need for men, Moresha hoped. But until then, Moresha knew Miranda would never yield to her desire to be exclusive, and so Moresha was left in the untenable bind of choosing between leaving the woman she loved because she could not accept the situation or accepting the situation and, with it, Miranda. And what was true love, if not unconditional?

Distracted, Moresha gathered her coat and purse and stepped into the sunshine of yet another incongruously lovely but bitingly cold winter day. Even the sun shone differently in Reason, beginning each winter day with the tantalizing promise of warmth, never to be fulfilled. "Bitch," Moresha muttered as she started down the porch steps and out to the driveway, but she wasn't entirely certain whether she was talking about the sun overhead or the woman in the house behind her. She knew without looking that Miranda was watching her from some window, and she imagined that there would be curiosity, fear even, in her eyes. Maybe she thought this time Moresha would not return. Fuck her. Or fuck him. Whatever. Let her wonder. Moresha kept walking, and her heel ground more sharply into the pavement in anger, knowing she would be back, and sooner than she wished.

There was nowhere to go. Moresha sat in the driveway, gripping the steering wheel, and willing herself to move. The keys were in the ignition, the car was on, heat was pouring out of the vents, and still she sat there. She had to leave, but she could not think of where to go. Not a single place. There were no groceries to buy, no letters to mail, no dry cleaning to pick up or deliver. Nowhere to go. Still she sat, waiting, knowing that Miranda was watching, but unable to move.

The knock, when it came, sounded loudly against the window, though Sincere had deliberately and gently used the palm of her hand. Moresha startled, then quickly pasted a polite smile on her face and reached over to roll down the window. Even shielded from the wind by the house, and with heat blasting through the car, Moresha could feel the iciness of the day seeping into the bones of her fingers. Still, she recognized the pretty, slender Black woman she had seen before visiting the older lady who lived across the street. She had often waved, but never spoken or visited.

"Sincere," the woman reached out one hand toward Moresha, and tactfully withdrew it when Moresha continued to stare, her smile belying the liquidity of her eyes. She waved toward the house across the street where the porch was, for once, devoid of company. "My godmother lives across the street. You're Moresha, right?"

Moresha finally spoke in confirmation, her voice sounding husky and unused.

"Listen, I won't tie you up, I know you've got places to be." Sincere looked at Moresha with compelling intensity, as if she understood more than she acknowledged. "I walked on over here from the bus stop, ain't been over to my house yet. Mama Kinney, my godmother, she jus' asked me to pick up a prescription from Wilson's, but my truck is still at home. I saw you getting ready to go an thought you might be heading that way?"

At once, Moresha comprehended that Sincere was asking for a ride. Her mind searched busily for an excuse, but found none, and Sincere pressed full advantage against her momentary lapse. "Thank you, you can jus' drop me wherever you're going, I'll find my way from there." Sincere hugged a coat closely to her body and rounded the car to the passenger side door. With regret, Moresha remembered that she had relaxed her guard since coming to Reason. The doors to the car, as well as the house, remained unlocked, despite the habits of years of city living. Sincere let herself in and Moresha felt herself moving in automated response, shifting gears and backing into the street.

"Oh! It's so warm in here!" Sincere gratefully relaxed her body against the seat, closing her eyes briefly and holding her hands out to the vents. She spoke with irony, her lips curving at the corners in amusement. "Funny, ain't it? Sun out shinin', but even its warm rays are indoors, hiding from the cold!"

"Wilson's, you say?" Moresha asked, suddenly relieved to have found somewhere to go.

"Or somewhere thereabouts. Don't let me make you go out of yo way. I ain't all that particular." Sincere stared out the window. "This town ain't but yay big, anyway, so I can find my way from wherever you leave me."

Moresha forced a more genuine smile. "I'll drop you where you goin', it's not a problem."

"Good, then." Sincere sat up, smiling widely at Moresha. "'Cause I was jus' tryin' not to impose. But the truth is, in this cold, I'd be half-dead if I had to walk more'n a block." Sincere frowned at Moresha, and the earlier intensity returned. "You a'ight? You seemed a bit upset when I approached."

Moresha's jaw tightened. So this was why Sincere had invited herself into the car! Moresha changed the subject, offended by the thought that she'd been so thoroughly manipulated. She forced herself to relax. "You been living here awhile?" she asked, her voice mimicking the casual familiarity with which all of Reason's residents seemed to speak.

Sincere nodded. "All my life. Reason born an raised, as they say." She pointed to a vacant, boarded up building as they passed. "Used to go to preschool right there, Gercha Wilks Academy, elementary school jus' a lil' down the street." She nodded again, but this time with finality. "Folks don't leave Reason. I'll likely be buried out in the cemetery on Bell Street, right beside my mama and Ray."

"Ray?" Moresha picked up on the slight change in inflection when Sincere voiced the name.

"My mother's husband." Sincere seemed lost a moment before she continued softly without direction. "My father."

There was pain there, but it was most certainly private and Moresha decided not to push. She did, however, have other, more pressing questions, and the brief talk with Sincere seemed too good an opportunity to pass up.

102

"Your godmother, the woman across the street…" she began without looking at Sincere.

"Mama Kinney."

"Yes, Mama Kinney." Moresha tasted the name. "How long has she lived there, in that house?"

Sincere's eyes narrowed. She could recognize when she was being pumped for information, but she saw no harm in answering the woman's questions. *Maybe then she'll answer a few of mine,* she thought, remembering Rich. "Oh, long as I been alive. Her husband bought that house years and years before I was even thought of. He raised three children of his own in it, too, not a one of which you ever likely to see."

"They don't come around much?"

"Don't ever come 'round. Like I said, they were his, not hers. They were grown before the two of 'em married. I'm 'bout as close Mama Kinney got to kinfolk. And she all I got, too." There was warning in her tone, but Moresha could not perceive the reason.

"But the house…" she pressed, redirecting the conversation. She was far more interested in the structure than the people living in it.

"What about it?" Sincere asked lightly, unthreatened by the question.

"Not your godmother's house, the one I live in." Moresha paused and took a deep breath, abruptly deciding to proceed in honesty. "Sometimes I feel like there's more to it than four walls, like there is history still living there. There's this feeling in the rooms, a sort of remembered pain."

They pulled into the driveway of Wilson's. Sincere waited while Moresha pulled into a space and parked the car before quietly answering. "That sounds about right." She nodded, quickly deciding how much to tell.

103

"You been in Reason, what, a month or so now? One thing you learn quickly about this town, the whole town has history. Every last person, from the littlest babies to the eldest of our old folks. Even the animals and the buildings. Stories that are common knowledge and a few that are well-kept secrets. Why else you think we all still here?"

She snorted. "Ain't no industry in Reason, an only a few jobs. Used to be more, back when there was only some places Blacks could go, when racial mixin' was unheard of an we all had limited options. Times and circumstances forced us all together. Then suddenly all that changed, and our little home-grown and local-owned businesses got bought up by big chains." She waved toward the grocery store. "Life left us behind, but we all still here. Why else you think? History is what binds us to one another, the reason we stay and, for some of us, the reason we still tryin' to leave. It's not like other places, not in that way. There is not a person in Reason who you can take at face value, newcomers like yo'self included. Everybody got a reason for bein' here, some of us got two or three."

After a moment, Sincere continued quietly. "That house you live in, it's no different than the town. History is all that holds it together."

Moresha thought a moment, then rephrased her question. "But if I wanted to know more specifically—"

"Look," Sincere interrupted, and reached under the seat to grab her purse. She was suddenly impatient with the direction of the conversation. "You will never learn this town by talking to people. Ain't nobody in it gone tell you what you wanna know, mostly jus' cause you wanna know it. What you sense about that house ain't dead, it's as alive as you or I. Walking, breathing, hating.

But I guarantee you this much, whatever it is, it ain't stuttin' you. Maybe somebody else, but not you."

Moresha wondered if she was referring to Miranda, but Sincere moved quickly before she could ask, pushing open the door and letting in rushing, ice-cold wind. She turned back to look at Moresha, her eyes narrowed against the wind. "Everything you need to know 'bout this town, you gotta find it out by livin' in it. No other way. None at all." She smiled to soften the refusal. "But I sure do appreciate the ride, all the same. And the opportunity to speak. I expect it won't be the last?"

Moresha chuckled suddenly, knowing when to quit. Sincere had referred only to what she might *need* to know, not what she just wanted. She suspected she might actually like this woman who had so neatly avoided her questioning, and for the first time since arriving, she actually hoped she might stay long enough to find out. "Not at all. I'm sure another such opportunity will present itself real soon. Real soon," and she smiled as she watched the car door slam behind her.

Sincere reflected on that comment as she rushed from the car into the store. A body could pass on to the next life, still waiting for opportunity. No, opportunity was a device, a tool to be created and used when the occasion warranted. Like what just happened. Sincere now knew that the woman named Moresha had no true knowledge of Miranda's purpose, and no understanding of why Miranda was here. But she was a smart, perceptive woman, that much had been evident, and given time and the opportunity, she would certainly understand. Sincere quickly smiled. Moresha would be creating that opportunity as soon as she got home, and Sincere would wait. When the time was right, she would find the *opportunity* to discover exactly what that purpose was.

In the interim, however, meeting the woman had raised more questions than it answered. From Sincere's point of view, it was difficult to see what attracted the two women to one another. Certainly, looks could not be a large part of it. Miranda had grown into her promised beauty, true, but Moresha seemed the type to look beyond that, to see a person from the inside out. Intuitive, but more than that, genuine. Even Sincere had felt dissected when the woman looked at her with those piercing blue eyes.

She would be less than honest if she didn't acknowledge that Moresha certainly had nothing physically attractive about her. Well, besides her eyes, which were compelling in an odd way. Her figure was flat, functional, almost mannish in its lack of curves. Her face had been an odd assortment of features put together in a way that didn't quite seem to match. Her skin had been blue in some places, pink in others, as if showing the marks of life and living. If she had ever been beautiful, or even passing pretty, it must have been a phase she'd grown out of quickly. Now, any beauty that remained was in her spirit, the type of beauty only someone who loved her could grow to appreciate.

It was possible that Miranda had *grown* into her relationship with Moresha, but somehow Sincere didn't think so. There had been a nervousness about her questioning, the implication that she couldn't have gotten the same information from Miranda. Their relationship seemed new, fragile somehow. But surely it couldn't be that new? Moresha had, after all, followed her to Reason, and the two were living together, so certainly there must have been some length and substance to their relationship prior to their arrival.

Too, Moresha had seemed to accept Rich's presence in the house. This morning she had seemed questioning, angry even, but far from ready to leave. Sincere wondered what kind of woman would stay in such a situation. It was clear that the depth of any love shared between the two women primarily flowed one way. If Moresha accepted Rich's presence in the house, it would not be because Miranda treated her so well.

Sincere shrugged to herself as she stood in line to await the pharmacist. With her limited experience, she couldn't figure out male-female relationships, let alone probe the complexities that must be inherent in a relationship between two women. Whatever the reasoning behind Miranda's return, Rich's presence, and Moresha's acceptance, she would not figure it out any time soon. It was a conundrum for another day, when she had more facts at her disposal.

For now, though, she would keep her eyes and ears open, and she would be prepared. Miranda's presence in Reason was not idle; clearly she expected to accomplish something, and Sincere knew that whatever it was, would involve her. It was inconceivable that it would not, given their shared history. So without knowing either Miranda's agenda or her goals, Sincere knew she would need to be prepared for anything. The task was daunting, but not impossible, and Sincere determined to watch Moresha even more closely than Miranda. When Miranda did make her move, Moresha would almost certainly be the first to know, and Sincere right after her.

Chapter 7

She woke him by his senses. His mouth was filled with the taste of her, her tongue battling his own, her lips hungrily capturing his and licking at them before she bit down in reproach. Her hands moved busily between his thighs, touching him roughly, moving and manipulating him, forcing a response. Her thighs moved against his and she pushed away the sheet with her feet, not allowing for the possibility of refusal. Not that Rich would have. From that instant of awakening, he wanted to touch and taste her as much as she wanted him.

His hand rose between them and briefly touched her breast before she grasped him by his wrist and pushed him away. He could feel the cottony-softness of her sheets brushing against his skin, heightening his senses. He was stronger than she, he knew, but her order was as clear as if it had been spoken aloud. He did not try to touch her again, but let her continue her exploration and assault as she desired until his head and his body were so filled with her, there was no discernable location where he ended and she began.

Their coming together was violent, almost, but tempered by her lesser strength. She moved and positioned Rich as she desired, and even knowing he could resist, that such resistance would be the privilege of superior strength he did not have. Could not have. Beneath his acquiescence lay fear; the fear that she, angered by his resistance, would reject him. Worse, that she would refuse to allow him to stroke and please her body, as he so desired to do. So rather than risk her unknown and unpredictable reaction, Rich's body acquired the pliant capabilities of a doll, holding contortions and positions as she required. For his complacency, he experienced what was certainly the most supreme pleasure: a feeling of overwhelming fullness, the knowledge of becoming complete.

When she finished with him, he lay alone again, drained and bereft, aching for the pressure of her body lying against his chest. His body was attuned to this woman. He imagined he could actually detect, with the transparent down covering his body, the slight shift of air parting when she moved. His nostrils flared, inhaling the complexity of her scent: stale cinnamon, sex, and something else. Something he recognized but could not name. His eyes noted little details like the sheen of moisture on her right thigh and the way it reflected light. He felt connected to her, somehow, as if his seed on her body marked her for all the world to see as his own. From somewhere in the house, a door opened and closed noisily, and she moved to the window, parting the curtains and standing there in her beauty. Something about the action felt right, as if she was deliberately broadcasting his ownership before the public. Heat radiated from a space somewhere in his chest and Rich realized immediately the significance; he was truly, incredibly, unchangingly in love with this woman. *This woman!*

Rich suddenly wanted to stand with her there in the window, to hold her in his arms and declare himself. He would marry her, of course. The thought brought a flush of pleasure, and more, as he imagined that even now his seed could be traveling through the hairy thinness of her fallopian tubes, creating life within her. The realization was provocative and sexy all at once. He looked down to note with some surprise that he was hard again, ready to reinforce what now seemed less a fantasy than an absolute.

He made some sound, a groan perhaps, and Miranda turned. She stared at him, then glanced down to see his cock, aroused and reaching toward her. She smiled, comprehending, and that smile was almost enough.

The curtains fell again into place, removing the morning sun. Miranda moved toward him, reaching, touching, knowing. He could not help himself. His body moved toward her instinctively, wanting. Her nails scraped lightly against the inside of his thighs, and then came the exquisite sensation of being cupped by her in her small hands. Rich could feel his seed rising, threatening to undo him. She removed her hand and replaced it with his own, and desire abruptly confronted confusion.

He must have closed his eyes at some point in the process, because he opened them now in startled awareness to see that she had removed herself and sat, expectantly, on a nearby chair facing the bed. Her thighs were parted, advertising her womanhood, exposing her scent. Rich's hand closed around himself in involuntary reaction, tightening, cutting off the circulation of oxygen and blood. He could feel himself moving hurriedly, pumping and surging toward a culmination, but could not seem to stop. Even in this state of near-fulfillment, his mind registered the uncomfortable knowledge that she was watching him as he pleasured himself. He had never done this before with a woman. He would have expected the experience to be exciting, perhaps, a prelude to something more substantial. Now, though, before this woman, he felt somehow ashamed, as if the act relieved him of his humanity and replaced it, instead, with the raw and unrestrained sexuality of an animal, one that even he was powerless to control.

It was over in a moment, further completing Rich's shame. He was afraid to look, but he could feel the sticky fluidity of wasted seed flowing over his hand and between his fingers. His grip relaxed, his body, too. He lay there, breathing, listening to the hum of air in the room, and the soft sounds of Miranda's presence. He noticed immediately when she left, felt her vitality withdraw from the room, and the emptiness it left behind. Still, he waited a few moments more before opening his eyes and stretching his body. He swung his legs over the side of the bed, his eyes searching the room for the items of clothing he had arrived wearing last night. They were not there. Instead, his eyes lit upon a dark spot staining the okra velvet of the chair Miranda had occupied only moments before. He moved closer, ran his fingers over the spot to confirm what he already knew. As humiliating as the experience of pleasuring himself before this woman had seemed, Miranda had apparently been both excited and aroused. The proof was there, staining the chair, testifying to his shame.

Hungry, he had no difficulty locating the kitchen, even though he moved about the house with the timid knowledge that he did so clothed only with bed sheets wrapped around his waist. His clothes had disappeared somewhere in the evening's activities, and he would have to ask Miranda to locate them. He only hoped that Moresha was not there, waiting to unman him with one critical, withering look at his manhood. He had, after all, just survived a marathon of lovemaking. It was not his fault that his manhood had shriveled into sedated nothingness, resting for what he hoped would be an equally active evening to come.

Miranda must have heard him coming, for she had already begun preparing a late breakfast. She stood before the stove, still naked, briskly and efficiently whishing liquid in a small pan. Sunlight streaming into the windows suggested, and the clock above the stove confirmed, that it was almost noon. Shit. Lorna would be wondering, and he had a vague recollection of a meeting scheduled for this coming afternoon; a house he had been trying to sell for the past eight months. Even as he remembered the importance of the meeting, he knew he would not attend. His mind could not yet imagine leaving this woman behind, and somewhere in the recesses, he acknowledged a slight suspicion that she would lose all interest once he disappeared from view. Out of sight, out of mind.

Somehow, seeing that she was naked relaxed him and he felt comfortable enough to remove the bulky sheet. The feeling was irrational, considering that she was naked in her own home, and he was naked before a woman he barely knew in a house he'd never set foot in until three days before. His mind shied away from that knowledge. He knew her, of course he did, he was in *love* with her!

Miranda's greeting was all smiles and honeyed kisses, even as she held her hands away from him, still holding cooking paraphernalia in each. He tried to catch and hold her to his body, but she danced away quickly, turning her back on him and giving him a lovely, but somehow insufficient view of her backside and her nipples bouncing in profile.

"My clothes, you happen to know where they are?"

Rich said, and stood awkwardly waiting for her answer.

Miranda waved the whisk in dismissal. "I'm sure that's Moresha's doing. She must've put them in the wash. You don't need them. Sit down, sit down! The food is almost ready."

Rich obeyed, although the vinyl seat cushion felt strange against his bare skin. It was an awkward sensation, but he didn't seem to have a choice in the matter.

"You like eggs," she said, and sat a plate in front of him, but it wasn't really a question.

Rich ate quietly, without comment, smiling at her to make sure she knew he appreciated the gesture. It had been a while since a woman had cooked him breakfast, and he found that he enjoyed the thoroughly domestic implications, especially coming from this woman. While he ate, she sat across from him and watched him, head propped against her fist.

"You ain't gonna eat none?" he asked, already knowing the answer. Women never ate around him, as if he were some kind of disease that disrupted a body's natural functions.

"I've already had my breakfast," she said, and bared her teeth in such a way, he almost thought she was referring to him.

Rich was anxious to finish eating and speak with her. He had a lot of questions about who she was and where she'd come from, and would she marry him, now, before somebody else discovered her presence? But first, he thought he'd better resolve the issue that was Moresha. It was understandable, though perhaps a little strange, that she and Moresha had taken to one another when there were perhaps no other men available. But now, he

113

was here, and although he still harbored some doubts about how satisfying she had found their lovemaking, he knew that he could give her more, much more, than Moresha ever could. She was, after all, only a woman. She could not fill Miranda the way he could, and she was therefore unnecessary, and certainly a bit inconsistent with his picture of perfect domesticity.

He found, however, that he was too hungry to quickly finish, and so he ate two more helpings of scrambled eggs, toast, and grits before finally pushing back his plate. "Girl, you gone make me fat and round 'fore long. But then, maybe all that physical activity we been up to'll burn it off." He rubbed his stomach and pushed away from the table, briefly tightening and displaying his muscled chest. This was usually a source of attraction for most women.

Miranda, though, didn't seem particularly impressed. She rushed forward to collect his dishes, then washed them before setting them out to dry. He noted the action. She would make a good wife.

"I need to call the office—" he began, but she interrupted.

"You won't go in today."

Rich paused. Yes, he had been planning himself to simply call in, but it didn't seem entirely right that she should presume his decision. She turned toward him, at the same time leaning back over the sink, and his objections disappeared. Her breasts rose, straining the muscles of her abdomen, emphasizing the narrowness of her hips. Of course he would call into work, but not right now. She wanted him and he wanted to be with her, and there was, he supposed, nothing objectionable about a woman making her wishes known. Nothing at all.

Later, when he tried to broach the subject of More-

114

sha, she touched him. And when he asked her about her last name, her tongue brushed against his lips. Much later, when he said he thought maybe they should talk more permanently, her fingers played piano keys in the dimpled spaces above his backside. The questions, unanswered, faded to the recesses of his mind, lost in the preeminence of this passion, consumed by the desire she aroused within him. If he doubted her answers for a moment, he had only to remember the fervor of her response, the way her body had lifted and swelled with him, the way she had taken care to bring him to complete satisfaction multiple times.

They stayed together all afternoon, making love throughout the house, marking every surface with memories and the scents of their lovemaking. He was sleeping upstairs in her room when Moresha returned, peacefully oblivious to the sensuality of their greeting, the way Miranda used her hands, hands she had so recently used on him, to stir Moresha. Moresha's purse and keys lay, forgotten, near the door where they had fallen while the two women touched and tasted one another in the dining room, balanced precariously against the white linen covering the table. For a moment, Moresha almost forgot the man she knew still lay above, awaiting Miranda's desire. But then she caught the faintest scent on Miranda's body, the remnant of passion she knew she had not inspired. Despite that, she could not prevent the joy of her response. It was always this way; Moresha's fear of losing Miranda mixed with her excitement at the confirmation of her love to form a strange, profane sort of desire. Miranda would only use that desire to fuel her passions as she lay and copulated with whatever man she happened to be fucking at the moment, but Moresha could not prevent her own reaction any more than she could stop Miranda from wanting to be filled by a man. Miranda was who she was, and Moresha could not help being caught up in this strangely erotic, selfishly demanding kind of love.

Miranda fed Rich dinner in bed and he realized, suddenly, that he had neither showered nor dressed the entire day. His mouth felt dry, foul; he had not thought to bring a toothbrush or an overnight bag with clean underwear. Yet, still she seemed to want him. The fire of her touch removed any lingering sense of self-consciousness. Tomorrow, he promised himself. Tomorrow he would take care of the many things left undone: catch up on his work, locate his clothing, brush his teeth. Maybe he would even go home and shower. Tomorrow would be soon enough. But right now, right this minute, his senses were again overwhelmed by the experience of Miranda, and the readiness of his response. He had never been this way with a woman before; but then again, he had never had just this woman before. She was beautifully unpredictable, demanding one moment and giving the next—a living fantasy. He couldn't help being satisfied, even if he still doubted she felt the same.

Jody came to visit late Friday afternoon, expecting to catch Rich at his office. Lorna, his secretary, took great satisfaction in informing her he had called in for the day.

"Well, is he out with a client?" she demanded without pause on her way to his door. Rich had not informed her of his visit with Miranda on Tuesday, and she had been more than a little bit peeved when she heard it around

116

the way. She thought he had understood that she expected him to report back to her.

"Client!" Lorna snorted, stopping Jody in her tracks and shooting a skeptical look. She rifled through a stack of paper, ignoring Jody momentarily while she enjoyed the superiority of her position. "Well, I guess you could call her a client, but that ain't how *I* would term her."

"It ain't?" Jody asked, confused, coming back again to stand before the secretary's desk.

"Naw, girl, ain't you heard the news? Or you ain't been out much lately?" She looked Jody up and down, staring pointedly at her clothing. Jody had taken care in her dress today, anticipating this visit, but now she self-consciously remembered that the shoes were slightly scuffed and the dress last season. Still, it was one of her nicest outfits, chosen because it showcased her body at its best, and Jody defensively stared Lorna down. If she didn't have a man right now to take her out and about Town, it was because she had chosen otherwise. It was *not*, as Lorna undoubtedly assumed, because she lacked offers.

For once, though, Lorna was not intimidated by this woman who had often treated her as if she was beneath her notice. Lorna had some bite to her tongue, too, when she so desired, but had always been restrained by Jody's power over her boss. Released from that particular fear, she paused a moment to contemplate exactly how she would let this news drop with just the right timing, and what words she would use. A feeling coursed through her, heating her skin and she recognized it immediately for what it was—satisfaction.

"Folks say they saw him out at the Hallelujah Club last night, all but doin' the do wit some woman in a booth. Heard tale she that woman live out 'cross the street from Mama Kinney, and while I ain't seen her myself," Lorna leaned over her desk, drawing Jody closer, "I do hear she's somethin' pretty." She shook her head in false castigation. "Shameful, really, the way them two was carryin' on. Ain't never knowed Rich to be so up on a woman he lose his head *and* his reputation, all in the same night."

She leaned back, all business again, hands clasped atop her desk and voice brisk and dismissive. She almost looked professional, but for her words. "Now, you know I don't much credit gossip, but I *will* tell you this…he ain't even bothered callin' 'til well-nigh noon, and when he did, I swear to God, she musta been handlin' business while he was right there on the phone! I ain't never heard his voice hit that particular note, and you *know* I done seen and heard a lot of that man over the last six years."

Jody stood there, shaken, reminded suddenly of her visits and attempts to seduce Rich right there in his office. That was after her interest had started waning. He had never conceded, always reminding Jody that the walls were thin and Lorna was on the other side. She felt awkward in Lorna's presence, confused, wondering if Lorna could possibly know all that. How thin, exactly, were these walls? And how could Rich be with Miranda? For God's sake, she had told him to meet the girl, not *do* her. Anger heated her face and prevented her from making a more graceful exit. Instead, she rushed out without further comment, hearing the bells that rang behind her as an echo of the laughter she knew Lorna could barely restrain.

Chapter 8

The weather was capricious, warm and welcoming one day, cold and forbidding the next. It allowed for no prediction, no opportunity to enjoy or observe. Mama Kinney was used to the ever-changing nature of the weather in Reason; she had grown up knowing and loving it, but still unable to predict it. When she was younger, she had woken early on Saturdays to talk to morning, waiting for it to rise, communing with it in that close and uninhibited way of two women who are wary of one another, but friendly all the same. She would sometimes ask for small blessings, like sunshine in the middle of winter, and every now and then the weather would comply.

Most folks had learned to expect what was least expected living here in Reason, and bright, sunny days in the middle of winter were nothing if not expectedly unexpected. If an ice storm came in the middle of summer, folks in Reason would just get out their snow boots and put the chains back on their cars. The only thing they'd learned to count on, as far as the weather went, was that every year there'd be two seasons, summer and winter, and nothing in between.

Even knowing this, Mama Kinney prayed hard on Friday night that rain would come on Saturday. Not passive, sprinkling rain, the kind of which had been falling intermittently all week, but the sort of drenching, forbidding rain that kept stray dogs cowering under foundations and people locked behind closed doors with the oven open and all furnaces on for heat. That kind of rain, pouring angrily down from the heavens, something that would stop the tide of curious people Mama Kinney knew enough to expect come morning. Women who had worked hard all week taking care of somebody else's children, washin' somebody else's ass, and cleaning somebody else's house, wouldn't dream of wasting their weekend doing the same at home. Those women had nothing better to do than laze away a Saturday afternoon, gossiping and watching the house across the street for whatever new thing might occur.

But if the weather was a woman, she was nothing short of perverse. The storm that'd been dropping light rain all week passed over, stopped shortly by to visit, then gathered itself and continued on to dryer climes like a polite neighbor who knows when she's worn her welcome. Morning came in peacefully dawning, all brightly-patterned sunshine and wet-scented earth. Even the cold, biting wind was mostly gone, replaced by a gentler breeze that tickled the nostrils and toyed with your hair. Mama Kinney sighed in disappointment, knowing better than to complain, lest the day get brighter. There was only one other person in Reason who would look out at the sunshine and share her disappointment.

Sincere called shortly past seven and got straight to the point. She was all business and details, saying that she'd be over by nine and asking if Mama Kinney needed anything. "Bring supplies, would you?" Mama Kinney asked in defeat, knowing Sincere would understand exactly what supplies to bring. "I'm running low on more'n a few items, what with the week it's been."

"Don't worry, Mama, I'll bring in supplies and maybe a few reinforcements." Before Mama Kinney could question her on that, the phone went dead in her ear. Mama Kinney hung it up and sighed, knowing she had only a short bit of time to eat, wash, change, and meditate before the tides came in.

Sincere arrived as promised, fifteen to nine with a grocery bag filled to overfull with various food items: a box of Bisquick, butter, eggs, cinnamon, brown sugar, hot chocolate mix, marshmallows, and, curiously, three bottles of Phillip's. She had apparently been up and ready for some time, and made a stop at the grocery store before arriving. Mama Kinney frowned as Sincere unloaded her bounty onto the table, and the lines between her brows creased deeper as she noticed the quick, mischievous smile Sincere flashed. Sudden comprehension dawned and Mama Kinney laughed out loud.

"We got maybe an hour or two at most before they start comin', so you'd better get that in the oven soon!" Mama Kinney said hobbling over to lean heavily on the counter. She fished inside a cabinet for two large mixing bowls and laid them out on the table. She stood back to watch Sincere do her thing.

Sincere had far surpassed Mama Kinney's cooking abilities by the time she was fourteen, and was particularly known around town for her cakes and pies. Aside from church bake sales and summer picnics, it was rare for the town to taste one of Sincere's creations. When they arrived, everyone would want a slice or more, despite the early hour.

Sure enough, when folks began crowding onto Mama Kinney's porch some forty-five minutes later, more than a few stomachs grumbled loudly at the delicious smells wafting from the kitchen. The women looked nosily through the screen door, waiting to see what would come out, and Mama Kinney sat back in satisfied anticipation. Her arthritis was acting up again, probably due to the erratic weather, and she willed the coldness and sensitivity in her bones to recede, at least long enough for her to play social host. The laxatives would ensure that the meeting came to a swift end, but Mama Kinney knew she'd have to entertain this group of women for at least another two hours.

"So, I hear that car been parked out there since Thursday. An ain't nobody seen the backside of that boy for the same period of time. Folks is startin' to worry."

Mama Kinney nodded, confirming the gossip. "Saw him go in myself on Thursday, ain't seen him since." She took a sip of tea and hid her eyes to cover her discomfort with the topic of conversation.

"You been watchin' closely?" This from a younger woman whose name Mama Kinney could not quite remember. The woman squinted at her, and watched for her answer through narrowed eyes. Mama Kinney rolled her eyes.

Lady answered for Mama Kinney with a skeptical raise of her brow. "What you think?"

The woman opened her mouth to respond but, thankfully, Sincere emerged from the house carrying a large tray piled high with golden squares of coffee cake. She set the tray on a small card table against the wall and stood back as the women clamored forward, briefly forgetting the purpose for their visit in the rush to grab a piece. The respite was welcomed, and Mama Kinney exchanged a look with her goddaughter.

Lady took her customary seat beside the table and sliced into her cake with a fork. Lifting a large bite to her mouth, she paused and looked up. "Mama," she addressed the older woman respectfully, lowering her fork without tasting. "Would you like some cake?"

"Can't," Mama Kinney said shortly, though eyeing

the cake. "These diabetes, they likely to put me in an early grave."

Lady looked closely at Mama Kinney, then Sincere. Mama Kinney had been diagnosed with diabetes goin' on three years ago now, and this was the first time Lady had ever known her to turn down something sweet. 'Specially with Sincere otherwise occupied, seeing to her guests, as she was now. Something was not right. Lady frowned at the piece of cake, and noted that Sincere, too, was not partaking. "You know, Mama, I think you might be right." Lady patted one oversized hip. "I ought not be eatin' all these sweets my damn self. Ain't good for my weight." She pushed her plate back onto the table, where it disappeared immediately into someone else's hand.

"Well, excuse me if I don't share yo worry," Reese said, arriving. She leaned over Lady to grab her plate off the table. "My diet gone have to start tomorrow, when Sincere here ain't passin' out these goodies."

"You *know* that's right!" somebody said, and everyone aside from Lady, Mama Kinney, and Sincere, began eating. There was another large pan of coffee cake warming in the oven, but Sincere knew it'd be eaten as soon as she brought it out. There were eleven women, total, on the porch right now, but she knew there'd be more to come.

The cake did not distract them long. As they ate, they plied Mama Kinney with questions about when, exactly, Rich had arrived, what he'd been wearing, how he'd looked, whether he or anyone else in that house had passed butt-naked by a window lately. No possibility seemed too wild or outrageous and the women, just today, had no shame in asking.

"I heard they been doin' all kind of nasty stuff in

123

broad daylight, windows open and all!" Joyce talked over a full mouth. She was working on her second slice of cake.

"May told me she walked past here last night, on her way home from work, and heard the strangest sounds comin' right on through the screen, and it was just before dinner, too!"

"Thas triflin'. Them two women, ain't no tellin' what they got goin' on in that house, or what they been doin' to poor ol' Rich. What's wrong wit his sisters? They ain't tell him he shouldn't be messin' around wit no skanks...'scuse my language, Mama."

"Now wait a minute." Mama Kinney spoke with gravelly-voiced authority, clearing through the chorus of voices by pounding her cane hard against the railing. The woman who'd been leaning against it jumped, then moved circumspectly away. "Ain't a one of y'all met this woman, y'all don't know if she a skank, a skeet, or a purified virgin!" she said in rebuke, staring the women down.

"I met her," Jody volunteered, stepping forward onto the porch. Everyone had been so busy talking, no one had heard her approach. "Had a nice talk wit her, too. Um, hmm. An I can tell all of y'all from personal experience, the woman ain't nothin' but a stuck up bitch! And a man-eatin' one, at that!"

"Tell it like it is, girl!"

"Who knows what kinda thang she got goin' over there. Done had Rich locked up in that house for two whole days now, we don't even know if he still alive!" Jody let her suggestion drop on the group, then smiled in satisfaction as the women reflected varying degrees of horror. It was a possibility; a crazy, unlikely possibility, but a possibility nonetheless. And without knowing any-

124

thing about Miranda or her white woman friend, Moresha, it was a possibility they couldn't rule out.

Lady's laughter broke the silence, drawing everybody's eyes. "Y'all mean to tell me y'all gone sit here an let her feed y'all this crock of shit?" Lady laughed again, ignoring the women watching her, waiting for her to continue. When her laugher died down to chuckles, she finally did. "Y'all don't see that Jody here jus' a lil' bit jealous? That was, after all, her man just a few weeks back."

"That was more'n six months past, Lady," Jody said in protest, on the defensive now. "And please remember that I got rid of *him*, not the other way around!" But the seed had been planted.

"You ain't never been that selfless, Jody. Don't matter if you kicked him to the curb and moved on to the next, you still wouldn't want him wit another woman." This from Jenna, who'd tried to remain unnoticed most of the afternoon as she sat and watched the house. Still, she couldn't resist this one, public opportunity to get her digs in Jody, even if she knew it might result in a very public take-down. "Plus, what'n't you the one sent him over there in the first place?"

All eyes turned to Jody, waiting. She fidgeted, moving stiffly against the banister. "I might have suggested he go on over there, but I never intended for him to stay!"

"Regardless, you wouldn't sent him over at all if you really thought she was all that bad." Having said her peace, Jenna returned her attention to the peach house, only partly listening for Jody's response.

"Tell the truth and shame the devil!" someone shouted into the silence.

"Anyhow, it's only been two days. For all we know, Rich could be havin' the time of his life, gettin' the benefit of two women instead of one." Rhoda, a slender, light-skinned woman whose face was marked with the evidence of teenage acne, winked slyly as she made the suggestion. She, along with several other women on the porch, had often been the target of Jody's insults and disdain, and she wasn't above taking advantage of the situation to show the other woman up.

Jody stared at them, her mouth open in disbelief. "I can't believe y'all! A man disappears without a trace into the house of two women *we don't know* and y'all jus' gone sit here and let things be? Y'all don't feel a sense of Godly urgency? Rich *is* one of our own!" she reminded the women, pulling her purse tightly under one arm and standing straight up in their midst. "Y'all might not care enough to be concerned, but I do! I'm goin' over there right now and make sure he's alive. That's the least I owe him!"

She turned, and the women blocking her path shifted, more than willing to allow her to go. The drama would be well worth it, and more than one of them secretly hoped Jody might finally get what was coming to her.

"You stay right here," Mama Kinney's voice rang out with finality, immediately altering the smugly expectant expressions on the face of several of the women. Sincere moved closer to Mama Kinney, silently supporting her authority. "Go'on and sit down, girl, have you a slice of cake. Every one of us, including you, Jody, knows that boy is jus' fine. Ain't nobody done nothin' to him he didn't want and didn't like, an I'm not about to let you go on over there and start somethin' you can't finish. Leave that boy in peace, and get yo nose back out of where it don't belong."

Jody stood stiffly, her back toward Mama Kinney, watching the house with narrowed eyes. For a moment, she considered directly defying Mama Kinney and going anyway. She knew in her soul that Rich couldn't be there with his consent, and everything in her urged her to go forward and rescue him from that bitch across the street. Who knew what kind of strange, unholy things she and that white woman were doing to him, even right now, as they all stood there talking and laughing and carrying on like nothing was wrong. She could go over there, righteously put a stop to it, show everyone what had been going on, right beneath their noses. But Mama Kinney would not permit that sort of transgress on her authority to go unpunished, and Jody knew she would thereafter be unwelcome on her porch, and several other places, for that matter. Mama Kinney was, after all, an elder and highly regarded throughout the small town. Still, it might very well be worth the risk to prove to everyone that she, alone, had known the truth about that woman across the street. While everybody else was busy giving her the benefit of the doubt, assuming Rich was in there havin' the time of his life, Jody had seen the danger behind those eyes. She knew Miranda's pretty face and sweet smile could deceive a simple man like Rich into believing she was all things good and innocent. He wouldn't see the danger until he'd already been caught in the web.

Only the slight possibility of error prevented her defiance. What if she was wrong? She didn't want to be publicly shamed before these women, having rushed over to expose the truth of what was really nothing but a man's fantasy of having not one, but two women. She knew, of course, what Miranda really was, and sooner or later, everybody else would know the same. But Jody couldn't be certain that rushing over there, right now, would expose it. And without that absolute certainty, how could she risk so much?

Jody turned back quietly and gracefully complied with Mama Kinney's order. She took a seat someone had vacated and crossed her knees before her. She was every inch the lady, and both Mama Kinney and Sincere breathed a sigh of relief. They had been afraid that Jody would choose this very moment to show her ass, and they were grateful that she'd for once perceived the wisdom of discretion.

The women, on the other hand, evinced nothing short of disappointed anger and deep disgust, but they could not direct it at Mama Kinney. So, instead, they directed it in equal amounts at both Jody and Sincere, knowing that something important had just occurred involving both women, although unable to decipher exactly what it was. Though both women remained somewhat quiet throughout the conversation, the women took turns goading them, trying to get a rise. Sincere smiled graciously, serving another tray of cake when more women arrived. Mama Kinney's presence prevented them from speaking openly about what had almost occurred. Jody quietly seethed in the background, refusing to rise to the conversation. Soon, a few of the women who'd been there longest began looking about anxiously, holding their stomachs and quietly excusing themselves from the gathering. One by one, they walked stiffly but quickly away, headed in the direction of their respective homes.

The departures were a catalyst. The other women, in turn, each took their leave in the same curious way, leaving the less-alert women on the porch to continue their talking and eating. The composition of the group gradually changed to latecomers, with the exceptions of Mama Kinney, Sincere, Lady, and Jody, and even the latecomers took their leave. Jody was amongst the last to go, not wanting to give up her post watching the peach house, but unwilling to be alone with only Lady, Mama Kinney, and Sincere. With only the usual group around, Mama Kinney wouldn't bite her tongue and Jody was uncertain of what she might say. And so she left, already thinking of a way in which she could bypass Mama Kinney's order and do exactly as she pleased.

When only Lady, Mama Kinney, and Sincere remained, Lady finally rose. "I won't be the one to say it, but don't think for a minute those women won't figure out what y'all did to them. They'll all be on the toilet shittin' tonight, but tomorrow they'll be back out runnin' their mouths, and sooner or later they'll figure it out."

Sincere smiled widely at Lady, relieved to be alone again. "Oh, don't tell me you disagree! They woulda been here all night, waitin' to see what they could see when the lights go on in that house. Like the three of 'em gon' put on some sort of freak show, right there before the open windows."

Lady couldn't help but laugh, her good humor returning. She began gathering up the dishes on the table. "I'm not judgin' y'all, mind you. I'm just sayin', it surely whatn't the only way to clear 'em out."

Mama Kinney eyed her skeptically, and even Sincere looked like she disagreed. Lady held up a hand to forestall them both. "Like I said, I won't be the one to tell. But they'll all know come morning. They women. They ain't got nothin' better to do in life but run they mouths once it stops runnin' out the other end."

"And if they do start talkin', thas a problem we'll deal with when it comes 'round. For now though, I can't help but admit I'm lookin' forwards to a long, hot shower, *without* all these women constantly talkin' and bickerin' on my own front porch! Let 'em go to somebody else's house, for a change!" Mama Kinney shuffled into the house, holding the door open behind her for the two of them. Sincere and Lady each carried in a pan or platter, devoid of even the smallest remaining crumb, heavily laden with coffee mugs of assorted shapes and sizes. They set the trays in the kitchen sink.

Soon after, Lady, too, took her leave, disappointed that nothing gossip-worthy had occurred. Well, aside from that little episode with Jody. But for a moment, Lady had almost hoped that she and her boys would be displaced from their infamous role as the most scandalous household in town. Lady had let herself believe, just for a moment, that the strange combination of two out-of-town women, one of them white, doin' whatever was to be done in that house with one of Reason's most eligible young bachelors, would be enough to focus attention elsewhere. Just long enough for her to make a few small changes. She and her boys had occupied a position of notoriety for so long, it was difficult to try and create some bit of privacy. And having finally settled her heart on one of them, Jonas, she didn't want to mess it up before the two of them could slip away and get married. She knew instinctively that any amount of scrutiny would be too much, and she sighed, knowing that it would have to wait a moment more. There were still too many eyes looking and ears listening for her to take a chance on revealing herself too soon.

At the house, Sincere and Mama Kinney shared a sigh of relief that everything had turned out well. Here it was, not even dinnertime, and already the porch was clear and they were alone. If their luck held out, Lady's prediction would prove false and none of the women would discover that their sudden departures had been contrived. Sincere knew that was asking too much, but the greatest penalty for her deception would be that her cakes might sell for a little less money at the Easter bake sale. It would be a small price to pay. She would have to make up the difference with a larger offering, and pray God's forgiveness.

For her part, Mama Kinney felt no remorse at all. Though she usually hated dishonesty, it had been a necessary evil. The women, she knew, would have rolled out sleeping bags and stayed the night if she'd let them. She'd done them and their families a favor by sending them on home. And especially since they'd all narrowly averted disaster with Jody. That situation was a time-bomb, and Mama Kinney just hoped it would not blow up in everyone's face. This girl, Miranda as she called herself now, couldn't possibly know what kind of dangerous games she was playing. Reason was a peaceful town, but the people had a sharpened sense of justice.

Chapter 9

When even Sincere had gone, Mama Kinney
moved back through the hallway and took a seat on the
couch in the living room. She sighed heavily and closed
her eyes, feeling the comfort of well-worn cushions
embrace her like a long-time friend. She supposed she
should get used to the extra visitors; it seemed like
Miranda was hell-bent on getting the attention of folks
in Reason, and they were more than willing to comply.
The town had not seen such excitement for years, and it
would likely be years to come before they'd see it again.

Still, Mama Kinney couldn't shake the feeling that
this was one intrigue that would not end well. There was
a burning that had been evident in Miranda's eyes, that
wouldn't be satisfied by mere attention and awe.

The light in the room shifted unnaturally,
inconsistent with the dim glow being thrown by a small
lamp on a table. Mama Kinney looked up, unsurprised
this time to see Miranda's shape emerge from the
shadows. She watched as the woman took a seat on the
couch, not waiting for an invitation. "So you found the
time to visit again? Can't say I'm surprised."

"Chalk it down to softness and old memories.
Comin' over here, reminds me of back when Sincere and
I was jus young girls playin' hide an seek through the
hallway." Miranda looked slowly around the room, as if
noting the changes years had wrought. "Funny, common
sense told me things would've changed in all these years.
That buildings wouldn't look so big as they had when I
was little an folks'd be jus a little bit older and some of
'em gone." She shook her head. "Still, seein' the changes

when I got here was somethin' new."

She sighed. "Guess I changed a bit, too, got a little older and, hopefully, a bit wiser wit the years."

"One would hope," Mama Kinney said shortly, without any real confidence. The two women sat silently a moment, contemplating one another, each lost in her own thoughts.

Miranda took a deep breath and exhaled. Her words, when she spoke, were abrupt, breaking the silence and interrupting Mama Kinney's thoughts. "So you been thinkin' on that question?"

Mama Kinney reached for her cane in sudden agitation, striking the wooden floor with its tip and sitting forward quickly in her chair. She leaned heavily against a nearby table, and a lamp atop it trembled slightly and flickered in the dark. "I ain't afraid of you, girl. I'm too old to be scared of anything now. Ain't nothin' more you can do to me that life ain't already did, an more. I'ma meet King Jesus sooner or later, an it don't much matter whether thas tomorrow or twenty years from now. Go'on an say what you got to say, Jean."

"Miranda."

"Jean!" Mama Kinney insisted. " Girl, don't forget, no matter how you call yo'self now, I know who you really are. Inside *and* out." Mama Kinney knew she was pushing, but she couldn't seem to help it. The woman provoked some answering anger in her that had been long dead almost twenty years now. She had some nerve, coming into Mama Kinney's house and thinking to cow her into some sort of unjustified fear. She had done nothing she wouldn't be proud to admit in daylight, but she would not explain herself to this girl. She certainly didn't seem to be without her own share of sins.

Miranda paused, staring at Mama Kinney in the un-

133

even light. Although her face was partly hidden by the shadows, Mama Kinney sensed her smile. "You do, don't you? You know a lot of things now. Knew a lot back then, too, as I recall."

"Yo recollection might not be so accurate. Seem to me like you couldna been more'n nine or ten las time you was here."

"Eight. I was only eight when I watched my daddy kill my mama." Miranda heard Mama Kinney's swift intake of air. "You never thought watching such a thing might hurt such a little girl?"

Mama Kinney regained her footing in the conversation, remembering who it was she was talking to. "You wasn't my responsibility then, girl, and you ain't my conscience now. I ain't did nothing wrong, I didn't owe nothin' to you."

"You sure you wanna take that position, Evelyn? You don't think you mighta had the slightest responsibility for all what went down so many years ago? And before you answer that, consider that we all grown folks now, and time has exposed more than you mighta wanted known back then."

"Hmph! Time ain't told you nothin' 'bout my affairs that I ain't already brought out into the light."

"You sayin' you done told everyone about yo part in what went down? They *all* know everything? Even Sincere?"

Mama Kinney was silent, unwilling to let Miranda know that her words had struck a nerve. Of course she hadn't told Sincere everything. Despite their closeness, Mama Kinney couldn't bring herself to speak aloud what Sincere already knew about her father's death, or worse, to admit her part. "What you here for, Jean? What exactly do you want? Money? Blood? Just the pleasure

134

of makin' folks spit?" Mama Kinney paused but she did not respond. "If it's money you want, I can tell you right now I ain't got enough. Money won't cure what's wrong wit you, girl. Won't scare away the demons runnin' through yo head at night."

"Demons, Evelyn? We talkin' 'bout me now, or *you*?"

Mama Kinney sighed, frustrated by the games. "Look, girl, I'm gettin' older every second now. My mind ain't quick enough to follow all these questions and reasonings you keep implyin'. You wanna tell me somethin' I don't already know? Or ask me somethin' you don't know? You got a point for being here in my house? Otherwise, you know how to see yo'self out."

Miranda shifted on the couch across from her and another lamp flickered, flooding the room with its light, and allowing Mama Kinney to fully see Miranda's face. Despite the intervening years, Miranda's skin was as smooth and unlined as it had been when she was a girl, but for the interruption of a small, puckered scar across her bottom lip. Her dark brown eyes seemed dull in the thin light, but it was evident that she had grown into the beauty promised at her birth. Mama Kinney wondered if anything of her father had been survived in her genes, because it was her mother's print you could see.

"Cat got yo tongue, Evelyn?" Miranda smiled, enjoying the look of discomfort that had passed over Mama Kinney's face.

"It's my own damn house, girl. I'll say freely whatever I like." Mama Kinney heard her voice, heard the emotions revealed in it, but could not completely disguise her feelings. Miranda had provoked her from the day she was born, and she was certainly no less provocative now as an adult. She decided to change the subject. "Answer me this, Jean…you and that girl over

135

there, what in the world are y'all doin' in that house? And wit Rich, too? What he ever did to you?"

Miranda looked at her in some surprise. "Nothin', nothin' at all. Less you know somethin' I don't?"

"He ain't had nothin' to do wit yo parents, if thas what you askin'. He was jus' a boy when the whole thing happened."

Miranda nodded. "I would ask you why you care, but I 'spect it's just common courtesy. No, Rich is just scratchin' a itch I got, comin' into town. He'll be gone again soon enough."

"And the girl?"

"Moresha? What is it people say we doin'?"

"People say a lot of things, most all of 'em unsavory."

"Too proper to repeat them, Evelyn?"

"I don't dignify gossip."

"Really? Is that why I can see y'all sittin' out here on your porch, talkin' and laughin' and watchin' the three of us, 'cause you don't *dignify* gossip?" Miranda waited, but Mama Kinney made no response. She sighed, rapping her knuckles against the end table decisively. "Whatever they sayin', it's more'n likely true."

Mama Kinney nodded, as if she had expected no other response. "Yo grandparents wouldn't've approved, you know. Y'all two got folks talking, thas for sure. Folks that ain't got no claim to decency themselves is talkin' about how you and that girl living together in that house, flauntin' y'allselves before God and the entire town. They gone keep talkin', too, long as you keep on in this path."

"And? You wanna tell me why I care?"

"Talk ain't never good for those bein' talked about."

"It ain't always so bad as that. Bein' talked about is better than being forgotten." Her words hung thickly in

136

the air between them, recalling the prior discussion.

"You mighta been lost, girl," Mama Kinney said quietly. "But you ain't never been forgotten."

"Lost? That how folks explained me gettin' shipped off to foster care?"

Mama Kinney shrugged, well aware of the hypocrisy in the way all trace of Reba, Sandal, and their Baby Girl had been erased from the town's collective consciousness. She almost felt sympathy for the young girl that had been swept up in the tragedy, through no fault of her own. "You ain't lived long enough to know this, Jean, but memory is a tricky thing. Sometimes, if you wanna believe somethin' happened a certain way, your mind'll recall it so it did." Mama Kinney used her cane to gain her balance and rose. "Yo grandparents was good people. You might not've agreed wit what they did, but sometimes that's just the benefit of hindsight. To everyone in *this* town, when yo grandparents said you was lost, that's jus what you was. Lost."

"And shoulda stayed that way, I suppose?"

"You said it." Mama Kinney ambled over to the doorway. "Mornin' be here soon. Wit so much goin' on in yo house, I'm sure you got plenty to do."

Miranda nodded and stood, the moment almost congenial. "That I do, though I enjoyed this time to talk. It was rather...enlightening."

"That it was," Mama Kinney said, shuffling through the hallway. "Though I can't say I'm all that anxious to do it again soon." She felt the air shift when Miranda left, and she was grateful that she had. It had taken more than a little faith to turn her back on the woman, and she was not at all certain that this would be the end of it. For all the questions asked today, Mama Kinney had the firm impression that there had been many more. These nighttime visits were futile.

Chapter 10

It was Sunday. Moresha woke at dawn with uncommon excitement, her entire body nearly vibrating with happy expectation, her senses certain that Rich was gone. *Gone!* The feeling was heightened by the sensation of smooth skin brushing against her, and Moresha looked down to see Miranda's body snuggling deeply into the irregular contours of her own. She was beautiful. Moresha studied the contrast of their colors, Miranda's deep, muddy brown against the paler, vein-streaked blue of her own. She was reminded of oceans, of watching waves and water slip between her fingers and disappear with the tide, leaving behind only sand and tiny pieces of its essence. It was just that way between them; for moments at a time, she would feel Miranda slipping from her, going in small increments, leaving behind pieces of abandoned knowledge, promises that she would return. She always did.

Joy spurred her movement, and she drew Miranda to her with more force than finesse. She didn't care. She kissed Miranda's hair, her eyes, mouth, neck, touched every part of her at once, consumed by the desire to be underneath her skin. Her body clung to Miranda, legs moving feverishly between her thighs. Rendered insecure by Rich's continuing presence, she had abandoned her usual tendency to sleep nude. Now she regretted the thin fabric of her nightgown that stayed between them, separating her and her love. She removed it without conscious effort, anxious and hurried in her movements, wanting. Miranda awoke with immediate awareness, and Moresha was glad of it. She could not wait.

Her fingers felt urgently beneath the sheet, seeking her love's heat. She found it at once, stroking, suggestive in her movements. Her fingers moved, parting Miranda, pressing against her wetness, slipping inside her body and stroking her. She opened, pushing down, ready. Moresha captured the peak of one breast in her mouth, laving with her tongue, mimicking the movement of her fingers. With her other hand, she held Miranda's hips still, controlling the small bucking movements she made.

Moresha was hurried, true, but she could not stop touching Miranda, even knowing that she was prolonging the time until their coming together. Still she delayed, waited, wanting to simultaneously touch and taste every part of her. A stream coursed through her body, reminding her that she loved this woman, bodily and mentally, touching her with eager anticipation, knowing she would not bruise, hoping to mark her heart the way she marked her skin.

She ground herself against Miranda, feeling their collective wetness collide and swell, touching each of them intimately. Between them, the short tautness of their clitorises met. Miranda reached her peak more quickly, hands moving desperately against Moresha's skin, pinching sharply, then releasing, holding Moresha to her as she climaxed and returned. Moresha came with her, more slowly but just as intensely, her body convulsing, her mouth forming cries of gratitude and relief, which lacked clear expression. Her vision blurred, then focused again on the face of her love, smiling, watching her as she came.

The two lay side by side, loving one another in silence. With the last remaining vestige of her strength, Moresha rubbed the small indentation of Miranda's lower lip, searching that part of her with leisurely exploration. She had admitted her love before, but never felt it as strongly. Miranda's eyes were closed, lashes brushing thickly against each cheek, breath feathering out into the space between them, resting but not asleep.

Moresha's mouth opened, but her thoughts stopped short of tumbling out. She had been concerned. Miranda had kept men before, for no more than two days at a time, often much shorter. Sometimes only hours at a time. The duration varied with the men, dependent only on Miranda's need and their ability to fill it. Somehow, though, Rich had been different. Miranda's reaction to him had been different, more complex, with subtleties and nuances that infected each interaction. She had seduced him right there in front of Moresha, forcing her to watch, using those same suggestive scents and smiles and the touches she sometimes used to coax and coerce Moresha into whatever something she wanted most at the moment. It had been frightening, Miranda's sudden and temporary disregard for her feelings. Moresha had been uneasy about the relationship, secretly afraid that this might be the beginning of the end.

She knew, of course, that Miranda was incapable of feeling anything beyond casual interest in any man. On one of her darker days, Moresha could secretly admit that Miranda had never felt deeply for any person, herself included. She was simply not that type of woman. She organized her feelings, divided them into separate boxes, and deliberately disposed of anything remotely resembling love. That was just her way.

And yet, she had looked at Rich with such need in her eyes. Moresha had felt a physical ache, like a blow beneath her belly. She had touched him as if only the sweetness of prolonged seduction warranted her delay;

141

as if she would eat him right there, with Moresha to watch, partaking of that something she seemed so hungry for. It had been there at the ends of her smile, in the way her hips swung, lightly, singing, when he was there. And he had followed so easily behind her, loving every second of her attention.

Even before she had returned home to find Miranda's hips singing, though, there had been a change, something indefinable. She would only deny it if Moresha had asked, so she did not. Instead, she had watched the changes occurring in Miranda, the sudden evasiveness and the distraction. Although they had been subtle, she had noted them immediately, recognizing the changes taking place within her lover. They had begun on that morning only six months before when Miranda blithely and unequivocally announced they would be moving. Where, she would not say. But it had been immediately clear that she knew, even if she would not tell Moresha, and that she would not be dissuaded from her purpose.

Their arrival had been tense. Moresha was not used to blindly following anyone, and her relationship with Miranda had been a trying time of completion. This was how she had learned to love selflessly, unconsciously, without reservation. But Miranda had always conditioned that love, and Moresha knew no other way to hold her than to accept those conditions. When after two years of what Moresha recognized was the sort of deep and abiding connection between two souls, Miranda had requested this final condition, Moresha had been helpless to refuse. She had agreed to the move, calculating expenditures, planning. Miranda had insisted on going first, alone, and even that time apart had been too much. Moresha had dropped her off in Reason under cover of night, then immediately left. In her nightmares, the house had swallowed Miranda, tangling her behind the boarded-up windows, leaving Moresha without. She had lain awake through those weeks apart, afraid, wondering if Miranda would be there when she arrived, wondering if she would want Moresha there beside her. This was the pain that she now recognized as the evidence of love, the waiting and the insecurities.

And then finally it had been time to return. Moresha had not hesitated; even the uncertainty of what would meet her when she got there was not enough to prevent her from throwing away her job, her home, her friends and neighbors, everyone, and coming to meet her love. And as always, Miranda had been more than worth the sacrifice, substantial though it was. She had welcomed Moresha without reservation, relief making their reunion lovemaking more urgent, more loving. Moresha had been afraid to trust the hope, growing somewhere in her heart, that maybe now Miranda had found a place where she could finally let herself fully experience the freedom and exultation of unbound love.

Then had come Rich, and that exultation and joy had turned, twisted, so that Moresha was no longer certain that she was the object.

But that was over now. Miranda had stayed true to character and had only used him for a brief time. Even the invasion of their home was not so awful in retrospect, brief as it had been, and Moresha could excuse the slight disrespect, such was her relief. Rich was no different than any man before, and Miranda, sweet Miranda, was still the same woman.

Moresha pulled Miranda closer, ignoring the way her body stiffened in sleep and pushed away. This was the most beautiful thing about loving, consistency.

She awoke in a brief panic, knowing instinctively that Miranda was gone. Her eyes opened, flitting throughout the room, searching. Her heart pumped frantically, as if on the verge of collapse, anxiety speeding the rhythm of her pulse within her throat. She jumped from the bed, in the same move pushing off sheets and confining blankets, her feet moving before they touched the floor. She felt as if she was in a horrible drama film, trapped in that instant when the music alerts the audience that death is imminent, but the main character is still blithely unaware. The only difference was, *she knew!*

She rushed from the room, headed to the stairs, but paused when she heard the sound of soft laughter behind her. She turned, and her heart finally collapsed within her, leaving a void in her chest that she rapidly filled with breathing. Miranda stood there, a blindingly-white towel wrapped around her head, and nothing else adorning her beautiful body. "Where in the world are you headed?" she asked, smiling. "And wherever it is, please don't tell me you plan on wearin' that!"

Relief crowded the words in her throat and made it impossible to respond. Shaking her head, Miranda walked slowly back into the bedroom, and Moresha followed behind the rhythmic sway of her hips. She looked down at her nakedness and cleared her throat, waiting.

From inside the closet, Miranda's voice was loud into the silence. "I thought maybe we could go to church today. It *is* Sunday, you know."

Moresha frowned, surprise making her unsure of what response was merited. She had not been to a religious house of worship since she was a small girl. As a teenager, her sexuality had emerged and people had assumed she would have no interest. Moresha had been comfortable in this assumption, since it demanded nothing. "Church? Why would we go to church? And what's wrong with just staying here, like we always do?"

Miranda emerged from the closet holding a dress that wavered brightly between aquamarine and green. Moresha recognized the dress, and what it signified. Warning bells sounded somewhere in her mind.

"You *would* say something like that, Moresha." Miranda held the dress to her body, looking searchingly in the mirror. "Careful now, life might make you into a heathen."

Moresha was stung by the words, spoken jokingly. She had an innately spiritual nature, though she had never subscribed to any one religion, least of all the religion of her birth. She opened her mouth to respond, then closed it abruptly. For the first time, she noticed that Miranda had lost some small amount of weight. It showed in the bare thinness of her shoulder blades, the way her neck seemed longer, smoother. It was lovely on her, of course, but unusual all the same.

Miranda mistook her silence for assent and nodded, still looking into the mirror. "Good, good. We need to leave in about twenty minutes. You'll be ready?" Her eyes met Moresha's in the mirror. Moresha nodded, feeling as if she was engaged in the useless endeavor of holding back a tide. She was reminded suddenly of her earlier impression, staring at the patterns of their skin. *Please,* she prayed, forgetting momentarily to direct it to anyone. *Please let her leave something behind.*

Moresha stayed in the shower too long, but when she got out, on the bed lay another brilliant dress, this one intended for Moresha. Beside it was a slip, a bra and panties, and an unopened package of pantyhose. *Pantyhose!* A pair of shoes lay casually on the floor, something new that Miranda had apparently purchased for Moresha some time before. Moresha left the underwear and shoes where they were but took the dress back to the closet, opting instead for a sober and shapeless black dress, simply adorned with a silver broach above one breast. She lingered longer over the shoes, touched as she was by the thoughtfulness of the gift, even knowing Miranda was well aware that Moresha would never wear such brightly-colored things. They were patterned to look like alligator skin, dyed a deep purple, with six-inch heels. Moresha slid them into a corner of the closet, and instead chose a pair of sensible black flats that complimented her dress.

Miranda walked into the room and stopped short, disappointment etched on her face. Her lips tightened as she beheld the clothing, and Moresha immediately regretted the moment of rebellion. She was instantly contrite, and thought maybe she could change back, but Miranda spoke and effectively closed off that option. "I see you're ready. Let's go, then," she said, and moved quickly from the room in the same breath. Moresha followed behind her, less certain of her footing.

Outside, the wind bit at exposed flesh, punishing her for choosing a woolen shawl over the warmer tan-colored trench coat she more often wore. But she had not wanted to attract any notice at all, and the coat would have been bright against the black of her dress. The clouds gathered, threatening rain, and Moresha silently hoped that they would make it back home, or at least to the church, before it broke. Across the street, she could see the neighbors, and the woman Sincere, sitting on the porch, holding court even in this weather. She nodded toward her, instinctively wanting to conceal their brief association from Miranda. Without understanding why, she was certain Miranda would not approve.

The sky held off its rain only long enough for them to enter the car. Then it poured down, sheets of thick, heavy rain that obscured the road and isolated their car. Moresha was grateful Miranda had chosen to drive; she still could not navigate the streets of this town with absolute precision, and less so in the rain.

Still, she recognized Mid-Town when they arrived by the grocery store where she'd dropped Sincere off the day before. A few blocks later, what looked to be a main intersection, and the distinct steeples of two churches vied for attention from opposing sides of the street. The rain let up just enough for her to make out the size and shape of the building, and the brick-red exterior, before Miranda pulled into a parking space on a side street.

The driver side door opened automatically, and Moresha leaned forward, craning her neck to see by whom. The image was fleeting, obscured by a dark umbrella, the body unrecognizable in its distance. She waited a moment, her heart beating hard against her breast, her mind insistent, but she refused the ugly thought. He was gone, an unwelcome memory, and she need not fear his reappearance.

That was, of course, more fantasy than fact, for as she ran through the rain to the awning of the church's front doors, Rich and Miranda moved quickly before her, the navy umbrella dancing tauntingly in the rain. He swung the church doors widely open, welcoming both women inside. He was solicitous of Miranda, removing her coat before escorting her up the staircase to the main auditorium with his hand on the small of her back.

Moresha was left to hang her own shawl, now sodden with rain. She trailed sullenly behind them, still stunned by his appearance. Her mind raced at the implications. Why is he *here*? Had she made a mistake in thinking it was over? Was he still going to be a part of their lives, and for how long?

The church smelled of cloves and of dampness, but the smell was more soothing than unpleasant. It induced Moresha to set aside her questions for a moment, instead concentrating on the more imminent danger of walking into this church with these two, not knowing how the people would receive her, and worse, not knowing what Miranda had planned. The pair walked together in affectionate harmony, touching, and Moresha felt suddenly bereft. How had she lost Miranda so quickly?

Despite the loudness of the tambourines, and the care they took to avoid drawing attention to themselves as they slipped into a back pew, Moresha knew the second everyone became aware of their presence. There were no obvious signs; no conspicuously turned bodies trying to get a better look, no whispered comments. Still, there was a current that had gone through the congregation at their entrance, such that Moresha knew, *she just knew*, that they had been exposed. She sat stiffly, Miranda to her right, Rich on her other side, not knowing how to act in such a foreign experience.

She could see the surreptitious glances being cast their way by several congregants, and she worried that their presence was distracting others from their worship. Moresha still retained a certain respect for religion that was the residue of an orthodox upbringing. Now she sat awkwardly in the pew, clutching her handbag to her lap and trying to ignore the stir they'd caused. The pastor sat on a raised dais facing the congregation. He leaned over to ask a question of an usher standing nearby. His gaze fell on the three of them, and Moresha dropped her eyes to avoid his own. This was why she stayed away from churches. People could be vicious in their judgment under cover of religion.

A woman stood and sang out, "I woke up this mornin' wit my mind," and the rest of the congregation joined in. Moresha stumbled on the words, trying belatedly to catch up, but the effort was wasted. The words kept changing, and she seemed to be the only person in the church who did not know them. She fidgeted in her seat, one shoe rubbing against the other, her hands toying anxiously with the strap of her purse.

Miranda's hand reached over and covered her own. She looked down, comforted. She was conspicuous in this church, the only white person, the only person who did not belong. Even Miranda blended in better, despite her gaudy summer dress, among these people. But it was obvious Miranda had no intention of blending in; she had, of course, chosen to attend the small church with both of her current lovers. Moresha had the unfortunate feeling of being caught in the crossfire. She had seen the women standing, gossiping on the porch across the street. She knew their living arrangement and Rich's continued presence engendered speculation, but she was helpless to prevent it.

The music paused a moment, a low hum still sounding through the church. The pastor stood, his robes flowing around him, making him appear as if he glided on air. The church stood, too, and Moresha got to her feet, belatedly following along. Miranda and Rich took their time complying, as if defying the unspoken command somehow gave them an advantage. Prayer commenced, and Moresha took relief in the knowledge that, at least for a moment, they were free from observation. She sighed, knowing her anxiety would not defuse until they left this building, and Rich, too. His presence seemed to embolden Miranda, and Moresha was unused to seeing this provocative side of her.

"Turn with me in your Bibles to..." the pastor said when the prayer was over and the congregants all sat again in their pews. There was a sound of fluttering, like the noise bees make when they swarm. A woman in the front row stood, her voice ringing loudly in the quiet.

"Now concerning the things whereof ye wrote to me: It is good for a man not to touch a woman."

"Well!" somebody sang out in rejoinder, but the woman barely paused.

Moresha was distracted from the words by Miranda's fingers moving rhythmically over her hand, her wrist, her arm. The sensation was uncomfortable, like a small insect moving along her skin. She shook her arm briefly in annoyance, trying not to seem as if she were rejecting the caress altogether.

"...let every man have his own wife and let every woman have her own husband." A chorus of "Amens" followed, and the woman continued. "But if they cannot contain, let them marry: for it is better to marry than to burn," she finished, and regained her seat. Her final word hung thickly in the air, making it feel hot.

Miranda moved beside her, shifting in her seat, and then Moresha felt her hand massaging the muscles of her thigh. Her body answered, softening, and she turned to stare at Miranda in confusion. *What was she doing?*

Miranda seemed unperturbed by the silent question; her eyebrow cocked and Moresha could see that her other hand had disappeared somewhere in Rich's lap. Suddenly upset, Moresha forcefully pulled at her hand, dislodging it from her thigh, and placed it with distinct emphasis in her own lap. She would not do this here; whatever Miranda's game was, Moresha refused to play a part. Even the risk that Miranda would turn to Rich, instead, was not enough to compel Moresha's cooperation. She had had enough of the up and downs this morning. She was tired of it all and wanted just a little bit of calm and maybe the luxury of peace.

She felt Miranda's shoulders lift beside her in a shrug, and she moved closer to Rich. The preacher's voice rang out. "In this passage, the Bible clearly lays out God's plan for Man. Man is intended for Woman, and she for Man. Now, I don't care what the world around us might say, we are talkin' about God's plan for mankind. It's documented right here in the Word of God!" A chorus of "Amens" reverberated through the church, and more than a few glances were cast their way. Moresha suddenly realized that the pastor was talking about them. They were the subject of this week's text!

In mortification, she folded into herself, trying to be smaller, afraid that her size and presence would not allow. "The Word don't change. God don't change. He said it in the beginning and church—" he paused dramatically, waiting for the escalation in momentum. "I'm tellin' you today. Sexual immorality in this life will get you sent straight to hell in the next!"

"Amen, pastor!" someone shouted from the front. *Oh, hell*, Moresha thought, her cheeks burning in embarrassment. *Why wait?* There was plenty of room right up on the pulpit to erect a spit and string the three of them up to roast.

Beside her, Miranda giggled loudly, foolishly ignoring the mounting tension in the church and the preacher's targeted sermon. Moresha couldn't decide whether to be

151

amused or indignant. She'd obviously planned this awkward moment, dragging Moresha into it, knowing what would happen. And Moresha had let her, so caught up in love and the belief, mistaken, that Rich was out of their lives. The movements to her left became quicker, more urgent, and Moresha was afraid to turn and find out what that signified. She knew that hoping no one else was watching was pointless; they were obviously the most notable guests to visit this small church in some while.

The congregation apparently liked what their pastor was saying, and they signaled their agreement with everything from loud Amens to clapping and stomping. If the scene hadn't been so tragic, Moresha had no doubt she'd be more interested. She had never been in a Black church before, and the style of worship was different, louder and more physical. She was frustrated now, wishing they could leave, but knowing Miranda would not permit. She clasped her hands together in her lap, waiting with unhappy anticipation, unsure of what to expect.

Moresha concentrated on tracing with her fingernails the tiny lines that crossed each hand until suddenly she realized that the church had grown curiously silent. In sinking awareness, she turned and looked, her mouth dropping open in stunned surprise. Miranda had outdone herself this time. She sat, almost fully upon Rich's lap, her face nuzzling against his neck, and his hand somewhere beneath the hem of her dress. And the two of them were kissing full on the mouth, smilingly, as if there was no problem. Moresha was aware of a slow buzzing in her ears, and the heat rushing through her body, marking her turn crimson red. She suddenly wished that, rather than just picking a different dress, she had absolutely, unequivocally, insisted on staying home.

The ride home was made without comment or apology, each woman defiantly ignoring the other. In her heart, Moresha was sick. The day had begun with such promise, but now had been completely ruined by what had happened at the church. There was no explanation, no reasoning for Miranda's behavior. Moresha felt as if she were caught in that same sick terror movie, except now it had been turned into some sort of comedic drama, and only she remained ignorant of the nature of the joke. Unwilling to experience further embarrassment or wait for either of the ushers moving quickly toward them from the pulpit, she had grabbed Miranda's hand and pulled her forcefully from Rich's lap, compelling her toward the door and ignoring her indignant protests. Rich had followed closely behind, not wanting to let Miranda go without him, but Moresha had barely noticed and not cared at all. Her only concern had been to minimize the disruption and embarrassment their presence had already caused.

Miranda, for her part, was distinctly unrepentant, but Moresha knew her well enough to expect an apology in deed, if not in words. She had already decided she wouldn't accept. Nothing could suffice to remove the stain of embarrassment caused by that scene in the church, except to move away. Far, far away.

Still, she knew Miranda's nature. They arrived at the house without incident, and Moresha was not entirely surprised when she pulled up to park behind a long white car, trimmed flamboyantly in gold. Rich met them at the side door, waiting to be let in, a desperately needy puppy begging for his treats. Though the rain had stopped while they were in church, his clothes were still wet, lending to the image. Moresha's mouth twisted in distaste, knowing she had no say as to whether or not he could come in. For the moment, then, she would ignore them, and gracefully so. But she would not concede the war.

They tumbled into the house in disarray, Rich and Miranda both laughing, Moresha more sober in her black dress. The dress seemed even more appropriate now than it had this morning, what with her day having been so dismally bleak. She removed her shawl and carried it up the steps, leaving the two behind in the kitchen and ignoring their whispered comments. She knew what would happen next, and she shut the door of her bedroom against the sounds of their lovemaking as if there was no act more appropriate to celebrate their victory at the church.

The headache that had begun when Rich greeted them at the church suddenly slammed to the fore of her head and pressed against her eyes, obscuring her vision. She closed the curtains against the sunlight, now breaking through the clouds. The sun, the clouds, the rain, Miranda, Rich, all would be there when she awoke. For now, though, she would take a much-needed rest and shore up against whatever lay ahead. And, knowing Miranda, she was certain it would be something equally dramatic.

Unwilling to join the two for dinner, Moresha instead

woke in the early evening and headed for the kitchen to locate something she could smuggle, cold, into her bedroom. She opened her bedroom door and listened, judging the silence to mean that the two were probably sleeping after an afternoon of sex. The thought sickened her, twisted the memory of this morning, and she resolutely moved past Miranda's closed bedroom door without stopping.

The refrigerator held only the unappetizing remnants of Thursday night's courses, and Moresha ignored them in favor of a wedge of cheese she found hidden behind the milk. It would have to do. She grabbed it and rummaged through a cabinet, finally locating a box of crackers. Her dinner supplied, she turned, hoping to reach her room before she risked running into one of them.

She turned right into Rich, who had apparently overcome any pre-Miranda modesty, and was walking about the house, proudly naked. Moresha startled, letting out a small cry in her surprise, horribly aware of herself, her weight, her thinning hair, and most of all her womanhood. Even Moresha had to admit Rich was lovely, and though her body produced no sexual response to him, she had to fight back the desire to run her hands along his body, just for the pleasure of judging his presentation. Any artist would be hard-pressed not to desire him as a model, and Moresha was no exception. Still, her antipathy for him reared its head and quickly reminded her that they two were locked in a battle for Miranda's affection, and Moresha wasn't at all certain now who would win.

Her mind raced ahead, compelling her to speak, knowing that this was a rare opportunity indeed. "Excuse me," he said, and moved toward her, and

Moresha jumped back, afraid he would touch her. He did not, but her movement seemed to suddenly remind him that he was unclothed. His hand quickly moved to cover his male parts.

Despite herself, Moresha was curious. She could not understand why Miranda could desire such a thing as lay hanging limply from his body, unthreatening in its posture. She had explained it once, telling Moresha about the way it filled her, and how it reached back inside of her to a place that Moresha, with all her inventiveness, never could. The admission had been hurtful, but enlightening. Now though, looking at it, Moresha could not picture just how it was all accomplished. The thing looked impotent, unable even to stroke to arousal that part of Miranda that Moresha took such time to engage. Moresha narrowed her eyes and spoke out of confusion, her words laced with bitterness and a small hint of jealousy for what she couldn't seem to have. "What are you still doing here?" she asked, already knowing the answer.

Rich frowned at her but answered anyway. It appeared he'd quickly gotten over the intimidation of that first night, and he looked at Moresha as if she had no right to ask.

"What does it look like I'm doin'? I'm gettin' somethin' to eat!" He opened the refrigerator, ignoring her presence.

Feeling slighted and unreasonably angry, Moresha struck out with words. "She *will* get tired of you, you know. It's only a matter of time." Moresha watched as his body stiffened in affront and he turned from the refrigerator to face her.

"Be honest, Moresha. You wouldn't care a rat's ass if she did." He crossed his arms before his chest, for the moment forgetting that he'd left himself uncovered. He shook his head, and looked at her with false pity. "No, what you're really worried about is that she won't. You're worried that I can give her something you never could, that she won't be satisfied with what's between your legs, and instead, she'll leave you for what I've got between mine. Admit it, woman. You're worried that what Miranda needs is a nice, strong cock, and you just aren't capable of providing that."

Moresha turned away, unwilling to let him see that his comments had struck home. Unable to let him win this round, she shot back, "She won't keep you! She never has." She turned again to face him, smiling nastily, inching toward the doorway. "Maybe you're right, too. Maybe she does need that. But you should know by now that she can get it elsewhere. Hell, half the population has one! You think this is the first time she's ever brought someone home before? There've been men, many of them, stronger, bigger..." She glanced down at his member, still lying in repose, "and *better* in bed than you. And every time, when she gets done with them, she just throws them away. Like a piece of trash. Don't think that you'll be different. Believe me, you're not the first man to live in that particular delusion, and you surely won't be the last."

Feeling the need to escape, unable to stand her own viciousness and still unable to stop it, Moresha clutched the cheese and crackers to her nightgown, moving forward, to the door. His words stopped her before she could leave.

"And yet, all those other men are gone, and I'm still here. What does that tell you, Moresha? What does that mean?"

She answered without turning, fear sharpening her

words. "All it tells me is that you're that much closer to leaving. Just have your bags ready and waiting when it's time, 'cause she won't give you much notice." She left without looking to see if her words had caused the desired amount of damage, preferring to make her exit while she could do so in dignity.

Rich, for his part, stood alone, uncertainty lingering in the back of his mind. He wasn't deliberately being obtuse. It was only that, even after these days in her presence, he still didn't know what she wanted.

Sexually, he had tried everything he could to satisfy her, to push her beyond reason and into ecstasy. Still, she had withheld herself from him, refusing to submit to her passions. Without knowing what she wanted, how could he possibly give it to her? And if he didn't give her what she wanted, would she really keep him around, especially when no other woman had?

Chapter 11

The phone lines burned hotly in Reason all throughout Sunday night, as members of Bethune Baptist called other members and then their family, friends, and whoever else would listen to the scandalous goings on that had occurred, right there in church, right in the middle of Pastor's sermon on immorality!

"Pastor stood there in the pulpit, mouth wide open, girl, fly coulda gone right in an he wouldna known no better," one tithe-paying member told a known sinner with whom she happened to be close friends. "He started to stutterin' so fast, you woulda thought he was speakin' in tongues!"

"Wish I coulda seen that! That fool quickest person I ever knowed wit some words, could sweet talk my granny right outta her drawers." The sinner laughed loudly, knowing that her friend was among the many women in town who had dropped their drawers for the velvet-tongued preacher.

"Well, I done told you before, girl, you outta get saved and come on down to the church house. You mighta been there to see!"

"If I'da known y'all had such carryin's on, I mighta woulda, too."

The member responded, seeing her opportunity, and quickly led her friend in a brief recitation of the Sinner's Prayer of Repentance. So despite Miranda's scandalous antics in the church, or more properly because of them, the small church enlarged and gained several of Reason's less reputable citizens, each vowing to be in service the following week, even if they didn't commit to anything

159

beyond that.

By Monday morning, everybody who knew somebody had called anybody who would listen and told and retold the tale, with two exceptions: by tacit agreement, everyone refrained from calling either Sincere or Mama Kinney. A few of the women who'd visited on Saturday had spoken frankly with their friends, and between them they had all come to one conclusion: Sincere's freshly baked, irresistible treats had done a number on all of their stomachs. They disagreed as to whether or not they thought it'd been done on purpose, a few of the women preferring to think it mighta just been an egg that'd been too long in the icebox or some mealy flour. But either way the conclusion was the same: none of the women would risk having them do it again, whether out of mistaken hospitality or spiteful meanness, and so not a one of them called and gave Mama Kinney or Sincere a head's up on the local gossip.

Consequently, Sincere departed quietly for work, noting with some surprise how few people stood at the bus stop, waiting to go into Town, but assuming she'd forgotten some local holiday. No matter. As a nurse, her schedule did not always coincide with holidays, and she even worked on Saturdays and Sunday, whenever there was a need. A number of the town's other, less diligent residents, called into work with various ailments: coughs and colds that had been caused by the unpredictable weather. A few came down with more serious maladies, explaining to their respective employers that they couldn't be certain of just when their gall stones, back injuries, or chronic diarrhea would clear up, such that they could return to work. Who knew how long this thing might drag on, and what scandalous things might occur come Tuesday that they would *not* want to miss?

Thirty-some-odd women converged on Mama Kinney's porch early this time, coming in with sunlight, bringing their own baked goods, lest they should be seduced again to try whatever leftovers remained. Mama Kinney greeted them with reluctant and surprised hospitality, certain of nothing more than that she could lay this entire visit at Miranda's door. The women quickly confirmed her belief, savoring the opportunity to scandalize one of the sole occupants of Reason who hadn't already heard.

"Right there, she was right there on his lap!"

"I heard she had one hand down his crotch."

"And the other on that woman- what's her name again?"

"Whatever, girl it ain't important. Fact is, I heard she was tonguin' 'em both down, right sittin' there in the pew!"

"Shut up, girl! You *must* be lyin'."

"I know you ain't callin' me no liar," the woman responded. "I ain't got to lie, girl, everybody seen it! The whole damn church!" She looked out at the crowd for confirmation, and more than a few of Bethune's members nodded their heads in response. "You ain't lyin'," they chorused loudly, and the woman sat back with restored dignity.

Even Mama Kinney, besieged with unwelcome visitors, couldn't help but get caught up in the gossip. She had seen Moresha and Miranda on their way to church, had wondered at it, but Lord! Even Miranda didn't seem *that* bold. And Rich!

"My question is, what the *hell* is up with Rich? I mean, it ain't like him to be doin' all kinda public nonsense. He always struck me as bein' just a lil' bit smarter than that."

161

This from Jenna, who shook her head with the comment.

Reese looked at her skeptically with raised brow. "Rich? Our Rich? We talkin' 'bout the same boy? 'Cause if we is, let me be the one to tell you, he ain't got no more sense than a cockroach, and that ain't none at all!"

Jenna bristled noticeably, her arms crossing over her chest in an automatic and defensive gesture. She thought, and then said, "He built that business!"

"An he gone run it into the ground, too, you mark my words. The boy ain't got nothin' goin' on up there, you can see it in his eyes. Give you that glazed over look, like he don't know whether he comin' or goin' but he movin' all the same!"

"Can't say he a complete fool. I side wit Jenna on that one." Minnie, a woman who'd had a brief affair with Rich before her recent marriage, chimed in. "I will tell you this much, the boy don't know nothin' 'bout no woman. He couldn't tell your titties from your ass, and he liable to poke you in either." Belatedly, she remembered the presence of the church congregants, but they only nodded along with everyone else. She smiled sheepishly at Mama Kinney, silently apologizing.

"That's what makes me so nervous," Rena said, stepping out toward the center. "She probably over there, doin' whatever nasty things she can to him, and the poor boy wouldn't know the difference. She could be into voodoo, for all we know!" Several of the women crossed themselves, unconcerned that the movement was distinctly Catholic.

Across the street, the side door of the little peach house opened, and out walked Moresha, head bowed in concentration, ignoring the women on the porch. They sat, every one of them, watching her move quickly past

162

Rich's white car to the powder blue Buick, to stand there fumbling with the keys. The porch was silent, barely breathing, everyone attuned to her actions. Getting the car opened, she slid behind the wheel and the engine roared to sudden life, warming.

They stood there for some moments, frozen in the tableau, everyone waiting for something else to occur. Someone let out a deep sigh and the other women collectively hushed her, afraid they would miss some minute word or sound across the street.

Moresha got out the car again, leaving it idling in the driveway, and turned to return into the house. But before she could, the door opened again and Miranda walked out, carrying a small bag. Even from across the street, the women on the porch could read the frank sexual promise in the way her hips moved with suggestive precision. Several of them had never seen her before, and they pressed forward eagerly, wanting to know something about this woman everyone was talking about.

Miranda did not disappoint. She walked forward, handing the bag to Moresha, and leaned over to whisper something in her ear. The two of them stood, close together in the driveway, unspeaking, something indefinably intimate in the air between them, and then Miranda did the most remarkable thing. She reached a hand toward Moresha, pulling her face toward her, and her lips and then her tongue traveled in easy, unhurried enjoyment over the other woman's mouth. Moresha stood awkwardly in her embrace, her posture stiff but softening as the moment drew on, her arms rising, involuntarily, to embrace Miranda before she got back into the car. She idled a moment more, letting it completely heat, before putting the car in reverse and slowly backing out of the driveway.

Miranda, for her part, simply waved and beamed brightly at Moresha, until the Buick had pulled around the corner and out of sight. Still she stood a moment more, hand still raised in half-salute, staring defiantly at the women across the street before she finally returned into the house.

"Good God a'mighty!" Mama Kinney said quietly, letting the words escape in an involuntary whistle through clenched teeth.

Her words seemed to break the spell that Miranda had cast, and the entire porch erupted in immediate reaction as women scrambled to regain their seats. A few, convinced that they might miss something the next time, still clung to the posts, reluctant to take their eyes off the house where the two strange women did even stranger things inside.

"Now, she *know* she know better!"

"When I would do good, evil is ever before me." Mable, one of the older church members in the group, shook her head. "God said it, I believe it!"

"She outta be ashamed, airin' that kinda sinfulness, right out here in public!" someone else said, outraged.

Mama Kinney raised a brow. "Seem to me like she ain't the only one ought to show a lil' shame. Every one of y'all came out here today for no other purpose than to see exactly that." Mama Kinney stared the women down, trying to shame them herself.

The tactic actually worked for a moment, and one of the younger church members nodded. "We outta go on over an share the gospel, save her soul from hell."

"We couldn't save that girl from burnin' if we hosed her down wit water and double-wrapped her up in ice. She bound and determined to meet the devil, she'll probably enjoy the male company." Mary shook her head in resigned condemnation, already having decided her position. "'Sides, is some sins even God won't forgive."

"Mary," Marina said, shocked, but Mary staunchly defended her position. "You know it, too! That kinda thing, that's just unnatural. Women lovin' women! Thas jus' nasty. They outta outlaw that type of thing."

"There might be a law, at that."

"Naw, girl, they do all types of things out in the cities. I know. My cousin Victoria be callin' me up, tellin' me about the things she sees. Y'all think *this* is scandalous!" The speaker, a woman with light brown hair and pretty, even skin, shook her head.

"Nasty or sinful, I don't know," Lady said, laughing lightly to dispel some of the tension that had fallen over the porch. "Got to say, though, for myself, I loves me some—" she broke off, looking at Mama Kinney, before finishing lamely out of respect, "men."

"You ain't the only one," Mable spoke up, her hand waving across the street. "She must love it, too, else why she got Rich in there? Must be she ain't satisfied wit what that other woman givin' her."

"Can't say I blame her, either. If I was into that sort of thing, can't say I would gone an take up wit her. I mean, she 'bout the ugliest thing this side of hell. Aside from the fact she *white*," and here Rena paused, as if she'd just made a revelation. "The woman has *got* to be at *least* ten years her senior, and it look to me like more'n a few of her parts is startin' to sag. Gotta wonder what she see in her, 'cause it must be more than looks."

"Well, I done seen my fill of both of 'em," Reese said, standing. "I gotta go call my sister, she gone *hate* havin' missed this!"

Her comment reminded the women that they had

duties that needed attending to. Others stood, too, unwilling that someone else should spread the word before they got the chance. Mama Kinney's heart rose in her breast, then plummeted as she heard one of the women say, "Nah, y'all gone ahead. I'ma see what else happens out here, today." Several more women kept their seats or moved toward seats that had just been vacated, and they all settled in as if they planned to stay.

Unable to think of a reason to object, Mama Kinney instead resigned herself to a day of involuntary entertaining. Her bones swelled within her, protesting, feeling the cold, reminding her of every one of the past sixty-eight years. She sighed, listening to the women gossip excitedly around her. Despite her age, her days did not seem to be getting any shorter.

Within the house, Rich watched Miranda standing, looking out through the curtains toward the street. He had slept in a bit, his body feeling drained from the excesses of the day before. He sighed, realizing today was Monday, and that he was already late for work. Lorna would be more than a little peeved at the task of explaining to his clients why, exactly, he was running late. He would need to hurry.

He stood, unconcerned about his nakedness after four days with this woman, and walked up behind her. He casually draped his arms around her and nuzzled her neck, deeply inhaling her scent. If love could be captured by the senses, this would be it.

But she moved quickly and stiffly away from him, dropping the curtains back into place before he could see what she had seen outside. He looked at her in wounded confusion, uncomprehending.

"Don't touch me," she said simply, and moved away.

Rich smiled easily, his heart speeding a bit, concerned. "Baby," he began, trying to assuage her irritation, but she moved toward him suddenly, the fabric of her dress rubbing roughly against his chest. She reached out and stroked him, holding and manipulating him until he stood at ready attention.

He moaned and pushed her hand away. "Naw, baby, today is Monday. I got to go to work."

Her hands refused to stop, and instead found and teased small dimples in his flesh, sensitive areas that corresponded with his various senses. The pleasure of it was awful and sweet, all at once. "Call in," she said, her voice husky with command, and he was reminded of a similar order on Friday. *Request*, he reminded himself. She had only *asked* him to call in.

"Not today, baby, I really have to go in. Money jus' don't make itself," he said, still enjoying the pleasure her hands worked across his body. One of her nails flicked across the tip of his dick, pressing him open, teasing him. His knees weakened.

She moved with him, pushing him back toward the bed, crowding his thoughts and his emotions. His knees, already weakened by the excitement, buckled completely when they hit the soft mattress, and his body fell hard onto the bed. She knelt before him and his mind stopped, hung up on one word: *yes!*

And she did, using her tongue and mouth in ways he'd never before experienced, mouth threatening to swallow him whole. He felt lost in her, his mind unable to think for the dense fog swirling around him, refusing to ease. The sensation of it was exciting and scary all the same. Her lips whispered into the space where his thighs met his groin, brushing him with their softness, promising more. He gave in, unable to continue in resistance, his body begging his mind to let go. His hips lifted, pressing more deeply within her mouth, but still she met him thrust for thrust, her mouth opening and widening, taking him in. He could not stop, could not keep his hands from pressing her more fully on him, demanding more until he came, surging deeply into her mouth, spilling his seed. And she took that, too, refusing his retreat.

When he came to, he realized he still lay half on the bed, his feet dangling limply along the side, her head resting intimately on one thigh. She smiled up at him, her eyes sleepy and unfocused, and he wanted to shout out his love. This woman was everything, and he would be a fool if he didn't marry her. What other woman could ever be so happy, so satisfied, to service only him?

He smiled down at her, shaking his head in regret. Still, he knew he had to go to work. He couldn't miss another day. "My clothes, baby? Where you put them?"

"For what?" she said, still smiling dreamily up at him.

He chuckled in response, knowing she'd assumed his acquiescence meant he'd stay. His fingers brushed against her forehead, finding and massaging her scalp through the thickness of her hair. "Baby, much as I'd love to stay, I gotta get to work. It's Monday," he said again, certain she'd understand.

But she didn't. Instead, she frowned at him, leaning back on her knees. His skin felt suddenly cold in the space she had vacated. "You call in," she said again, and this time he detected a hint of steel beneath her voice.

His body stiffened in automatic response before he forced an easy smile. "You know—" he began, but she cut in.

"You leave this house today, don't plan on comin' back," she said, her voice calmly conveying the message.

Now it was his turn to frown. Moresha's words echoed in his head, and he wondered if she was already growing tired of him. "Don't be like that, baby," he said, and reached for her, but she made a small negative movement with her head and stood. Her body moved fluidly through the door and he stood, too, uncertainly.

She returned, carrying with her a pile of clothing. She dropped the clothing in the middle of the floor and stood over them, daring him to retrieve them. Instead, he reached for her, hoping he could soften her response, gentle and cajoling in his movement. But she stepped back again, deftly avoiding his hands.

"You can get your shit and get out," she said, her smile belying the harshness of her words. "Or you can join me back in bed and we can make love again. And again."

The thought of making love with her was blessedly erotic, but he could not shake the feeling that he was being manipulated, or worse. He did not like the way she commanded him, as if she expected his obedience. But she moved toward him, removing her own clothing as she walked, and his eyes were captured by the sight of her body, suddenly naked, but for a small, infinitely intriguing pair of panties. Despite his resolve to return to work, he felt himself caving, submitting to her demand. She wanted him, and he wanted her, again. Suddenly, work seemed less urgent, and he decided Lorna could simply do her job. She would have to wait until tomorrow, though, because apparently, he would not be going in today.

By the time Rich did call Lorna, she had worked herself into something of a mood. She was not at all happy about the prospect of another day explaining to irate clients that he would not be in.

"But what about Mr. Morris?" she said, asking about a client he'd been trying to satisfy for at least a month.

"He'll just have to wait, Lorna. Give him my apologies."

He could hear the frustration in her sigh, but she wisely chose not to question his motives. He was relieved, unable to explain them right now.

Her hesitation was obvious, and then, in little more than a whisper, she asked, "But you're okay, Rich?" She paused, giving him less than an opportunity to answer, then rushed on. "I'm just asking 'cause, you know how people talk. They're sayin' some odd things, Rich, that you been seen doin' all kinda things! I know it's not true, of course, but still it's not like you to be out this long, and especially over a woman."

Rich stiffened, suddenly feeling like there were too many women in his life, all trying to manage and control him. "Goodbye, Lorna. You gone an take the afternoon off, after you make those calls," he said, and hung up, feeling suddenly like a bastard. She had only been worried, and he had been too harsh. He would have called back to apologize, but for Miranda's sudden entrance.

"You've called, then." She smiled at him brightly, her eyes hiding her thoughts. "Good," she said, and that simple word was full of meaning.

Chapter 12

Sincere stopped by Mama Kinney's house on her customary visit before returning to her small apartment. She found Mama Kinney sitting in darkness in the living room, staring at the closed curtains and into nothingness. The scene frightened her for some indefinable reason, and she anxiously began turning on lights until the room was restored to its normally bright atmosphere. Mama Kinney didn't seem to notice, and Sincere looked more closely at the curtains, just to ascertain that nothing was there.

"Mama?" she whispered questioningly. Mama Kinney, startled, looked up.

The older woman sat forward in her chair, still unspeaking, and Sincere took a seat on the couch across from her to wait. She obviously had something on her mind.

Finally Mama Kinney spoke. "She was down at Bethune yesterday. Made a big, scandalous scene. Disrupted the whole service." She paused a moment to let Sincere digest the words, then continued. "I hear that old rat, Pastor Mitchell, tried to give her a lesson on sexual immorality. Thought he'd teach her somethin' he don't know nothin' about." She smiled at that, remembering.

At seventy-nine, Pastor Mitchell was still a good-looking man, lean and well-built, even if he was showing his age, but Mama Kinney knew what was hidden on the inside. She might not have known when she was nineteen, but she had looked closely at him one day years later and seen the devil dressed in clergymen cloths. And she'd not gone near that particular bit of hellfire ever since.

"And then right there, right in the middle of his sermon, she somehow got herself into Rich's lap, the two of 'em doin' unspeakable things in *God's House.*"

Sincere could imagine the fairer-skinned pastor turning red with outrage, and the gaping jaws of sanctimonious congregants. She laughed out loud at the image.

Mama Kinney snorted in disgust. "And that white woman—"

"Moresha," Sincere corrected, out of respect for the woman she'd met briefly on Saturday.

"Yeah, that one. She had to pull Jean out of the church. Good thing she did, too. No tellin' what other nonsense that girl woulda been up to otherwise, given more time an a willing audience." Mama Kinney, too, chuckled at the imagined scene.

The room was quiet a moment, each woman entertaining separate thoughts, until Sincere finally said, "What is she *doing?* I mean, she knows better."

"She been gone a while, Sincere, and it is the seventies. Not everybody knows we still live like this in small towns."

"She ain't been gone *that* long! And small town or big city, that kinda carryin' on in the house of the Lord ain't appropriate nowhere." Sincere studied Mama Kinney closely as she spoke, to gauge her response. "An she was born here. She know how people talk. Just look at what happened with her parents. Her memory ain't *that* short."

Mama Kinney shook her head in silent agreement. Whatever her reasons for doin' what she'd done, ignorance wasn't likely to be one of 'em. "They all came out, too, every one of 'em, just to see what they could see. Standin' here cranin' they necks, talkin' as if they know somethin' more'n what they know. The whole lot of 'em, as if they ain't had nothin' more productive to do wit they day. Waitin' for the show to start." She waved a dismissive hand and sucked her teeth. "As if they ain't got enough shameful behavior goin' on between 'em."

Sincere knew enough to read into what her godmother hadn't said. "What'd she do?" she asked, dreading the answer.

Mama Kinney snorted. "What didn't she do! She came out here with that white woman," and this time Sincere didn't interject. "...tongued that woman down right there in they own driveway! Like she jus' wanted everybody to see! The girl ain't got no shame, no shame at all!"

Sincere sighed heavily and lowered herself deeply into an overstuffed living room chair. With pastel-colored flowers on an off-white background, the chair matched a sofa and a second chair, in which Mama Kinney currently sat. The pattern had always seemed incongruous in the simple house, as if Mama Kinney had no patience left, by the time she finished decorating the rest of the house, to choose more suitable living room furniture. Sincere spoke quietly, suggesting another possibility. "Maybe she did want everybody to see. Maybe she don't care no more *what* people say."

"Well, if she want people to talk, all she needs to do is continue doin' what she doin'! Her grandparents would turn over in they graves if they could see her carryin' on like she is, right here for the entire town to see. They was decent folks. They never woulda appreciated they granddaughter, they own blood, makin' such a mockery of they memory."

173

Sincere kept her thoughts to herself, knowing this was one thing on which she and Mama Kinney would never agree. In her opinion, Miranda's grandparents had shamed themselves long before now by their treatment of their granddaughter. And having rejected and hurt her, they would certainly be in no position to object to her behavior and its effect on their sainted memories.

Mama Kinney hugged a blanket more tightly about her shoulders and sighed. She sat back in her chair, suddenly deflated. "It's been a long day," she said, and the way she lingered on the word 'long' made Sincere look at her more closely. She seemed and sounded exhausted.

The two of them sat quietly in the stale and waning light, watching shadows chase each other on the wall. Sincere was suddenly conscious of the space between them that had been created by life and living. Mama Kinney had sixty-eight years for her twenty-eight and had squeezed more life into each day than Sincere could into a month. She knew and understood things for which answers only existed in the abstract. She was not a fool, and in Sincere's lifetime, she had rarely been wrong. Still, in this Sincere knew she was prejudiced. She, like everyone else in Reason, had been quick to judge the girl by the actions of her parents, and even now Mama Kinney could only see Miranda as the product of her parents' actions, not as a distinct person, with separate motivations. Mama Kinney, in her bias, could not see Miranda as she was now.

And what she was now was dangerous. Dangerous, but not stupid. For whatever reason, she had intentionally staged both of those scenes for the benefit of her audience, and Sincere knew instinctively that she had done so in conscious, calculated planning. She had not struck Sincere as an impetuous woman, but one driven by some stronger emotion that required satisfaction, whatever the cost.

Mama Kinney had some knowledge, true, but she, too, was just a woman. She was not infallible. And in this she had misjudged. Jean, now Miranda, was not imprudent. No, she was intentionally flaunting her lifestyle and her actions in front of everyone, fully aware of the talk her actions would engender. Whatever her reasons, they were not innocent or incidental. And Sincere suspected they would be destructive for more than a few people involved.

A light snore shook Sincere out of her contemplation and she smiled, realizing Mama Kinney had fallen asleep. It must have been a long day indeed, for Mama Kinney to fall asleep right there on the couch! Sincere, too, was suddenly tired, and anxious to be in her own home and bed. She carefully turned out the lights and shook Mama Kinney awake, then helped the older woman to her bed.

"Sincere?" Mama Kinney said, stopping her before she could leave the bedroom. "Baby, hand me my Word." Sincere smiled at this, thinking that long day or not, Mama Kinney would always make time to consult with the Word of God before another day could arrive. She handed Mama Kinney her Bible and stayed a moment more, as she'd not done for years, to listen to her read the words out loud. Tired, Mama Kinney chose a short passage from the book of Psalms, the words comforting in both their familiarity and message.

"Blessed is the man that walketh not in the counsel of the ungodly, nor standeth in the way of sinners, nor sitteth in the seat of the scornful..." She continued on, and Sincere allowed her thoughts to be lulled into peacefulness by the words. Whatever her worries, they were reassured by the passage. Even if Miranda's plans were dangerous, surely God would protect them all. Mama Kinney had always delighted in the Word of the Lord, surely God would bless her for that much devotion. She silently prayed, listening to the words, reminding God of the promise of this passage, urging Him to fulfill it. And when she finished, her heart was lighter, her mind at peace, and she felt nothing less than blessed in the knowledge that everything would undoubtedly work out.

Sincere slipped out of the house and closed the door quietly behind her. She heard the lock click into place and marveled at the change. Reason was not the type of town where people locked their doors, even now, with all the changes in the world. Beyond Reason, life was becoming more chaotic and fast-paced and less secure. But here, in this town, it was if time had simply stopped passing. People worked and lived and ate and laughed with the same simplicity as they had a century before, with minimal intrusions from new technological advances. They blended seamlessly into the town's atmosphere, causing no answering alterations in the values and motivations of the town's residents.

Still, Sincere couldn't help being a little bit shaken by Miranda's return to the town. What she was after was anybody's guess, but the threat of her presence was almost tangible. Sincere sighed, standing in the darkness of Mama Kinney's porch, watching with some regret the house across the street. She had never found closeness with a woman, had never achieved that amicable camaraderie that was shared between female friends. She had spent much of her life alone, surrounded by people who loved her, but never loved by someone who *understood* her. As an adult, she had distanced herself from both men and women, having been made a little bit wary by the circumstances of her life. Mama Kinney was the only person with whom she shared more than a detached friendship and, with a generation between them, they sometimes lacked understanding.

Sincere was tired of feeling so old, and so alone, but helpless to change her nature. She could love, certainly, deeply and loyally, without reservation. The problem was in *being* loved. She had yet to have someone, male or female, of her own age love her with the same devotion.

She had hoped, for a moment, that that would change. Standing before Jean on her porch, her heart beating in rapid movements in her chest, she had looked at her old friend and seen nineteen years slip away into inconsequential nothingness. She had longed for the embrace of friendship, that kind of happy giddiness that washed away time and misunderstandings, all at once. She had even smiled at Jean expectantly, offering herself fully and conveying everything she felt and thought unashamedly in her eyes. All the love she'd ever felt for her friend had swelled up in her breasts, threatening to consume her with its intensity.

But then Jean had smiled at her politely, and at Jody, and introduced herself as Miranda. She had stood back, conveying her own message with silent body language. Then she had looked again at Sincere with eyes narrowed and such loathing in them that Sincere had been taken aback. *She hates me*, Sincere had thought, and something within her had withered and died, right there on that porch where she'd played and laughed and been with

Jean, now Miranda, so many years before.

Who are you, Sincere wondered to the darkness, knowing it would not answer. Since her arrival, Sincere had constantly struggled within herself, the honest part of her longing to go to her old friend and speak frankly about whatever misunderstanding lay between them, preventing them from loving. She had wanted to tell her how much she'd missed her, how she'd never forgotten her, how she had watched daily for an entire year, hoping she'd return. And when Moresha arrived and it was evident what the relationship was between the two women, Sincere had wanted to remind Miranda that she was not so small-minded to care. If there was room in her life for another female friend, Sincere was happy to accept whatever space and time was left. She had her own sins and fears; she was in no position to judge.

But life was making that impossible. Sincere had no doubt that, even with her godmother's obvious disapproval, she would have eventually made her way across the street and across the years to Miranda. She might yet do the same. But Miranda seemed hell-bent on a destructive path that had shocked and scandalized the residents of the small town, and Sincere had the sinking feeling that Miranda had meant her actions as an affront to her, as well. That somehow she had wanted to distance herself from Sincere and was doing this by acting outrageously in ways Sincere could neither understand nor condone. It was frustrating, to say the least, to spend her entire life waiting for that closeness, that love between friends, and to be offered it and have it taken away, all in the same moment.

Jean, or Miranda, was walking a fine line between scandal and offense, and Sincere knew she might be in need of a true friend real soon. Moresha seemed like a genuine and wonderful person, but she would not be able to protect Miranda from the people of Reason. Reason protected its own, and Moresha was not one of them. No, if Miranda was going to survive this path she'd chosen for herself, she would need a less-questionable ally, someone who could work within the town to keep them from turning against her. *She will need me*, Sincere thought, encouraged.

But the thought was suddenly tempered by another: no matter what her access or how persuasive her arguments, she could not undo the damage that had been done so far, nor that she was certain was to come. Miranda didn't seem to want her allegiance, and was doing everything possible to turn the entire town and all its people against her, including Sincere. It would not work, of course; if Miranda remembered anything about their friendship, it must have occurred to her by now that Sincere had faced down considerable opposition and pressure to maintain it. Even Mama Kinney had been adamantly opposed to the relationship, and had tried for months to prevent the two girls from seeing each other before she'd finally given in and turned a blind eye. Other children had been cruel, ostracizing the young girl without ever knowing why. They had only known that their parents, grandparents, and friends all thought the girl was bad, for whatever reason, and they had acted in accordance.

No, it would take a lot more than just scandalous antics to make Sincere turn against the woman she still considered her friend, despite the intervening years. Sincere did not love lightly, and she could not discard her love quickly and without cause. If Miranda knew anything at all, she *must* know that.

Which was exactly why Sincere had locked the door

behind her when she left Mama Kinney's house tonight. There were very few things Miranda could ever do that would turn Sincere against her, but hurting someone else she loved was certainly one of them. Not that Miranda had any reason to hurt Mama Kinney, nor did Sincere have any reason to suspect as much. No, it was just a fear, an unspecified feeling that had settled in Sincere's gut and wouldn't go away. Sincere *knew*, without asking, that Miranda wanted to sever her ties with Sincere. And she was certain Miranda knew that would not be easily done. The situation was untenable, and Sincere could not predict its outcome. Perhaps Miranda would be satisfied with Sincere's unwavering, but distant and unspoken love. It had not and would not interfere with her course, whatever that would be. Perhaps. But hatred was as powerful an emotion as love, and Sincere wasn't certain which of the two emotions was stronger within her friend.

Shadows shifted in the night across the street, and Sincere saw the side door of the little peach house open and close quickly in the dark. She stood in stillness, trying to make out a shape. Nothing moved, but goose bumps rose on her arms and she had the sudden awareness of being closely watched. It was Miranda, of course, but Sincere could not see her in the dark. Feeling exposed by the bright porch-light, she stepped back, willing the shadows to close around her, but the movement did not dispel the feeling. Finally, the door opened again, the light inside broken by the shape of Miranda reentering the house.

Sincere stood a moment more, saddened by the missed opportunity, wondering why Miranda had not approached. She shrugged resignedly with the sinking realization that she could spend a hundred years puzzling over the motives of this woman, and still never understand what she had become. Best not to try at all, and simply to protect herself and those she loved as much as she possibly could.

Chapter 13

Fucked. That was the most apt description of how Rich felt upon awakening Tuesday morning. Upward, backward, and thoroughly. Exhausted, more than a little bit hungry, somehow diminished, both as a man and as a human being. His skin was sensitive, raw in places she had touched, bereft in places she'd neglected. His body ached for her, for the sweetness of her skin against his own, but his spirit was repulsed by the possibility. He had nothing left to give and, somewhere in his mind, he acknowledged that this had been true for at least the last two days. Yet, still, she had taken more, provoking responses from his tired body that he would have deemed impossible before now. Before her. And still, even in their lovemaking, he knew he had failed to touch her heart. Every day he'd woken thinking today would be the day, but this day he accepted the truth. Miranda was a complex woman. She would take time and energy to woo, to make her trust him, and he wasn't sure he had either to give her today.

Even without opening his eyes, he could feel her there, watching him, waiting for him to awaken. Even now he didn't know what she wanted from him. Well, besides sex. He had done that, given all he had, and he was tired. All he wanted now was to rest and rejuvenate, to hold her and touch her and be. Just to be. *What was wrong with him?* Was he becoming a woman, then, wanting to lie here peacefully with her in intimacy? Wanting *not* to make love to her, with her, for once? Wanting to talk and learn the woman he knew he loved?

He was loath to admit the truth. Somehow he knew

she would not appreciate the admission. For the past four days, she had been relentless in her passion, always demanding, as if the idea of non-sexual intimacy was a concept unknown and unexplored. He feared that she would laugh if he explained his feelings, or worse.

He had learned to do his thinking before opening his eyes in morning, knowing that she was there, watching. She was always there. It was an uncomfortable feeling, and one he had tried to alleviate by asking her not to do it. But then she had moved against him, making his body rise and sing against hers, and he had forgotten his request. She could see through him, could read his mind; she knew the thoughts that lay behind his eyes. And so he had learned to think before opening his eyes in the vain hope that he could thus prevent her from knowing his thoughts.

"Get up," she said. He opened his eyes immediately at the malice in her voice. His eyes searched the bedroom, looking for her. She sat, perched on a wooden chair beside the door, a long blue skirt hiding her ankles from his view. He frowned. She did not often wear clothing in her own house, he had learned that much by now. Something was wrong. Her eyes seemed a reflection of her mood, stormy and yet resolute. Long fingers, fingers that had touched him in the most intimate ways, tapped against her knee, conveying her impatience more effectively than words. "Get up," she said again, and he moved in fluid quickness, unwilling to risk her displeasure.

He walked toward her, naked, feeling awkward, before a familiar print made him stop cold. His clothing sat on the edge of the bed, folded neatly, and he almost smiled gratefully before he understood the significance. He frowned, thinking rapidly. She had refused to return his clothing since he arrived five days ago, keeping him naked in her presence and always ready for lovemaking. The two of them had walked about the house naked, unselfconscious. He had grown comfortable in her presence, unconcerned even when the light exposed the slight bulge he'd just noticed beginning to gather around his hips from all her good cooking. A puckered scar marred the smooth skin on the back of his thigh. But when she looked at him, it was as if she never noticed, as if she could only see that he had exactly what she needed, what she could never get from Moresha.

Panic washed over him and he turned to her in desperation, turning his back on the damning clothing. "Miranda, baby-"

"Rich," she said, stopping his words with precise finality. "It's time to go."

He went to her, wanting again to see that look in her eyes that said she needed him, but she stood and nimbly moved away. He moved with her, unwilling to let her go. "Baby, you don't mean that. Look what I got for you," he said, gesturing downward, but his body was too exhausted to rise.

She arched a brow, her eyes following his hand, and then back at his face. Her mouth twisted in what might have been a grim and mocking smile.

"Now, wait, baby, just give me a minute," he said, stroking with abrupt and jerky movements that revealed his desperation. Given the right incentive, he knew he would be ready again. Hadn't it been this way with her these past four days? He always felt as if he'd had enough, as if nothing could make him respond again, but then she would come to him with expectation and enticement in her eyes, and he'd be ready all over again.

"Oh give it up," she said, crossing her arms over her

breasts. "You could make that thing stand up and salute me an I wouldn't give a damn. I'm done." She didn't have to say "with you" but he heard it all the same. She turned to leave.

"You don't mean that," he said again, reaching down and grabbing her arm. "You need me."

She looked at him again, that single brow mocking him, giving lie to his claim. His hand fell awkwardly to his side, releasing her. "Need you? For what?"

Rich looked down at himself, frustrated by the timing. He felt as if he was fighting for his life, and yet his body had a mind of its own. "It'll rise again, baby, you know that," he said, flinching at the pleading in his tone. Still, he was afraid a less-than-genuine response would destroy any chance he might have. Pressing his case, he said, "*She* won't give it to you like this. She *can't* give it to you, baby, she ain't got it to give. You need me," he said again, but even his own body was unconvinced.

She looked at him without speaking, and he stood awkwardly, afraid to hope, but more afraid of giving up. Her words, when they came, barely rose above a whisper, but the anger in them was apparent nonetheless. "Don't you ever mention her again. Moresha gives me everything I need. Everything you never could, and never will," she said, and walked out. From the hallway, he heard her say, "Get dressed, and get the fuck out. Now. Otherwise, the entire neighborhood will see what you ain't got when I throw you out my house, bare-assed and naked."

Rich stood in the room, watching her leave, stunned by the finality of her rejection. She didn't mean it. She couldn't. She wouldn't just up and decide one day that everything was over. There had been no warning, no

185

waning of her interest. No reason to think last night that he would wake up to this in the morning.

He felt sorry for himself. Women were always leaving him, but this one was special. If only he had reached that part of her, the inside of her emotions, maybe then he could have bound her to him and made her stay. Instead, he had failed in even that endeavor, though he'd certainly tried his hardest. What was *wrong* with him, that every woman he wanted didn't want him? He looked down at himself, angrily eyeing his dick. It had been good enough to get him inside, but not good enough to keep her. How was it he'd fallen in love with a woman he couldn't have?

But as he thought it through, it occurred to him that maybe he could. Miranda had said she was done with him, yes, but she would need him again. Moresha had said as much on Sunday, in the kitchen, that Miranda regularly had this need. Surely she would want to fill it with someone who was known to her, someone who loved her. She *must* have felt something to have kept him there so long. And even if she didn't, she would need a man again. She would need him, and he would be right there, ready to give her exactly what she needed. And this time, whatever the cost, he would make her love him.

With a renewed sense of hope, Rich made his way down the stairs, fully dressed now and more confident about the situation. He would take his time and woo Miranda, utilizing every skill and ability he possessed. First, though, he would go home and rest up, and get ready for the upcoming seduction. Her passions were endless, and he wanted to be ready to meet them with equal capability.

She stood in the hallway, waiting for him, and he nodded to her congenially, casually, thinking it was best not to show his hand just yet. And wasn't there some old adage about women always wanting what they could not have? He stepped quickly around her, opening the door with ease, but he couldn't resist looking back for one last hopeful moment. "Miranda, don't you—" he began, but she shut the door in his face before he could finish the request.

He stood there a moment, fighting desperation and the persistent fear that this might, indeed, be the last time Miranda would welcome him into her home and her body. He shook himself mentally and tried to regain his earlier confidence. Of course this would not be the last time. Of course she would welcome him again. He needed only to find that one thing that she wanted above all else, that one thing neither Moresha nor any other man in her past could give her. When he found it, she would come back to him. She would love him this time, too, he knew she would.

Turning, he was almost blinded by the sunlight pressing hard behind a cloud. The intensity of it was astonishing. Rich felt as if he'd not seen daylight in months, years even. He stood there staring out, allowing his eyes the moment needed to adjust to the brightness.

When they did, Rich almost wished he had remained blinded after all. The sight of seven or eight women watching him with wide eyes and open mouths from across the street was enough to chase the last of his confidence away. They had seen her shut the door in his face, he knew they had. They would make their own assumptions, none of which would be good for him.

187

He stepped lightly with false gaiety, waving back toward Miranda's house although he knew she wasn't looking. It was necessary either way, if for no other reason than to salvage what remained of his reputation and dignity. He could not court the woman properly with a dozen interested parties watching his every mood. He would have to shape the gossip, make them think that he was simply leaving for the day and returning on the morrow. They would have to think, at least, that Miranda was still his woman, despite her rejection.

The image wasn't difficult to carry off, but it crumbled when he got into his car and turned it on. In his heart, he knew this rejection had been a lot more serious, and that he would need to fight to get her back. He also knew that she was a beautiful woman, and he would not be the only interested man in Reason. He needed to act quickly and boldly to stake his claim, and he needed to let all the gossips and everyone else in Reason know that this woman was his and his alone. Only then would he have the space and peace of mind to maneuver her back into his arms.

Across the street, Mama Kinney and the women on her porch finally began speaking again, certain now that whatever drama there was had already concluded. "It don't never get borin' 'round here, do it, Mama?" a woman named Sissy asked into the quiet that followed Rich's departure.

"Not since *she* moved in, it ain't," Mama Kinney responded, because it was expected.

"She probably take that sort of drama wit her everywhere she go. Wish she'd move in next to me, then I could stop makin' this trip down to yo house." Reese reached down to toy with the fastening of one shoe.

Mama Kinney eyed her skeptically. "You best be careful what you wish for, God might just give it to you. And believe me, entertainin' y'all bunch of biddies and gossips every day on end can be a tiresome job. Make me wanna take a nap jus' thinkin' on it." Mama Kinney covered a long yawn with one hand.

Lady leaned forward and looked at her more closely. "You alright, Mama? You seem a little…off," she finished, unable to find a word that adequately captured the look of sheer weariness on Mama Kinney's face.

"Ain't been sleepin' much lately," she mumbled her reply. The long nights and early mornings had weakened her system, and the unpredictable weather was making her joints ache with pain. "I'm a little bit tired, been playin' hostess to you all daily."

"Oh!" Lady said in some surprise, recognizing the gravity underlying Mama Kinney's response. She gathered herself and stood. "You need to go lay down, Mama. Let your body rest. Let me take care of these ones." She reached out an arm toward Mama Kinney, who gratefully took it and used it to haul herself up. Lady waited patiently while Mama Kinney balanced herself on her cane.

Lady put Mama Kinney to bed, helping her shed her clothing and draw on a nightgown. She turned on the heater, too, just so Mama Kinney wouldn't catch cold. Despite her bulk, there was a fragility to the old lady laying on her pillow, resting her eyes that hadn't been there before. Lady smiled, remembering how much in awe of Mama Kinney she'd been when she was a bit younger. Now she was of an age to see Mama Kinney simply as another woman, prone to the same human failings and foolishness that often plagued her. She moved toward the bedroom door, preparing to leave, understanding that Mama Kinney needed her rest.

"Lady?" Mama Kinney said sleepily, and she turned at once in response.

"Yes, Mama?"

"My Bible, baby...up there on the dresser." Lady handed it to her at once, surprised that Mama Kinney still intended to read it, despite the tired and sickly look about her face. She propped herself up in bed, weariness slowing the movement, and began reading. Lady quietly let herself out, closing the bedroom door behind her.

"Y'all can't take a hint?" she said when she returned to the women still gathered on Mama Kinney's porch. "Y'all didn't hear the woman say she tired and need some rest? Or are you all too selfish to really care?"

"Oh, saw it off, Lady," Fat Mary said, waving a dismissive hand and fishing beneath her seat for her purse. "We was jus' waitin' for you to come back on out, is all."

Lady stared her down in silent rebuke, having seen right through her reasoning. Still, the women each began gathering their things, preparing to leave.

"Me, I jus' can't wait to see what she gone do tomorrow," a burly woman named Mable said with gleeful anticipation.

"You betta plan on watchin' the show elsewhere, then, cause you ain't comin' 'round here to see." Lady shooed the women off the porch and they began walking down the street in a tight-knit group. "You can tell everybody else the same thang, too. Mama Kinney needs her rest, so don't a one of y'all show up here."

They made a collective sound of protest but she silenced them with one last comment. "I'll be watchin' out. An whichever one of y'all get past me, Lord help you if you run into Sincere. She liable to kick yo ass with steel-toed boots, and I swear to God I'll hold yo fat ass down while she do it."

Lady called Sincere at work to tell her about the day's occurrences, just so she could know what was happening before she returned home.

"I appreciate the call, Lady. Mama Kinney wouldn't've told me everything, 'specially 'bout her not feelin' well."

"Tell truth, Sincere, she ain't look so much sick as tired. Just dead-dog weary, if you know what I mean." Sincere did. "I told those *ladies* not to come on back tomorrow, if they fear God and the two of us."

Sincere laughed. "You ain't got to tell me how they responded. Those women are the most selfish bunch of hypocrites—" Sincere broke off, suddenly aware she was gossiping like the women she'd just condemned.

"You ain't got to say it, baby, I know the rest." The two hung up in perfect understanding of the nature of women. Despite her joking response, though, deep inside Sincere was troubled. Worried, even. Mama Kinney might be old, but tired wasn't like her. Not at all. The woman had more energy than Sincere, sometimes, when she chose to display it, and Sincere couldn't think of a single time in her life when she'd seen Mama Kinney sick. No, there was definitely something wrong.

One thing was certain: come hell or high water, Sincere had to move back in. She had to get back closer to Mama Kinney. There was an unspecific fear compelling her, edging her to that realization, and Sincere knew she would feel safer moving closer to Mama Kinney. Despite Mama Kinney's objections, she needed Sincere now, whether she knew it or not, and Sincere definitely needed her. Now all that still needed to be done was convincing the stubborn old woman that her moving back in had nothing to do with mutual need at all, and everything to do with convenience.

Chapter 14

Rich gave Miranda all of Tuesday to cool off, figuring that some sort of typical female malady was behind her mood. In his experience, women often threw such fits of emotion, suddenly becoming angry or tearful or sad or agitated, always without reason. It was unnecessary and unproductive to speculate on the causes. The important thing was, they always got over it.

To ensure he was ready to return when she did get over it, Rich called Lorna as soon as he arrived home, and told her he'd not be in that day. She complained, of course, and said his clients were irate and work was piling up. Rich listened with only half an ear, already planning his next moves. He would spend the afternoon resting and recuperating from the previous five days, renewing his stamina for their future rounds of lovemaking. These past few days had been wonderful, of course, but draining all the same. In the morning, he would have flowers delivered. Roses were out of season, of course, but the florist would certainly have something else equally as lovely. Perhaps some shopping, then, to pick out—

"Rich! Are you even listening to me?" came Lorna's voice, whining her displeasure over the phone.

Distracted, Rich responded with, "I likely won't be in tomorrow, either, Lorna," and quickly hung up the phone before she could object. This was, of course, much more important.

He woke on Wednesday morning feeling refreshed and ready to resume his pursuit. He called the florist first, ignoring the proprietor's nosey questions and supplying nothing beyond the most basic, necessary information. He could hear the unsatisfied curiosity in her tone, but he ignored it all the same. He had learned to be selective in hearing the words women spoke.

The florist called him three hours later to report that the flowers had been refused. Rich frowned at the phone in confusion and disappointment.

"My driver said she said she didn't want 'em, 'specially when he told her who they're from. Unfortunately for you," she added with malicious satisfaction, getting revenge for his earlier dismissal, "you've got to pay for them all the same."

Rich told her he would be in to pick them up and deliver them himself. Perhaps she would be more receptive if they were hand-delivered by him.

But Miranda laughed and said with a dismissive wave, "Go home, Rich, I'm done with you." She shut the door in his face, just as she'd done the day before.

Disappointed, Rich returned to his apartment to think and regroup. Giving up was not an option. He stared into space, letting the small apartment grow cold and dark around him, searching his mind for some gesture, some idea that would win her heart. He discarded ideas he thought were too mundane, or worse, just outright stupid. But he had never had to try so hard to win a woman over in his life, and good ideas were not quickly forthcoming.

By the time dawn began to streak across the sky on Thursday, lighting it with fiery brightness, the flowers sitting neglected on the table had begun to wilt. Something about them touched him. He felt just as dejected as they looked. A deep red rose petal separated and drifted to settle on the table, forlorn.

Suddenly, he smiled. It was a brilliant idea, one he was

certain would gain him entry into her home and her heart. She needed a spectacular, grand showing of his love to convince her that he cared for and needed her more than Moresha. Picking up the lonely rose petal, he stroked it with his fingers, memorizing its velvety-soft texture. The flowers would not be wasted after all. He had hit on the perfect plan.

Having learned his lesson, Rich ordered flowers this time from a small shop just outside of Reason, in an even smaller town called Mosely. The proprietor didn't know him from a cockroach, and treated him no better, assuming that an out-of-towner wouldn't know enough to contest his rates. Rich happily paid the inflated price of avoiding gossip and carried out his bundles, satisfied with the purchase.

The blue Buick was gone from the driveway when he arrived, and Rich breathed a sigh of relief. Moresha's presence would impede his plans. The only remaining question was whether the house was wholly empty, or whether Miranda was still inside.

Anxious not to show his hand too soon, Rich made his way cautiously around the side of the house, hiding between shadows and peering inside the windows. From all he could see, the house appeared empty. Just to be certain, Rich knocked loudly at the back door and hid himself, waiting for her to appear. He knocked again after a few minutes, but the response was the same, and Rich smiled, seeing that luck was with him and everything had fallen into place.

He tried the doorknob and found it locked against

him. He stood uncertainly in the daylight, bemused. *How was he going to get in?* He could try the front door, but he was trying hard not to be seen and, anyway, it was even more likely to be locked. The kitchen curtains fluttered softly and he turned, realizing that the window stood open, available. It was some distance off the ground and a delicate operation, but one Rich successfully mounted nonetheless. He tumbled into the house all elbows and knees, bumping painfully against the countertop and the linoleum of the floor. He took a moment to rub his bruised joints before putting himself, and his plan, into action.

He went quickly and efficiently about his work, trying not to attract the neighbor's notice as he labored to bring each of a dozen rose bouquets inside the house. He set them in strategic places about her bedroom to ensure that their presence, and their scent, would overwhelm and entice. Finally, he brought the last dozen, the one that had been rejected the day before, into the house and shut the door. He took his time with this one, treating it with careful patience, painfully aware of the parallels between it and himself.

When he was done he waited, optimistic, but unsure of what to expect. Despondency warred with hope, making his feelings vacillate sharply between the two extremes. The uncertainty was almost painful, but he was afraid to pray she would come quickly and show him her response. Without knowing what to expect, adrenaline coursed through his body, preparing for her entrance.

His stomach grumbled painfully, reminding him that he'd not eaten that day, or the day before, or the day before that, but he was unconcerned. Eating would have to be a secondary pursuit. Right now, he was engaged in a far more important task.

He heard her enter the house and walk about, completing mundane tasks. He glanced out the window, making sure that the blue Buick was still conspicuously absent. It was. He toyed with the rose petals on her bed, straightening them, then frowned and straightened them all over again, wanting the presentation to be perfect. He stroked himself insistently into arousal, urging a response, and his body, for once, cooperated. Anticipation of her entrance hung thickly on the air, making him anxiously expectant.

When she arrived, the moment was almost anticlimactic. She opened the door in a burst of lavender sunshine, pausing on the threshold in surprise, her reaction hidden in her eyes. He was nonplussed, unsure of how to proceed, but hoping the sight of him aroused and ready on a bed of roses was enough. But her face was unreadable, impassive.

He stood and advanced, ignored her step backward. "Baby, I wanted you to know this is for real," he said and reached out to pull her forward by one hand. Pliant now, she allowed herself to be seated on the bed in the midst of rose petals that he had tried to arrange into a heart, now indistinguishable. "There's nothing I wouldn't do for you. I love you," he said, smiling sheepishly and lowering himself to one knee.

"I want to marry you, baby, give you my name. It might look like I ain't got much, but I own my own business, I got money in the bank, and I would be more than happy to take care of you, now and forever. I love you. I want you to be happy, and I want to be happy, so please do me the honor of becoming my wife." The request was delivered sweetly, sincerely, and Rich waited, his heart thumping painfully in his chest, aware he'd just said those words for the first and, he hoped, the last time.

Afraid to look into her eyes, Rich instead, concentrated on the smooth and flawless skin of her hand, waiting for her response. Finally, her hand began to tremble and shake and he looked up, alarmed, expecting tears. Instead, her face was twisted in laughter that emanated from inside her and burst into the bedroom loudly, ringing in his ears. He frowned. He hadn't expected laughter. But then he smiled and joined in, too, nervously, uncertain of why.

He had thought she might be angry he'd let himself into her home and call the police, or worse; or that she'd be overjoyed with the request and the opportunity to live decently, respectfully. But laughter? Where did that fit in?

"I'm sorry," she barely ground out, wiping her eyes with the effort. "This has *got* to be the funniest thing a man ever said to me," and she broke off again on another stream of laughter.

He frowned again, realizing that her laughter was not a good sign. "I mean it, Miranda, I'm not playin'," he said earnestly, trying to convince her.

"Wait 'till I tell Moresha 'bout this," she said between laughs, her hands reaching up to tug at her cheeks, trying to quiet her laughter.

"Miranda!" he yelled in desperation. This was *not* going right!

She suddenly stood, her expression now serious and devoid of laughter. "I'ma give you only a few minutes to clean this shit up and get the fuck out my house, Rich. What the *hell* were you thinking, coming in here like I'd welcome you, ignoring my wishes. Don't you *ever* do it again, you hear me? If I catch you in my bedroom again without my express permission, I will cut that little worm off from your body and throw it out the goddamn window."

Stunned, Rich stared up at her, uncertain how to respond. "Miranda, I love you," he said again, holding the words out to her like some sort of talisman.

She retreated, walking over to lean against the door. But all she said was, "Good."

His eyes narrowed in reproach. "You don't care, do you? You don't care one bit that I love you, that I'm willing to go through all this trouble for you?" His hand swept the room, revealing his handiwork, and he almost flinched at the evident desperation in his voice.

"Miranda, I swear to God, I can't live without you. I *won't* live without you, I love you just that much!"

She only shrugged. "You come in this house again, you won't live at all. Yours won't be the first blood spilled in this house," she said, and Rich suddenly realized that she knew the house's seedy past.

"Clean up after yourself and get the fuck out, Rich. Moresha will be home soon." She left the room quickly, without looking back, unconcerned.

Miranda visited Mama Kinney again that night, slipping seamlessly into a house that had been locked against her. Mama Kinney was unsurprised by the intrusion.

"I been wonderin' when you was gone find yo way over here again. I know how much you like our visits," Mama Kinney said, knowing she was there without turning to look. Instead, she pointedly ignored the woman and focused on washing the few dishes that were waiting, undone, in her sink.

She heard the scrape of wood against linoleum and Miranda took a seat at the kitchen table. "I certainly enjoy the company. Life since I returned, has slowed down a bit. It's not quite as exciting as it was before."

Mama Kinney snorted and turned on the tap to rinse a plate. "Excitin' for who? I ain't seen folks in this town act this lively since..." but she broke off, at once realizing how inappropriate it would be to mention to this woman the excited speculation that had followed the deaths of her parents.

Miranda was silent a moment, as if she perceived the reason for Mama Kinney's abrupt break in conversation. Mama Kinney finished the dishes and watched the water slowly draining out of the sink. She wasn't sure what to say to this woman, especially now. Despite herself, she was beginning to see what Sincere had liked about her: the girl had passion and uncanny perception, and it appeared from their previous verbal sparring that she had inherited her grandmother's wit. Still, something about her seemed dangerous, as if she was a snake, coiled and ready to strike. You could approach her, mesmerized by her beauty, thinking she was harmless, and come back missing a hand, or worse. The analogy sent a remembered fission of fear down Mama Kinney's nape and she turned, suddenly reminded to never turn her back on this woman.

"Saw that boy come by today," she said, turning and watching Miranda closely for her reaction.

Miranda waved her hand dismissively at the topic. "Who the hell cares?" she said callously, unconcerned.

Mama Kinney responded with quiet rebuke. "I care. Everybody in this town cares. You really been gone that long, you forgot how Reason takes care of its own?"

"Like how this town took care of me? Like that?" she said. Her words made Mama Kinney suddenly afraid. "I'm done with Rich, he's not something I wish to talk about tonight," and for the life of her, Mama Kinney could not make herself voice a disagreement.

There was a feeling hanging in the air between them and Mama Kinney struggled to define it. Fear. On her part, at least. She could feel this woman's silent intimidation and she was tired of fighting against it. Miranda was overpowering in her presence, and though Mama Kinney could hold her own against much stronger women, the long days and longer nights had taken their toll. She was tired, and she wished Miranda would simply come to the point. She waited.

"Sit down," Miranda ordered. Mama Kinney obeyed, despite the inappropriateness of this young girl issuing her commands. Miranda leaned over the table toward her, and Mama Kinney could see the intensity in her eyes.

"I want to tell you more about what I *do* remember. I want to tell you about me…about that little girl you used to hate, an I want to tell you 'bout yourself. 'Bout what you did wrong, and you can listen closely and see if there might not be something you can do to fix things to right."

Mama Kinney sat back in her chair, and didn't answer. It seemed tonight she was to finally learn why, exactly, Miranda felt she owed her something.

"I remember it was a school-day," Miranda began, staring at Mama Kinney without seeing her. Her eyes were unfocused, as if she wasn't really in Mama Kinney's kitchen at all, but in another time, some nineteen years before. "But for whatever reason I hadn't gone to school. My daddy left that morning. He kissed me on my forehead before he left out to work." She smiled in recollection, absently rubbing a spot above her eyebrow. "He woke me up that morning and said, "Baby girl, who am I? An in my sleep I turned to him and said, you the most handsomest angel this side of heaven, and you also is my daddy. And he smiled at me and kissed me again, as if everything was golden. He left me," she said again. Mama Kinney thought she was referring to more than just Sandal's early morning departure for work. She paused in the storytelling, and the silence became awkward between them until Mama Kinney almost spoke herself.

"Mama slept late that morning. It wasn't the first time, she had been doin' that a lot lately. She didn't wake up until some time around noon, and by then it was too late for me to go to school. So I didn't. I made myself some breakfast, put on some clothes, went outside to play, and waited for Sincere. I was waitin' for her to get back from school and tell me what I had missed. I was waitin' for my mama to wake up. When she did, I don't think she even knew I was home still. She didn't say nothin' to me, didn't even see me when she woke up. I didn't want to get in her way, didn't want her to yell at me. So I stayed outside, playin' in the mud, hiding myself so she wouldn't see me, afraid to go inside and get my doll. Then Daddy came home early. I saw him walkin' a block away, and I loved him *so much*. I thought maybe he would play with me. Or maybe he would help me get my doll from in the house. I came out of my hiding place, but he just walked past me, didn't barely speak, jus' went right on in to see my mama. I followed him in, too, because I thought maybe he would see me then, play wit me inside. But when he saw me, he told me jus' to go

202

back out, and I didn't know *why* he didn't want to talk to me." She shook her head at the memory. "It didn't make sense, my daddy always had time for me. So I hid in the pantry, right between the mop and the broom, smellin' all the stuff my mama used to clean the house. I wasn't s'posed to be in there, not that day, not ever. Daddy said the things in there could hurt me. They started yellin' at each other, screamin'. Daddy was so angry, his eyes was hot an he kept wavin' his hands. And Mama just stood there, smilin', yellin' right back like she ain't had sense enough to close her mouth. She got up in his face, real close-like, stood in front of him an told him he couldn't stop her from leavin'."

Miranda rocked backward in the chair, hugging herself. Her eyes seemed bright in the lighting. "He pushed her, an it was the *first* time I ever seen my daddy put his hands on Mama, or anyone else for that matter, I swear it! But he pushed her, an she fell backward against the sink. She didn't stop smilin' though, as if she didn't care that he was jus' that angry. I sat in the pantry and I watched her and I wanted to get right out of there and slap that smile off of her face."

The venom in her words shocked Mama Kinney to her core.

Miranda's voice changed; became matter of fact. "Then Daddy got that gun, an I didn't have to slap her or anybody else, 'cause he blew that smile right off her face. He made sure she whatn't gone never leave us. An she didn't." Miranda finished the story, her eyes refocusing on Mama Kinney and piercing her where she sat.

She let those last words linger and settle between them. Mama Kinney's mind was stuck on the image of her, as a girl, sitting in that closet, watching her father shoot and kill her mother. Despite the antipathy between them, Mama Kinney couldn't help but feel regret and sympathy for the young girl. Maybe she had been too quick to judge.

"You know what you did, now," Miranda said, and the words were not a question. Mama Kinney's mind had been slowed by the emotion and the imagery, but eventually she realized what Miranda had said. She was in the pantry, in the kitchen! She must have seen Mama Kinney come in, must have seen her take that ring!

Miranda saw her awareness and nodded in confirmation. "I want it back," she said simply, and Mama Kinney suddenly understood.

"I don't have it," she said automatically in dejection, but stopped herself before she revealed who did.

Miranda's brow raised and she stared at Mama Kinney in skepticism. "Don't tell me you lost it. It meant enough to you that you came and took it from *a dead woman's neck!*" she said, her words accusing.

Mama Kinney wasn't sure how to respond. Yes, it had meant that much to her, but for different reasons, reasons Miranda knew nothing about. The ring had not belonged to her mother at all, but to Ray. It had been his wedding ring, and Mama Kinney had not wanted Cassandra, or worse, Sincere, to find out how deeply his betrayal had gone. Miranda would not have known this, of course, and explaining this to her would only tell her who did have it. Mama Kinney couldn't be certain what she would do with that knowledge.

"I don't have it," she said again, but her eyes shied away from meeting Miranda's.

The younger woman sat back in her chair, considering. Mama Kinney knew she thought she was lying, but there was no way to explain. The situation was untenable.

When she finally spoke, her words were a relief to the heaviness of silence. "I want that ring. It was my mama's ring, and now it belongs to me. You had no right. *NO RIGHT* to have taken it away. It wasn't yours."

Mama Kinney flinched, thinking that Miranda knew so little about what she'd done. Arguably, she'd had no right to have interfered at all in what was going on between Reba and Ray. But she'd done it anyway, blinded only by the need to protect her best friend and, ultimately, her goddaughter. She had not known how things would end. But even knowing, she likely would have done the same. It had been her only choice, and she'd had no responsibility to safeguard little Jean.

She chose her words with care before speaking, remembering to address Jean by her chosen name. "Please, Miranda, it's time to let all that go. Livin' in the past will prevent you from enjoyin' today, I know! I got sixty-eight years worth of past and regrets, an if I let myself think on it too much, I'd drown in it all. You got to let all that go. You got to move on. Gettin' back some tiny bauble that used to be yo mama's won't bring her back, an it won't make up for her not lovin' you."

But her words backfired and made Miranda angrier where she sat. Her face twisted and her eyes flashed, and Mama Kinney's heart sped up in answering terror. For a moment, she was certain the woman would kill her where she sat, she looked at her with such enduring hatred.

But when she spoke, her words were quiet, belying the look in her eyes. "My mama loved me," she said, and her words seemed suddenly sad. She stood, towering over Mama Kinney, threatening in her stature. Still, her words were deflated of their earlier intensity, and Mama

Kinney had the impression that the irrational moment of anger had passed.

"My mama loved me," she said again, and Mama Kinney nodded, just to pacify her. "It was not a bauble, it was a diamond ring. But I wouldn't care if it was, it wouldn't matter to me if the ring wasn't worth two cents. It was my mama's ring, and now it's mine. An you been holdin' onto somethin' all these years that whatn't never yours to keep."

She smiled down at Mama Kinney. "An now, jus 'cause I'm a generous person, I'ma give you the chance to right the wrong you did so long ago. I'ma give you the chance to put everything back the way it shoulda been, an we can all forget what all else you owe me. That way, you can go to your grave wit a clear conscience, an I can start my life again, without this between us. See? Everything can work out for everybody involved."

She moved to the door, unconcerned that Mama Kinney still sat, paralyzed, in her chair. Something about the way she'd said the word "grave" made Mama Kinney think she was speaking of something that would occur sooner, rather than later. "Now," she said brusquely, ending the conversation. "I'ma give you a coupla days to find it. You figure out just where you *lost* it. But when I come back, I don't want to hear no more excuses and I won't tolerate any lies. I want what's mine, an if you won't give it to me, I'll get it myself."

She left, disappearing into the house, going the way she'd come. Mama Kinney sat, knowing it was pointless to wait for the close of a door, unable to make herself move.

She wasn't sure how long she sat there, waiting for her body to obey her mind. She prayed without words and without thought, begging for God's forgiveness and, more selfishly, for His mercy. She didn't have the ring, in that much she'd been honest. And she knew she could not get the ring, especially without an explanation that was likely to cause more grief than it would alleviate. No, explaining to Sincere that Miranda wanted the ring back would only make Sincere confront her, and Mama Kinney had no idea how that would turn out. For the same reason, she could not tell Miranda the truth about why she did not have the ring. The more time that passed, the more likely it was that she would figure things out on her own, and she could not trust Miranda to act sanely or with kindness.

But there was another reason why she couldn't let Miranda find that out. If Miranda knew the extent of her role in causing that tragedy, so many years before, she might not be satisfied with a mere ring. She would want more than that; she would want Mama Kinney to pay for the pain she had caused.

Mama Kinney couldn't remember exactly when she had realized what all was going on, but she remembered when she realized the situation had escalated. She had walked Sincere over to play with Jean and stood with her while she knocked on the door. Reba had answered, looking at Sincere first and then at Mama Kinney with disappointment. Mama Kinney had known by then, of course, about the affair. She knew that Reba had expected Ray to accompany his daughter today, but he'd been held up at work. Instead, the duty had fallen to Mama Kinney, and Reba's displeasure couldn't have been more obvious.

But Mama Kinney had barely noted it, mesmerized instead by a flash of brilliance about the woman's neck. She recognized the ring at once; Cassandra had a more feminine version almost exactly alike. Reba had stepped aside, and Jean had come out, and the two girls had disappeared around the house, intent on their play. The two women had stood there frozen on the porch, Reba following the direction of Mama Kinney's eyes and understanding immediately her silence.

Mama Kinney had begun to speak but Reba interrupted. "You like it, don't you? Ray gave it to me, just this week."

The admission was unexpected. "That's his wedding ring!" Mama Kinney burst out, outraged at the thought, but Reba simply laughed.

"I know. He says he'll get me my own ring later, when we go. For now, though, it'll have to do. At least it's real, unlike this piece of shit I been wearing for the last nine years." And she'd held up her hand, dismissively indicating her own wedding ring. Sandal and Reba had married so young, of course he'd not been able to afford much. Still, the ring was lovely in its simplicity, even if it did look cheap compared to the one around her neck.

"You don't really think that man gone leave his wife for you?" Mama Kinney had said, disbelief written on her face. "He an Cassandra been married goin' on twenty years now!"

"An he been unhappy wit her the last nineteen!" the woman had shot back.

Refusing to be cowed, Mama Kinney had responded with words intended to cut. "An he been fuckin' everything in skirts for the past twenty-one! You think you the first woman Ray ever done skipped out on his wife for? If you think that, you a bigger fool than I thought."

"The only fool here is you, Evelyn. Of course I know about Ray an his women, the whole town knows. But I also know this...ain't another woman 'sides his wife he ever give a ring, and he ain't never made the promises to her that he done already made to me."

Mama Kinney had stared at her with dismay, recognizing the truth in her statement. When Cassandra married Ray, she had done so with full disclosure. She had known from the beginning what she was getting, and Ray had never even tried to make her believe in his fidelity. He had cheated on her while they were dating, but she had ignored her best friend's warnings all the same. "He got a job, he'll be a good provider," she had said with absolute practicality, and refused to believe that she deserved more. Then she had reminded her friend that she was in no position to criticize, trapped as she was in her own loveless marriage due to her own mistakes.

Still, Cassandra had trusted Ray for at least that much, and she would be heartbroken and destitute if Ray left her. She still had all five young children to support, and while their oldest was almost out the house, Cassandra did not make enough as a laundrywoman to provide for them all.

Mama Kinney's conversation with Ray had been no more productive. He had told her to mind her own business and to stay out of his. Reminding him of his vows had accomplished nothing, especially since they'd been broken years before. When she threatened to tell Cassandra, he had invited her to go right ahead, daring her. But she and he had both known that Cassandra had neither the time nor the energy to confront this situation, serious though it was, and Mama Kinney was loath to burden her friend with something she could not change.

Finally, in desperation, Mama Kinney had reached out to the only person she thought *would* respond to the situation. She had waited until his lunch hour to approach Sandal at his job, explaining to him the situation, begging him to stop it. He had not laughed, had not seen anything the slightest bit disdainful in the situation. She wasn't even certain he had heard her when she finally admitted the suspicion that had been lingering in her mind, forcing recognition. It had been there in the way Reba moved, tired, as if she'd been weighted down, and she had stood in the doorway, one hand on her hips, the other settled over the slight curve of her stomach. Sandal had moved away, walking out of his job without explanation or excuse. His supervisor had called after him, but he had not turned around. Mama Kinney had been left to stare after him, wondering what he would do, but certain that he would do *something*.

She had been slower getting home herself, and had approached the house to hear a loud sound disrupting the peaceful quiet of the neighborhood. She had waited, recognizing the sound as a gunshot, hoping otherwise. But a few moments later she'd heard the second shot, and she had immediately understood.

She had approached the house with trepidation, knowing she was responsible for whatever scene greeted her upon entering. She had placed everything in motion, and she was immediately sorry for the result. Still, she'd been cautious in her entry, unwilling to atone for her actions by getting shot, herself.

Reba had been dead on the kitchen floor, her eyes staring open in shocked disbelief, as if she'd seen what was coming and dared it anyway. Mama Kinney shook her head, reflecting on the woman's stupidity, and moved into the house. She reached immediately for the ring where it lay on the dead woman's breasts, not even thinking the action through. It had felt heavy in her hand, and warm from Reba's body.

210

But then Mama Kinney had felt the sensation of someone watching her, and fear had made her move quickly out of the house without checking to see what had happened to Sandal. She ran across the street, terrified that she would be shot in the back, not stopping until she'd reached the safety of her home. She'd locked the doors behind her and crawled into a corner of her bedroom, still uncertain of her safety.

By the time the police had arrived to question her hours later, she had finally composed herself enough to tell the lie without blinking. No, she'd been gone when the whole thing occurred. She knew nothing about the reason. No, she wouldn't be willing to provide a home for the suddenly-orphaned girl but, yes, she could give them the names and numbers of the girl's closest relatives. "You're welcome, officers, happy to help," she had said.

She had gone with Cassandra to identify her husband's body, found a day later, and to make arrangements for his funeral. Surreptitiously, she had slipped the ring back onto his finger, silently berating him for his refusal to heed her advice when there was still time to have prevented this tragic turn of events. He had lay still, willing to listen to her now that he had no choice.

Mama Kinney had intended the ring be buried with him, but Cassandra had noticed it and chosen otherwise. Mama Kinney understood. The ring was one of the family's most valuable assets, and Cassandra had been too practical to let sentiment win out over the knowledge that, as a widow, she would now be the sole provider for her family. With help from her best friend, though, she'd never had to sell the ring to support her children. Instead, she had passed the ring down to her daughter, to the only one of her children who would grow up without her father.

Which was why Mama Kinney found herself in this untenable situation. Miranda was convinced that the ring rightly belonged to her mother, and Mama Kinney wouldn't correct her belief.

She finally moved, pushing back from the table and standing awkwardly. The room seemed empty and cold, bereft. Miranda's presence seemed to linger in the walls, making Mama Kinney feel afraid in her own house. Defiantly, Mama Kinney made her way to her bedroom. Come what will, that woman would *not* hurt Sincere!

Chapter 15

On Friday, Jody finally decided she'd given Rich enough time to get over his unhealthy relationship with Miranda. Even if he hadn't, she thought spending time with her might just help him along. How deep could the relationship have been, anyway? It had only lasted all of five days.

With that in mind, Jody packed a picnic basket with several of his favorite dishes: freshly-fried chicken, cold potato salad, rolls, and even a sweet potato pie, although the potatoes had been difficult to find so far out of season. She stayed up Thursday night, ignoring the ringing telephone, performing what was surely a labor of love. Peeling potatoes, marinating chicken, slicing vegetables and what small amounts of fruit she had been able to find at the local grocery store. At eleven o'clock, she'd finally gone to sleep, knowing that any lack of sleep would undoubtedly show on her face. Just to make sure it did not, she'd carefully washed away her makeup and softened her skin with just a bit of cocoa butter cream before tying up her hair and going to sleep. In the morning, she had awakened and finished cooking, giving herself enough time to carefully shower away any hint of the smell of chicken grease from her skin. Her perfume had been carefully chosen to intrigue, but not overwhelm, and her clothing was unseasonably light but very fashionable, giving her the air of someone untouched by mundane concerns about the cold. With one last glimpse of herself in the mirror, she left her house, humming lightly as she drove the short distance to Rich's office over on Main, expecting a beautiful day despite the cloudy skies overhead.

The bell rang when she entered, announcing her arrival with satisfying clarity. Lorna looked up, and Jody was suddenly reminded of why she had taken such care with her own appearance. The woman looked nothing short of haggard. Given Lorna's behavior on their last visit, Jody couldn't move herself to sympathy. Her hair, professionally sculpted into a small bun at her nape, was coming unraveled, and her clothing was wrinkled and unkempt. She had apparently forgone makeup, and sleeplessness showed in the dark bags under each eye. Jody self-consciously ran a hand over her long jacket, appreciating both its warmth and its style.

"Rich ain't here," Lorna said wearily, returning to her work with barely a glance. Jody felt slighted at the woman's short dismissal, even while her mind processed what she'd said.

Confusion caused her to frown. "Well, where is he? I brought him lunch," she said, patting the side of the basket in illustration.

Lorna let the silence stretch out a moment before replying, eyeing the basket and Jody with a sort of half-hearted dislike. Finally, she sighed and shrugged tightly. "Hell if I know where he is. But he ain't here. He ain't been in since last Thursday."

Jody's frown deepened as she understood the import of what Lorna had said. He had not come into work, even after leaving Miranda's house on Tuesday. What in the hell was going on, and where would Rich be, if not here?

Lorna's head dropped to her desk, and for the first time Jody felt something more than disdain for the secretary, something almost like compassion. Almost. "I'll go talk to him, Lorna," Jody said, her sharp nod punctuating the statement. "He'll get his ass in here by Monday, that's for sure," and she left, headed for his apartment. She did not notice that Lorna barely raised her head to acknowledge her words. The secretary wasn't sure whether to feel skeptical or hopeful, but she had too little energy left for either emotion.

Despite Rich's success selling other people their dream homes, he still lived in a tiny brick apartment above a small deli on the East side of Reason, within walking distance of his office. He had told Jody once he was waiting for marriage to buy a home so that his wife's tastes might be reflected in the purchase. The idea was thoughtful, but Jody was too practical to fully appreciate it. Rich wasn't getting any younger, and a thirty-year mortgage might see him to his grave.

She stood in the narrow entry to his apartment and called out to him, knocking once briskly at the door, her voice loud in the silence. From within, she heard rushing feet and stumbling, then the sound of something crashing to the floor and shattering. Rich let out a loud curse and she smiled, knowing that he was anxious to see her. Good, then, maybe this *was* just what he needed.

But Rich's face fell when he saw her, and he made a brief movement as if to shut the door. Jody stepped nimbly inside before he could, her eyes adjusting to the darkness, her nostrils offended by the smell. All of the curtains in the small apartment had been drawn, and the darkness was extreme and overwhelming. Clothing was strewn across the couches and chairs, and a lamp lay broken on the floor. Without thought, Jody automatically knelt and began picking up the shattered pieces of terra cotta, comprehending at once that the lamp had been a casualty in his rush to open the door.

After a moment's pause, the door finally clicked shut

behind her, and Jody turned around, her eyes searching the darkness for Rich's familiar shape. It was indistinguishable from the other shades of darkness in the house, and she reached over to light another lamp on a table beside the couch, placing the shattered pieces of glass beside it. Rich moved backward, shying from the light, his body flinching at the flooding brightness. He squinted at her in the darkness, disappointment showing clearly on his face. "I thought—" he began, and made an involuntary movement with his hand, gesturing toward her.

Jody stood and raised a brow, looking him over. His face was shadowed with the beginnings of a beard, his hair uncut and unclean. What appeared to be an off-white robe was tied loosely about his hips, and Jody could see he was naked underneath. "You thought what? You thought I was *her*?" she said, and her mouth twisted on the word. She was not used to being mistaken for another woman, and certainly not with disappointment.

He did not respond, but moved away from her, retreating into the hallway, not bothering to see if she was coming along behind him. "Whatever you're here for, Jody, get it and see yoself out."

Jody followed him into his bedroom, not allowing the dismissal. "That's all you're going to say, Rich? That's how you greet an old friend? Not even a hello?"

Rich looked back at her with evident skepticism. "Hello," he said. "Goodbye."

Jody made a small, falsified moue with her mouth, even as her back stiffened with the insult. She was going to have to deal more firmly with Rich, lest he take her intervention for granted. He flopped face forward diagonally onto the bed, grabbing and hugging a pillow closely, unconcerned about the way his robe had slipped

216

and exposed the firm calf of one leg. Jody stood awkwardly in the doorway, feeling ignored and just a bit intimidated. Something indefinable about Rich had changed, altered in just that short time. A bit of his confidence had slipped, disappeared and left this weak, hollow man behind. *How was she going to break the hold this woman had over him?*

She walked back into the hallway, her mind racing forward, planning as she straightened up the place. She had left the picnic basket near the entrance. Now she retrieved it, bringing it with her into the kitchen, expecting that room to be in a more extreme state of disrepair than the rest of the apartment. Instead, the kitchen was unusually bare and almost empty. There were no dishes in the sink, and the trashcan was clean. Jody comprehended immediately that Rich had not eaten since he returned home. No matter. If anything, Jody's back and her resolve strengthened. She would simply have to undo the damage Miranda had done and put Rich back together, if for no other reason than that her pride would not let her admit that a woman other than herself, had broken him.

She set about cleaning the house, returning it to its usual state. She unloaded the contents of the basket into the refrigerator for him to enjoy later, throwing away expired cartons of milk and stale hunks of cheese before washing it down with cleaning supplies she had found under the sink. She wiped down counters, swept the floor, dusted, mopped, and bagged up clothing for the wash. She found a vacuum cleaner in the closet behind the door and used it to clear away any remaining particles of glass. Perspiration heated her cheeks and made her clothing cling to her body, but though she'd always been careful about her appearance, she had never been too cute for hard work.

Finally, when all was done, she stood surveying the place with a critical eye, looking for any remaining items out of place. The apartment looked just as it had months before, when Jody had said goodbye to Rich and their brief relationship, and walked out the front door. Satisfied, she collapsed onto a nearby couch, taking a moment's respite, kicking her shoes off in relief.

"You still here?" Rich's voice, when he spoke, was unexpected and hoarse. Jody had not felt him enter the room.

"And you're very welcome I am," she replied without opening her eyes, ignoring the content of his words.

He walked past her to draw again the curtains she had opened during her cleaning spree. Jody sighed in frustration and stood, looking around. The house was clean, the man was surly, and it was time to go. Her basket lay neatly where she'd left it underneath an end-table, her keys and purse discarded near the sole unbroken lamp. She slid her feet back into her shoes, bending over to retrieve the other items, not bothering to push back the strands of hair that fell and brushed over her eyes.

"Baby," Rich said in that gravelly way that signified hunger. She stood abruptly and turned, uncertain. She recognized his voice and his look from their previous relationship. His eyes were unfocused, moving quickly across the contours of her body, and Jody was suddenly aware of the provocative way her dress clung to her skin, drawing his attention to her breasts. She was certain the moment seemed contrived, but it honestly had not been. Never one to waste opportunity, however, she moved forward in liquid seduction, in one movement removing her shoes again and padding over to meet him where he stood. She smiled, her eyes and her body deliberately conveying the message of her invitation. He groaned and pulled her to him roughly, and Jody could feel the length of his hardness escaping from the loose confines of the robe, seeking her warmth. Satisfied by his apparent hunger, she gave herself over to him, letting him begin the encounter.

His breath was foul in her face, his body smelled of week-old sweat, and the short hairs of a beginning beard brushed abrasively against her skin as he held her and nuzzled her neck, but Jody forced herself not to recoil. If this was what would break whatever hold Miranda had over him, Jody was more than happy to oblige.

Their coming together was accomplished with a series of grunts and hurried, ungentle caresses. Lacking his usual finesse, Rich bent Jody backward over the arm of the couch, his fingers feeling impatiently beneath her dress, and pushing aside with rough fingers the thin fabric of her underwear.

"Slow down, hon," she said, but his mouth came over her own, silencing her words with careless efficiency. He ground against her and her body opened for him, despite the almost-painful pressure of the movement. Her hands moved against his chest, her fingers entangling in the terry cloth, though whether trying to slow him down or push him away, she couldn't be sure. Instead, she felt him there, pushing inside her, the entry to her womanhood giving way to the painful insistence, her mind registering the feeling of tearing. She cried out in pain, but he kept going, moving against her feverishly, his body rhythmic in its urgency. Her legs dangled awkwardly in the air, brushing against the couch, her hands pushing at his chest, her mouth still filled with the invasion of his tongue and the sound of her cries trying to escape. Still he moved against her with ruthless force, her body yielding with helpless defeat.

Finally, he stiffened and she felt his release inside her. His arms softened, abruptly depriving her of support. She collapsed backward onto the couch, feeling bruised and suddenly cold. He fell heavily atop her, his chest angled between her thighs, his head laying in the softness, against the fabric of her dress, still bunched and covering her belly. She could feel him still within her, though he now seemed soft and non-threatening.

Her mind would not stop thinking, playing out the details of their coupling in horrifying detail, reminding her of her pain. She wasn't sure what to make of what just occurred, or how to feel. The muscles in her arms seized in recollection, compelling her to push him away, but she resisted. He had needed this. Rich had never been like this before; in their previous sexual encounters, he had always been gentle, studied in his lovemaking. It had been yet another of his less intriguing attributes, and one of the reasons why she ultimately had left. If anything, it had been she who was the aggressor, trying to provoke him into more spontaneous passionate displays. Still, this had been entirely too passionate. Was this how that woman liked it then, rough and abusive? Had she taught Rich to behave this way? Was his transformation *her* fault, then?

Rich's breathing fanned out across her breasts, teasing at the fabric still covering her nipples, and Jody finally decided it had been okay, this experience. She was not hurt; well, not in any way that couldn't be repaired by a long soak in warm water and some gentle washing. And he…he was better, of course, restored to who he had been before, Miranda's hold over him broken. In the end, they had all come out better for the experience, and

Jody would not begrudge him.

She reached down and rubbed a hand over the back of his head, but it had barely touched him before he flinched away. He stood abruptly, withdrawing himself from her body, leaving it cold. He turned away without speaking, his jerky movements telling Jody that he was pulling together the loosened ties of his robe and recovering his body. She frowned, not understanding.

She could still feel the slippery moisture of his seed between her thighs. She rose, too, slipping her legs down from the arms and unfolding her body from the couch. Her muscles screamed in a peculiar sort of agony, unused to such abuse.

"You should go," he said, his back still turned to her, and his voice sounded even more gravelly than before, as if he were on the verge of tears.

Her eyes widened and she approached him from behind, reaching out toward him. "Rich?" she said questioningly, her hand barely settling against his shoulder before she felt it heave, shake, and crumble. She withdrew her hand quickly in appalled realization, backing away from him, more terrified by the hoarse male sobs coming from deep within his throat than she had been by his aggressively passionate touch. Her mind panicked, urging her to leave, and she did, grabbing her keys and purse from the table and dragging her shoes with her feet toward the door. She stumbled on her way out and paused a moment in the hallway, leaning against the closed door. Hatred burned within her, directed at Miranda. Whatever she had done to Rich, Jody would make her get it back, tenfold. You reap what you sow, Jody thought, and nodded, planning. She would find Miranda and make sure that bitch got exactly what was coming to her, a return for what she'd so callously done to Rich.

Jody realized that she'd left the basket in her haste. From within, she could still hear the sounds of his heartbreak, and it spurred her into flight again. Her sense of urgency renewed, she quickly fixed her shoes more securely on her feet, and flew down the steps, running away from the broken man who in no way resembled the Rich she'd known and cared for, only a few short months before.

Chapter 16

Sincere called Mama Kinney Friday afternoon
before she left work to tell her she would not be
stopping by. "I got too much to do, Mama, things've
been crazy an I still haven't packed up my bedroom."

As if from a distance, she heard Mama Kinney sigh.
"You do what you got to do, baby," Mama Kinney said,
and that was the end of it. Sincere frowned, staring at the
phone when she hung up. Something wasn't right, she
could feel it in her bones. But she didn't know what.
Everything was as it should have been, but Mama
Kinney's voice had seemed curious, strained even.

Sincere's frown grew deeper. Maybe Mama Kinney
was having second thoughts about allowing her to
return. Thinking over the brief conversation, she
decided that was it. Mama Kinney had almost seemed
disappointed that Sincere would not be coming tonight.
Maybe she wanted the time to talk Sincere into holding
off longer.

Sincere's lips tightened with displeasure. If that was
her plan, Sincere would not allow it. She had waited long
enough for Mama Kinney to concede. She would not
allow Mama Kinney time and opportunity for a retreat.
No, it was good that she was not planning to visit
tonight. She would have to find an excuse for tomorrow,
too. And on Sunday, when she arrived early in the
morning with her suitcases and boxes, there wouldn't be
a thing Mama Kinney could still do. She would have to
accept, then, that Sincere had returned to stay. And this
time it wouldn't be so easy to get rid of her.

223

The darkness had again become overwhelming. The sounds of night continued, unabated, beyond the door, and yet Rich could not bring himself to engage them. Rich sat in a chair, contemplating the couch in silent darkness, inhaling the scent of female sexual response that still scented the air. He could still imagine her here, though it had been brief. He reconstructed the memory with slow deliberation, positioning her in his mind as she had been that night. A flash of something caught his eye and he turned, expecting her gold shirt, but it was only a cockroach crawling up the wall, having assumed from the quiet that it was alone.

If it was possible, he felt even more exhausted now than he'd felt on Tuesday. On Tuesday, when he'd awoken, his body had been filled with the languid sleepiness of a man who had spent several pleasurable days in bed with an amazing woman and who anticipated many more. Tonight, though, he just felt sick, disgusted with himself for not being what Miranda needed after all. She had told him as much, laughed in his face and mocked his display of love. Her voice and words played over and over again in his memory in disturbingly complete detail: *You're nothing to me. I don't need you. I don't even want you. I'm done with you. You're nothing to me.*

In the pit of his stomach, Rich was afraid she'd spoken truth. He had sized himself up as a man, and he always seemed to come up short. Jody had thought so, and every other woman before her. Now, when it really mattered, Miranda thought so, too. Despite his business, and his money, and his good, God-given common sense, he was apparently still too common for her. But he had already known that, hadn't he? He had recognized the truth of it on that first day, that Miranda was beyond his comprehension and certainly beyond his capabilities.

Maybe he should just cut his losses and run. If he ran far enough and fast enough, he might be able to outdistance her voice telling him she didn't need him.

But he warred within himself. She needed him, of course she did. She just didn't know it yet. She needed him as much as he needed her, and he would make her see. He would teach her how to admit the truth.

It was Moresha. She would have to go. Once Moresha was gone, out of the picture, she would be open again, seeking and needy. She would need someone to love her in that uncompromising, unconditional way he recognized in Moresha; she had an addiction to it, it was evident in the way she treated Moresha. She had so carelessly flaunted him before Moresha, but she had always stopped short of complete alienation. She needed Moresha, needed her love, and if Moresha was gone, then, she would need him instead.

In the dark, Rich dreamed. She came to him, naked, her breasts swinging like heavy pendulums, his eyes mesmerized by the rhythmic movements of her areolas. She was beautiful, magnificent in ways that had nothing to do with the superficiality of her looks. While he was staring at her breasts and measuring the width of her hips in anticipation of his entry, though, she was spinning silken strands and wrapping them around him. They tightened in a sort of painful pleasure around his body, preventing his movements, and he was hard, so hard, waiting as she lifted and offered one plump nipple for his tongue to lave. The nipple became hard and puckered in his mouth, and it tasted of softness and sweetness and warmth. But then it turned cold and hard and unyielding, and he looked up to see that it had changed in color and texture, too. It was a dusky pink and the breast it topped was a pasty-white and marked by the highways of blue veins. From above him, Moresha's blue eyes bore into him and absorbed his horror while her mouth opened in surprised ecstasy. Her body moved against him, and he could feel her wetness pressing against his pelvis. His tongue pushed at her breast, rejecting it, but she reached behind to grab his head with rough hands, pressing it against her breast. His arms struggled against the bonds of silk, but he discovered that they were as strong and unbreakable as chains. His breath came in desperate gasps and he wanted to push her away, realizing that she was going to suffocate him in her passion. But she was unyielding and her passion was not yet spent, and somewhere in the dream, as he felt his eyes rolling back into his head and his mind, submitting to blackness, he heard the sound of Miranda's mocking laughter.

By Saturday evening, Miranda had come to a decision. Mama Kinney had had enough time to produce the ring, and she had refused. Whether her refusal was borne of stubbornness or hatred, Miranda couldn't know, but her only concern was that it had, indeed, been refused. And something about Mama Kinney's manner told her she would not change her mind.

Miranda's lips tightened grimly as she let herself into the house. Mama Kinney was proving to be a stupid woman, not at all like she remembered.   Miranda remembered how Sincere had all but worshipped her godmother, and Miranda had sometimes seen Mama Kinney through her eyes. To Sincere, Mama Kinney could do no wrong and always knew the answer to whatever question she wanted to ask. Even their playtime had been dictated by Mama Kinney. "Mama Kinney said that if you boil the potatoes first," Sincere had told her one day while they were playing 'house,' "the skin will just fall off like that. You see?"

But Miranda hadn't seen. To her, Mama Kinney had been a bitter and mean woman, not given to kindness, one full of judgment and hate. Each time she stood up to her now, she felt as if she was doing a little more to vindicate the girl who'd been the object of Mama Kinney's resentment.

Now she intended to triumph once and for all. Mama Kinney's stupidity had led them both to this situation and forced her decision. While she didn't regret the necessity, she did regret the timing. It was too soon. There had been other things she needed to accomplish in Reason, but now they would all have to wait.

It was a frustrating scenario, and not at all how she'd imagined doing this.

Of course, she had always known Mama Kinney would have to die, if for no other reason than because justice, and the memory of her parents, demanded it. And she had known, too, that Mama Kinney's death would raise questions. But she had expected to have the ring by now and be on her way out of Reason before the body was even discovered. Now she would have to spend time looking, searching for the ring, and hoping she was not discovered in the interim.

But even if her mind balked at the necessity, her body was ready. She could feel waves of anticipation coursing through her. It was killing time. She felt energy pooling at her hips, and she walked with deliberate movements, enjoying the way skin rubbed against skin. It reminded her of something, a memory long past. Maybe this was her father's blood, this enjoyment of the act. She smiled, approaching the living room where she could hear Mama Kinney breathing. You couldn't pay for this sort of completion, the wonder of sweet, sweet satisfaction.

Chapter 17

As a child, Miranda had often admired the everyday reality of death, the kind of daily routines it left interrupted when it came in quietly and stole away life. The kind of death Miranda had witnessed briefly that day nineteen years ago, before she had been carried her away from everything and everyone she had ever known, and taken straight to hell.

Mama Kinney's kind of death. A coffee cup, made with the painstakingly-careful but imprecise hand of a child, sat next to her on the table, half-filled with some type of brown liquid. A small plate, a fork, and a pot lay waiting in the sink for Mama Kinney to wash, unaware that she could not. Miranda caught a movement and turned, but it was only the unclear pictures of a muted television, which Mama Kinney had apparently been watching before Miranda had permanently muted the volume. How would anyone know when to dust the living room or change the bedding, now that Mama Kinney was gone? Who would wash the dishes, cut off the television, and carry on life as Mama Kinney would have, if she were still alive?

Miranda found herself lovingly performing these tasks, as she might have done for her parents, had she been allowed to stay. She would have lovingly washed her mother's blood from the linoleum, patched the hole in the wall where the bullet that passed through her father had come to rest. As it was, she was certain that it had been done carelessly, by some backwaters, illiterate lackey whose only purpose in life was to serve someone else. The carelessness of the unknown maid had angered

Miranda when she had opened up the house. It had been evident in the way the furniture, covered only partially with white sheets, had become discolored and decayed with dust and time. Dirty dishes had been trashed, rather than washed, and appliances had been emptied but not cleaned. There had been deep pinkish-orange stains on the kitchen floor; Miranda had cleaned small flecks of what might have been her father from the bedroom walls. If she had been allowed to stay, she would have lovingly cleaned the mess, carefully preserving the house that constituted her sole inheritance, and continued in the everyday routines of her small family. But then, had things been different, she would not be standing here, wondering who would perform those same tasks for Mama Kinney, now that she, too, was gone.

Miranda found herself searching through the linen closet for a small washcloth, which she used to carefully wipe away the saliva that had dripped from Mama Kinney's mouth and pooled in a crease of the clear plastic covering her couch.

She had expected Mama Kinney to be heavy, but not impossible. Thankfully, her bedroom was downstairs. Miranda dragged a cheap but durable swap meet piece of carpet that she had seen lying in the hallway into the living room, and spread it lengthwise next to Mama Kinney's chair. Then she retrieved two pillows off the couch and arranged them on the floor. Satisfied that the pillows would cushion Mama Kinney against any inopportune bruises, she gently reached out and shoved the dead woman onto the floor.

Mama Kinney fell heavily, causing the room to vibrate softly before settling once again. Miranda steadied a table with one hand before studying the way the body lay on the carpet and the floor. Mama Kinney formed an imperfect X with the rug, but her back was in the proper position. Miranda needed only to shift her head and shoulders slightly, then reposition her feet so that she lay fully upon the carpet for moving. This having been done, Miranda began the arduous task of dragging the laden rug down the hallway and into Mama Kinney's bedroom.

In the room, Miranda found herself faced with the anticipated dilemma of getting the heavy body up onto the bed. She sat down, leaving Mama Kinney laying face up on the rug, and studied the situation, planning. Mama Kinney's eyes stared up at Miranda in silent accusation, but Miranda had seen death too often before to feel ashamed. Finally, she decided on a combination of pushing and pulling, so she rested a moment more to prepare herself for the task, then got up to begin her work again.

It was not an easy task for a small woman. Mama Kinney had at least a hundred pounds on Miranda, and she dropped the body altogether twice before finally moving the shoulders and hips fully onto the bed. She was not happy about the possibility of bruising, but finally decided Mama Kinney's dark skin would hide any that occurred. She stood beside the bed and placed Mama Kinney's feet and legs onto the sheet before rolling her body forward to the left side of the bed. When the body was in its proper position, Miranda carefully pulled the blankets up and arranged them neatly around, then stood back to admire and assess her handiwork. She was sweaty, tired, and out of breath, but she had done it. Mama Kinney looked exactly as she had a week ago, when Miranda had slipped into the house and watched her as she slept. Well, almost exactly. Something was missing, Miranda knew, but she shrugged, thinking it would come to her later.

The most difficult portion of the task having been performed, Miranda set out to complete the other more mundane pieces: repositioning the rug in the hallway, washing those few dishes, turning off the television. When all was done, Miranda, exhausted, sat down to rest in the same chair in which Mama Kinney had died lest than an hour before. She closed her eyes and wondered again about death, about how unexpectedly it came in, taking away life and rendering the mundane tasks of daily living suddenly unimportant. Death, unless it was prayed for and anticipated, always left things undone.

Miranda realized she was thirsty. Opening her eyes, she spied the cup of brown liquid Mama Kinney had been drinking before her death. Miranda briefly considered the irony, then shrugged her shoulders before carrying the cup to her lips and taking a deep drink.

She choked. The liquid, indeterminable before, was apparently hot chocolate, and it was now, bitterly, disgustingly cold. Grainy bits of chocolate had settled on the bottom of the cup, depriving the drink of its former flavor, so that it now tasted like watered-down piss. Miranda dumped the cup in the kitchen sink, then washed it and placed it carefully into the dish rack. There would be no things undone in Mama Kinney's house when she was discovered dead in her bed tomorrow night. Miranda would make sure of it. Not because she owed Mama Kinney, but because it was what she had owed her mother and father.

She took her time, searching through the house with leisure, lingering over pictures and memories and looking for the ring. There was no jewelry box, so Miranda carefully searched through each of the dresser drawers. There was nothing there. She turned and perused the room, wondering where an old woman might keep her precious things.

She eyed Mama Kinney's body on the bed, but shook her head. After the struggle of getting her into the bed, Miranda was not up to repeating the experience. She looked again through the drawers, pressed against the floorboards and even the walls, but the search proved fruitless. Miranda glanced at the clock, noting the passage of time. Moresha would be waiting, and there was really no rush. Miranda had watched and carefully noted Sincere's schedule; she would not arrive until the evening time, on her way back from work. With Moresha gone tomorrow, Miranda could search through the house in her own time without interruption and without arousing anyone's suspicion.

Satisfied with that conclusion, Miranda took a moment to walk through the house, carefully checking to make sure everything was in its proper place. She went back into Mama Kinney's room and eyed the woman in bed critically. Still, something seemed different, out of place, but she could not remember what it was. She frowned, hating to leave any suspicions, and frustrated by her inability to recall. It was important that everything appear exactly as it should, and that no small thing be left out of order. Her work in Reason was not complete, and she could not afford any mistakes just now. She concentrated deeply, trying to resurrect in her memory exactly what she had seen last week when she watched Mama Kinney sleeping. The room had been dark, and Miranda had been unwilling to turn on the light and risk Mama Kinney waking. She turned off the light now and stood watching a few minutes more before she shrugged. She would try again to remember tomorrow, but sometimes, even the most routine people made changes. Whatever it was, it would likely be written off as one of those routine changes. If it had not warranted Miranda's notice, it would likely not arouse anyone's suspicion. Miranda, usually unwilling to leave anything to chance, found herself caught in an untenable situation, but one she could not relieve. She let herself out, closing the back door behind her and moving quietly through the night, slightly uneasy, but satisfied with the outcome. There was always life after death.

Chapter 18

Rich stood inside the kitchen, suddenly aware his plan was no plan at all. He had not thought this through. He had not decided how he would approach Moresha, or what he would do. He had been relieved to find the door unlocked this time, since he'd not considered how he would get in. Now he felt stupid, inept, and ashamed. He didn't even have a weapon, for God's sake. He knew he wasn't doing this right at all.

He looked around, noting the neatness of this place in the dark. Brass-colored fish hung from the wall, their indiscernible eyes peering at him in conviction. The window had been left open slightly, and the curtains fluttered briefly on a breeze before settling again against the wall. He remembered the sunflowers, cheerful and bright. Moresha's touch, she'd said. His jaw tightened.

The refrigerator stood, observing him, and he stared back, remembering. He remembered her gown, flowing lightly and brushing against her feet, the sturdy cotton of it shielding her body from his view. Not that he had wanted to see. And there had been those eyes, staring him down, promising that Miranda would tire of him. Now that she had, he imagined her laughing in triumph, enjoying the sweet temptations of Miranda's body and the fullness of her spirit. Moresha had won this round, and she believed there was nothing he could do, but she was wrong.

His resolve strengthened, he quickly rifled through the drawers, looking for something he could use. A set of silverware winked up at him in the darkness but he shook his head. It would do no good to simply wound her. She would tell Miranda it was him and Miranda would reject him all over again. No, if he was going to kill her, he would have to do it right.

In a drawer full of odds and ends, Rich finally found the tool he needed. A sharp hunting knife glinted and curved in the darkness, and the weight of it felt heavy in his hand. He frowned, wondering briefly what the very masculine knife was doing in a house of women. But then his lips twisted and he picked it up. Moresha was part man. Maybe it was hers.

He made his way up the stairs, pausing outside the bedroom he had shared with Miranda only a week before. He almost changed his course and went inside, but a memory made him pause. Instead, he continued on to the door behind which he knew Moresha lay sleeping. He would have to be quick. She was larger than him, and he had no doubt she would be capable of fighting him off if he left her enough time to react. He would not. He would enter with stealth and quickness, and the entire thing would be completed before she realized it was happening. And he would leave, slipping out of the house quietly to return again on the morrow, full of sympathy and comfort. Miranda would need him then, and he would be there, available.

Still, his hand paused on the doorknob, suddenly uncertain. His bottom lip trembled in the dark and he flushed. *What was he doing?* This was not him at all. He was not a murderer. He had never killed so much as an ant intentionally, how had he imagined he could kill another person? The thought of sliding a knife between the folds of her skin now repulsed him, and he stared at the knife in his hand in uncomprehending revulsion. *How had he come to this?*

It was love, of course. Miranda was the woman he

would do anything to have, the best thing life had ever given him. He was not ready to admit defeat. He needed her, not just sexually, but spiritually. Something in him had been wrapped up in her, and he no longer felt complete without her.

But he would need to find another way. He was not a murderer. He loved her, true, but he would have to find another way to convince her to return to him. He would not bring himself so low.

He felt the air shift and part behind him only a second before she spoke. "Not man enough to do that, either?"

Rich turned, searching out the shape of Miranda's body in the darkness, filled with equal parts dismay and excitement. She had caught him standing before Moresha's door, holding a knife, and yet all he could think was that they were here, again, both of them in this house. His heart leapt inside him, and his body responded to her nearness. His nostrils flared, barely catching a hint of her scent on the air and something else.

"You were going to use my father's knife," she said. "How quaint." He could feel her mocking eyes staring at him in derision. His own eyes dropped to the weapon, which now looked less sinister, less capable.

"I…" he began, but could think of no excuse for his presence or the knife. Surely she didn't think…?

But she did. "Get out, Rich. Get out before I hurt you, or worse, you hurt yourself." She stepped close to him, her arms brushing against his shirt in an agonizingly tempting touch. Her scent grew stronger, and he identified the smell clinging to her clothing: nighttime. She moved over him, her body moving sinuously against his own, and her arms wrapped around his head, pulling him down to her. He groaned mentally, his eyes closing

237

in the sensuality of the moment. The door to her bedroom was not far away. Her lips moved over his ear, licking and tugging at it, then biting it in reproof. She whispered now, and her words came to him from far away. "If Moresha were dead, and every man on this earth had disappeared, and you were the only one left, I still wouldn't want you. *I wouldn't touch you.* How could I want something I already have?" She stepped away from him suddenly and he teetered in imbalance, bereft and lonely.

"But you keep that knife," she said, moving away. "Maybe you'll grow some balls and decide to try again. Not likely, but you never know." She disappeared into the door of her room without looking back, expecting his compliance.

When she was gone, Rich stood awkwardly where she left him, ashamed that she had seen his weakness. He hated her in that moment. He could kill her, he thought, and everything would cease. She would not be there to taunt and tease and reject him. He would be sane again, free from the need and temptation of her presence. Except....

Except he needed her, and that need was heavier than his feelings of resentment. And she had known, too, and had left herself exposed. She knew he could come in there at any moment, and she knew he was armed. But she also knew he wouldn't do it, and she had turned her back on him in challenge.

Rich's shoulders sagged in defeat, knowing that she was right. He had no will for this. He would have to try again, but without threatening Moresha. He would win this game fairly, not by default.

He moved through the hallway and back down the stairs, forcing himself to resist the temptation to go to her. She would not respond, he knew that much, and anyway he needed the time to clear his mind. Adrenaline still pumped through his body, making him sweat, and he did not want her to see any more weakness in him. He couldn't be sure how he would respond if she rejected him yet again.

He kept the knife, though, just as she'd suggested. He had already decided he would pursue her fairly, without hurting Moresha, but deep inside he knew he was fighting a losing battle. His mind was beginning to accept what his heart could not, that she truly did not want him. It was a difficult thought, but it remained insistent and strong. Still, he wasn't yet ready to give up altogether. He would try and try again, and later, if all else failed, and if it came to it, yes, he might have to use this knife.

From within her bedroom, Moresha listened to the sound of his footsteps retreating and finally exhaled the air crowding her chest. She had heard Miranda slip out of their bed and room hours before, and she had thought at first that Miranda was simply going to spend the night in the room she'd insisted on claiming for herself when they moved to Reason. She had worried for a moment that she might have done something to make Miranda not want to spend the night at her side. But then she'd heard her footsteps padding quietly down the stairs and the soft sigh of the kitchen door closing as Miranda had gone out into the night. She frowned, realizing that she would not have heard the door at all if she'd not been so alert to the sound.

Worried, she had toyed with the idea of going out to Miranda, but she had quickly set it aside. Miranda was hiding things; that much Moresha knew. Moresha vaguely remembered once or twice reaching out at night to find an empty bed, even after Rich had gone. Now Moresha wondered if there might be another reason for her disappearances, something else she was hiding besides a man. Moresha could go after her, but the stakes were too high. If she caught Moresha following her, trying to learn her secrets, she would only become more adept at hiding them in the future. No, Moresha would have to look elsewhere for answers; they'd not be forthcoming from Miranda.

Still, she had waited in the darkness, listening for the sound of her returning. There had been a noise, the soft sigh again of the door, then the slightly louder noise of someone rifling through drawers. The stairs had creaked with each step and Moresha had turned over in bed, prepared to project the image that she was asleep when Miranda came back into the bed. But the steps had paused on the threshold of her bedroom and she had waited, still and silent, without breathing, for Miranda to enter.

Then she'd heard Miranda's voice in the hallway, and the sound of Rich's answer. Something within her had shriveled and died when she'd realized he was back inside the house, and they were together. She had crept to the door, pressing her ear against it, listening. What she heard reassured her as Miranda's voice had lifted in dismissal. She heard Miranda retreat into her bedroom and Rich's footsteps go beyond, and down the stairs, and she'd been satisfied. Whatever had provoked him into coming, it was obvious that Miranda, at least, remained constant in her rejection.

With a lighter heart and a smile hovering on her lips, Moresha now made her way back to the bed, certain again of her position. Miranda might not love her yet, but she didn't even *want* Rich. The knowledge was affirming. Rich was not a threat to their peaceful, if uneasy, existence together.

By the time Miranda finally returned to their bed in the predawn hours, Moresha was peacefully sleeping away her fears and exhaustion. Miranda ran her fingers lightly over her lover's back, careful not to disturb her, her fingers toying with the nakedness of her skin. She smiled in the dim morning light.

Finally unable to help herself, though, her hand reached up and cupped Moresha's breast, teasing the nipple, while her mouth moved urgently against her neck. Moresha turned to her, sleepily reaching for her, touching her in dreamy awareness. Moresha's hand reached out and missed, barely brushing across her hip. Her breath caught on a snore as she submitted herself again to sleep, and Miranda laughed softly into air. Assuming Moresha was tired, she didn't try to awaken her. Instead, she used this opportunity to explore the contours of her lover's body, her tongue and fingers dipping with gentle softness into indentations and curves, stroking each stretch of her skin. Too exhausted to respond, Moresha lay there absorbing the experience of Miranda coming to her in a dream. Except in this dream, Miranda held her softly with relief and kindness, and whispered quietly into her ear, admitting her love. Moresha smiled sleepily. She much preferred this dream-lover Miranda to the woman her subconscious mind knew would greet her in the morning with distant affection and demanding expectation. If every dream could be like this, she might never wake up.

Chapter 19

Sincere's smile was bright as she arrived at Mama Kinney's house and let herself in. "Mama?" she called out, setting her purse down in the hallway. There was no answer, and Sincere moved quickly into the house, closing the door behind her against the cold air.

Sincere shivered and stepped into the living room, looking for the control to the house's heating system. Mama Kinney had had the system installed just a few years ago, complaining that age was making her bones more sensitive to the cold. She usually turned the heating on at night, before she went to sleep, but apparently she'd forgotten the night before.

A feeling of apprehension settled low in Sincere's stomach, giving lie to the thought. Even if Mama Kinney had forgotten the night before, she would surely have turned on the heat as soon as she awoke in the morning. Sincere moved toward her godmother's bedroom, forcing doubts from her mind, but they refused to be quieted. And then, as she stood there staring at her godmother's form in the bed, the thought became more insistent, pushing her into a panicked rush. She grabbed Mama Kinney's shoulders roughly, trying to shake her awake, but the body was stiff and unyielding to her touch. She screamed her godmother's name over and over again, louder each time. Panicked tears began to stream freely down Sincere's face and the feeling in her stomach suddenly became tangible, overwhelming. She dropped her hands from Mama Kinney's body and ran into the hallway, but she stumbled on the rug and didn't make it to the toilet. Instead, she spilled the contents of her stomach onto the bathroom floor, the scent of it making her wretch over and over again until her stomach hurt with emptiness and even the tears on her face had dried.

Oh, God, she thought, moaning and falling backward on the floor. She narrowly missed the refuse of her stomach, but she was too distraught to care. *Dead!* her mind screamed at her. *Mama Kinney is DEAD!* Her mind repeated the thought over and over until it became a string of words that made no sense. *Dead? How can Mama Kinney be dead?* Confusion clouded her mind, refusing the thought. She had misunderstood, misinterpreted something. Mama Kinney wasn't *dead.* Maybe she was sleeping.

Sincere crawled on her hands and knees through the house, back to the bedroom where her godmother lay. But the scene was the same. Mama Kinney was dead, and her body lay undisturbed, peacefully resting in the position Sincere had left it. Overwhelmed by a sudden tide of grief, Sincere found only enough strength to pull herself onto the bed and crawl beneath the covers. She held Mama Kinney's body to her tightly, crying out her sorrow and pain, unable to form coherent words with either her mind or tongue. She fell asleep, rocking the body against her, waiting for it to come back to life.

Sincere stood alone in the front yard, watching as they loaded Mama Kinney's body into the back of a waiting ambulance with muted lights. Someone asked, and she quickly signed off on a writing tablet before nodding and handing it back to a waiting attendant. She seemed lonely as she stood there, watching Mama Kinney go. Lady pressed Sincere's face into her bosom, and Sincere did not object. She knew Mama Kinney was dead, but she was still angry when the ambulance pulled away without turning on its sirens. Hopeless. The entire world felt hopeless.

Later, when Lady was gone, Sincere waited alone for the memories. The house was full of memories. Sincere was almost reluctant to stay, seeing the imprint of Mama Kinney's spirit on every item and in every place. It only made her absence more pronounced, and Sincere's heart only became heavier within her breast. Her mind refused to let her live in the hope that it was all a bad dream; brutally, efficiently, it insisted Mama Kinney was dead, and would not be coming back. This house was hers, with all its accompanying memories, and she would need to get used to the feeling of living so close to her godmother's spirit.

She sat in the darkness of the living room, staring into space. There was grief, yes, the kind that was overwhelming and persistent, refusing to be denied. But there was something else, something her mind only now made identifiable. Guilt. Sincere frowned into the darkness, uncertain. What did she have to be guilty about?

She had not known when her godmother died. She might have even been awake when Mama Kinney likely took her final breath, and still she had not known. She had not sensed when the earth shifted and tilted on its axis, releasing Mama Kinney's spirit. She had been so happy this morning, smiling and expectant. *How could she be so unaware? How could she not have sensed when Mama Kinney's spirit had departed, leaving her alone in this world?*

It didn't seem entirely right. She and Mama Kinney

had been so close, surely she should have felt when Mama Kinney took her final breath. It should have hit her, knocking her to her knees where she stood, forcing her into awareness. *She should have known!*

Instead, she'd gone blithely about her business. What was wrong with her, that she could lose the person she loved most in this world and not know, not feel it, until she saw it with her eyes? How strong was their connection, that it could be broken and leave no awareness, no ache in its place?

Sincere sighed heavily, wiping at her eyes. They were dry now. She had nothing left to give. The house, in its emptiness, comforted her; it missed Mama Kinney, too. Sincere's stomach growled suddenly, and she realized she had not eaten all day. But she had no heart to cook, knowing she would have to eat the food alone. She would order out, but she didn't want anyone, even an impersonal stranger, invading this moment. And anyway, people would be calling as soon as she plugged the phone back up, so she likely wouldn't be able to make the call. It was inevitable. She had refused to answer the knocks at the door, leaving the house completely dark in hopes that people would assume no one was there. She didn't truly care what they assumed, as long as they didn't bother her in her grief.

Hours passed without Sincere moving. Her body protested when she rose from the couch, having been seated there for almost three hours. The pain was distracting, but only for a moment. Then Sincere stretched and headed into the bedroom, knowing that her body needed sleep and craving the relief and thoughtlessness it would provide. She stopped in the hallway, listening. Her eyes strained against the darkness, but nothing moved. Still she waited, standing still, until she was finally satisfied that she had imagined the noise that sounded something like a woman's swift intake of breath. The house was old and drafty in places, and there were bound to be noises in the dark. When she was a child, when she'd spent the night, the noises had been scary, prompting her to spend her nights in Mama Kinney's bed.

Now she put on one of Mama Kinney's smaller nightgowns and crawled again into her bed, smelling the sheets as they settled back from their disturbance. She leaned forward, touching her forehead to the same place, imagining Mama Kinney in the space opposite her. It was a hollow image, but it allowed her to finally close her eyes and fall asleep.

Moresha was still awake when Miranda slipped into bed beside her, but she did not say anything. Miranda was hiding something. That much was certain, though Moresha was almost afraid to ask what it was. The most likely scenario was that she'd slipped out to meet with Rich, but somehow Moresha didn't think so. She had seemed so definite in her dismissal, so emphatically sincere. No, there was something else Miranda wasn't telling her, something that had begun as soon as she'd arrived in Reason.

This was not the first late-night outing Moresha had witnessed. Where she went was a mystery; Moresha had not yet been able to catch and watch her as she left and didn't want to ask when she returned. Where Miranda had gone was a looming question, and what she did when she got there was an even bigger question with an answer Moresha wasn't sure she wanted to learn. She only knew that whatever it was would not turn out well, and she wished she could take Miranda away, back to their small flat in the city and the life they lived before they came to Reason, before it got to that point.

Despite Sincere's warning, Moresha *had* spent some time in the library, looking through the history of this town. There had been one or two interesting items, but Reason was a small town and there was not a whole lot of news. Still, Moresha had been caught by some newspaper articles she came across, describing a long-ago murder-suicide. The players had been people Moresha neither knew nor wanted to know; the story had been sordid, full of sex, lies, and betrayals. What *had* caught Moresha's attention was not the story, or the people, but the house. One of the articles had contained a picture of the police milling about a stately, two-story corner house. Moresha had quickly donned her glasses, squinting at the house with disbelief. She recognized the house immediately as the little peach one on the corner of Starlite and Lane.

The articles had detailed the story of a young black woman who'd cheated on her husband and paid the ultimate price. One or two of the articles had the distinct flavor of approval, as if they thought any woman who did such a thing deserved her fate, though they purported to be news. Aside from the deceased residents and the sexy story, though, one article had mentioned that the young woman had had a daughter. And Moresha had known, without ever asking, who that daughter was.

It explained a lot, like how Miranda, penniless and homeless and sleeping in a train station when they'd met, had owned this house. And why she had insisted on them moving to Reason at all. It had even explained the way Miranda seemed to insist on flaunting herself and her lifestyle in front of these people, as if goading them into the admission that they cared enough to be ashamed. What it did not explain was the reason they were still here, or what Miranda expected to accomplish.

Moresha had known enough not to ask outright, but she had tried in a roundabout way to get *some* information or admission out of Miranda. She had mentioned it over breakfast two days before, asking Miranda if she'd known that two people died in this house. Miranda's lips had thinned and tightened as Moresha relayed the story of the love-crossed young Sandal and Reba, but she said nothing. "Sandal! Isn't that the strangest name for a man? Or maybe that type of thing is common in these parts?" Moresha had asked innocently, watching her closely.

"I wouldn't know," Miranda said, and smiled. "I only know about women, and one in particular," and she'd given Moresha a look meant to tease and distract.

Moresha had shaken her head, refusing. "Now, I'm not scared of ghosts, mind you," and she paused, jabbing into the air with a spoon. "But I certainly do believe in spirits. And once or twice I've felt those spirits in this house, breathing and laughing and living as if they still got tomorrow. Somebody ought to tell them they dead, maybe then they'll go away," she said, and swallowed a spoonful of oatmeal.

Since Miranda had not responded, Moresha let the topic go, knowing that Miranda would tell what she wanted to when she wanted. Moresha would simply have to wait. But while she was waiting, there was no reason why she couldn't do her own investigating, and find out what she could. After all, Miranda was the one who'd started first by keeping secrets.

Chapter 20

Sincere knew that a small funeral would be impossible, so instead she arranged with the funeral home to have a private sitting with the body a few hours prior. She didn't cry, but sat there looking at the body, communing with Mama Kinney's spirit, alternately praying and wishing and hating her for leaving.

The past four days had been long. There had been arrangements to be made, people to notify. Sincere had been surprised by the genuine displays of grief shown by various people; Mama Kinney had always seemed to her a lone tree, set apart from a forest of people. Sincere had known to expect the formal show of grief. Mama Kinney was, after all, a respected elder. But she had looked into the eyes of some of the people who had come by to express their sympathy, and had seen something else. It was the sort of remembered feeling that never manifested in life, the respect and admiration and love, tinged by a certain element of regret. Sincere was comforted by it.

Nonetheless, she had never felt more alone. Mama Kinney had been everything, and Sincere felt as if a necessary part of her body had been brutally excised and she would forever be unable to recover. Would it always be this way, this longing for Mama Kinney's scent and her presence in the world?

Time passed, and Sincere kept watch. They would come, likely more than she knew, and they would bring words and touches and reality. Mama Kinney's family, a few distant relatives that she had rarely mentioned and never spoken with, might even show up, waiting to see if she had left anything for them. She would not have, of course. Mama Kinney had been too practical to leave anything a surprise, and she had always discussed her death and her will with Sincere. She would have made certain that it was uncontestable, and that Sincere would not have to face a legal battle along with her grief. For that much she was grateful; the process of mourning had exhausted her of any desire to fight, and she knew it would only take the slightest assault to make her collapse beneath the weight.

The funeral was a simple affair, briefly held and quickly finished. A song or two, the eulogy was read. Sincere declined to speak, preferring instead to remain unremarkably on the front pew, grieving privately. The people who knew her understood that she would desire to mourn Mama Kinney without an audience, and so they hastened the service and gathered the people together for the long ride to the burial grounds.

Sincere was the first to leave, signaling an end to the funeral as she rose and followed the pallbearers and Mama Kinney's body. She was cloaked in the traditional black, with the short brim of a black hat and a small transparent veil covering her face. She preferred silence, and gathered a black wool shawl closely about her shoulders as if she were gathering a mantle of grief. They would understand. Lady and Jody fell in step behind her, followed by Tricee, Reese, and Joyce, their presence quietly supportive. It occurred to Sincere how few people had truly known Mama Kinney. Of all who had attended the funeral, Mama Kinney had only cultivated an intimate relationship with Sincere. Everyone else had known the image, but not the woman.

And she had been some woman. Sincere remembered how, when she was five-years-old, Mama Kinney had gone about telling everyone how smart she was simply because she had known enough not to let the owner of the corner deli scam her with a fatty, less choice bit of meat. "Um, hm," Mama Kinney had said when she told her about the exchange, sucking on her teeth. She had not said anything directly to Sincere, but later she had overheard Mama Kinney telling her mother, "That daughter of your's, she got more brains than the both of us put together!" And because she had believed it, Sincere, too, had come to believe it.

Sincere could remember how, three years later, she had run from school straight to Mama Kinney's house, upset about the news she'd heard on the playground. Mama Kinney had held and rocked her all night, whispering how God would be her father now, and how lucky she was that she still had two mothers. Sincere had woken in the night, cramped from her position, to find Mama Kinney still awake, holding and rocking her, singing her dreams to goodness. From that night, Sincere had all but moved in with Mama Kinney, feeling sheltered by her stout presence against the harsh reality of her father's death. Cassandra had not objected, and out of respect for her, Mama Kinney had never spoken openly about the financial support she'd freely given, even after Cassandra's death. When Sincere had learned of it from her siblings and asked Mama Kinney, she had only responded, "Now why would I ever do a thing like that?" and walked away.

Leading the procession toward the open doors of the funeral home, Sincere almost didn't see Miranda and

Moresha standing toward the exit, heads bowed respectfully. When she did, she stumbled, looking, and wondered why they had come. Neither of them had known Mama Kinney, at least not as adults, and it seemed odd that they would feel compelled to attend the funeral. Suddenly realizing she was holding up the procession and staring, Sincere moved awkwardly forward, filing the questions away for another time.

Sincere's heart felt full and heavy, her limbs moving sluggishly to carry her to the waiting cars. A few distant cousins of Mama Kinney's from Courtney had shown up to the funeral, undoubtedly expecting to receive something, and Sincere knew they would expect a limousine escort. Rather than share the process of her mourning with anyone, even Mama Kinney's blood relations, Sincere had instead requested a separate town car for herself. Now she stood back, watching as Mama Kinney's body was lifted and slid onto a rack installed in the back of the waiting hearse. She smiled. Mama Kinney had refused to drive or be driven for at least the past six or so years. She would appreciate the irony, were she alive.

A driver discreetly got her attention, signaling that they were ready to begin the procession. Sincere waited a moment more, allowing herself to acknowledge the longing in her soul. For a crazy second, she wanted to be inside the coffin, too, snuggled closely beside Mama Kinney as she had done on cold nights as a child, but she willed the desire away.

The interior of the car was black, as if the funeral home owners had not wanted anything to potentially disrupt her grief. No matter. The car could have been gaudy shades of red and it would not have drawn her notice. She positioned herself in the middle of the seat and watched the hearse driving ahead, still trying to digest the sudden feeling of loneliness that Mama Kinney's death had provoked.

As slowly as they traveled, Sincere's vision was momentarily distracted by a brief flash of white through the window. Outside, the long shape of a car emerged, speeding past her and careening violently into the hearse before it continued down the street. The driver of the town car screeched to a halt, forcing Sincere's body to jerk forward. Her foot became tangled under the passenger seat, and her purse slipped from her lap, but she barely noticed. Her attention, instead, was focused horrifyingly on what she saw outside. The hearse, blindsided by the white car, had jumped the curb and slammed into a fire hydrant. It sat awkwardly on the sidewalk, its rear still in the street. The back door hung lazily off its hinges, and Sincere's eyes searched frantically for the coffin.

Her mind registered the sound of the driver calling, telling her to wait, even as her hands fumbled with the door. She could not get it open quickly enough to suit. She was spinning into a shocked disbelief, she knew, but felt helpless against the flood of emotion that compelled her to move. She jumped out, racing to the hearse in uneven heels, not understanding that one of her shoes had broken. Still, she did not pause. In the short distance between the two cars, she searched the road for what she feared she would find. As she rounded the town car, there it was: splintered, fractured pieces of the wooden coffin lay strewn across the road in array. And there, lying in unordered disarray, was the body of Mama Kinney, her wig dislodged from her head and her dress gathered and revealingly bunched at her waist, showing all the world her womanhood. Even as she moved forward, tears flowing in undignified display, Sincere felt the pressure of a dozen restraining hands, pulling her back, keeping her from the only person she had ever loved. And then that was all she felt, as the world collapsed around her, gathering her into a comforting darkness.

"What the hell are you doing in here?" Jody asked, closing the door to Mama Kinney's bedroom behind her and leaning her body against it, lest Miranda should think to escape. Now that she had the opportunity to confront the woman, she would not allow any interruption or interference.

Miranda's body stiffened and she turned to face Jody, her eyes reflecting her recognition. "The bathroom—" Miranda quickly improvised, but Jody interrupted.

"Ain't nowhere 'round here. So you wanna tell me what you're doin' in this room, searchin' through Mama Kinney's things?"

Miranda looked at the woman in dismay, her mind searching desperately for a proper excuse.

But Jody didn't seem to care about the answer. "You know who I am?" she asked, still standing against the door with her arms crossed over her chest. Even outraged and upset, she couldn't help but notice the beauty of black against Miranda's dark skin. The woman exuded lushness, with full breasts that rose with every breath, a neat, trim waist and wide, childbearing hips. Jody reminded herself that evil was often cloaked in pretty. The devil was recorded to have been God's most beautiful angel.

"You came to visit that first day," Miranda said and smiled, but her smile didn't warm her eyes. "You're a Jehovah's Witness," and Jody nodded shortly, hating her for the reminder.

"It's nice to see you again, though I regret the circumstances." Miranda moved forward, congenially extending one hand.

Jody stopped her with an abrupt, jerky movement. Miranda's hand fell back to her side and she frowned. "I'm also a friend of Rich," Jody said, and understanding dawned in Miranda's eyes.

Her mouth tightened. "I'm done with Rich," she said simply, as if admitting as much would quickly end the conversation.

"And so what? That's it, then?" Jody's voice rose shrilly in the silence of the room. Miranda only shrugged.

"You *used* him!" Jody said, advancing in accusation. "You used him and threw him away!" she said again, and rage made her voice shake.

Miranda nodded. "I used him, and now I'm done. So he's available, if that's what you're looking for."

Jody stopped short. She could not believe the woman! She spoke about Rich as if he were a toilet, and had treated him no better. "I'm *not* tryin' to get him. Like I said before, I'm *just* a friend. You, on the other hand...I don't know what you are." Jody's eyes narrowed on Miranda, as if she was trying to figure the other woman out.

"I'm a woman," Miranda said simply, and spread her hands wide. "No different from you. I eat and sleep and bleed and love same as you, and I have no doubt one day I'll stand before God's judgment seat all the same."

"Some people go straight to hell," Jody said, frustrated by the woman's unshakable demeanor and ready admissions. She had imagined this confrontation differently.

"I'm sure I won't be the first," Miranda said, her voice turning, taunting. "Maybe you'll meet me at the door?"

"Or maybe I'll send you there myself!" Jody said, and moved forward. But Miranda didn't back away, and Jody stopped short. She stood awkwardly in the middle of the room, unsure of herself and what to do next.

Miranda's eyes bore through Jody, adding fear to her uncertainty. "You won't be the first to try. But take care if you do...I won't go easy and I might take you with me." She moved around Jody, heading for the door. Jody was incensed by the dismissal, but unable to make her body move. Miranda was smaller than Jody, but she seemed more dangerous and less rational. She had even turned her back to Jody, as if daring her to make good on her threat. But Jody's body was paralyzed, and she could not.

"You need to go," Jody said in a small, quiet voice, speaking her thoughts aloud. "You need to *get out!*"

Miranda stood stiffly, hand on the doorknob, considering. She turned to face Jody again, not pretending to misunderstand the woman's statement. "You want me to go? You want me to leave town?" she asked, staring Jody down.

Jody nodded, her eyes betraying her defeat.

"You help me get what I want," Miranda told her. "Soon's I get it, I'll be gone. I promise." Miranda quickly turned and left before Jody could question her and find out what it was. She stared at the door, feeling as if she'd just been trapped into a bargain with the devil, and she had no foreseeable way of getting out.

It was that same sensation of hands holding Sincere that brought her back, forcing her into awareness. These hands were gentler, though, and urging rather than restraining. Sincere opened her eyes, already knowing. It was unfortunate, this inability to lie to herself. Dishonesty was unnatural to Sincere, and her mind was brutally and uncompromisingly blunt with the knowledge. Understanding came in impressions: Mama Kinney's body, laying lifeless in her bed; the ambulance, advertising the finality of her death in their refusal to sound the sirens; the relatives, waiting for a hand-out she knew would not be forthcoming; whiteness, and then the feeling of being thrown forward; Mama Kinney's thighs, lying exposed in the street; the hands, pressing, restraining. Those hands. At the recollection, Sincere's heart let out an anguished wail that ended in her throat, stifling sound. Someone held a cup to her mouth, forcing her to drink. The liquid felt thick on her tongue, disruptive. It was quickly replaced by the refreshing smell of mint and the clearer taste of tea. Sincere swallowed a bit and coughed. Her hand came forward, pushing the cup away, even as she turned her head. She did not want to be revived or refreshed.

"Sincere, you and I both know you're too sensible to sleep this through," Lady said, pushing. In her heart, Sincere sighed. Yes, she did know. She sat up, looking around her, recognizing her own room on the second floor of Mama Kinney's house. She shook her head. No, it was likely her house now. Mama Kinney was gone.

There was a burst of laughter beyond the door, inappropriate in the silence. Lady turned around, scowling.

"They still here?" Sincere asked, already knowing the answer.

Lady nodded. "They won't clear out until the food is gone. Last I saw, there were platters yet to be ate. And why in the world did you make all those damn cakes and pies?"

Sincere shrugged, but Lady understood. The days following Mama Kinney's death had been lonely and grief-filled. Sincere's job had insisted she not come in, and Sincere had not known what to do to occupy her mind. Somewhere in her recollection, she had distinctly heard Mama Kinney's voice saying, "An idle mind is the devil's workshop," and so she had filled her mind and her hands with the mundane task of baking. Unable to eat, she had left them for the wake. There had been twenty-two dessert dishes in all.

Sincere almost asked about the accident, and how they had handled cleaning up and tidying Mama Kinney's body, but she stopped herself. Any of a dozen people would have seen to those details, ensuring that the body was properly buried and cared for. Sincere had the brief memory of being woken in the car, a pill pushed between her lips. She assumed it had been a sleeping pill, for even now it was difficult to shake the grogginess and the heavy blanket of confusion.

"They need you for the reading of the will." Lady reached forward a hand, offering assistance.

Sincere nodded but refused the hand, choosing instead to struggle up alone. It would be her permanent condition, she might as well get used to it now. Still, when she stumbled she was grateful for the imprint of Lady's hand on her back, ensuring that she would not fall.

Downstairs, people continued eating quietly, speaking in hushed whispers in corners. They noted Sincere's presence with silence, nodding and patting her arms as she passed. She shied away from the hands that reminded her so clearly of that awful moment standing on the sidewalk before she had fainted.

Sincere paused in the doorway of the living room, briefly startled. Deacon stood in a corner, shuffling papers, with another younger brother from the church. The two relatives, as expected, sat on a couch, waiting in agitated silence. But it was the presence of Miranda, standing quietly by and staring out of the window, that threw her. What was she doing here, attending this intimate function?

Deacon answered the question before she could ask, announcing loudly, "Evelyn, um, Mama Kinney, asked that both you and Ms. Foster attend. She has left items for both of you in her will." Deacon nodded toward the relatives. "I thought it best that we all read it together, just so there are no misunderstandings."

"What?" Sincere asked, uncomprehending.

Deacon cleared his throat in response. "Why don't we go ahead and get started? This has been a particularly trying day for many of us." He looked back at Lady and nodded, and Sincere felt herself being ushered to a small loveseat opposite the relatives. The cushion depressed beside her, and she thankfully realized that Lady had opted to stay in support.

The first several items were unremarkable, things that had been formally left to Sincere, but which she knew Mama Kinney intended for her to personally pass on to various individuals. She and Mama Kinney had talked about this many a time before, and she had a detailed list of what was to be given to whom. When she was just a child, Mama Kinney had made Sincere a joint tenant on all her bank accounts so that those items, at least, would not be restricted and taxed through the process of probate. It was only those personal items that remained to be passed on.

" 'My home, and all possessions therein, I leave to my goddaughter Sincere, with the restriction that she vacate the home immediately, and may not reenter until three days after the reading of this will, and that she thereafter list the house for sale within one month, such sale to be completed by the one year anniversary after my death.' " Deacon paused in his reading, watching Sincere in silent expectation.

Sincere sat, frowned, not understanding. Why would Mama Kinney have prevented her from entering the house for three days? Understanding came in increments of awareness, each more disturbing than the last. She had always assumed that the house would go to her; she had all but lived there since she was a girl. But for Mama Kinney to give her the house, then force it to be sold! Sincere's mind fought against the truth, refusing to acknowledge this betrayal. Mama Kinney would not have done that to her.

She stood, shaking her head as if to clear it, speaking even before her thoughts found the proper words to express her emotions. "You can't possibly be serious!" she said, shaking Lady's restraining hand away. "She wouldn't have done that to me!"

The small churchman beside Deacon looked at her pityingly, and even the relatives seemed sympathetic. Deacon, alone, stood resolute. "Sit down, Sincere. You know as well as I do, Evelyn was an intelligent and caring woman, and she would not have done any such thing without a distinct reason."

"What reason could there possibly be?" Sincere wailed, and her voice sounded shrill in the silence.

Deacon shrugged his shoulders helplessly, looking to Lady for support. He had been given the edict, but no explanation. Still, he felt as if he owed it to Sincere to say something comforting, but he could not find the words. Instead, he continued with the reading. "Sincere, you may not live in the house at all. Evelyn was very clear about that. You may not spend the night in this home."

Sincere opened her mouth, closed it again with a snap. Anger narrowed her eyes. "And what if I ignore what she says, who's gon force me to sell this house?"

Deacon's response was cold, unfeeling. "The house and land will revert to a local charity, effective immediately. They've already been notified, I am sure they would be happy to collect their interest."

Sincere heard little else after that, her mind still searching for explanation. Why would Mama Kinney have taken away the one thing she wanted above all else, the one thing she could claim by right as well as by experience? It made no sense.

Deacon distributed several letters to the relatives and even to Miranda, but there was none for Sincere. This seemed a final betrayal, that Mama Kinney had chosen not to explain herself to her goddaughter.

"Miranda, Mama Kinney also left you her jewelry box," Deacon said, handing the woman a large, heavy wooden box that was made to look like a miniature dresser. Sincere's eyes flew to Miranda, and in that moment, she hated her, too. Jealousy. That was what she felt, jealous that anyone else would have a part of her godmother when Sincere felt like even the memories of her were already slipping away.

"Give it back," she said, and stood. She rounded on

261

the woman, pushed her before the men could react. "Give it back," she screamed, poised for an attack, her fingers bent into claws. Miranda moved nimbly out of her reach and allowed the men to come between them. Sincere barely heard Deacon's rebuke, but the anger was gone as quickly as it had come and she collapsed again into a heap on the couch. She felt Lady's big hands moving over her forehead, her eyelids, soothing as she cried.

The reading of the will done, Sincere had no strength left to play hostess to her guests. Instead, she sat in the fading light of the living room, listening as Lady and Jody gathered and ushered everyone out, doing the job much more efficiently than Sincere could ever have accomplished. For that much she was grateful; her friends served as the necessary buffer between her grief and the world. All she wanted right now was to be alone to grieve, to understand why Mama Kinney had done what she'd done. She wanted to lay down in Mama Kinney's bed and miss her, purely, without an audience and without the need to hide her tears, though she knew she couldn't spend the night. She waited there as the sun went down, until the house was quiet and silent, and all that remained was the lingering presence of Mama Kinney's spirit.

Chapter 21

Frustrated, Miranda slipped quietly from the house and stood, gazing into the dark. Nothing had gone right since she arrived in Reason. First Mama Kinney had refused to admit her wrong, then she'd turned Miranda's search for the ring into a public fiasco. Everyone in town would know about the jewelry box, would wonder why Mama Kinney would give it to a stranger. It's true, Deacon didn't seem to know much about the ring, but he had privately given Miranda a key to the house and told her that, per Mama Kinney's instructions, she was to have access to the home in the three days following her funeral. Mama Kinney knew she didn't need a key! In her letter Mama Kinney explained that the ring was in the house, but said if she couldn't find it in three days, she didn't deserve it. Miranda had burned in hatred toward the dead old lady. How could she know what Miranda deserved or didn't?

Three days, but Miranda already knew the search would prove fruitless. She had already gone through the usual locations, had rummaged through her jewelry box even before the woman had given it to her, and the small safe she kept under her bed. No, there was only one person who would know where Mama Kinney kept her treasured things, but Miranda had already made clear to Sincere that they would not be friends. How could she go to her now?

The wind brushed across her face and she startled, her imagination conjuring up ghosts. She almost laughed at herself. There were no ghosts in this life, except the specters of lingering regrets and memories too strong to go without struggling. Death was final, but history...that could last forever.

Still, she stood watching the house from her front porch, waiting for Sincere to leave. She moved carefully into the shadows, taking refuge. She was a creature of the night; she could see and hear more clearly in the dark.

Now she called out to Rich, unsurprised by his presence.

"You know, I saw you at the funeral. I saw your car hit that hearse." He came out of the shadows and stepped close to her, and she allowed it. "You were looking for me?" she asked, her silken, honeyed tones suggesting the answer. He had always been looking for her. He'd come into this world seeking her, loving her from his mother's womb.

"I saw your car, Rich. I saw you keep going, after you hit the hearse. *I saw you.*" She moved close to him, her hand reaching up to stroke the stubble of his beard, her palm cradling his chin. She allowed her body to move toward him, her hips meeting his, brushing, teasing. They danced together in the dark, swaying into one another, the wind wrapping around them and pushing them closer. The natural sounds of nighttime formed a symphony in the background, moving them with urgency.

"You love me?" she asked sharply, forcing his eyes open again, her fingernails suddenly biting into his skin.

"I love you," he said simply, too deeply in to worry about self-protection.

She nodded again, then reached up and kissed him. The kiss was so sweet and soft, it was at odds with the woman. It seemed to say so many things that she could not, make promises she either could not, or would not, fulfill. Her arms joined around his neck, holding him loosely, and his hands encircled her hips. Her breath between them smelled of cloves and of goodness. He inhaled, smelling her sweetness as it mingled with the night air.

"You know what I need, Rich," and he agreed without thought, certain that he did. "I need you to get it, I need you to give it to me."

"Yeeesssss," he said in that same slow way he had on that first day, when he'd been sitting at her kitchen table, caught up in the spell of richness that was her. "Yeeesssss," he repeated, and he meant it in his heart.

She smiled at him and stepped slowly away, moving again toward the door. Her mouth and her words formed an invitation. "Come back to me, Rich. Come back tomorrow, when Moresha is gone. Come in to me, baby, and give me what I need."

"Yes," Rich said again, and she was happy. She had just needed to apply herself, the answer was always there. This situation would not outsmart her. Mama Kinney would not outsmart her. She would find that ring and get it, she just needed a little help. She knew that Rich would do her bidding without question and with complete loyalty. That was enough.

Grief woke Sincere every morning with a headache and immediate awareness. *Mama Kinney was dead. The funeral had been a catastrophe. The will had been a betrayal.* She couldn't even sleep in Mama Kinney's bed. A deep wave of depression had settled into her breast. Sincere could feel it in her bones, pressing heavily on her chest, preventing her from rising.

But when she'd had enough, Sincere knew how to make herself forget: work. And that she did. She began with her own small apartment and then, when the three-day banishment was up, she did the same to Mama Kinney's house. She forced herself not to be sentimental. She washed away Mama Kinney's scent with bleach and pine cleaner, and filled cardboard boxes with clothing. She decided she would first ask the church if they needed anything, and the remaining items she would donate to another charity. She worked, ignoring the insistence of Mama Kinney's memory, refusing to remember.

Now, though, she knew it would be her task to completely empty and clean the house, and to ensure that Mama Kinney's personal effects were taken care of. She did not relish the task, but she knew it was the last thing she would ever have to do for the woman who, for twenty-eight years, had been more a mother to Sincere than her own. She handled the items lovingly, as if she were holding memories in her hands, willing away her sadness with quick and thorough hands.

Sincere looked over the kitchen again, noting the changes and searching for anything yet left undone. A single cup sat in the dish rack, a lonely reminder of Mama Kinney in the otherwise-pristine kitchen. Sincere hesitated to pick it up. The cup had been Mama Kinney's favorite. Sincere had made it for her in class when she was in the fourth grade and had given it to her, proudly beaming when Mama Kinney hugged the cup to her chest and declared it the best she'd ever had. Mama Kinney had set it down, hugged her tightly, then kissed her on her forehead. She was old enough to be embarrassed, but this time she was not. She had felt so close to Mama Kinney, then, held in her arms, so treasured.

Now Sincere looked at the cup and frowned, wondering why it was in the dish rack. Mama Kinney had been overly protective of the cup, afraid it would drop and shatter and, with it, the memory of the gift. Consequently, she never left it out. She had always stored it either in the refrigerator during summer and in the oven in the winter. That way, the cup was always immediately ready to receive whatever her drink of the season was.

Sincere shrugged to herself. No matter now, Mama Kinney would not be using the cup anytime too soon. Not knowing what to do with it, she left it where it sat, alone, next to the sink.

In turn, Sincere scrubbed the downstairs bathroom, living room, dining room, and hallway. She cleaned the upstairs, too, dusting her own bedroom and stripping the bedding and curtains. She hadn't slept there in years, not since she'd returned from college. Mama Kinney had kept the room in the same patterns and conditions as when Sincere had left, but she insisted Sincere move. With her own apartment so close by, there had been no reason for Sincere to stay the night. The room had remained, unused, presumably for guests. No guests had ever come, but Mama Kinney had not insisted on clearing out the room and Sincere would not have let her if she had. Despite herself, she had always fully expected Mama Kinney to eventually come to her senses and allow Sincere to return home. It was a shame that had not happened, even after her death.

The second room upstairs had been used by Mama Kinney as a sewing room and was still full of fabric and unfinished patterns. It had been some time since Mama Kinney had been in there last, preferring instead not to worsen the pain in her joints by climbing the stairs. The room was cluttered with piles of finished dresses, coats, and other various garments, and a red ball sat atop a rusted ironing board, stuck through with needles. The room looked exactly as Mama Kinney left it; as if she would return tomorrow to finish an outfit she'd made for a sister at church or for herself. Saddened, Sincere carefully packed all of the items, placing the finished pieces in a box separate from those that had been left undone. She didn't think she would have the heart to finish them, herself, but someone at church might find a good use for the fabric.

Cleared of its debris, the room looked almost as it had years ago, before Sincere had gone off to college, back when Mama Kinney could still get up and down the steps with little trouble. This was the room where Mama Kinney had slept through Sincere's childhood, and where Sincere had snuggled close to her godmother on cold nights. When Sincere had left, Mama Kinney moved downstairs, citing the beginnings of arthritis. But Sincere knew that her pain had not gotten bad until sometime later, and she suspected that the move had been the product of combined loneliness and the need for a change of scenery. Unable to relieve either, Sincere had never challenged her contention, preferring instead to allow Mama Kinney that small bit of privacy.

Now she closed the doors of both bedrooms, knowing that it was probably the last time. More cardboard boxes stood silently in the hallway, waiting to be removed and taken from the house. She would not come back up, except to bring them down.

The bright sunshine of midday and the opportune grumbling of her stomach, both served to remind her suddenly that she had forgotten breakfast and it was now time for lunch. The bedroom was waiting, but Sincere gratefully accepted the alternative. In the kitchen, she fixed herself a light meal of tuna fish and crackers and sat down for a leisurely lunch, changing her mind about the mug. She used it now to hold her herbal tea, sipping it slowly and feeling closer to Mama Kinney as she did. She sighed helplessly, forgiving.

She busied herself with a variety of small tasks, but found by late afternoon that she could put it off no longer. She stood in the doorway of the small room that Mama Kinney had slept in, inhaling her scent, remembering. Grief and loneliness swamped over her, and she suddenly felt the same crushing weight that had kept her in bed this morning, pressed into the mattress. Now it pushed her to her knees, and Sincere knelt helplessly in the doorway, giving into the tears and waiting for time and exhaustion to ease the force of her pain.

She had loved Mama Kinney so deeply. She could not remember exactly how many times the two had spoken of her death, and all that would be done, Mama Kinney slowly preparing her. Still, the suddenness of her death had been so complete, so without warning that all of the preparations had been secondary to her grief. Despite it all, or perhaps because of it, Sincere had this terrible feeling of being alone the way a newborn babe might if taken from his mother's breast before he had finished nursing. Deprived, and angrily so. But there was no one to be angry at. A thought snaked through her mind, that Mama Kinney would be alive if only Sincere had been there. Sincere ruthlessly pushed it away, knowing that even she could not hold off death, though even that knowledge would not have stopped her from trying.

When the pressure eased, she pushed herself up,

leaning heavily on the doorpost, clinging to it and reality. There would be no visitors today, so Sincere would have to hold herself together. With stern firmness, she forced herself to recollect, knowing that the only thing standing between her and complete despair was absolute determination. She drew on it, holding it to her in desperation, knowing it would help to ease her burden.

It took her longer to clean this room, reluctant as she was to remove the many traces of Mama Kinney's personality. There were so many reminders of who she was that Sincere was loath to remove them, knowing that they would not be treasured by another the way Mama Kinney had treasured them. Sincere made two boxes, separating the things she would give away from those she would keep. The box of items she would keep filled and became two, then three. There were small, innocuous items like a small box of mismatched earrings that Mama Kinney had thought too precious to throw away. Pictures of Sincere at various stages of childhood were wedged into the border around the mirror, and Mama Kinney's Bible lay open on a nightstand. Sincere picked it up, knowing immediately that she would keep it, although the worn and old book had likely cost next to nothing when it was new. Mama Kinney had another, more ornately elaborate Bible, trimmed with gold and engraved with her name, one which Sincere, herself, had given her. The Bible had been expensive, but Mama Kinney was a simple woman and though she'd made pretty her response for Sincere's sake, she'd always gotten more use out of this one. This one had been made for everyday use.

Sincere's fingers ran lovingly over the cover, and a memory traveled across the edge of her mind. She turned to the bed, remembering how just a few days ago she had entered the room and found Mama Kinney's body. How often she had come before and found her, peacefully sleeping, glasses still on her face and the Word of God open beside her on the bed. Sincere's frown grew deeper. The Bible had been on the dresser when she entered, opened but untouched. Just to be certain, Sincere located and thumbed through a small writing tablet Mama Kinney kept on the nightstand, too, for her ready use. The tablet was filled with pages of notes, dated consecutively until they stopped, abruptly, two days before she'd found Mama Kinney's body.

Sincere shook her head, confused, not understanding what her mind was telling her. She refused the thought, bowing her head and resolutely finishing her cleaning without further thinking it through. She packed more quickly now, refusing to reminisce, ignoring the thoughts that held, determinedly, clinging to the fringes of her memory. She finished and pushed all of the boxes into the hallway and out into the last two rooms beside the front door to wait until morning, chest burning with exertion. The muscles in her arms ached, and her knees felt wobbly and unable to sustain her weight.

A moment later she stepped out onto the porch to listen to the singing of the wind. The night air teased her, raising goose bumps on her arms and drying sweat beneath her armpits. Sincere stood a moment, enjoying the breeze and the moment of quiet, before she returned into the house to finish.

Miranda found herself making her way again through the shadows of midnight, back to what used to be Mama

Kinney's house. Now it belonged to Sincere. She let herself in, stepping lightly, careful not to make a sound. The lights in this house had gone out two hours before, but Mama Kinney had had a habit of sitting in the dark, staring into space and presumably thinking. It was possible Sincere shared this habit.

But she found Sincere where she might have expected, sleeping in Mama Kinney's bed. It was curious that Sincere would sleep down here, instead of in the room upstairs that had always been hers, but Miranda shrugged, thinking it was no different and might even make things easier. She knew better than to look a gift horse in the mouth, so she would not question her fortune.

She stood in the doorway, looking at Sincere from afar, listening to the rapid rise and fall of her breath. She slept on her side, facing the wall, and Miranda moved quietly forward, considering the perfection of her form beneath the blankets. Her heart moved within her, making her stop in her tracks. Was it possible that she still retained some measure of love for Sincere, even after such a brief and childish relationship and the bitterness of the intervening years?

Sincere's breath rose and caught on the air, then settled back into cadence. Hearing it, Miranda deliberately shook herself, hardening her heart. Sentimentality and feeling were never as effective as action, and Miranda would not sacrifice her purpose in returning simply because it might have the inadvertent effect of hurting Sincere. Sincere would do well to stay out of her way and allow justice to take its course. If she did not, she would no doubt get swept up in the tide.

She came to stand before Sincere, watching for herself the soft parting of Sincere's lips and the way her nostrils flared and contracted with regularity. The rhythm was reassuring, telling Miranda that Sincere's dreams remained undisturbed, despite her presence. Miranda moved quietly to the nightstand, sweeping her eyes across its surface, before looking to the dresser. Both surfaces were bare but for the necessities, a small lamp and a large mirror. Even Mama Kinney's pictures and toiletries, which Miranda remembered had cluttered both spaces before, were now gone. They must have been packed and put away. But where was the ring?

Miranda carefully pulled back the nightstand drawer, trying not to make any noise, but the sound of wood scraping against wood was loud in the room. Sincere moved in her sleep, wiping a palm over her face, and Miranda stood still, waiting. Sincere did not awaken, but the moment was warning. Miranda would not risk forcing a confrontation, here in the middle of the night. She closed the drawer quietly, moving out of the room. She would have to find a way to search the house further without making that happen.

Chapter 22

Sincere stopped by Rich's office, having decided she would yield to Mama Kinney's wishes. The metallic tinkling of a bell greeted her as she made her way into the office, struck at once by the smell of oranges and the freshness that always came after rain. She stood resolutely, waiting for the receptionist to notice her, dripping rainwater from outdoors onto the thin carpeting.

"Oh!" Lorna said when she noticed Sincere standing awkwardly by the door, and rushed forward to assist. Sincere removed her coat, hanging it on a rack next to the door. "Sincere! What are you doing here?"

"I came to list the house, Lorna. Is Rich here?"

"What house?" Lorna asked at first, then awareness widened her eyes. "You puttin' Mama Kinney's house on the *market?*" Lorna asked, her expression conveying her disbelief.

Sincere's chin rose and she nodded. "I-" she began, then took a deep breath and started again. "Mama Kinney left instructions for it to be sold."

Lorna's expression sobered as she regained her seat. "I'm sorry about her death, Sincere, I know how much she meant to you."

Fighting back a sudden urge to cry, Sincere simply nodded and waited while Lorna searched her desk for the appropriate papers. She stood again suddenly and gestured to a chair. "You want to sit, Sincere? You look a little tired. Some water?" She rushed out of the room, from somewhere else producing water and handing it to Sincere. The water spilled over as it exchanged hands.

Lorna stopped and stood, smiling sheepishly at her clumsiness. "I'm sorry, Sincere. I'm just a little bit surprised, is all. Rich asked about that house many a time, but your godmother was adamant. Said she was holding it for you." Lorna shook her head. "Can't imagine why she would want you to sell it."

Sincere raised her hand to her temples, as if to ward off a headache. Life had been a constant headache of late. Suddenly, she knew she wasn't yet up to this. "Lorna, can you just have Rich bring the papers to me?" Sincere said, and rose.

The secretary was immediately sympathetic, but a look crossed her face before she carefully answered. "I'll see wat I can do," she said, determined.

Sincere didn't notice. Instead, she nodded and rushed back out into the rain, back to all the things that had to be done.

Sincere woke, groggy and confused, to the sound of banging at her door. She turned over, wishing it away, but it continued, insistent. She finally sat up and looked around the room, remembering. Her breath came in gasps, but the ache in her heart was beginning to ease. It had been ten days. Surely that was long enough.

The banging continued and Sincere went to open the door with a scowl, unhappy with whoever was on the other side. Rich stood there, a frown marring his face, and Sincere was suddenly aware she was standing there in her nightclothes. She was still wearing one of Mama Kinney's gowns, and her figure was lost in its voluminous depths. It hung and gapped loosely over her breasts, and Sincere reached up, embarrassed, covering any amount of exposed skin. She frowned, confused by Rich's presence.

Rich coughed discreetly into his hand, turning away. "Sincere, Lorna told me to stop by. Can I come in?" he asked, still politely looking elsewhere.

Sincere remembered suddenly that she'd invited him, and the manners Mama Kinney instilled in her for so many years wouldn't let her answer as she wished. She stepped courteously aside. "I-" she began, then paused. She had just woken up, and she wasn't sure she was at all presentable. She didn't want to breathe on him before she brushed her teeth. She stepped back a bit, distancing herself and waving him into the living room. "Give me a minute," she said, "I just need to change into something more... appropriate." She disappeared before he could object.

There were boxes lined against the hallway walls and filling each of the rooms. The house was a cluttered mess. Sincere looked over the boxes in confusion, wondering which one held her own clothing. In the end, she shrugged and began to search, rummaging through several boxes until she finally had gathered together a number of mismatched items. She grimaced, looking at them. They were not completely suitable, but they would have to do. She had already kept Rich waiting far too long.

She ran into the bathroom and quickly brushed her teeth and used a wet rag to wipe the sleep from her eyes. She made a face in the mirror, thinking what Mama Kinney would have said about her letting a man see her this way. She smiled ironically, looking down at her clothes. As tacky as they were, Mama Kinney would have approved. The pants were an old pair of stretch pants she mostly used for cleaning house and staying at home; the shirt was an old t-shirt with faded words across the breasts. Both items clung to the angles and curves of her body in a way that showed the pounds she'd lost these several days past and made her feel almost naked, but she'd had no choice. It had been between this and a long, thick wool coat she'd found in the same box. Given the choices, this one had seemed a bit more modest.

She joined Rich where he waited now in the living room, bringing with her two cups and a pitcher of water. "I apologize, I don't have more," she explained, pouring. "I been cleanin' and throwin' so much away, I haven't had time yet to shop."

Rich chose not to ask, sensing theemotion beneath the words. He took a long gulp of water and cleared his throat. "I wanted to check in with you 'bout your listing the house," he said, hoping the prompt would be enough.

She sighed, taking a sip of her water. She choked, and Rich moved forward to help but she waved him back. "I'm sorry," she said, regaining her composure. "I been so busy, I think this is the first bit of water I've had in the past two days." She drank another sip, this time keeping her composure, the water running cool and smoothly down her throat. Her stomach grumbled, taking this moment to remind her that she'd not eaten, either.

Rich considered her a moment, then made a quick decision. He stood. "Sincere," he said, drawing on old familiarity and watching her face. "It's obvious you haven't been eating, and you yourself admitted that you haven't been drinking any water. I'm not going to have this conversation with you until you get some food in your belly."

Sincere's chin went up in pride, but Rich headed her off. "I won't take 'no' for an answer. I can't have you sign these papers in this condition, I'd be accused of taking advantage!" He moved, already gathering his things and heading toward the door.

"But—" she said, but he shook his head and held up a hand, forestalling her words. "No 'buts,' I'll be back around eight, tonight, I've got some other thangs to do today. I'll send something over before then for lunch, but I don't much trust you to actually put it in your mouth. So you better be ready when I get here, or I'll drag you out however you are!" He pulled the door shut behind himself, leaving Sincere staring behind him, words of protest on the tip of her tongue.

In the end, she let him go without saying more, too tired to argue even this one. Besides, she knew she needed to get out and she knew she needed to eat. Doing both, and with an old friend, couldn't hurt. For once, she didn't mind being taken care of. And more importantly, just right now she didn't want to be alone.

Not wanting to be too obvious, Rich called instead of going by, though he'd wanted to see her, wanted once more to stroke her skin and kiss her lips. But he also knew the best way to get what he wanted was to give her what she wanted, that much he'd learned about women. He heard the satisfaction in her voice, understood her instructions. Yes, he knew how to please her well.

They ate at Rainey's, by tacit agreement avoiding any discussion of Mama Kinney's death and instead spending the time making small talk and trading gossip. Rich understood she had not been out and about since Mama Kinney's death, and he filled her in on town happenings. He ate heartily, and insisted she do the same, and Sincere surprised herself by putting away of a large, well-done steak, mashed potatoes, and corn on the cob. It was a heavy dinner, but appropriate after two days without food. The only awkwardness was caused when Jenna came to take their order, lingering over them and reaching down to brush her palm against Sincere's hair in sympathy. She barely glanced at Rich, knowing him for a friend and not perceiving any male interest in his presence. "I am *so* sorry," she said simply, and Sincere's throat clogged with emotion.

Jenna herself had dispelled the tense moment, brusquely asking if there was anything else and eyeing Sincere critically when she murmured 'no.' She had nodded to herself, still staring at Sincere, and Sincere was unsurprised when a second plate of food arrived with Jenna's quickly stated "on the house." Jenna had apparently decided she needed to be fed. Sincere looked helplessly at Rich, who pointed with a fork toward her food and just said "Eat!"

"Don't worry 'bout impressin' me, Sincere, I always love a woman who can put some food away," he said.

"I'm not trying to impress you!" Sincere said defensively, not wanting him to read too much into this moment. But suddenly she remembered Miranda and realized that was impossible. He was still too deep into Miranda to notice even if another woman was trying to gain his attention.

For a moment, she thought he was remembering

Miranda, too. His eyes darkened suddenly as he stared absent-mindedly at a square on the patchwork tablecloth. Sincere let the silence stretch, until it was about to break. She reached over, covering his hand with her own.

He shook himself and smiled brightly, looking at her plate. "I see you making progress!" he said, but Sincere just laughed.

"Rich, I'm a woman, not a hippo. No matter how long I haven't ate, I can't put all this food away in one sitting."

He nodded and signaled to Jenna, telling her they needed a couple to-go boxes. Despite Sincere's protest, he shoveled in all of the table's leftovers, telling her she could eat it, over the next couple days.

To her surprise, he did not immediately drive her home. Instead, he took a rambling path, up through some hills, showing her houses that he'd sold and telling her about the quirks of the owners. She paid little attention, confused by the trip and uninterested in his conversation. She knew he was keeping her out, trying to distract her, but she wasn't sure why. This wasn't a date. Maybe he didn't yet want to leave her alone.

When they finally arrived at her house, she tried to talk about the listing but he again side-stepped the question. "We'll have the discussion later, Sincere. Right now, I'm tired and it's late."

"But that was your doing!" she exclaimed, disappointed.

"Don't matter, you went along," he said, and flashed white teeth her way. For a moment, Sincere saw in the moonlight that thing about Rich that had Jenna and Jody and Miranda's panties all ready to drop.

She shook herself, confused, and nodded, anxious to

get back on even footing. She knew he was only trying to help, trying to take care of her. Hadn't everyone in town been doing that of late?

But later, she found herself smiling as she helped herself to more of her leftover dinner from Rainey's. She was at war with herself, simultaneously regretting the loss of her privacy but also enjoying the attention. This was what she knew about Reason, that people here helped and loved one another, and she couldn't hold it against the townsfolk for helping and loving her.

Miranda wasn't satisfied. The house had been a mess, already ransacked before she'd arrived. Sincere had left her clothing and Mama Kinney's items all over the place, half-pulled out of boxes, jumbled and out of place. She had stood a long while, trying to make sense of the disorder, aware before she started that her task was likely futile. She hated that Sincere had already started packing Mama Kinney's things away; she had no idea where to look.

At least there was Rich, and he was turning out more useful than she'd expected. Not only had he kept Sincere away from the house for several hours, he'd given himself a ready excuse to do the same at any other time she might wish. That much was helpful, but Miranda was still unhappy. She had already searched through Mama Kinney's house before it was packed; now she'd searched through her possessions after Sincere had taken them out and organized them. The ring wasn't in the box with Mama Kinney's other jewelry. It wasn't anywhere to be found. She needed more information, intelligence.

Suddenly she smiled, making a quick decision. It was time to tell Rich a little more about what she wanted to know. Rich was just the thing to loosen Sincere's lips, and Miranda was happy she'd kept Rich around, after all.

Moresha wasn't stupid. Or, at least, not the way Miranda seemed to think. She knew enough to know Miranda was scheming, though she had no idea what her scheming was for. Moresha slept light, noting Rich's visits, noting that he remained downstairs every time. Miranda wasn't fucking him, so what was he doing coming around?

Moresha knew Miranda had been sneaking out, and she knew what Miranda was capable of. She had watched Miranda move through the shadows, her body clinging to the night, and seen her enter the house across the street. The old lady's death had startled her when she knew, but she had quickly set aside her surprise. No one but she seemed to know of Miranda's trip across the street the night before Mama Kinney's death, and Moresha would not tell. She loved Miranda beyond that. Besides, she was not a judge. Everyone who knew said Mama Kinney had died of old age, who was she to say different?

One thing troubled Moresha. The path Miranda was on was self-destructive, that much she could see. She knew how this would end, how that the most likely person to be hurt in all this was Miranda, herself. Moresha could not let that happen. Miranda was already fragile; Moresha didn't want her to break. She would have to wait, and pray in the interim. Of all the parties involved, she knew the least.

Moresha couldn't predict how much time she had, but she well knew how to use it. She went about her daily work, washing and preparing vegetables for cooking, setting aside seeds for planting. She set a pot to boiling on the stove, filling it with pasta and combining ingredients in a small pan to make the sauce, all the while planning. She would be close behind Miranda, wherever she went, and one step ahead of everyone else. And if she had to run someone over on her way getting Miranda out of Reason, well, she just hoped to God she didn't leave any identifying skid marks behind on the road.

Chapter 23

Sincere interrupted the insistent ring of the phone on it's fourth round, just before the caller hung up. She'd burned her hand trying to rush to the phone and grabbed a stick of margarine before running out the kitchen. Now she held the margarine to her hand, trying to calm the burn, and muttered an unwelcoming and less than gracious "Yeah?" into the phone.

Lorna was on the other end, and her familiar voice made Sincere remember her manners. She shifted. "Yes, ma'am?"

"Sincere, Rich told me to give you a call, he got some papers drawn up he want you to sign."

"Papers?" Sincere questioned, unsure.

Sincere heard Lorna nod. "I don't know them, he prepared them himself and they in his office, locked, but I assume it's got somethin' to do with the sale of the house."

"Oh," Sincere said, at once feeling stupid and relieved. "Ok, well I can come about four," she said, mentally calculating her time.

"That'd be too early, Sincere, Rich wants to go over these papers with you himself, and he won't come in until after 5." Sincere didn't hear Lorna's disapproval. "He said to ask you to come around 6."

"6?" Sincere echoed, wondering about the lateness.

"Yes, ma'am. If you need to change the date..."

"No," Sincere was suddenly absolute in her resolve. "No, I'll be there."

"Good!" Lorna said, and hung up. For a moment, Sincere stared at the phone in her hand, smeared yellow with margarine. She wasn't sure what to make of it, but she also knew it was time to handle business. She would not shy from this transaction.

When she arrived at his office promptly at six, though, Rich was locking the door on his way out. Sincere made a sound of protest and Rich turned around, startled but not surprised. "I got yo paperwork here, Sincere, but you already know I'm going to insist on dinner first."

Sincere sighed. Yes, she had known, had even dressed for it. For whatever reason, this man seemed intent on taking care of her. She had already determined to give in.

They traveled together in Rich's car, which sported a fresh, bright coat of white paint. Sincere hugged her coat tighter around her breasts, knowing they'd get to their destination before the car would heat up. In just minutes, they were there.

This early in the night, the Hallelujah Club was just a bar with a full-service menu and music playing somewhere in the background while whatever band that would be playing later that night fine-tuned their instruments. Sometimes the band might treat customers to a couple of warm-up songs, but they saved their best for when the drinks would begin to flow, loosening pockets and wallets. Sincere steeled herself, readying for the noise and crush and laughter she knew would be soon to come.

Rich hesitated before opening the door and Sincere thought he needed reassurance. She wasn't ready, but she would act like she was. Fake it 'til you make it, she thought, shrugging within, and moving forward just slightly. It was enough. The two of them went inside, pausing a moment by the door to let their eyes adjust. When they did, Sincere saw that there were just a few patrons milling about, smoking and beginning their evening drinking, and the stage was empty. There would be no band tonight. Sincere's shoulders slumped, relieved, but also curiously disappointed.

Rich reached across her shoulders to remove her coat and Sincere smiled in gratitude, thankful for the help. The dim light inside felt less taxing on her eyes, which she knew were red from a combination of crying and lack of sleep.

Rich glanced briefly at his watch as they sat down and his eyes panned the room. Sincere knew she was not the focus of his attention tonight, and that was okay with her. If she thought about it, they were both caught in a sort of mourning, he for his love and her for Mama Kinney. Two sides'a the same coin, both a sort of death. Sincere was at once empathetic, and for just a moment she considered opening the conversation up about Miranda. But she knew better. She didn't know much about men, but Mama Kinney had told her more than once they don't tend to like when others see their vulnerability. And love always exposed a sort of vulnerability. She decided on a middle ground.

"My daddy died here," she said, staring at the sign above the side door that was brightly marked "EXIT."

She'd caught Rich's attention, but the change in him was subtle. "Oh?" he said lightly, as if he hadn't known.

Sincere nodded. "I was barely old enough for it to matter, barely old enough to remember him." She smiled a moment, wistful, considering her only significant memories of her father. "He was a vain man, I think. I know used to die his hair black, because I remember seeing some gray hairs still left in his beard and his mustache. I didn't see it at first, but Jean pointed it out to me..." she trailed off, not sure she had wanted to mention Jean.

"I remember," Rich said quietly, unsettled by the memory for some reason he couldn't quite pinpoint.

Sincere looked up at him sharply. "You do?" and her look was accusatory.

Rich stumbled, his words uncertain, feeling her out. The bartender approached, waiting tables this early in this night, and the tension was broken. They placed their orders, each of them confused by their own thoughts. Rich wasn't sure he wanted her to continue. "Anyhow, I don't remember much more than that. He wasn't never around much when I was small, not until he took up with Jean's mama. Of course, neither Jean or I really knew about that back then, we were so happy just to have time to play together. Mama Kinney didn't never want me playing with her, otherwise, so outside of school that was really the only time we got to be friends. She was more real to me than my daddy."

Quiet stretched out between them, the bar beginning to come to life. A few more people wandered in. Rich wondered aloud about their food. Sincere was still caught by her memory. "I miss Jean, sometimes, Rich, I do. I miss her more than I ever did my daddy. When he was buried, my mama gave me his wedding ring to remember him, but truth be told, I've never really looked at it and thought of him. When I touch it, when I hold it, all I think about is her. How she left when my daddy did, both of them at once."

But something else had caught Rich's eye now, and he leaned forward now, his gaze narrowed on her breasts. Sincere flushed, embarrassed, conscious that she'd been fondling the ring that lay snuggled between her breast as she spoke. She dropped it now and looked away, regretting that she hadn't worn her white turtleneck sweater. She knew the skin of her breasts were displayed above the neckline, as if she'd wanted him to see. But the blouse she'd worn tonight, though a little less modest than her usual dress, had been a gift from Mama Kinney.

Looking back at him now, Sincere leaned quickly back in her seat, shocked to find his hand reaching out toward her breast. He looked up at her face, not reading it at all, and Sincere could see he was miles away in his thoughts. "Rich!" she said, swallowing hard.

He stood abruptly, uncertainly. "Sincere, just gimme a minute," he finally said, and rushed off toward the bathroom, leaving Sincere behind, bewildered and confused. Sincere sat there unhappily, feeling herself, her emotions. There had been surprise when he eyed her breasts, yes, but also a sort of heat. Sincere wasn't sure how to interpret that. There had never been heat before in her dealings with Rich, that sort of awareness of being a woman in the presence of a man. There had never been that sort of heat before between her and *any* man. But Rich?!?!?

A few feet away, Rich slammed the payphone with frustration. He knew where Miranda was, knew before dialing the number that she wouldn't answer Sincere's phone. But he had to try anyway. Still, he was plagued by self-doubt. What if the ring wasn't the one she was looking for? What if he was making a mistake? He was following Miranda's instructions, keeping Sincere out of the house one more time so she could search, and he wasn't supposed to return her any time soon. But *he knew!* This was the ring she'd been looking for, and she'd never find it if it stayed here on Sincere's neck. He wasn't sure what to do. If he brought Sincere back early and it wasn't the ring she wanted, he might blow his last chance to get back into her graces.

He returned to the table with purpose and threw several bills onto it. "Sincere, I got to go," he said, already going to get her coat. Sincere just stood, even more confused now. Whatever awareness she'd had of him as a man had apparently not afflicted him. He was all business now, abrupt movements and quick resolve. His hand on the small of her back propelled her toward the door.

"Rich!" she exclaimed, putting her hand up against the doorframe in protest. He stopped short of forcing her out, although she could see his impatience written plainly across his face. "Our coats, Rich. And what about our food?!?"

Rich looked at her, and it was as if he were seeing her for the first time in several minutes. His eyes softened, but then his gaze strayed downwards to where her necklace caught the dim light of the room. "I'll get your coat, Sincere, the food'll have to be. I promise I'll make it up to you one day, but I got to get you home right *NOW!*" he said, moving her forward out of the door before the sentence was finished.

In the car, Sincere felt her stomach grumble in protest, but she ignored it, knowing she had no choice. She sighed deeply, knowing Rich's rush served her own purposes, as well. She needed some time alone to think, but at least now she had something more than Mama Kinney's death to think about.

Sincere let her head fall back on the seat, her eyes closed, her inner thoughts anything but restful. The horn blared loudly in her driveway. She startled, her eyes flying open as Rich stopped the car. She looked at him in inquiry. "Sorry," he mumbled, and shrugged. "An accident." He leaned forward to get something off the floor under his legs, and his shoulder pressed again against the horn, this time a little longer. "Rich!" Sincere rebuked, exasperated. "You gone wake the neighbors!"

"Sorry, sorry," he said, but Sincere noted he'd come up empty-handed. Anxious now to get back inside, she reached for the door handle.

"Wait!" Rich said sharply, and Sincere looked at him. Suddenly she softened, sensing something desperate in his manner, realizing. Maybe he was trying to gain Miranda's attention. She smiled now, more patiently, willing to play along.

They lingered outside some moments more, discussing the sale of the house, the paperwork that had to be signed. The natural light of day had long since died away, and Sincere knew anyone observing their interaction inside the car would not know the truth of the chastity of their dealings. For a moment, Sincere hoped maybe seeing her with Rich would make Miranda pay attention to her, too. The loneliness of living without Mama Kinney would perhaps be eased if Miranda would come to share it. Suddenly, Sincere longed for a shoulder to cry on. Throwing caution to the wind, she invited Rich inside.

He stumbled over his response, uncertain, but she smiled softly, encouragingly. "If you really wanna give her a show, Rich, you gotta do it right!" and with that she was quickly outside the car.

Rich scrambled to keep up, and caught her as she was putting the key into the lock. "Wait!' Rich said again, grabbing her elbow. Sincere turned with some exasperation, but her attention was caught by a movement in the bushes.

"Did you see that?" she said, and Rich didn't turn around. Quite out of nowhere, his lips were suddenly hard on her own, his arm unyielding around her waist, and Sincere wholly forgot what she had thought she'd seen.

For a moment the kiss was awkward, dry. Sincere's mouth refused to open, a thousand shocked thoughts flying through her mind at once. But then it was as if they both became aware of the fabric between her breasts and his own, and then his tongue flickered out questioningly at the corner of her lips. She softened, forgetting about Miranda and Mama Kinney and the house and her troubles. Forgetting, too, that this was Rich holding her, kissing her.

She yielded, her defenses down, her body needing to be touched. Her thigh rose softly against his own, her hips parting without warning, her vulnerability exposed. He seemed caught as well, his hand moving up her back, the other hand feeling along her belly, moving insistently up to hold the weight of her breast. She moaned and his manner became suddenly more aggressive, more insistent. His keys dropped to the ground, and the sound of it rang loudly in Sincere's ears. Suddenly aware again, she pulled away. After an initial resistance, Rich's arms fell, releasing her.

They stood awkwardly in the dark shadows of her porch. Sincere wasn't entirely sure what to do next. He'd been kissing her to make Miranda jealous, Sincere knew, but somehow the kiss had gotten out of hand. Sincere knew he was probably as confused as she. She longed suddenly for Mama Kinney, the only person who could have helped her sort this situation out, and she gasped as she felt choking sobs making their way up through her breasts, felt them stick in her throat.

Rich moved forward, reaching out to her, but she quickly brushed him away, forcing the door open and

291

quickly shut behind her before he could fully react. She leaned hard against the door, falling to the floor, giving full reign to the sobs bursting forth, the grief that was somehow strangely mixed in with this new awareness of her sexuality.

On the other side of the door, in the shadows of the night, Rich stood confused, uncertain, aware but not caring so much about the presence he sensed behind him. He tried to gather himself, his thoughts, but was interrupted by the caustic sound of her whisper, loud in the night's quiet. *"That was NOT what I asked you to do!"*

Rich whispered too, trying to apologize, to appease this woman. *"I didn't mean it, baby, you know I only want you!"*

In the dark, he felt more than heard her laugh, but her voice was still upset. *"I don't give a damn if you sleep with that broad, but I TOLD you to keep her OUT of the house, and instead you brought her BACK!"*

"Baby, though, I had a good reason! I tried to call you but you didn't answer."

"You know good and damned well I wasn't going to answer that woman's phone. Are you ignorant, or just plain stupid?!?!? Ugh!" and she moved quietly off Sincere's porch, her steps light and sure, missing every creaking board. He followed closely behind her, trying to match her movements and failing. But then, Sincere already knew he was out here. Miranda was the one who needed to hide.

"I told you!" he said, his whisper a little louder. "I had a good reason!"

Suddenly she turned to him, and there was not enough room in the small space between them. He stepped back. "I don't much give a damn what reason you *think* you had, I didn't *tell* you to think, I *told* you what I wanted you to *do!*" she said, already annoyed and regretting him. She stared at him, waiting for his acquiescence. Her work wasn't done, and she might have need of him yet. But she knew better than to use someone who insisted on having their own mind.

Rich hesitated a moment, in the cold still aware of the heat of Sincere's response. He had known Sincere since childhood and what he knew about Miranda was that she was dangerous. She would hurt anyone who stood in her way. He sensed that, and knew his next words would decide Sincere's fate. But he also knew where his loyalty lay.

"She has the ring," he said, his head low. "She has the ring, it's hanging around her neck. She wore it to dinner tonight."

Miranda was so quiet, Rich wasn't sure she understood. He rushed on. "The ring," he said, "White gold with a "Z" through the middle, three diamonds on either side. That's what you said. She told me they gave the ring to her after her father's death, to remember him by. Now that I think on it, I've always seen her wear it." Here he stumbled, aware he'd made a misstep. "Well, I didn't know that was it. I never really looked on it. Matter fact, I'm not sure it wasn't always different rings, it coulda been. Matter fact, I'm not really sure that's the ring after all…" he trailed off, unsure what else to say.

"It's the ring," Miranda said simply, calculating, accepting his conclusion. Truth be told, she didn't remember much about the ring, just it twinkling when her mama help it up into the light. "Thas gold, baby," she'd said. "Real gold, worth a few dollars, and real diamonds, too, not like those shit wannabe diamonds yo daddy tried to give me." The brief memory of Reba swaying in the weak light, holding the ring and dancing without music on the same linoleum that was later stained with her blood, caught Miranda off-guard.

She thought out loud. "Question is, how I'm going to get it."

Rich could hear the steel of her voice and a coldness passed between them that had nothing to do with the night air. He knew enough to be afraid for Sincere. "I can get it," he volunteered, "just give me a few days."

"No," she said. "I will get it," and she smiled. "Tonight."

Rich looked on helplessly behind her as she disappeared into the night, not knowing what to do. He saw the shadows move between Sincere's house and the house across the street, and he knew Sincere was okay for now. But he wasn't sure how long before Miranda came back. Suddenly he remembered Mama Kinney.

He got into his car reluctantly, sitting in the silent darkness, unhappily reviewing his options until he saw the curtains twitch, and a beam of light fell across the hood of his car. It was quickly gone, but he knew Sincere was probably wondering why he was still out here in her driveway, an hour after she'd gone inside. With no other choice, Rich started the ignition and slowly backed out, not knowing where he was going, so long as it was away from here.

Chapter 24

Some hours later, the shadows outside Sincere's house were again moving in the wind. Quietly asleep, Sincere didn't hear Miranda slip into the house, and wasn't aware of her feet padding lightly through the hallway. In her sleep, she felt a weight against her breasts, a dark shadow over her eyes, and she whimpered a little, her fingers reaching out to clench against the sheets. "Mama?" she murmured, and shook awake.

She got up, padding softly to the kitchen, not caring about the coldness beneath her bare feet, the wind whispering on her legs. She'd barely had the strength after her cry to get dressed for bed, and instead had settled for removing everything except her blouse and underwear, knowing the heavy blankets would be enough to keep her warm.

In the kitchen, she poured herself a glass of tap water, not bothering with ice, and took her water into the living room, to sit in the dark. She found Mama Kinney's chair without stumbling and sat heavily, knowing she would not go back to sleep. She knew, too, there was a Bible in the drawer of the end table next to this chair, she had but to tug the chain of a lamp to find solace, relief from her pain. But she did not.

She sighed in the dark. "I think I hate you, Mama," she said, and at that moment it was almost true. Almost. She couldn't get past her feeling that Mama Kinney had left her, willingly. She had always expected Mama Kinney to fight death, to force it away so she could stay with Sincere a little while longer. Instead, she'd left years before her time, quietly slipping away without notice, without a fight. The thought sat bitterly in Sincere's chest.

"Wish you'da left some explanation, though. Just a note or something. I don't know why you did this to me, Mama, why you makin' me sell this house. Why you takin' everything away from me. It's like you don't want me to have nothin' left of you." A dry heave worked its way through her chest, but Sincere had no tears left. She'd been crying daily since Mama Kinney's death, but suddenly she knew there would be no more. She was out of tears.

There was a whisper in the dark and Sincere suddenly looked up, peering into the darkness, a chill creeping across her skin. "Who's there?" she said, her fingers finding the chain on the lamp.

No one answered, and after a moment Sincere relaxed again, laughing to herself crazily, hysterically. She held up her glass in quiet salute, acknowledging the dead. "For a minute, I thought you'd answer me," she said. "That'da scared me shitless, even if you are my godmama." She laughed again, putting the glass down on the table and moving quickly to the window. She wanted to see the moonlight glowing on the grass.

Instead, she saw Jody's car parked discretely across the street, a couple houses down. She frowned, confused. Why was Jody's car in this neighborhood at this time of night?

The car eked slowly forward, and Sincere suddenly realized it wasn't parked at all. Just, the lights were out. Behind the wheel, in the moonlight, she could just about make out a man's shape. *Rich!*

She laughed again, this time without the hint of hysteria. Shaking her head, she made her way back to the bedroom and found her clothes where she'd thrown them, across the trunk at the foot of Mama Kinney's old bed. Leaving her smart pumps, she instead pulled on a pair of woolen socks and slipped her feet into a pair of Mama Kinney's slippers. Not wanting to alert Rich, she made her way through the small passage she had used as a child, when Miranda had been Jean and Jean had been forbidden. Mama Kinney had never known how often Jean had spent the night, Sincere had seen to that.

Rich jumped at the sound of Sincere's nails against the passenger window and sharply stepped on the brakes. The door was opened, and Sincere slipped inside before he could refuse. "Rich," she said, and smiled gently at him. "You are never gone get the girl if she knows she's already got you!"

Uncertain how to respond, Rich just looked at her dumbly, confused. Sincere jerked a thumb toward Miranda's house. "I seen you following her before, Rich, you gotta cut that out. And sitting outside her house? You think just cause you in Jody's car she don't know it's you?"

Rich just stared at her and muttered a curse under his breath. Sincere sighed. "Pull up in my driveway, Rich. That way, she'll think you've come to visit me. After the way we carried on earlier, that outta help your cause a little." She smiled at him.

Rich smiled back, relieved. He hadn't been sure how to go about protecting Sincere without pissing Miranda off, but this opportunity was perfect. If Miranda looked out, she'd see Jody's car and know Sincere had a visitor. Meanwhile, once he was inside, Rich could think how to go about getting that ring. His gaze dropped, but he could see nothing in the darkness of the car.

They were discreet when they entered the house, quiet. Sincere was grateful for the company, reluctant though he'd seemed. She didn't really want to sit alone, hearing shadows in the dark. And she knew she could help Rich on this. For all his experience, the man didn't understand women much at all.

Comfortable now, lighthearted, even, Sincere's movements through the house were more certain now. She went back to Mama Kinney's bedroom where she'd been sleeping and called to him over her shoulder. "Rich, I gotta warn you, it's still the middle of the night and I can't say how long I'll be good company. I just can't," she said, changing as she spoke. Unwilling to be uncomfortable, she removed her clothes but put on a heavy flannel nightgown, just to maintain her modesty.

She rejoined Rich in the living room where she'd left him, and he was seated in her old chair. She laughed to herself, shaking her head.

"Mama Kinney'd be beside herself now to see me in here half-dressed with a man in the middle of the night!" she said, finding her way back to Mama Kinney's chair to sit.

Rich smiled now, too, at ease. "Would she now?" Rich asked, just because he knew it was his turn to speak.

Sincere nodded. "She was always going on about how I needed to get myself a life and all, a man. I know everybody thought she was just a good old lady, Rich, but somma the stuff she said behind closed doors 'd make you blush." Sincere got into her story-telling. "Right before her death, she was nagging me about this new doctor at the hospital, every time she saw a good-looking single man she'd be at it, Rich. Even you!"

"Me?" he asked.

Sincere nodded. "Yep. She'd told me more than once that I outta have a go at you. I mean, she didn't really think we'd make a good couple, just said you'd be a good l-" Sincere blushed suddenly, cutting off what she'd been about to say. She reached for her water.

But Rich was starting to enjoy himself. "I'd be a good what, Sincere?" he asked, unwilling to let it go.

"Well!" Sincere said and got up, moving restlessly through the room to the window. She peered out again into the dark, but this time the street in moonlight looked familiar, everything as expected. Sincere looked up at the house across the street.

"Oh, I'm not gone let it go that easy, Sincere, I wanna know what she said!" Rich said, but Sincere shushed him.

"C'mere," she said, fanning her hand to usher him toward her. "Look! I think it's her!"

Rich suddenly remembered his purpose, rushing forward to the window and pushing the curtains closed again and pulling Sincere off to one side.

"What'd you do that for?" she snapped at him, still whispering. "The goal is to *let* her see us, *that's* how you get the girl, Rich!"

"Why are we whispering?" Rich asked, and now it was Sincere's turn to be confused.

She laughed again and this time she spoke normally. "I don't have the faintest idea!" she said. "I guess sometimes I still feel like she's here, listening in the night."

Rich looked around, and he could feel the presence, too. His eyes went automatically to the shadow of Sincere's neck, searching for the ring. His hand followed his eyes, brushing aside the collar of her shirt.

Startled, Sincere stepped back. She stood looking at him a moment, quiet, then made a decision. She found his hand between them and with her own guided it back up to her neck.

Rich wasn't sure what he was doing. His fingers traced the thinness of her collarbone, and his body stepped forward of its own volition to fill the space between them. His palm found the softness of her breast, and even the thick flannel between their skins did not cool the heat.

"Sincere," he said quietly. "If you want this to stop, you goin' to have to tell me."

Her own body moved forward in answer, offering herself to him. She knew within herself she was tired of being alone. Rich groaned suddenly and crushed her to him, giving in. His hand became more insistent, finding the buttons of her nightshirt, clumsy in his haste.

"Wait," she said, and moved away, pulling him after her. They found the bed easily, and she removed her nightshirt herself while he removed his own clothing. Suddenly shy, Sincere was glad she hadn't turned on the light. His hands found her breasts again, now bare, in the darkness, and for a second time he kissed her deeply.

Neither one had the presence of thought to get under the blankets and they fell back lengthwise across the bed, the pillows at their side. Sincere reveled in the feeling of Rich's hard body against her own, and her hands stroked his shoulders restlessly, wanting. His tongue invaded her mouth and her hips rose suddenly from the bed, pushing up against his own unconsciously. Rich moaned deeply, and their kiss became more urgent.

He touched her, his fingers parting her gently, and Sincere felt a wave flooding over her. She couldn't stop herself. She bit his lip, lightly, then turned away, the sheets cool against the warmth in her cheeks. Her hips pushed up and down, up and down against his hand until they abruptly paused, still high in the air, and she felt a wet river flow suddenly from that secret place between her thighs. She hid her face in the pillows, unable to stop.

When her hips had stilled, his hand began to move again, his wrist brushing lightly back and forth where he cupped her, his finger slipping delicately inside.

"No," Sincere, said, pushing at his hand now, but he didn't stop. Instead, his mouth found her own again and he whispered against her lips, "Don't stop me, baby, please." Confused, Sincere let him kiss her again, and felt a tension building again inside.

He covered her with his body and his fingers opened her. At first, Sincere wasn't sure what was happening. Or maybe she was too lost in the feeling. But her eyes flew open and her hands pushed against his chest when she finally understood what she felt inside her was no longer his finger.

"Rich!" she said, but it was too late. He stared at her, confused too by the tightness around him, the constriction he'd encountered. Suddenly he understood. "Sincere!" he said, his voice thick with surprise and passion.

But he could feel her pulsing around him, and the tightness of her body was an irresistible sensation. He knew in an instant he would regret it, but he couldn't stop himself from pumping inside of her, his body searching for release. When he found it, it was overwhelming, and he cried out his ecstasy in the dark, even as he felt his seed release within her. His weight collapsed against her.

Moments passed before he could hear anything over the beating of his heart, but then he groped for a light, his lips turning downward in dismay. "Sincere!" he said, and his fingers found the lamp switch, but she turned away from him. "Baby, I'm so sorry. If I'da known- I'm so sorry!" he said, his hands reaching out to her, trying to stop her from crying.

She let him pull her to him without resistance and buried her face in his chest. He felt no tears against his skin, only the rapid movements of her breasts as she gulped for air and cried. He didn't know what to do, aware he'd made a cake of the situation. Here she was, a twenty-some-odd-year-old virgin mourning over her godmother, and he'd come in and taken more than she had offered. He felt awful.

Her breathing became gradual, normal, punctuated by light hiccups, and Rich knew she'd fallen asleep. He lay beside her in the dark, thinking, unsure of what to do next when he heard Miranda speak to him out of the dark.

"Well, that was…interesting. To watch, anyway."

Rich sat bolt upright, then stilled when Sincere began to move against him, shushing her like he would a baby. Miranda laughed softly, and her voice had travelled. "Don't worry," she said, "She won't wake."

"You don't know that," Rich whispered, gently pushing Sincere away from his body.

He felt, rather than saw, Miranda's shrug. "It doesn't matter, anyway. Where's my ring?"

"Your ring?" Rich echoed, feeling slow. "Uh, it's not on her."

The room was quiet for a moment, then a lamp threw soft light across brown skin. Rich grabbed at a sheet, embarrassed. "Don't bother," Miranda said flatly, "I've already seen what you got."

Still, Rich was ashamed she'd witnessed him making love to Sincere. All at once, he realized she didn't care, and likely never again would. Sadness crept into his chest at the thought, the knowledge that it was surely over between them. If seeing him make love to another

302

woman could not make Miranda jealous, she had no feeling for him left.

A thought occurred. "Wait...how long have you been in here?" he asked, almost hopeful.

"Long enough," she said and smiled. "I got here before you."

Rich registered confusion amidst his fading hope. He remembered the twitching of the curtain in the bedroom upstairs, across the street. He frowned, realizing Moresha had been watching. *For what?!?!?*

The dim light revealed the slender column of Sincere's throat, bare of any jewelry. Rich stared, then looked around for a jewelry box but saw none. He looked to Miranda, dismay filling his eyes.

"Wake her up," Miranda said, but Rich hesitated, unwilling. He was beginning to realize there was no future with Miranda, but his feelings toward Sincere, especially after this night, were less definitive.

He gently nudged Sincere, whispering her name.

Miranda moved without warning, striking Sincere across her face. Sincere sat up in the bed, sputtering, and looked in confusion toward Rich, first, then Miranda.

Suddenly she grabbed at a sheet, remembering she was naked. Her eyes focused on Miranda. "Get out," she said, but Rich wondered if she was speaking to him, Miranda, or them both.

Miranda just ignored her and sat down on a small chair near the window. "So glad you're awake, Sincere. We really weren't having much fun without you," Miranda's eyes stared directly into hers.

Sincere cleared her throat and looked to Rich. A shadow crossed her eyes but was quickly hidden. "This has gone too far, Rich. Y'all need to go."

"Yes'm," Rich said quickly, and stood, and narrowly

stopped himself from falling after he stumbled over the blanket he'd wrapped around his body.

"Sit down, Rich," Miranda said, and he did. "We're not goin' anywhere, Sincere, not until I get what I came for."

Sincere rolled her eyes. "Ok, I have had enough of this! Rich, I was happy to help but this is too much. It's late and I'm going back to sleep. If the two of you will recall, I just lost my godmother. Some goddamned privacy would be much appreciated!" Her voice had risen in anger and near hysteria, the emotion of the night hitting her all at once. She turned her back on them, gathering the sheets more tightly around her naked body, and determinedly closed her eyes.

Suddenly Miranda's face twisted in anger and she moved again, grabbing Sincere by her hair and yanking her head hard across Rich's lap. "Don't you turn your back on me," she screamed, "Don't you dare dismiss me or you'll end up like your bitch godmother!"

Sincere's hands flailed behind her, grabbing at Miranda, and the sheet dropped around her waist. Tears of pain made her eyes look glassy, unfocused. Miranda suddenly dropped her hold with a brutal shove, and Sincere's body went crashing to the floor in a tangle of bed sheets and brown skin. She held her head, backing against the wall. Now her attention was caught by something Miranda had said, and the accusation shone as brightly as the tears in her eyes.

Miranda actually smiled, understanding the question before it was asked. "You wanna know what happened now, how Mama Kinney died? You wanna know why I killed her?"

Terror and something else flashed now in Sincere's eyes. Rich stood again in the space between Sincere and

Miranda, trying to stop what he knew was about to happen. "Just leave it be, Miranda," Rich said, holding up his hands toward the woman. "Leave it all alone."

"No," Sincere said, speaking behind him, and he turned to her, wanting to convince her, too. She looked him in the eye with absolute focus. "I wanna know. Everything."

When he turned back to Miranda, still pleading, she was smiling. Suddenly, Rich saw the coldness in her heart and wondered how he had ever thought to love her. There was nothing loveable about her, not in this moment.

But Miranda began the story in a place they'd not expected. "Mama Kinney took my mama's ring, Sincere. Oh, what, you didn't know?" she asked in response to the widening of Sincere's eyes.

"Yes, Sincere, your sainted *godmother* stole my mother's jewelry from off her neck when she was dying! That's how good Mama Kinney was. And then, when I got to town, she *refused* to give it to me! I came here night after night, told her to give me back my mother's ring, *my ring*, and she actually refused!" Miranda stood now, pacing between the walls, and Rich was afraid of her agitation. He didn't really understand what she was saying, this story about her mother and Mama Kinney, but he understood her. He looked at Sincere, hoping she was on guard, but she stared at Miranda transfixed, her eyes seeming far away.

"You were there," Sincere said simply, all at once understanding.

"Of course I was there! I watched my mama die, Sincere, watched my daddy shoot her. Of course I was there! And I watched Mama Kinney come in and squat down and take my mama's ring! Like she had no shame, no shame a'tall!" Miranda's voice got louder and more insistent with every word.

"It wasn't her ring," Sincere said, quietly, and Miranda stopped her agitated pacing to stare. "It wasn't her ring," Sincere said again, this time louder.

Miranda's eyes narrowed to dangerous slits. "You calling me a liar?" she asked, incredulous. "It was my mama's ring, she used to wear it around her neck."

"No," Sincere said. "It was my daddy's ring. He gave it to yo mama when they were havin' an affair."

"That's a lie!" Miranda said, and moved toward Sincere to strike her again, but Sincere moved just as quickly this time and met her partway, her hand catching Miranda's wrist in midair. She twisted it just a bit, and it was Miranda's turn to register pain in her eyes.

"Don't you put your hands on me, Jean, don't you do it again! I will give you what you want, but you gone learn to ask for it nicely. You've turned into a selfish bitch, but I'm still the same person you knew back then. And you will leave here empty-handed if you try to force me, you hear?" Without taking her eyes from Miranda, Sincere spoke harshly to Rich. "Turn the light on," she said, and he moved to accommodate her request.

But when he would have moved back, she spoke again. "Rich, turn it back off. No, on again." Rich thought for a moment she was crazy, but her eyes never left Miranda. Now he finally moved to his clothing, not knowing or understanding what was between the women but suddenly feeling exposed.

"Sit down," she said, and released Miranda with a slight push, causing the smaller woman to fall back into her chair. Miranda's anger could be felt, but she was wise enough to keep quiet. Sincere had long since dropped her protective sheet and now stood, the aureoles of her breasts bounced slightly with each breath she took.

"I'm gonna tell you the truth, Jean, because I think you need to hear it."

"Miranda," Miranda corrected, but Sincere just looked at her. "You will always be Jean to me," she said, and a vague memory crossed through Rich's mind. "Although I see now that you never were the girl I thought I knew. Yo mama and my daddy were having an affair all those years ago, that's what they were doin' while you and I were outside playin' in the yard."

"That's a lie!" Miranda repeated, but Sincere just looked at her with pity in her eyes. "Jean- Miranda, whatever, you too old not to understand these things now. That's the whole reason why yo daddy killed her, he found out about the affair."

"No!" Miranda said, but Sincere shook her head, and spoke slowly, as if explaining to a small child. "He killed my daddy too. They found his body the next day after your parents died. It's true, Miranda, and you know it is."

Miranda shook her head as if to clear it. "The ring..." she began.

"Was my daddy's. He gave it to yo mama. I don't really know why, but Mama Kinney musta gone back there to get it. I don't know how it happened; all I know is, in the end they gave it to me."

Miranda's eyes snapped up, looking into her own. "I want it back, Sincere," she said. "Now."

"Don't you see, Miranda, you killed a good woman for nothin'! All because you still livin' in the past."

"I'm living in the past?" Miranda screamed, and stood. "I'm living in the past? You, Sincere, you never left the past! You never left this house or this town or your godmama! All these people here, they hated me! But you, you were supposed to be my friend and yet you loved them! You loved them more than you ever loved me!"

"That's not true, Jean! I looked for you—"

"I wasn't hard to find! You never looked for me, Sincere, you forgot me the moment I left. My mama, my daddy...I lost everybody who ever loved me. These people, this town, Mama Kinney, she took everything from me! But I paid her back. In the end, I win."

Sincere had had enough. Screaming now, she rushed at Miranda in anger, her hands encircling the smaller woman's throat. Rich moved too slowly, and his weight, alone, was not enough to break her hold.

Miranda began to black out, losing consciousness, a lone thought flitting across her mind: *was this what Mama Kinney had felt right before she died?*

At once, Moresha was there, forcing Sincere's fingers apart and her arms behind her. Awareness began to overtake Sincere, clearing the haze. She realized how close she'd come to killing Miranda, and her arms were suddenly limp at her side.

Moresha dropped her where she stood, understanding that the rage was gone now and the danger had passed. She rushed to Miranda, while Rich tried to gather Sincere against his chest. Miranda's eyes were glassy, unfocused, and her fingers were still desperately scratching at her neck. "Stop," Moresha said, and tried to still them with her own. Tenderly, she raised them and kissed Miranda's hand, then bent down further and kissed her neck. Miranda's breathing was less harsh now, returning to regular, and her eyes had focused on Moresha's face.

"Stop," Moresha said again, and this time kissed her gently on her lips, her palm caressing Miranda's cheek.

Suddenly, a small green box struck Miranda in her

chest. "Get her out of here," Sincere commanded Moresha, but Miranda didn't move. "It's in there," Sincere said, and nodded at the box. "The ring, the truth. The past. All of it's in there. Now that you got it, you can get your ass outta Reason, too. Ain't no reason to stay around, now you got what you came for, Jean."

Moresha opened the box, a small diamond winking at her in the dim light before she snapped it quickly shut. She nodded at Sincere, accepting what she did not understand, and helped Miranda to her feet. There was no more protest from Miranda now, and she felt tiny in Moresha's arms.

"Get out," Sincere screamed after them, and Moresha knew she meant more than just her home.

When they were gone, Sincere collapsed against the wall, giving free reign to her emotions now and the tears that had itched at her eyes. "I had hoped we could be friends again," she said, shaking her head, knowing now their friendship had ended before it had begun. In one night, she'd lost for good her best friend and all her childish illusions. Still, she'd gained, too. The bout of mourning passed quickly. She'd already shed too many tears.

Rich spoke hesitantly into the quiet. "Sincere?" he said, questioningly, unsure of the ground on which he stood.

Sincere's smile was tentative, but genuine. She stood now in the room, hugging the sheet under her arms, covered. "It's ok, Rich. It's ok. I knew when I welcomed you into my bed that you still had feelings for her. Let's just both forget the whole thing ever happened," she said, and stuck out one hand for him to shake. "Deal?"

But he didn't immediately reach forward. "No, Sincere, I'm sorry but—"

309

"Rich!" she said, exasperated. "I do *not* want to do this tonight. I'm tired and I'm drained and a lot has happened. So can we just put this all behind us and let it go? Please!"

Reluctantly, he took her hand, shaking it once, twice, but without emphasis. She seemed satisfied with this. He let himself out, knowing there was nothing else to do. Through an opening in the curtains, he saw a light flicker off in the small peach house across the street. He knew she was watching, but for once didn't care.

When he'd gone, Sincere lay in bed with all the lights on, too rattled by the evening's events to sleep. She wasn't sure she could trust everything with Miranda was settled, but she was fairly certain she could trust Moresha to keep a better reign on her, at least for tonight. Tomorrow was anybody's guess.

She dozed fitfully until morning, not feeling safe, but comforted nonetheless. Mama Kinney had not just abandoned her, she'd realized. The thought filled her heart with a certain measure of peace.

Chapter 25

Not a week later, Sincere came home from the grocery store, her arms laden with brown paper bags, to the sound of metal pounding against wood. For a moment she was concerned, but she knew there was nothing to fear in daylight. She followed the sound to where Rich knelt down in the grass on the side of the house, a nail held loosely between his lips and a hammer and another nail in his hands. He positioned the nail in the wood and brought the hammer down hard, narrowly missing his finger. He looked up when he heard Sincere call his name. "When you get done," she said, balancing a paper bag on her hip, "Come on in and get a glass of water," and he understood her thanks. He had been uncomfortable knowing that this passage existed, and that Miranda could come again into her house while she was sleeping. As she turned and walked back to the front door, he glanced up at the house across the street. But now he could no longer feel her presence, watching him or otherwise. He wondered if the link between them had been broken, or if she just was not there.

Minutes later, Rich met Sincere in the house and sat down at her table, a glass filled with ice and lemonade she'd just freshly made for him sitting before him. "You know it ain't the time yet for lemons and lemonade, Rich," she'd said when she handed it to him, "So you'll just have to make do with the powder stuff."

Rich had made a face, playfully, and considered Sincere when she swatted at him. He realized now he'd never seen her before. Well, he'd seen her but he hadn't really *seen* her. Not as a woman. He cleared his throat and gestured with a nod of his head. "They ain't moved out

311

yet?" he asked, trying to sound casual but already knowing the answer.

"I don't concern myself with them, Rich. If you want to know Miranda's doings, you'll have to go ask her yourself," Sincere said, washing vegetables in the sink.

But Rich insisted. "She must know you could turn her in to the police."

"But I won't," Sincere said, and turned to him. "And you won't either." It was a command.

Rich nodded absentmindedly, already knowing he wouldn't. "Still..."

"The past is the past, Rich, whether it's been a month or twenty years. Mama Kinney don't need vindication and neither do I," Sincere said, and turned back to her greens.

"But Sincere—" he said, persisting.

"You finished?" she asked, and snatched his glass just as he was bringing it to his lips.

Empty-handed, knowing Sincere's impatience, Rich stared down at the table, deciding to be honest. "Sincere," he said, "I worry about you."

Looking at his head bent toward the table, Sincere softened and walked back to where he sat. She handed his glass to him and commanded his attention with a hand placed softly on his back. "Don't be, Rich, I'm a grown woman. I know what I'm doing. I *am* Mama Kinney's goddaughter, you know she ain't raised me to be no fool."

He changed tactics and topics. "You not gone sell the house?" he asked, getting to the other reason he'd come. Lorna had told him Sincere called that day and said as much.

"Oh," Sincere said, smiling. "Deacon says I don't have to. I told him about the threats Mama Kinney was getting, and he said that a will that was made in such circumstances wasn't really valid. Duress, is what I think he called it. So I get to stay. Ain't that lovely?"

It didn't really seem lovely to Rich, but Sincere suddenly felt to him like a fast-moving train he couldn't grab hold of. He let it go. "Well," he said, "What time is dinner?"

She sighed, giving this much. "Six o'clock, Rich. And don't bring no drama, neither!"

But he just smiled, heading for the door. "Thank you, ma'am, 'preciate the invitation," he called back, as if Sincere had had a choice.

But Rich only brought flowers, and a smile, and a bottle of wine he convinced Sincere to drink over dinner. Sincere was trying hard to embrace a new, less restricted self, but still hesitant to try too much. She's never drank any kind of spirits before. But Rich was insistent, and she felt safe.

He was there again the next day, and the next, always with some pretext, always making himself handy, always in time for supper. On the day Sincere didn't cook, hoping he'd get the hint, he wouldn't take no for an answer and forced her to join him at Rainey's. On the day she'd simply failed to extend the invitation, he took a seat on her front porch and refused to budge until good manners forced her to let him in. Each time, he brought her gifts, the occasional bottle of wine, a ham on Sunday, steaks on Friday, and whatever else he wanted to eat. He learned that Sincere was as good a cook as Mama Kinney, an observation that had escaped him all these many years before.

After a while, Sincere even began to enjoy Rich's company and the two lingered sometimes after dinner as he cleaned up, his other contribution to the meal. When he kissed her again, she didn't pull away. And when he touched her, she suggested he stay the night. This time, they awoke to bright sunlight streaming through the window instead of dangerous whispers. The awkwardness between them faded, and after some time, Rich spent more time at Sincere's house than his own. But now the room they slept in had been changed, and Mama Kinney's personal items were gone, replaced with things belonging to Sincere and Rich. Even Mama Kinney's big bed, the one in which they'd found her body and the one in which Sincere had lost her innocence, had been replaced by a more modern, much larger four-poster, sturdy bed. Rich and Sincere had laughingly broke it in, their joy at coming together releasing that final dark memory.

Summer

Summer, when it came to Reason, was some-
thing to behold. Beautiful, but untouchably dangerous
nonetheless. In the beginning, though, in the early
months, it tended toward a gentler, calmer sort of
loveliness, like a young girl posing on the stairs before
leaving for the prom, smiling with just a hint of the
womanly ripeness soon to follow. It was just this sort of
promise in the beginning of each summer that enticed
old folks and children alike out onto their porches for
no other reason than to wonder at the manifold
blessings of the Lord.

On this particular Saturday afternoon in May,
however, the town was curiously silent. Streets were
bare, devoid of the sort of busyness that had marked
them only an hour before. Small indentations in the dust
on the sidewalks bore testimony to a thousand light,
quick feet that had gone walking, all following along the
same path. For once, no stragglers came in late. The
doors of Bethune Baptist Church had been in constant
motion all morning, swinging softly behind each arriving
person. Within the church, the residents of Reason
spoke in a low but constant buzz. The women were all
brightly arrayed in spring colors and wide-brimmed hats,
the men more soberly dressed but no less excited and
expectant. The children spent the morning being absent-
mindedly reprimanded each time they behaved in some
way that endangered their Sunday best. A few church
ushers made a half-hearted attempt to preserve order,
but their efforts went unheeded and ignored. The
community was beyond itself with anticipation, each

resident waiting with sharpened excitement for the coming spectacle.

In a small choir room near the entry of the church, six women crammed into the small space, laughingly sidestepping the train of the bride's dress. All but one of the women was dressed in deep fuchsia, trimmed with white, and adorned with matching white gloves, shoes, and small, pillbox-shaped hats. Despite their differing sizes and shapes, the dresses were well matched and complimented each of the women's respective skin tones. Even Joyce's normally-splotchy and uneven complexion looked soft and touchable beside the jewel-colored fabric. Lady said as much, and the woman smiled and simpered like a young girl.

Jody nodded in an uncharacteristic show of kindness to the other woman. But she ruined the effect when she said, "But I do wonder if that dress won't get singed by the time this thing is over. The good Lord is liable to open up the gates of heaven and rain down thunderbolts today, right here in Reason, right in the middle of this ceremony. Lyin' in a Baptist church," she said, and shook her head piously.

"You ain't even Baptist!" Joyce returned shortly, but smiled anyway.

"Ain't nobody in here told a lie, Jody," Sincere said, and moved toward the door. "Ain't no sin in lookin' beautiful on yo weddin' day."

"You can lie by yo actions as well as by yo lips," Jody said, and reached down to wipe at an imaginary speck on her shoe. "I'm jus' sayin', wearin' white ain't gone take away all of yo sins. Only Jesus can do that."

"Like I said before," Lady said, folding her arms defensively. "The color white has nothing to do with virginity, it only stands for happiness."

Tricee nodded in support. "I looked it up. It's the *veil* that represents purity, an since she ain't wearin' one, she ain't tellin' no lies."

"You can lie to yoself all you want to, but the Good Lord an I both know the truth." Jody smirked at the women and moved back quickly to dodge a playful swipe by Lady.

"The trick to livin' a lie," Reese said, handing each woman their respective bouquets and winking at Lady, "or in this case jus' wearing one, is to wear it well. An girl, let me be the first to witness, you *wearin'* that dress!"

With that, each of the women left the choir room to begin their walk toward the altar, three of them on the arms of men they barely knew and wistfully thinking of the day when they might do so as the one dressed in white. Despite her comments, even Jody knew she'd be wearing that color whenever the day came. Only Reese walked affectionately on the arm of her husband Luke, remembering fondly their own wedding day and determinedly ignoring all the changes wrought by the intervening years.

Her hand resting lightly on Rich's arm, Sincere only halfway listened to the music and the intonations of the preacher. So much had happened in the last few months, Sincere didn't know if she could trust herself or her feelings anymore. In a short span of time, she had lost the person she loved most in this world, the innocence of a childhood memory she had always cherished, and her chastity. But she had gained so much more. A new friend, and at this thought, she found Moresha's eyes in the crowd, firmly on her. She noted Miranda was again not beside her. This man, and she glanced up at Rich now but his face was fixed on the minister. But more than that, she'd gained a sense of herself. Sincere was finally coming into her own, and the feeling felt good. She wished Mama Kinney could be there to see it, but somehow she knew she already had.

She said a silent prayer, knowing it was sinful to pray to an individual, but she really couldn't help it. Somewhere near the heart of Jesus, Mama Kinney was staring down at her goddaughter, watching her. Smiling, and enjoying this moment. Mama Kinney would have been infinitely proud to watch Sincere standing here, beside the altar, although she undoubtedly would have been happier if Sincere were the one speaking vows. But despite the significance of this day, this moment was not hers to claim. So she smiled widely at Lady and Jonas as they said the words, letting Mama Kinney's approval show through it.

When the vows had been spoken, the small wedding procession made its way out of the church with a shout and a cheer. A few teenagers had quietly organized the children into two rows along the steps, and they all began throwing rice at the happy couple as they exited the church. The entire town crowded onto the steps and into the street to celebrate the occasion, surrounding Lady with a love and acceptance that she had never before been able to claim. Sincere knew it would be short-lived; folks in Reason had long memories and too little excitement, and they would not wholly forgive the scandal of Lady's previous living arrangement. Still, every one of the men Lady had once called her Boys had come for the celebration, and they all kissed the bride and shook the groom's hand as they made their way down the stairs. One had even stood up as best man. Lady had no enemies, had stepped on no one's feet. It seemed as if the entire town stood united in their celebration, and it was a sight too rarely witnessed not to enjoy.

Sincere felt an arm around her waist and she looked up, startled by Rich's closeness. For a moment, the old Sincere raised an objection to the nearness of any man and the implicit familiarity with which he touched her body. But then the moment passed and she relaxed into his embrace, telling him without words that she was ready to go home. "Ok, but only for a minute," he murmured before the two of them disappeared. They got to the reception much, much later and Lady just winked when she noticed Sincere was no longer wearing her fuchsia dress.

Lady and Jonas and Sincere and Rich weren't the only ones celebrating their love that day. That evening, Moresha and Miranda made love, enjoying the closeness of one another, translating emotion into action, barely noticing the elusive scent of the night wafting through open windows. There had not been enough time for them to grow used to the newfound honesty, the shared transparency of feelings shared between them. There was an awkwardness, but it was the awkwardness of new love, uncertain, but hopeful.

Moresha was less reserved now in the truth of her love, feeling Miranda's submission. If she rushed, it was because there was too little time left, and too many ways she still needed to express her love. If she was slower sometimes, it was because she wanted to savor the newness of this moment, the opportunity to love freely and with confidence.

In the back of her mind, there was a niggling doubt

reminding her that the strength of the hatred or anger or hurt that had motivated Miranda to return to Reason before had not completely healed, and that it might make itself known in some unanticipated way. Despite everything she knew, she understood there was still so much she didn't know, and never would. Miranda was a complex woman, and her feelings and thoughts were not easily predictable, but Moresha had always accepted and loved her as such. That would not change now, certainly, when for the first time there was reason to hope Miranda might return her love.

Besides, Moresha was not the type to live her life in fear, and of one thing she was certain: nothing she could ever learn or discover about Miranda would change her feelings. They were there, each time they touched, renewed in their urgency. She had known Miranda through so much pain, when Miranda had been soft and needy and uncertain of her direction. Moresha had loved her even then, terrified that Miranda's needs would destroy her and everything else she touched. But while Miranda had been unknown, unpredictable, Moresha had known herself, and her feelings. She knew, she just *knew* without explanation, that she would love her forever, without conditions and without reservation. There was no other reason for being.

Reading Group Guide

1. What role does sexuality play in the novel? Consider how Miranda, Sincere, Lady, Jody, and Mama Kinney expressed and interacted with their sexuality. What role do their varied expressions of their sexuality play in understanding their character, morals, and personalities?

2. What did you think of Miranda's ultimate motives for returning to Reason? Were these motives sufficient to justify her actions?

3. Was Sincere being realistic to desire a relationship with Miranda? Is it possible for a friendship of two children to survive adulthood?

4. Was Mama Kinney's dislike of Jean/Miranda justified? Discuss.

5. Arguably, Miranda's family and Miranda herself came to a bad end. Was that what the townspeople foresaw, or was it the product of the way the town treated the family? Was the town's treatment of Miranda's family justified, or was Miranda right to be angry about it? Do the ends justify the means?

6. Throughout the book, there are generational differences and divisions. Are there really so many differences between the ways of "old folks" and the perspective of the young? Is it possible for two women, in this case Mama Kinney and Sincere, to have a deep, abiding relationship in spite of that generational divide? Did Mama Kinney and Sincere really seem to understand one another, or was the relationship lopsided?

7. Imagine Sandal had survived long enough to meet Rich. Do you think the two men would have liked and/or respected one another? In their own ways, both men did desperate and perhaps crazy things for love. How do you think each would have judged the actions of the other?

8. Mama Kinney's porch served as a meeting space for discussion and gossip, but was there more good or bad that occurred in those meetings? How important is the space in which women gather? Aside from gossip, were there any positive things occurring in that space that might justify having it?

9. If Mama Kinney had simply given Miranda the ring, how do you think Miranda would have responded? Would Mama Kinney have survived?

10. Was Sincere really ignorant about the events that unfolded nineteen years before? Do you think knowing the details would have changed the way she responded to Mama Kinney? Miranda?

11. Was Moresha's love for Miranda unconditional, or is unconditional love even possible? How do you know?

12. Of the various women in the book, are there any you would or would not trust in your home? Why or why not?

13. What role did religion play for each of the characters in the novel? Were there any character(s) who demonstrated "true religion," and how is that defined?

14. Miranda set out to shock the town. Were her actions truly shocking, or was the town too thin-skinned? What makes you think as much?

Victoria Elaine Jones is a transplant to Dallas, Texas from San Francisco, California. A family law attorney with a thriving practice, she wrote her first novel, Reason, in her second year of law school. She is the published author of several poems and essays. A proud mother of two smart boys, when she's not writing or working, she practices being a better mother and wife to her husband, Emmanuel. She is currently hard at work on her next novel.

Go beyond the books!

@victoriajones

victoriajones

✍ A Thin Line *excerpt*

Just because she hated them, and because they had hated one another, Deidre buried them together. Not together like side by side pressed against satin lining, but together in the indignity of death. She imagined they would decay and become dust together, their bodies mingling with filth and worms and finally, each other. The way it might have been in life, but for their sins.

She took a certain pleasure in the roughness of the wood, the way the cold, musty fingers of fog stroked their way into the earth, stirring up its scent. The smell was new, fresh; the smell of life rather than death, but by now, she was already too far gone.

The coffin had been delivered at midnight, the rough-hewn boards of it not fit for its purpose. Coy would've hated it, she knew. He would've insisted on something better, something befitting his stature. But Coy wasn't here. Only this dry husk of a man, worn thin by life, if not death. Corpses have no desires, she thought, and smiled. Coy could not command her in death. Here, finally, there was freedom.

For as long as her memory, Coy had always been there. There had always been velvet ropes, soft chains binding the throats of the women he had loved with finality. Golden pedestals, bound feet, and no place to go. Still, there was no place to go. She had loved him, too, as purely as he'd loved her, but she knew she would need him gone to raise her seed. In the dark, her eyes searched for the shuttered windows of the room where he lay, and the peace that came from knowing where Coral lay settled the restlessness that rose briefly in her breasts. Coral was his grandfather's child. Her one regret was that Coy would never get to see.

Had they lived, she knew they would have found a way to love one another. She still believed, and there had been hope in finally having the truth revealed. When she had looked in Coral's eyes, seen Coy's quiet, unwavering stare blink back at her once, twice, for a short while she had believed there was hope. But now, in death, that hope was gone. Even the hate that had driven them, that, too, had vanished. In its place, there was only indifference, silence. Silence and death.

She got back to her work, unfinished. With soft movements and tender hands, she stripped them to nakedness, removed their outer and under garments, even their jewelry, the heavy golds and pearls and precious stones, and left them bare. Momentarily gentle, she washed the bodies, taking care with each, averting her eyes respectfully though she knew they couldn't see. The bodies were impossible to lift, but somehow she moved them. It took hours, or minutes, she wasn't sure. But when it was done, she folded them together in the box, the three of them holding hands in death as they would not have done in life. Coy embracing both women, holding them kindly, a sweet tableau of falsehood. She was alternately certain that she loved them, and hated them all the same. The pain was there, but it was not grief for them. They had not lost. She alone had suffered loss.

Grief pressed on her chest, dulled the pain in her hips where Coral once had rested, rocking himself to sleep while she busied herself. But there was nothing there now, no babies, no possibilities. Instead, there was only fortitude, resolution; maybe, if she examined it, a little bit of anger. She didn't. She couldn't stop herself long enough to wonder at her motives. Death was calling. She dug the grave deeper, working as hard as any man.

When it was finished, she was not. The sweat had long since begun rolling down the sides of her face and tucking itself in the space between her breasts. The physical exhaustion of her muscles had not quenched her thirst at all. She felt again that familiar restlessness, dissatisfaction. Their selfishness had cost everyone more than it was worth.

She would not have been able to move the coffin, herself, and she was relieved she'd had the forethought to have Frederick place it on a makeshift contraption. Now she lowered them into the ground, and with them, the dead part of herself. Her shoulders drooped, her anger losing momentum. They were gone now, in so short a time. There was nothing left, no remnant of death. Deidre collapsed onto the earth, lying beside the gaping hole, now filled, but still open. She wanted to crawl inside with them, the last of her past. She wanted to be buried in the box beside them, traveling into eternity, but she knew it was not possible. Coral and Frederic both needed her to live. She needed it, too. Instead, she lay beside the grave until morning, alternately crying and sleeping and unconsciously brushing aside the creeping things that came to investigate her warmth. It was a dead thing now, the past, and the time had come to live.

NOW AVAILABLE!!!

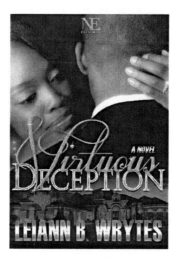

Only one thing stood between **Frank Mason** and his $20 million inheritance-- a wife. When he found, Lisa, he didn't waste any time marrying her, but their fairytale romance was not built to last. Lisa's infidelity doesn't go unnoticed, but Frank has his reasons for maintaining his silence. That's until he uncovers some new information about his step ford wife that lands him in jail. Only then does their picture-perfect life start to unravel, dragging every last skeleton out of his closet. **Lisa Raine** was an exotic dancer desperately seeking a way out. Frank Mason posed as the perfect escape. However, Lisa's ex-lover, Lewis, was not willing to let her go without a price. After years of paying Lewis to keep her past a secret, the money soon dries up, and both Lisa and Lewis are forced to alter their arrangement. Things take a turn for the worse and only one of them may make it out alive. **Michelle Lewis**, a private investigator, has managed to avoid mixing business with pleasure until an assignment sends her world colliding into the Mason's. When Brianna Mason is kidnapped, it is left to Michelle and her boyfriend to find her. Michelle unexpectedly stumbles across startling evidence that will irreversibly alter her and Brianna's life. Desperate for the truth, Michelle sifts through their families past, ripping old wounds, exposing forbidden relationships, and breaking years of silence to get it. Will the truth set them free or is it only the beginning of their parents arranged virtuous deception?

CPSIA information can be obtained at www.ICGtesting.com
Printed in the USA
LVOW07s2146130215

427029LV00004B/188/P